THE FLIGHT OF THE BUTTERFLY

A NOVEL

OBED OLIVARRÍA

metamorphosis
PUBLISHERS

OTHER TITLES BY OBED OLIVARRÍA

PSYCHOLOGICAL SUSPENSE NOVELS
Broken
Scars
Dilated Pupils

NON-FICTION
Divine Masterpiece
The Threefold Love

Names: Olivarría, Obed, author.
Title: The flight of the butterfly / Obed Olivarría
Description: Metamorphosis Publishers
Subjects: LCSH: Kidnapping–Fiction. | Captivity–Fiction. | Modern-day-Slavery–Fiction. | Prostitution–Fiction. | Criminal-Rings–Fiction. | Immigration–Fiction. | Adoption–Fiction. | Identity–Fiction. | Family-Secrets–Fiction.
BISAC: FICTION / Psychological. | FICTION / Thrillers. | GSAFD: Mystery Fiction | Suspense Fiction

Print ISBN: 979-8-9913504-6-4
eBook ISBN: 979-8-9913504-7-1
Library of Congress Control Number: 2024922950

First Edition

Book and Cover design by Obed Olivarria

For information contact:
http://www.obedolivarria.com

Printed In the United States

For Zaidy.

Thank you for being extraordinary.

Content Warning:
This story includes graphic content that some readers may find distressing or triggering. Topics covered include extreme violence, hate crimes, sexual assault, rape, graphic homicide, and instances of suicide ideation.

Author's Note:
The inclusion of these challenging topics is intentional and aims to shed light on the harsh realities of human trafficking, modern-day slavery, and the exploitation of vulnerable individuals, including minors. These issues, often hidden from daily view, demand awareness and understanding. My goal in writing is not to sensationalize, but to bring these truths into the open, fostering a deeper consciousness about the struggles faced by victims around the world. Please take care while reading, and know that these scenes are crafted with the intent to drive awareness and empathy.

THE FLIGHT OF THE BUTTERFLY

OBED OLIVARRÍA

Soaked in blood, wet, and trembling in the cold, the young girl pushed harder. She couldn't give up now. Not this close to freedom.

Hunkered behind an industrial metal trash bin, the shadows it cast protected her as the baby's head began to crown. She clenched her teeth, but a low moan escaped her cracked lips, and she bundled a portion of her gown into a tight ball, biting down on it hard. Breathing deeply, she pushed with all her strength. As she felt the baby slide out of her and onto the ground, closely followed by the placenta, the fabric in her mouth stifled her final cry.

On the damp concrete between her parted legs, the newborn lay, writhing. With shaking hands, the girl scooped it up and held it close to her, trying to warm it with her own icy skin. She looked around for a sharp object by a trash bin, found a discarded tin, and used its sharp edge to cut the umbilical cord.

The baby cried.

A quick check revealed that it was a girl. A gentle, tiny creature. Beautiful, yet fragile. And now the meaning of her life.

Hearing footsteps approaching, she slithered back, farther into the shadows of the alley. But she couldn't stop her own whimpering or that of her child's.

Trembling as she held the newborn, she watched the shadow of the newcomer lengthen. His silhouette came into full view under the dimmed streetlights beyond. Was this man her deliverance or her damnation?

Her eyes widened when she finally saw him.

PART 1

•

Gigi

CHAPTER ONE

Irvine, California
June 2019

Genesis 'Gigi' Gill chewed on the end of her pen and bounced her knee rapidly under her desk as she looked over the post she had edited for a coworker. It was an emergency article from one of her colleagues, regarding breaking news about the city's new bylaws. Her associate had requested help from Gigi's proficient eyes earlier in the day, and while Gigi wasn't one to work during time off, today was an exception. She was open to taking any work she didn't particularly enjoy, just to let her mind escape the unwelcome thoughts plaguing her.

Shaking away her nerves, she knew she had to trust her writing abilities. John Macy, their boss, needed it fast, but even so, she never faltered on quality. Satisfied with the turn out, she clicked send and rose from her desk. She stretched her tired arms and stood on her toes to reach the box of cereal she had stashed atop her wardrobe. Gigi had always complained about her size, being constantly in the midst of taller people. Well, except for her mother, who she jokingly blamed for her features, but loved regardless.

She cursed under her breath as the one person she had been trying to keep her thoughts away from managed to filter into her mind. Michelle Gill was the one woman in Gigi's life that she had always been comfortable with. Michelle wasn't just her mother, she was a confidant and a friend. She had dedicated her life to Gigi, and Gigi couldn't be more grateful for the attention that she had received from the woman. It was her that had passed along Gigi's love of art and painting.

Unfortunately, her mother was also dead.

Huntington's Disease, a genetic disorder, was the culprit who took her away too soon. She had been dead for the past two weeks and laid to rest a little less than that, and for Gigi, it had yet to sink in. There was one moment earlier in the week when she had picked up the phone to call her mother, and when she realized her mistake, she had burst into tears.

Gigi had been on bereavement leave since she got the news. Mr. Macy had graciously allowed her these past weeks, and though she was grateful for the time to collect herself, she knew she would have to return to work after the weekend, and she couldn't decide whether the jump back to normality would be comforting or jarring.

As Gigi slumped onto the end of her bed and dug her hand into the cardboard box in her hand. She opened the traveling book of Baja California, Mexico at the page she had saved, as her phone buzzed on her desk. She ignored it, knowing it would be one of two people, and shoveled a mouthful of dry cereal into her mouth. Dealing with her father and her fiancé had become an added burden to her period of mourning; the two most important men in her life, whom she adored, simply didn't understand the concept of *alone time*. Her father had been calling her multiple times a day, while her fiancé Jay kept coming to her apartment to check on her. He had brought her food twice already in the past twenty-four hours.

"At least eat something, babe," he had told her. "I made you this soup. I hope you enjoy it. I'll check on you again tomorrow."

"Thanks, Jay. I'll talk to you later. I just need some time alone," she replied the first time.

The second time she wasn't as nice. She did appreciate the gesture, though.

But Gigi's mind was somewhere else. For now, it was more important for her to discover how she had ended up in the home of Mr. and Mrs. Gill. The unconditional love her parents had given her, knowing Gigi was not their blood, intrigued her. But lately, it was the fragility of life, the reality of transmissible genetic diseases, and the fact that she would soon be starting her own family, that fueled her desire to find out more about her origins.

Gigi was nine years old when she first found out she was adopted. Prior to that, she had never suspected she wasn't her parents' biological daughter. She had always considered herself Chinese-American, since her adoptive father was white and her mother, Chinese. The news shocked her, but she understood why it was important her parents told her the truth. And now, with her adopted mother taken by a genetic disease Gigi would have most likely inherited had they been biologically related, she felt the urge to dig into her own past even more.

She needed to see her true parents, look into their eyes, and ask them why they had given her up. She needed to find out about their culture and history. She needed to understand her family if she were ever to understand herself—her genetic make-up, or if perhaps there was some disease running through her family tree too. Why had she been so prone to sickness growing up? How could she marry someone and bear his children if she wasn't certain about her genetic make-up?

Since she was told of her adoption, Gigi had always felt a need to reach out to her biological parents. Yes, to many it would seem irrelevant, considering that she was about to reach her third decade on Earth; but it was even more imperative she found out about her real parents before she could move forward in life. It was because of this mystery that she still had not set a wedding date with her fiancé. She and Jay had been engaged for six months now; he was more than eager to get the wedding preparations rolling, but Gigi needed answers first. She needed closure.

Gigi closed the traveling book and put it on the night stand. She played with the ring on her finger as she idly stared at her computer screen from afar. A new email came in, prompting her to set down her cereal as well and move back to her desk. She opened it quickly, as she had been eagerly expecting it. Weeks before her mother's death, she had done a DNA test. Her results were finally here.

She was a mix. Well, yes, she'd figured that much already.

"What else? Tell me more! I need specifics..." she mumbled to herself.

There it was. Her genetic composition was a collection of multiple possible scenarios, mostly consisting of Iberian European and East Asian descent. But this didn't say much, other than what she'd always assumed. Genesis Gill, an ethnic combination. Thick black hair and slanted, hazel eyes. Light skin, with olive undertones. Freckles. Most of her origins from Northern Spain and Southern China. Some Irish, a little Native American.

Gigi possessed an inquisitive mind ever since she was a young child. She wanted to know why things were called what they were and why people acted the way they did. It was this curiosity that led her to pursue a journalistic career. But the identity of her biological parents was the one question which eluded her. At least now she'd confirmed her heritage.

She closed the browser on her laptop. A desktop picture of Jay and her on the beach made her smile. Whatever her background was, she would make a beautiful family with this man. She stood up, her stomach begging out loud for something more than dry Cheerios. Anything would do. As much as she needed the time alone, she sure missed Jay's cooking right about now. She missed his company too.

She grabbed her phone and made her way to the kitchen, passing by a wall of family pictures. Her smiling parents. Jay and her camping with some friends. Gigi as a teenager, winning multiple local martial arts tournaments. Piano recitals. The family at her dad's bee farm. All images of a great life.

Her father was aware of how important it was for her to know everything about her biological parents, so he supported her quest. A week earlier, soon after they'd buried her mother, he had approached her in his backyard and pushed her to do something about it.

"How are you holding up?" her dad had asked as he lowered himself onto the swing chair beside his daughter. "Were you able to sleep last night?"

Gigi turned her reddened eyes to him and smiled. Her tears had dried, but the evidence of their existence prevailed. She shrugged as she returned her gaze to the setting sun. "I'm fine, Dad. And yeah, it's getting better at night. You don't look too bad yourself," she replied.

He smiled and shook his head. "Looks can be deceiving, sweetie. Trust me; it's been the hardest couple days of my life."

Gigi knew those words couldn't be truer, especially for her father. "I've always felt I take after you. You know, masking my emotions. Even Jay tells me I can be so cold at times. I wish I was more like Mom." She laughed, as if to somehow dull the effect of the harsh words.

"Gigi, you are more like your mother than you could ever know. You remind me so much of her. But... you're right; you did come out more like me in that sense. I guess we all deal with stuff in our own way."

A moment of silence passed between them. He gently kicked his legs to move the swing, wrapping his arm around Gigi for a hug. Unlike her mother, it was rare that her father would hug anyone, but she appreciated it. At the same time, there was always a purpose behind every action he took, and she knew this would be no different. She wondered what lingered on the tip of his tongue.

Before she could say anything, he broke the silence, "So, how is Jay?"

She glanced at him; this was certainly not the question that he'd had in mind, she was sure. "Jay is fine. He had to rush to work for an emergency after the service. But we're good."

"Hmm..." Her dad nodded. "And, um... have you given further thought to searching for your biological parents?"

That was it.

In all honesty, she had thought of it several times, but nothing concrete had formulated in her head since she'd brought it up a year prior. Her mother's quickly deteriorating state and Gigi's busyness at work had taken priority. Back then, her dad had supplied most of the information that she needed: she had been adopted from an agency in Baja California, Mexico that brought in kids from all over Latin America; they had picked her up from an orphanage in the border city of Mexicali; and her father was reliably informed that a teenage boy had been the one to bring her in as a baby.

"You always did get straight to the point," she said, laughing weakly. "Yes, trust me, it has been on my mind. But unfortunately, there's just too much going on right now, and I haven't really had any time to pursue it."

"I understand," he responded as he played with her hair. He would do this to her often, even at her age.

She playfully batted his hand away and ruffled the white hair on the back of his head. She had a feeling he had more to say, though. And he didn't disappoint.

"Your mother's death has me thinking, Gigi. You really can't keep postponing this quest you've been wanting to take on. It will bug you forever. If you are serious about wanting to know the answers, then this is something you need to do soon, before everyone who can help you trace them is either dead or unable to help anymore. I wish I had more to tell you about this, but like I said before, we weren't given much info when we adopted you."

Gigi nodded, noting his concern. It was a genuine one. She couldn't keep stalling on something of such importance, and she certainly couldn't keep making excuses to Jay either.

"I understand, Dad. And you are right; I still need to know for myself."

He reached for her hand and took it in his, interlacing fingers with his treasured daughter. He gave it a squeeze. "I just don't want you to have regrets, Genesis. You have always been an ace in investigations. And maybe it's time you use your talent to your own benefit."

She smiled at him and agreed silently.

"But there's more."

Her smile waned. "What do you mean?"

"Well, I gotta be honest with you. Mom made me promise on her deathbed to make you seek your origins before you got married."

"She did? Why?"

"She knew you better than anyone. She knew it would bug you for the rest of your life until you found out something. Anything."

Genesis lay her head on her dad's chest. "She did know me well."

Since that meeting with her dad, the thought of finding out more on her biological family had been resonating in her head. Genesis had yet to inform Jay of the possibility that she may be traveling across the Mexican border to visit the orphanage from where she had been adopted. For now, she was formulating a plan that would get her boss to allow her a trip there without it affecting her work. Her bereavement period had passed, and her career was very important to her. The *L.A. Chronicle* gave her everything she needed to get to the top. She wouldn't sabotage her career as a successful reporter because of her personal life, no matter how important this quest was. And she was determined to find a way to turn this into an official assignment.

As she reached the kitchen, her rumbling stomach reminded her that she hadn't eaten since the night before. Gigi had an unhealthy habit of forgetting to eat, especially when she had a project due. Once, during her teens, her mother had thought Gigi was intentionally refusing to eat and had put her on a food watch program.

She sighed as she realized her mom wouldn't be around to monitor her eating habits anymore and scanned through the fridge quickly. Gigi was a lousy cook, although it wasn't for lack of trying, so she ordered out a lot. Not finding anything appetizing, she closed the fridge door, adorned with her own purple-and-red watercolor paintings. She would have to get takeout—again.

She unlocked her phone and scrolled through her contacts; Jay often laughed at her for having the numbers of at least five different restaurants stored in her favorites list. Jay also joked that when they had kids, she would feed them with dishes from those same restaurants. And she would laugh about it with him; but Jay was thankfully no slacker in the kitchen. It was one of the many reasons why she was grateful to have him in her life.

"I don't worry about that, Jay. We both know that you will be the one to cook at home!" she would reply.

Her phone began vibrating just as she was about to dial one of the restaurants. *Speak of the devil.* Jay's nickname, *BlueJay*, popped onto the screen. She had ignored his last two calls and one voicemail for a reason. Unlike Jay, she reenergized by being alone. She was also more productive by herself.

But he was persistent.

She stared at the screen, wondering if she should ignore it again. But she knew Jay would keep calling if she did.

She slid her finger across the screen to answer and placed the phone to her ear, only to hear him let out a sigh. "Gigi! Thank God! I was worried something happened to you!"

Gigi rolled her eyes; sometimes Jay could be overdramatic. Okay, she hadn't answered his calls for the past couple of hours, but this wasn't the first time in their five-year relationship she'd done that. "Good thing I answered then," she replied flatly.

"How are you, babe?" he asked, his voice now leveled.

"Hungry, but fine. How are you?" She picked lint from her pajama pants.

"I'm fine. I am worried about you, though. Do you need me to come over and whip up something special for you?" he teased.

She could hear the smile in his voice. She was tempted to agree. She missed him a lot. But for now, since the article was finally done, she really needed to think up her plan to find her biological parents. And she knew that if he came over, she would only lose focus.

"Nah, it's ok. Charlie's Palace has me covered tonight. Thanks, though."

He laughed. "Chinese, huh? You think that's better than the *chiles rellenos* and Mexican rice that I have in mind? Oh, and it comes with *dessert* too!"

His words elicited a smile from her, knowing that *dessert* would be much more than chocolate sundaes. Jay was a very attentive lover in every ramification, and unselfish as well. He wasn't perfect, though. At times, he could be too sensitive, and Gigi would tease that he was the girl in the relationship. But still, he was the best lover she could ever ask for. Her handsome bear.

"As tempting as that offer is, I'm afraid I'll have to decline, Mr. Rodriguez. Not tonight, at least."

"Wow, you must have a ton of stuff to do, then. At least you got some time to paint."

"Yeah," she sighed. "At least."

"Hey, by the way, did Macy bring you back to work early?"

"No, this was my choice. I'm slowly easing back into it, but I'm still busy. You don't know the half of it," she replied as she looked once more inside the fridge, as if something new had magically appeared since a minute ago.

"Alrighty then... I guess I should just leave you to your work?" he asked with hesitation, as if hoping for a different response.

"You should," she agreed, her fingers drawing an invisible image over the watercolor butterfly painting on the freezer door. "I promise I'll make it up to you, babe. Soon, I'll be all yours."

"All right, babe. Good night, then. I love you!" he said with a defeated sigh.

"Good night." She disconnected the line before he could say anything else to try to convince her. She would most likely be convinced, as part of her wanted to just be with him and forget about life.

Gigi knew she could be cold sometimes; she couldn't be lovey-dovey or express affection in public or over the phone. Perhaps it was because she wrongly felt unloved for many years, thinking her biological parents simply didn't want her. She figured those closest to her knew and understood her apprehension to open up; the recent death of her mother had only heightened this closed-off habit.

Once she found a reason to go down to Baja California, she would inform Jay of her plans. He would understand. He always did. And, hopefully, she would be successful with her investigations. This quest could not wait any longer. And yes, soon she'd be free from this weight on her shoulders and give Jay all the time and love in the world again.

"Yeah, hi. Can I place an order for delivery, please?"

As Genesis made her way to work the following Monday morning, she thought a lot about Jay and the mission she had in mind. As pulled onto the interstate, her phone rang. The caller ID on the car's dashboard displayed, "*BlueJay*." His slurred voice came over the line as if he had just woken up.

"Hey, babe... I was wondering if you were up already."

Another quick glance at the dashboard told Gigi the time was 7:02 a.m. Jay knew she was always out of bed at 6 a.m., latest, to do her yoga routine. At times, she would wonder why she was so fixated on religiously working out when she was already in great shape. She wished she could be more like Jay, who ate whatever he wanted and never cared how he looked to other people.

"You're joking, right?" She reached out to lower the volume so his voice didn't blare through the speakers.

There was a pause on the other end before Jay gave a hearty laugh. "I know how much of an early bird you are, G. I just wanted to ask if I could stop by your office to take you out for lunch. I'm excited to see you, and we could use some alone time. You know, so that we can have a little time to plan the trip."

The car lurched as Gigi slammed on her breaks to avoid the car passing in front of her. She pounded a fist on her horn. "Idiot!"

"Huh?"

"Sorry. A crazy driver just cut me off, and I nearly bashed into his taillight. Um, I didn't catch your last sentence." She had, but she knew she hadn't share her intentions of embarking on any trip with him, and she didn't have a plan to go on one by herself. Well, at least, not yet.

"Wait, are you all right? Or do you want me to summon my superpowers and appear right there by your side so I can whoop that fool's butt?"

This made her smile. Typical Jay. Always wanting to be her hero, even though half the time, he seldom meant the threatening words he said.

"No, I'm all right, babe. Anyway, I don't remember talking about going on a trip with you," she stated.

"You don't remember because I just of it. What do you say? I'm dying to spend some time with you. What do you think of a weekend getaway?"

As tempting as the offer was, she shook her head, as if Jay was seated just beside her. "I don't think I can, babe. I have so many things going on and I've missed out on so much at work already. Besides, I really need to figure out my life. To be honest, going away on a fun adventure is the last thing on my mind right now."

"It's ok, G. I figured it was worth trying. By the way, have you heard the good news already?"

"What good news?"

"Oh, so you don't know! Never mind, then. I thought you knew. I don't want to spoil the surprise. You'll hear about it at work soon."

CHAPTER TWO

Los Angeles, California
June 2019

As John Macy, Senior Editor at the *L.A. Chronicle*, sat in his leather chair that morning, he smiled with pride. Thick volumes neatly lined on the bookshelves to the display of various awards and accolades at the far end of the office. On his desk was a letter, *Genesis Gill,* written boldly on it, and above that, a crest: the Los Angeles Anthropology Research Institute. He already knew of their response to Genesis's article on the monarch butterflies and their arduous, yet beautiful annual migration down to Michoacán, Mexico, but...

Macy knew all she ever needed when she had a brilliant idea was his support, and she would produce something wonderful each time. And although he never told her and never would, she was an excellent sleuth, an even better writer, and one of his favorite journalists on the team.

He poured himself a mug of steaming coffee, dropped a single sugar cube into his mug, stirred it a little, and savored the strong smell before finally sipping it. Settling his pre-coffee angst, he turned around and stood up to look out the northwest corner window, enjoying the view of the city skyline.

"Gill will be ecstatic," he said to himself. "I should rally the team and share the good news with them for when she gets here."

"Congratulations, Gill!" It was Billy, the skinny office clown who said it as Genesis walked past him by the elevators.

Gigi smiled, confused. "For what?"

Billy didn't reply.

Okay...?

As Gigi entered the working area, everyone stood up and applauded loudly, all grinning ear-to-ear. In the middle of the office space, where over twenty workers occupied the cramped maze of cubicles, stood John Macy.

She acknowledged their applause, thanked them with a confused smirk, and made her way to her desk.

What in the world is this? I left a couple of weeks ago with their consolation, and I am welcomed back with congratulations?

As she passed them, her co-workers patted her back and offered her further congratulations. She thanked them with smiles and quiet words, all the while eager to find out exactly what was going on.

The vibrant watercolor paintings adorning her small cubicle space welcomed her, bringing a new smile to her face as she dropped her bag and sat. As soon as she was settled, she opened her laptop, and John came around the corner.

"Gill," he said. "Don't you want to hear the good news?"

"Of course, I do! Sorry." She lowered the laptop screen. "What's going on?"

He smirked. "Later. I have a video conference right now. But stop by my office in an hour. I'll share everything then." He started to turn away as he called, "Also, welcome back." With that, he left.

"Okay...?" Gigi scratched her head. "Why so much suspense?"

But as curious as she was, there were other things eating away at Gigi's mind. Flipping open her laptop once again, she opened the web browser and searched *Mexicali*. Pictures of a sprawling desert border city flooded her screen. She relaxed to go through them. Her father had told her she came from an orphanage in Mexicali. A teenage boy had brought her there and had later disappeared, but all efforts to trace him had proved pointless.

After studying the pictures closely, Gigi moved on to search the names of orphanages in the city. Names like *El Niño Feliz*, *Oasis del Desierto*, *Tesoros Escondidos*, and *Fuente de Vida*, among others, appeared in the results, but she knew it was as useless as searching for a needle in a haystack. *Casa Hogar San Jose* was absent from all listings, just as her father had already told her.

Her mind flashed back to almost twenty years ago. She remembered it like it was yesterday, even though she was only nine at that time.

Orange, California
Winter 1999

Gigi was in her room cutting up newspapers and trying to clip them together to solve a puzzle she had set for herself, when the door unexpectedly opened. The first person to enter the room was her dad, closely followed by her mother. He smiled down at her where she squatted in deep concentration. She looked up to him, her innocent eyes glowing like a hopeful puppy's. It wasn't time for bed yet, so seeing her parents activated the little defiance she could muster at that age.

"Gee-gee!" her mother exclaimed. "You've been working on this for hours," she laughed. She towered over Genesis with her hands on her hips. Gigi studied her features: petite, a round face, and a smile that had deep dimples buried in it. The same smile Genesis had. Her mother always referred to her as Gee-gee, or Gigi. She said that it reminded her of a friend she had in her childhood, whom Genesis had taken after with her inquisitive mind and ability to ask deep questions.

But then her mother crouched low to look Gigi in the eyes. Her voice softened as she said, "I need to talk. I mean, *we* need to, your father and I... really need to talk to you, honey. It's something important."

"Okay," Genesis replied. She dropped what she was doing and sat cross-legged with her hands folded in her lap, sitting between her parents on her bed.

There had been many nights like this one when they would come into her room to tell her Bible stories, or simply to talk to her about what she had learned in class. She thought this night would not be any different.

"You know we love you and we would never hurt you," her father said, seating on the edge of Gigi's bed. "You came into our lives when all hope was lost, bringing happiness and laughter that brought light back into our home. Our lives were restored that day because of you." He was already in his flannel pajamas and he looked like he'd just been dragged from the bed. His hair was disheveled, and his eyes had deep lines of tiredness etched around them.

"You are an angel sent down from heaven," he continued, "and you have remained an angel ever since. For never have you ever given us a cause to worry, neither have you ever broken our hearts. You are deeply loved, and if we had the chance to have you again, we would have you, over and over. We'd always choose you. We would never give you up, and we also hope and pray that the revelation of tonight doesn't change your love toward us..."

Young Genesis simply stared at them in confusion as her mother gently brushed aside her smooth locks of jet-black hair. "We feel like you're old enough to know this now," Michelle completed.

By now, Genesis was listening with rapt attention. Their voices were bursting with emotion, and she could sense the caution each of them displayed before making a statement. Her mother had adjusted and readjusted her own hair, flipping it over her shoulder and twirling it in her fingers, over ten times already.

"What's the matter? Please, tell me. You're scaring me. Did I do something wrong?" Genesis said, standing up. She folded her arms and looked at her parents.

They exchanged glances before her mother invited her to rejoin them on the bed. Gigi slowly sat back, sandwiched between them—her dad to the left and her mom to the right. She placed her arms around her daughter and drew her close to her chest. She whispered a quick "I love you" to Genesis, smoothing her hair.

"Baby, we just wanted to let you know something very important. But no matter what, just know that you are ours, and we are yours," her dad said.

"Um, okay...?"

"What your dad is trying to say," her mother continued, "is that no matter what you are about to hear right now, we will always be your parents, and you will always be our daughter."

Gigi frowned. "What do you mean? Of course, you are my parents and I am your daughter. You guys are scaring me."

"Baby," Dad continued, "we feel like you are old enough to know and understand this. You are adopted. We adopted you when you were just a baby. Mom and I couldn't have..."

"What?" Gigi leaped from the bed once again and spun to face her parents. "That's not funny, Dad!"

Her mother sighed. "Genesis Michelle, Daddy and I just wanted you to know the truth. We understand this is difficult."

Gigi paused for a moment before slowly saying, "So... where did I come from? Who are my parents, then? I mean... like my... *real...* parents, I guess?"

"*We* are your true parents," Michelle said.

"Yes, I know, Mom. But... you know what I mean."

"We tried to trace your origin, your very beginning," her dad said. His eyes were shining more than usual, and he turned away. "Gigi, a few years ago, we wanted to know where you came from so that you would know the full truth one day. We wanted to know if your real parents might come looking for you at any point. We'd heard stories, you see. But the only information that was given to us was that you were dropped off a year before we came for you—by a teenage boy." He paused to let the information sink in.

"I don't understand," Gigi said, scrunching her face in confusion.

What she just found out was too big for her little mind to digest, even if she was smarter than the average child. He arms trembled. She wanted to scream, jump up, and run away; but how could she when they looked at her so fondly?

"I... I just don't understand, though," she said as a tear appeared on her face. "Everyone tells me I look like you, Mom! My size, my hair. I even have your dimples." She waved her hand toward her face.

"Yes, I know, baby. But..."

Gigi huffed. "Then who do I look like? Did my real parents not want me, or what?" The last part was louder. She was hyperventilating now, pulling air into lungs that too quickly wanted to reject it.

Her father grabbed her hands. "Gigi, *we* want you. We always have. We've always loved you, and you are our daughter, no matter what. Please know that."

The love she had been shown for as long as she could remember flashed through her mind in scenes: all the hugs and kisses before school; Richard Gill, her adopted father, slipping her extra helpings of dessert and bringing her jars of honey just for her; every comforting word Michelle Gill, her adopted mother, offered her whenever she came home sad from school. It all held new meaning now.

"But why would you love me, if I am not even your own flesh and blood?" Gigi asked with full tears now stinging her eyes. "I am not your real daughter!"

It was Mom's turn to speak again. She wiped some tears from Genesis's cheek. "We don't know what happened to your biological parents, baby. But like Dad said, please know that we love you. We want you. And you are, and will forever be, a Gill... our daughter. Always!"

Her mother's eyes held such sincerity, that Genesis could do no more than hug them both. The Gills—her parents. She was their daughter; she was one of them. They wanted her, and she wanted them. That was all that mattered. And from that day forward, there was no question in her mind that at least two people in this world loved her.

It wasn't until her teenage years that the thought of finding her biological parents took root in her mind. She didn't know if she even wanted to get to know her true parents if she found them, but she had so many questions. She wished Richard and Michelle, her parents, could fill the void she felt, but unfortunately, they knew very little, and they didn't have Gigi's investigative skills or curious drive.

This battle in her mind, what to do about her biological parents and whether it was right to find them, would trouble her for the reminder of her life. She wanted to know who she was, but at the same time, she didn't want to disrespect the people who raised her and loved her unconditionally.

Los Angeles, California

June 2019

Genesis exhaled as she stared at her work computer. Her hand rested on her mouse, the cursor hovering over the X at the top right corner of the web browser. Should she continue a seemingly pointless quest? Would any of her searches lead her to answers? She was lost deep in thought, questions crashing into her brain, when Jay's head poked over the top of her cubicle.

"Hey, babe!"

"Oh, my! You scared me!" Gigi took a deep breath. She quickly closed the web browser. "I didn't know you were here already."

"I just got here. We have a meeting with all the graphics people, but should be done by noon. So, what, are we still on for lunch?" he smiled.

"Yes, babe. The date is on!" she replied sweetly. She got up and gave him a kiss.

Seeing his face created a sensation of joy throughout her entire body, though she didn't always show it the way most people did. But her joy mixed with guilt as the voice in the back of her mind told her how she could be such a bad girlfriend at times. Many times. She truly loved Jay, but she always had problems expressing her feelings in the right ways.

I really don't deserve this man.

That thought crept through her mind constantly, but her ego would never allow her to voice it out loud. She didn't like expressing her insecurities, either.

She gave Jay a tight-lipped smile and sat back down. "So, I have a meeting with Macy in a little bit."

"Oh, yeah. I can't wait for you to hear. Tell me how it goes during lunch. I gotta run."

"I will. See you later, babe."

With that, she resumed her work.

Some hours later, a few blocks away from the office building, Genesis and Jay sat while talking in a restaurant next to the Grand Central Market.

"Congratulations!" Jay cheered as he raised his glass.

"Thank you, babe. Cheers."

Genesis took a sip of her wine, then quickly put the glass down. She still couldn't get used to the fermented tasted, having been raised in a very conservative home, free of alcohol. Growing up, she was a fervent church goer. However, her job as a reporter had taken her to places with different religions and values, and her worldview changed. She had discovered that most times, religion was used as a tool to bring about destruction and cause chaos in an otherwise peaceful world. Now, she believed that if religion didn't hold so much power, more people would be able to get along with each other.

With the exception of the day she heard of her mom's death, she hadn't prayed in years. That afternoon, crumpled in her bed, all she could mumble was a prayer not more than a few words. It was mostly a cry of desperation. A questioning of God's existence in this evil world.

"You're staring at your drink," Jay said, drawing her out of her reverie. "We're celebrating here, and you are... well, gone."

She smirked and looked down at her food, still steaming, but likely not for much longer. She had ordered a spicy tomato-basil soup and a quesadilla. Jay had opted for the fajitas. The restaurant was Mexican, and she had visited it with Jay almost bi-weekly for years, maybe because of the smiling faces of the workers, or maybe because something else pulled her toward the place.

She spooned a mouthful of the soup. "I was just thinking, that's all."

"Yeah, you've been doing a lot of that lately. But not enough talking. Which is unlike you."

"I know. Sorry, babe. I am here."

"So, tell me, what have you been thinking, my award-winning-journalist fiancée?"

Gigi laughed. "Well, about life, about death, about what happens after. I've been thinking a lot about the past *and* about the future."

"About *our* future?" Jay held her hand across the table.

"Yes, *our* future. Jay, we're okay. Don't worry about that. I promise." She raised his hand to her lips and kissed him.

"Phew. I was getting worried you're having second thoughts."

Gigi shook her head. "It's not that. The truth is that I'm just trying to figure out how to kill two birds with one stone."

"Okay...? Care to elaborate?" He pulled his arm back and sat straight.

Genesis looked up, behind Jay, and stared for a few seconds before exclaiming, "That's it!"

He turned back to see what she was looking at. "What? What's *it?*" He raised his brows.

"The news," Genesis replied, nodding her head toward the hanging television on the wall.

"What about them?" Jay asked while turning once more to look at the screen behind him.

"You know me," she said. "I'm always on the job." She looked up at the television but spotted Jay's worried expression in the corner of her eye. She rolled her eyes playfully. "That's how I can kill two birds with one stone. Look." She pointed to the screen.

The Spanish-speaking reporter was talking about immigrants that were being turned away. Video footage of a group of migrants being detained, followed by images of some tunnels, the large international fence, and protesting groups flickered through the monitor.

"Tell me what the reporter is saying, Jay."

"Um, okay." Jay turned his chair to face the monitor hanging up to read the close caption being displayed on the otherwise mute screen. "He is saying something about how some South and Central American migrants were smuggled to the States through degrading means."

Gigi's heart broke. "Keep going, babe. I want to know everything he is saying. I have an idea."

"Idea of what?"

"Just keep on translating for me, please."

Jay turned back his face again. "He just keeps going on about how many of these undocumented immigrants get lost without a trace, and more often than not, their bodies are eventually found in the desert." Jay took a break before continuing. "Okay, now they are talking about the inhumane living conditions many of these people endure once in the United States, but also how, for most of them, staying home wasn't an option for survival."

"That's so sad."

"I know, my love. Now, they switched the conversation. The reporter and the lady there are having a dialogue regarding the significance of the relationship between Mexico and the United States. They're talking about the wall that the president promised and what not."

"What exactly are they saying about it?"

"Well, let's see. They're talking about how in the border cities on the wall or the international fence, the economies depended so much on each other and how culturally they are really one and the same, with only a large fence in between. And now, they're getting into some political stuff."

The image then switched to the international fence which separated both nations, where the reporter stood, as he made mention of the possible building of a wall and how this would affect both sides. This much Gigi understood. Then images of tunnels came.

"Do you want me to go on? What's on your mind, G?" Jay turned back to face her.

"Please. Just a little more."

"Okay. This other guy is now saying that some tunnels that were found, used to traffic people and drugs, and how the wall wouldn't make a difference. He is saying that—"

"That's it!"

Jay was puzzled. "That's *what*? *What's* it?"

Gigi kept looking into the television set without replying.

"Babe? Earth to Gigi! Hello? Anybody there?" Jay gently nudged her and tried to turn her face away from the television. "You're not making sense."

"Oh, um... sorry. I just think this is so sad, but also very interesting. That whole thing about the wall the president keeps blabbing about, immigration, the border. The whole thing! I want to cover *that* story! I want to go there myself and find out what's happening down there on the border and report from there. Let the world know. I don't know. I feel like the public needs to hear more stories from people living there, and how it affects them. Hear their perspective. Plus, again, like I said, this way I could kill two birds with one stone."

Jay looked her in the eyes and smiled. "Okay. But what two birds are you talking about?"

"Jay, this is *it!*" she exclaimed while punching her fists on the table, making it shake."

"Come down!" Jay replied laughing.

"Sorry, I'm just excited. It's the perfect opportunity. This is exactly what I've been looking for. This is a trip that would give me the chance to search for my past and my origins. The perfect excuse. It would be a great story, very timely, *plus* I could take the time to finally do what I've been planning to do."

"Yeah, I'm still confused."

"The border, babe. The wall that Trump promised but never came to be. But how some still want it done. I can do a piece on that. But with a different twist. Maybe focus more on the economics on both sides, the people living there. Or maybe even something about those tunnels and how they are used for drug and people trafficking. I don't know. While at the same time, though, searching for my origins while I am there! It's a perfect plan. All I need to do now is convince Macy."

"Oh, you mean so the *Chronicle* can pay for it. You know Macy keeps complaining about how we are short on money and how no one reads the newspaper anymore, and you want it to fund your personal quest?"

"I mean, when you put it like that, it sounds horrible." She rested her face on her hands above the table.

"Yes. Yes, it does." Jay took a sip of his wine before continuing, "You know I support you, both in your professional life and in your personal stuff. That's what I am here for. And I know how much you care about finding more on your origins. All I am saying is that you might want to think this through."

"Babe, I'm not trying to be shady, I promise. I want to write this piece. I really do. It's just that otherwise, I won't have an opportunity to go there any time soon."

Jay took a bite of his food while staring at her, but didn't say anything.

"Babe, don't judge me like that."

"What? I didn't say anything."

"You didn't need to." She threw a small piece of her quesadilla at him. He laughed. "Look, Jay, once I'm in Mexico, I'll dig until I get to the bottom of it all, *and* I'll write an awesome piece. You have to admit, it's a timely topic." She swallowed half of her quesadilla whole, taking her time to chew her way through it.

Jay watched her for a moment before shrugging. "True," he said in between bites. "It could work. You just gotta pitch it right to Macy. He's in a good mood right now, and he's proud of you. So, I guess you are right... Maybe this *is* a good time to bring it up, after all."

"Touché." For the first time in a long while, she muttered a sincere prayer. "God, please help me make this work."

Jay smiled at her.

"What?" She said, blushing under his stare.

"Nothing. You're just cute when you get excited about something. That's all."

For the rest of lunch, Gigi couldn't shake the idea from her mind. *Mexico, I am coming!*

CHAPTER THREE

Irvine, California
June 2019

The buzzing of the alarm woke her. Groaning, Gigi rolled over on the bed, her arm feeling heavy. As she stretched her hand to turn off the alarm, there was a gentle knock of pain on her right shoulder. She winced as she snooze, then rubbed her eyes and gave a long yawn. A flurry of monarch butterflies covered her: a blanket gifted to her by Jay. He had bought it for her because he knew how much she loved the creatures.

Gigi turned to the nightstand; on it, balanced lightly, was the transparent plaque that carried her name: "Genesis Gill. For the most expository article, 2019." A piece about a creature as ignorable as the monarch butterfly. She smiled, as her mind made a brief detour to a night three weeks before. She pushed herself up and stepped down into the fluffy slippers that were always at the foot of the bed. Stretching and scratching her head, she walked with uneasy steps toward the bathroom, where she saw it on the mirror.

She had gone with Jay to the Dark Side tattoo parlor in Old Town Orange, at the edge of dawn. Even though she had never been drawn to tattoos, the article she wrote had made her want one. She asked for a butterfly on her back, close to her right shoulder. It was a beautiful piece of minimalistic art that Jay had designed—simple lines that shaped a butterfly. And she loved it! The procedure, however, had been more painful than she anticipated. Jay had to hold her hand all the way through, both soothing her nerves and keeping her still.

THE FLIGHT OF THE BUTTERFLY

After a short yoga session, Gigi started her shower. As the water heated, she took the chance to shave her legs. As she sat on the edge of the sink to do so, her eyes fell on the scar on her chest, the top of it just visible over the top the towel wrapped around her torso. It was a scar done to her by the medics who had battled to save her life about twenty-four years ago.

Orange, California
Fall 1995

Genesis, just five years old, was in kindergarten and doing well. Her teacher spoke highly of her keen observation skills and how she may turn out to be a force to be reckoned with because of her powerful mind and exceptional memory, but also her strong personality. One afternoon, Michelle came to pick Genesis up, excited to see her precious girl and spend the rest of the day with her. She watched Genesis sluggishly walk to the car and get in.

"Hi, baby. What did you do in school today?" Michelle asked, looking at her daughter in the rearview mirror.

The little girl did not answer. Instead, she stared at her palms. Michelle didn't think anything of it and got ready to go. She reversed out of the parking lot and began her drive home. She repeated the question when they were on the road; Genesis only made a little hum, still not looking up from her hands.

Michelle quickly looked back, and her heart froze. Young Gigi's face was blue, her right hand shaking. That moment, her small head dropped to her chest as she lost consciousness.

Panicking, Michelle quickly parked on the roadside, jumped out of the car, and raced to get the door open. She lifted her daughter and touched her head. She wasn't hot, but her breathing was coming in huge gasps.

"Oh, my baby. Not again! What do I do?" Michelle asked no one in particular.

The traffic on the road was flowing steadily. Michelle looked around for a pay phone, but saw none. The engine of the car was still purring like a cat when Michelle made up her mind. She strapped Genesis back into her seat and then jumped in the driver's seat. She illegally U-turned, disrupting several lanes of low traffic, but caring little about it. All she had in mind was the safety of the only child she had. She was her everything.

It was at the hospital, after the doctors had wheeled the little girl away, that she made use of the hospital pay phone to call her husband at work.

"Rick..." she started, her voice shaking.

"Are you all right, Michelle? What's wrong?"

"No. Genesis had a seizure, and she fainted again. I'm—"

"What? Where are you now? Is she okay?"

"I'm... we are at CHOC. She had another seizure here at the hospital, Rick. They're going to keep her overnight. She's having trouble breathing."

"Okay, I'm coming right away," her husband replied.

Twenty minutes later, Richard met her at the Children's Hospital of Orange County, where she paced around in the waiting room. Seeing Michelle's tears and shaky body, he wrapped his arms around her. The moment he stroked her hair and told her everything would be all right, Michelle completely broke down.

"She was all right," Michelle squeaked, her voice wavering. She spoke quickly, barely giving herself a chance to breathe. "I mean, she looked all right. I was talking to her, but she wasn't responding. I thought it was one of those days when her classmates made fun of her again because of her small size. I wasn't sure what it was. I just knew something was wrong. I figured we would talk about it with her at home; I didn't want to be pushy. You know how bullying is a very sensitive issue with her, and I just didn't want her to shut down and push me away this time." Michelle was trembling.

"Take it easy, honey," Richard said, stroking her back to calm her. "Genesis will be just fine. Remember, she's a strong girl. This isn't the first time we've dealt with this; we know how to get through it. She'll pull through again."

Richard continued to console his wife, but it was obvious that he was also worried. Michelle knew Rick was scared too, but that for her sake, he remained strong.

"I know she will," Michelle sighed, hugging her husband tightly. "But for how long will she have to battle these fainting spells? The doctors have to do something about it. Why haven't they figured out what's wrong with her yet? I can't lose my baby girl, Rick." Michelle sobbed into Richard's shoulder.

He patted her on the back and drew her close.

There were nights when both of them would sneak into Genesis's room just to make sure that she was all right. Even though the doctors had not been able to put their fingers on what was truly wrong with their little girl, they still took her for check-ups regularly. They took no risks with her safety and spent every waking minute of their lives worrying about her as she continued to grow.

"Mrs. Gill?" the voice of a male nurse made them break their embrace.

While Michelle's eyes were visibly soaked in tears, Richard's were misty, trying to hide the fact through a wavering smile.

"Yes?" Michelle looked at the nurse.

"Doctor Chung will see you now. Down the hall and turn left. His office is just after the elevator," the nurse said before moving through a pair of doors marked AUTHORIZED PERSONNEL ONLY.

The Gills followed the nurse's directions to an ER cubicle. They settled in the cushioned chairs across from the young doctor, holding each other's hands.

"Can you tell us what's going on?" Michelle asked before the doctor could speak. "What's causing this?"

Doctor Chung readjusted the collar of his lab coat and looked at the Gills with an empathetic smile. "I'll cut right to the chase. The good news is that the neurologist found no issues with her brain. But we did find something else. She has something called pleural effusion, as well as what appears to be some type of chronic obstructive pulmonary disease. Basically, she has liquid trapped in the space between the lining of her lungs and chest wall. She also appears to have some obstruction of airflow into the lungs. These things are usually a symptom of another condition, such as cancer, pneumonia, or some serious chest injury. Has she ever had any of these conditions before?"

"Well, not that we know of. We adopted her a little over two-and-a-half years ago. So, if she had anything like that before, we weren't made aware," Richard answered.

"But this isn't the first time she's fainted or struggled to breathe. The other doctor told us she might have epilepsy. But none of the MRIs so far have shown any issues," Michelle added.

The doctor looked at his notepad and wrote something there. He nodded. "You know, it's a miracle she's survived up to this stage. But I'm glad we detected it as there is treatment available."

As the doctor went on about the surgery, the Gill's listened with rapt attention. Michelle squeezed Richard's hand to stop herself from bursting into tears, and Richard looked out the window behind the doctor, pensive.

"Whatever it takes. She is our treasure," Michelle said. "Whatever it takes to help her."

Irvine, California
June 2019

The scar on Genesis's chest would remain with her as a reminder: A reminder of fragility; a reminder of strength; a reminder of new opportunities, of things of old and things of new. And every day, for the rest of her life, she would see it, and be thankful for her life.

As she exited the shower, her phone rang. Looking at the screen, she answered it immediately and pressed the phone between her shoulder and her cheek, exiting the steam filled room.

"Hello, Gill," John said right away.

"Good morning, Mr. Macy. How are you?" She already knew the reason why her boss had called and was eager to hear his response.

"I read through your email, and I must say it is very thoughtful of you to go to Baja to cover the border situation there. This topic has been on my mind, and we haven't sent anyone to follow up since Trump took office in 2016. In all honesty, I would have liked to follow you there; but, as you know, I have an office to run and lots of correspondents to answer to."

Genesis shook her head. She knew that Mr. Macy used to be a great reporter during his hay days; the number of awards and plaques that dotted his office served as verification. "Thank you, Mr. Macey."

"Gill, I believe in your sound judgment and your ability to stay away from trouble," John continued. "But you haven't gone international in a while, so I don't want you to forget the rules. I know you can pull this off, and I am ready to give you all the support you might need. But I do want to say one thing, though."

"What's that?"

"When you write the piece, don't get too political. I'm not trying to micromanage you, and you know I trust all my people. It's just that we can't afford to lose any more readers right now."

Gigi fiddled with the towel wrapped tightly around her. "Is there anything in particular that you would like me to focus on?"

"Well, the way I see it, you have two options: One, I'd like to know more about the immigration crisis, especially with these large groups coming from Central and South America making their way north, and with not so much focus on the wall or how it affects the local economies. There has been plenty written about that lately. As I'm sure you've heard, the cartels have tunnels there to smuggle their merchandise, so I am sure that people are trafficked through there too. See what you can find out about that. At least it could be a start to your investigation."

"Okay," Gigi said as she cleared her throat.

"But I mean it, Gill, make sure to stay away from politics. Besides, that's not your thing anyway, and we have other people on the team that already take care of that anyway."

"I promise. And what is option two?" Gigi put the phone on speaker on top of the bed and began dressing herself.

"The second option is that you can do a typical Genesis Gill piece."

"What do you mean?" she chuckled. "What exactly is a *Genesis Gill piece?*"

Is he complementing me or insulting me?

"You know, Gill, stick to what you do best. You write stories about human life, stories that touch the readers' hearts. You're good at emotional pieces. So, investigate while mingling, and give us a story about the lives of the locals: their daily struggles, their fears. Tell us about the pros and cons about living on the border and being transnational. Talk to foreigners that are stuck there. If you go this route, you could write a piece that would move readers."

There was silence on the other end. She didn't know what to say, as she finished buttoning her dress.

"Gill, are you still there?"

"Yes, sorry, sir. I'm here. Okay, Mr. Macy. I can do that without a problem. To be honest, I do feel like the world needs to know what's happening there and about all these people who try to cross for a better life. Maybe I can do a bit of both...?" It was more of a question than a statement.

Genesis sat on the edge of the bed. She picked at a hangnail that stood out on her otherwise neatly pedicured big toe. She imagined how pleased Mr. Macy would be when he saw the hard-hitting piece she would create... after investigating her own roots, of course.

But there was a part of her that didn't feel at peace with using the paper's resources to conduct her own personal investigation. She was professional and ethical, so it didn't sit well with her to be deceptive and do it behind Macy's back.

She felt guilt.

"Yeah, sure. If you can make it work, why not? Surprise me, Gill. Like I always say, let the story guide you."

"Um, sir. There is something else I need to share." She clenched her teeth.

"Go on."

"I, uh..." She took a few barefoot steps and inhaled deeply, pacing back and forth along the carpeted bedroom. She didn't know how to say it. Or what to say exactly.

"Gill?"

"Yeah, I am here. Sorry, I just wanted to say..." She hesitated again. She couldn't do it; the risk that he would revoke the invitation were too great. "I just wanted to say, 'thank you,' sir," she finally said. "For everything, that is. It's been difficult for me lately, as you know. And you've been very supportive through it all. Both with the monarch project even though it took so long, and then more recently with my mom's passing. And even now letting me go on this venture, even though I am just barely coming back. So, yeah, that's what I wanted to say. Thank you. You're just... a great boss, sir."

"You're welcome, Gill. You're one of the good ones." He sounded relieved. "I'm truly glad you feel appreciated."

"I do." She opened the closet to look at her shoes.

"Okay, then. Make sure to CC me when you send the estimate of everything you'll need for the trip. And, actually, don't bother coming to the office today."

"Really?" She had just finished putting on her heels.

"Yeah, might as well start working on this. I want to send you out on this as soon as possible, before it becomes old news or someone gets to it first."

"Yes, sir. You'll have a breakdown in your inbox later this morning."

"Oh, Gill, and one last thing. I'm thinking of sending Bob with you on this trip. He can take great pictures and perhaps even catch some good footage to go along with your written piece. We could turn it into an entire exposé, or maybe even a series. Come to think of it, if done well, this piece could really give us the edge and attention we've been looking for."

Gigi's heart palpitated. *Oh, crap!*

She grabbed the phone and placed it on her ear, taking it out of speaker mode. "Well, no offense, sir, but I think that I can take care of this by myself. I still have the Canon Mark V and the lens with me from the last trip, and if I can borrow it and take it, I'll make sure to capture those moments myself. That way, we could save a lot of money too. No use sending two people on a one-man job."

"Gill..." Macy sighed, apparently hesitant to go on. When he spoke again, it was carefully. "Bob will be more than just your camera man. I cannot with a clear conscious send a young, attractive woman on her own to an international gig. You didn't go alone to Michoacán."

"Mr. Macy, I understand your concern. And I appreciate it, I really do. But you know that patronizing me—"

"I'm not trying to be sexist, Gill. All I'm saying is—"

"I know, sir, I know. But I'm a grown woman who can take care of herself, and I'm not a rookie, either. It's not like this would be my first time abroad. Plus, Baja is basically an extension of California. I've been there plenty of times. Besides, have I ever failed you?"

"No, you haven't. But I don't want this to be the first time either—not that it would be your fault. But..." He clucked his tongue. "Nobody is patronizing you, Gill. Bob is going."

Genesis grunted silently as she stared angrily at the award on her bedside table. "Look, Mr. Macy, you are always telling us how things are tough right now and that the budget only gets smaller each year due to less sponsors and decreasing readership. In fact, if I can recall correctly, it was you who taught me to be tough and resourceful while in the field. And I know that I had the best teacher, so I feel completely capable. My photography skills are superb. You've seen my work. And trust me, I won't need Bob as my bodyguard."

Mr. Macy heaved a heavy sigh. "You can be so stubborn sometimes, you know. And a pain in the butt. You're lucky I like you, girl."

Genesis smiled. "So, is that a yes? As in, you agree with me. No Bob?"

Macy chuckled on the other end of the line. "No, Gill. I'm simply telling you that you're stubborn. Why are you so adamant about going alone? Is there something else you're not telling me?"

Crap!

"No! I'm simply trying to be conscious of the budget." There was a silence. An awkward, suspicious silence. Gigi sighed and ran a hand through her hair. She sat down on the edge of her bed. "Okay, sir. Let me be honest. The truth is I just need to do this alone. I've been spending a lot of time by myself recently, thinking. It has been cathartic. And I feel like I need to get away and stay busy to keep me distracted from my mother's passing. A project like this is ideal. Look, I wouldn't even want Jay to come with me. If it makes you feel better, I can check in with you more than the usual."

Macy exhaled on his end. Gigi got chills.

"Okay, Gill. Just... please be careful. And yes, I do expect to hear from you when you get there, more than usual. I already have enough migraines. Make sure to check in with me at least *twice* a day to let me know your whereabouts and plans; once in the morning, and again in the evening. That'll give me peace of mind."

Gigi collapsed fully back onto the bed with a silent sigh of relief. "I promise," she said.

"I'm serious, Gill. Don't make me regret this."

"You won't!"

"Okay then. Blessings. Be safe."

"Thank you, sir! I *promise* you won't regret this."

Genesis's heart raced, and she raised her arm triumphantly. But still, she did not allow her elation to show in her voice as she bade her boss goodbye. It was only after she had dropped her phone next to her the mattress that she let out a cheerful, "Yes!"

Convincing her boss worked out, after all. Yes, there was some deception behind it, as she hadn't told him the full reason why she wanted to go; but she had every intention of investigating the story she pitched to him. And she would write an awesome piece too.

The tough nut she had to crack now was Jay.

That evening, Genesis sat across from Jay at the dinner table at her place. She had finally agreed to let him come over and cook for her. Jay lived with his mom, and would remain there until they got married. After this, her then mother-in-law would be moving to Jay's sister's house.

Once they'd sat down for their first course, Genesis had barely eaten a bite of her salad before she blurted, "Sooo... I'm going to Mexico."

Jay's fork clattered onto the table. "Okay...? Is it official? I mean, I'm sure there is more to this."

Gigi didn't reply, as her mouth was full.

Jay continued as he picked up his utensil, "You know I'm always down for a getaway. Did you change your mind—"

"Jay, no," she said, shoving a lettuce leaf into her mouth. She didn't realize how hungry she was until she got a whiff of the lasagna cooking in the oven. "*I* am going to Mexico."

"What do you mean?" he asked, reaching across the table to cover her hand with his.

She squeezed his hand and then gently pulled hers away to wipe her face with a napkin. She cleared her throat. "I'm going for myself, and it has to be *by* myself. I know this may be hard to hear, but I don't know how long I'll be gone. I need this, Jay."

"But why do you *need* to go? Is this about your origins or about the story?"

"Well..." She waved her fork around as she thought. "Yes."

"Yes, what?" He put his fork down and crossed his arms.

"Macy is sending me on a quest to write about the border. The pitch worked! And I think it would be a great article. But, as you already know, there is more to this."

Jay stared at her in silence, brow raised, waiting for her to continue.

"Yes, okay. It totally is about my biological parents too."

"I knew it!"

"Babe, I really need to find out where I came from and put the pieces of my adoption together. You know this has always weighed on my mind, and if I don't take this opportunity now, I fear I never will. The whole border piece is the perfect opportunity to do this. You know, like I said before, kill two birds with one stone."

"I know, babe. I do. But does Macy know about this other part?"

Genesis nodded, then shook her head.

"Well, which is it?" he asked with a slight chuckle.

"Not... exactly..." she said hesitantly. "Of course, I didn't tell him I'm going to figure out my past. Although, I think he suspects something. Yet, somehow it's also like he knows I need this."

"Wow," Jay said simply, rubbing his face with his hands. "This is a lot to take in. I thought you were done traveling for work for a little while. First with your mom passing away, and then this. I was hoping we would finally dive into wedding planning again. Honestly, I feel like this is just another delay."

"Babe, that's not fair!" She now put her own fork down.

"I'm not trying to be mean, G. It's just that I really do feel like we just keep postponing the plans." Jay got up to check on the lasagna.

"I know, and part of me feels horrible for doing this to you. Honestly. But if not now, when?"

"You're not horrible. I mean, I get it. It's just I wish the timing was different," Jay said from the kitchen.

"I know." Gigi let out a heavy sigh. "Me too. Look, I promise you, once I come back, whatever I find or don't find, our life will go back to normal. And the wedding planning, and our weekend getaways, and then—"

"And spending quality time with my fiancée!" he interrupted.

"Yes, all of that. I promise." She beamed.

"Okay," he said upon returning to the table while smiling back at her. "And where exactly are you going?" he asked while placing the lasagna on the middle of the table.

"Mexicali," she said raising her eyebrows. "I'm going close to your hometown."

Jay's eyes brightened as he sat back down. "You do know I still know a lot of people there, right? Like, super close friends of the family. I know people on both sides of the border, Calexico *and* Mexicali."

"Yes, I know. Actually, Macy suggested Tijuana, as it's a busier crossing point. Biggest international border in the world. But the orphanage is in Mexicali, so I figured I can do more there. I remember reading about narco-tunnels and other stuff like that in that city crossing. So maybe that can be my angle."

"Okay, babe. Just be careful, and check in every day. I know this is important to you, and I want to support you. I'll make some calls too." Jay then went silent. He started cutting the pasta dish.

"What's wrong?"

"Nothing. It's just that..." He paused.

Gigi scrunched her eyebrows and stared at his concerned eyes. "What, babe?"

"I'm worried."

"Worried about what, my love? I'll be fine there. Nothing is going to happen to me."

"No, it's not that. I'm worried that you'll keep searching for answers and may never find any. And I just don't want this to consume you, G. I don't want you to bury yourself so deep in questions, that you forget who you are."

Gigi stood up and rounded the table. She grabbed the chair closest to him and sat down. As she held his hands, she said, "I know who I am, my love. I know the kind of person I am with you, and who I am as a journalist. I know Dad and Mom loved me unconditionally, just as you do too. But I feel like I can't enter into a marriage without knowing as much as possible about the people who brought me into this world. This is the first time I've really settled on diving deep into my past, and it's a good opportunity that I might not get again. I can't go on with this heavy burden anymore. I need it before starting *our* family."

Jay pushed a few strands of hair from her face and smiled. He nodded.

Gigi fixed Jay's collar and picked lint off his shoulder. "I promise you, Jay, I won't lose myself. And I'll be safe. I just need to know more about the woman that gave birth to me and understand my medical history. This whole disease thing with Mom worries me. What if I also have something? Why was I always sick as a kid? I know there's a chance nothing will come of it, but I have to at least try." She pulled Jay's hands with her. "I can't explain it, babe. It's just something pulling me to my roots. And I can't fight it anymore."

"I know," he said and leaned forward to kiss her cheek. "Just be careful. Now, let's eat this thing before it gets too cold."

"Oh, I will," she replied as she went back to her chair. This thing smells amazing." After a few moments, she added, "I mean, what's the worst that could happen anyway?"

THE FLIGHT OF THE BUTTERFLY

CHAPTER FOUR

Even though it wasn't going to be her first time going international, Gigi felt uneasy. This was, after all, the first time she would be going on her own, without the comfort of someone else to guide her, protect her, or at the very least, keep her company. Regardless, this mission was important to her, and she felt the need to do it on her own. Besides, this time she would only be literally a few miles deep into Mexico.

The time was 8 am, and the traffic on Jamboree Road, the street just outside her apartment complex, echoed through the covered shutters of her bedroom windows. Genesis carefully looked over what she had packed—the camera, lens, Dictaphone, passport, jotter, pens— all spread out on her bed next to a suitcase filled with clothes. Nothing fancy, just the normal, light fabrics and fresh items she would need in the scorching desert heat of Baja California in the summer.

A tune from her laptop prompted her back to the kitchen table where her soggy bowl of cereal sat. The message came from Jay. She smiled as she opened it.

Gigi,

I figured writing you a message would be best for this. But what I need to say is too long for a text, so I figured I'd just email you for now.

Babe, I know that once your mind is made up, you will see any mission to the very end. I know that tracing your origin became your dream the moment that you told me your story and how you were adopted. I saw it clearly in your eyes. Last night, the hunger to go to Mexico, to uncover a huge secret, troubled you. You were trying hard to hide it, but I saw it in you.

When you told me the details about your mission in Mexico, my heart sank. But seeing the seriousness in your eyes, I knew that trying to discourage you was never going to work. What you need right now is support, and that was exactly what I signed up for when I slipped that ring on your finger a few months ago.

I have contacted a family friend from Mexicali, Alejandro Dasani, who we all call Das. He will keep you company and take you around the city while you're there. Think of him as your fixer. I spoke with Macey about this already, and he's on board.

Das is a very good friend of my sister, and I trust him. He's a great guy. He'll be waiting for you at the hotel where you'll be staying. I'll share his contact info with you through a text. Call him when you get to the border crossing.

I believe you'll find what you're looking for; and when you return, I shall be right here waiting for you. And soon, we will find ourselves walking down the aisle side by side. Stay out of trouble, babe. And, please, be safe! Keep in touch and see you soon.

Te amo!

Your BlueJay.

Genesis took in a deep breath in and let it out slowly. She really loved this man. He had a way with words that made her feel tingly in her stomach. *Not bad for a graphic designer.*

Gigi had had a few boyfriends before she met Jay, but none of them were as sensitive and supportive as him. While getting attention from men came easy to her, eventually, most of them found her strength and independence off-putting. Jay, however, found it endearing. He was selfless, caring, and loving. He always took good care of her, while also taking care of his aging mother.

The text sharing Alejandro Dasani's contact information came through as she was walking out the door. She replied to the text with a heart and a short message: "I'm leaving soon. I'll call you on the way."

Equipped with snacks and a full tank of gas, Genesis began her journey down the I-5 going south. She hated this interstate, its traffic, and its terrible drivers. Normally, she would drive in the opposite direction, toward Los Angeles, so this was an adventure in itself.

Never taking her eyes off the road, she dipped her hand into her bag on the seat beside her, pulled out a water bottle and took a sip as she slowed to a stop behind a long traffic jam. She sighed; it was going to be a long journey. She took this as the perfect opportunity to call her BluJay.

Two hours later, Genesis turned East on the I-8, in the heart of San Diego. A mile into it, she dozed off, drifting into the other lane. When another driver honked his horn, she jerked the wheel back toward her lane. Shaking her head, she turned the radio on to keep herself awake; alternative rock seemed a good choice. She looked at the clock to check the time. She was about halfway there, but she felt like she had been driving for days, even though it hadn't been that long. The San Diego traffic didn't help.

She lowered the window on her side to feel the fresh air billowing through the car. The sun outside fell lightly on Genesis's skin. She took in a deep breath and then closed the window when a shiver crawled up her spine.

Just over an hour later, after descending from the mountains, she reached the 111 Highway in a flat desert land and turned right, going south toward Calexico. According to her navigation app, she would arrive to her destination soon. Genesis was glad she had done a little research on the temperature of Mexicali before embarking on the journey. Still, the heat that leaped at her so suddenly made her nervous.

When she stopped at a lineup to cross the international border, Genesis dialed the number Jay had texted her. It was local a Mexican number, area code 686. A smooth voice picked up on the other end, in perfect English.

"Hello?"

"Hi, I'm Genesis Gill from the *LA Chronicle*, and Jay's fiancé. I was told to contact you right before crossing the border. I'm about to cross and should be at my hotel in about fifteen minutes, according to my GPS."

"Hi! Thanks for calling. I will be waiting for you there, Miss Gill. Welcome to Mexico."

And just like that, the conversation ended.

Gigi didn't expect to go through any rigorous process of customs searching and clearing her before passing in to the other country. She'd done this several times, and never without any issue. She'd gone down to Ensenada, the wine country, and Rosarito for spring break.

She had her blue passport ready, but was met with a red light signaling for her to proceed through on the side for inspection.

Well, here we go, she thought. *This isn't the best way to start this trip.*

She hoped this wouldn't take long. This Das guy would be waiting for her in fifteen minutes, and she really wanted to make it to her hotel already.

She slowly turned her vehicle to make it to the secluded area on the left. Once there, an armed officer signaled her to park and turn the car off. She obliged and remained in her seat. The same officer then came and took her passport before asking her to come out of the car and wait by a concrete bench nearby. She didn't need to speak Spanish to understand what he was asking of her. Another officer came with a dog, who sniffed all around her car. The officer with the passport returned it to her and asked her something in Spanish.

Gigi's Spanish wasn't horrible, but she didn't understand the man. He spoke too fast.

Upon realizing her confusion, the officer switched to English. "What is the purpose of your visit?"

"I am a reporter for the *LA Chronicle*. And I'm here to do a story about the wall."

"Ah," he responded with a chuckle, "You mean that ugly fence?" He motioned with his head.

Gigi simply smirked as she put away her passport in her purse. The officer with the canine called her over and asked her to open her trunk.

Gigi complied and opened her trunk with the remote on her key and sat back down.

"How long is this going to take?"

"Are you in a rush, miss?"

"It's just that someone is expecting me soon."

"Well, if you have nothing to hide, this shouldn't take long. You know how long they've made me wait when I've tried to cross to the US? I'm sure you understand."

Gigi heaved a heavy sigh, but remained quiet.

She considered taking out her phone to call Das and let him know, but she figured it would look suspicious, so decided against it.

"You know, speaking about the wall," the officer continued, "I have something to say."

"Oh, yeah? And what is that?" Gigi replied as the canine officer signaled for her that it was okay for her to leave. She stood up from the uncomfortable bench but listened to the officer.

"First, your president is an idiot. Here's why, he promised that he'd build a wall. And here we are, years later, and he didn't build anything. Then, he said that the Mexicans would pay for it. But, of course, Mexico wasn't going to pay shit for this. And that's not even the best part!" The man laughed out loud. "There already is a massive fence in place so there was never a need for another wall. Though the funniest thing is that even if a fifty-meter-tall wall had been built all across the border from San Diego to Brownsville, it wouldn't have done anything. You see, jumping fences is a thing of the past, madam. Mexicans are experts at tunnels. That's where the real deal is."

Gigi was getting ready to go back to her car, but the officer's words caught her attention. "Actually, that's a great point. Is there anyone in your department that I could talk to about your thoughts on the wall. Or maybe anything about these tunnels that I've heard about. I'd love to hear from your perspective. You know, especially as an official from Mexican customs. Would you like to go on record, maybe?"

The man looked perplexed for a moment. He cleared his throat and then said, "I don't have time for this, sorry. As you can see, we are busy on the job. Besides, we've been briefed that we are to redirect any media to my boss, Mr. Lorenz. However, what I can do for a pretty lady like you is I can see if you can make an appointment with him."

Gigi gave him a fake smile. "Sure. I appreciate that."

"You're gonna need to park on that side, though. I'll get back to you in a bit." The man signaled her to move her vehicle to the side.

Gigi moved her car and waited inside. She turned it on to blast the air conditioning, as the heat was unbearable. She called Das, but he didn't answer. She left him a message letting her know she'd be late, as she'd been detained at the crossing, but that she was also following a lead.

Several minutes later, the same officer knocked on her window. She was startled as she didn't see the man coming. She lowered the window once she gasped for air.

"Mr. Lorenz said he'd see you right now," the man said.

"Oh! That was... fast. Really? Okay."

She got out of the car and followed the uniformed man inside the office building. The man left to return to his post, and a lady told her to wait there. But she didn't have to wait much, as about a minute later, an older, ununiformed gentlemen with gray hair came to greet her with a stretched arm to welcome her.

"Hi. You must be Miss Gill. Roberto Lorenz, nice to meet you."

"Hi. Genesis Gill, *LA Chronicle*."

"Please, follow me."

They made their way behind the main desk and into a small office. At least it was nice and cool in there and it smelled nice.

"You know, it's not very often that big newspaper comes our way," Mr. Lorenz said as he offered her a seat. "Would you like some water?"

"I just drank a full bottle in the car. Thank you, though."

"So, my man tells me that you're inquiring about the *wall*, as your people call it, and wanted an official's input for your article. I have a few minutes. How can I be of service?"

"Yes. Um..." Genesis took out her notepad and pen, as well as her recorder. She then reached to the man's desk and took a business card from the pile. She wrote the man's full name and title.

"Is it okay if I record this. It helps me for later."

"Sure," Mr. Lorenz said with a smile. "However, I would prefer to remain unanimous."

"Oh! Yes, sure. Thank you," she said as she started recording. "Mr. Lorenz, if you don't mind, first tell me about yourself. What exactly is your role here?"

"My official title is *Sub Titular de la Oficina de Representación*. However, please make sure my name and title remain unmentioned. I don't want HR up my ass later, if you know what I mean."

Gigi nodded, though she really didn't know what he meant. Why had he agreed then?

"Mr. Lorenz, can you tell me, as an official in the Mexican immigration, what are your thoughts about *the wall*? And how will this impact people here, and you in your profession?"

Mr. Lorenz chuckled. "It'll be a waste of time. Not that I think it'd be ever built. But if it ever was, it would be a waste of resources."

"Why do you think that?"

"Look out the window," he said pointing behind himself. "There's already a gigantic fence. Not to mention multi-million-dollar, top-notch security systems and personnel patrolling the area. The wall is simply symbolic."

"How do you figure?"

"It was simply a point of talk... nothing more than another issue thrown out for political gain by your president."

"I've heard talk about some tunnels. Would you care to share about that?"

Mr. Lorenz cleared his throat. He looked around, and cleared his forehead of some sweat. He motioned for her to stop the recording. Confused, Gigi obliged.

"Look, Miss Gill, I'll be frank. I'll tell you what I know about these tunnels. Much of this is common knowledge with the locals, to be honest. But being in the profession that you are, I would be very careful going around asking too many questions about these tunnels. Some journalists have disappeared because they dug too deep, if you know what I mean."

Gigi smiled. "I've been threatened many times before, Mr. Lorenz. I am well aware of the risks of the profession."

"Yes, Miss Gill, but this is Mexico. It's no threat. I wouldn't want anything bad to happen to you, that's all. Again, allow me to share, but don't go asking around too much about these things, for your own safety. Promise me that."

Gigi nodded. "Okay."

"Promise me, Miss Gill. One thing is local journalists disappearing... another thing is a reporter from the *LA Chronicle* going missing here. Nobody wants that kind of broadcast."

"I promise," she said. "Now tell me what you know about these tunnels."

"Well, Miss Gill, it's time for a history lesson. You see, when the city of Mexicali was founded, many of its original settlers were Chinese that had been working on the railways. Most of them came from Sonora, while some others were kicked out from the north. Either way, people didn't want them—not in the south and not in the north. So, they settled here in great numbers. It was an opportunity to start anew for them, and there was a lot of work due to the cotton fields. However, pretty soon, many of them opened opium bars and other things as such."

"Opium bars?"

"Yes, Miss Gill. Opium bars, and places for other vices."

"Interesting."

"Yes, indeed. And by other vices, I mean, alcohol, women, gambling, and such."

"I get it," Gigi said.

"In what is now the old part of the city, many of the Chinese people and several other business owners created an underground city, all connected through tunnels. You see, in places like Montreal, for example, there are underground stores and whatnot, for people to escape the cold. Something similar happened here, but it was to escape the heat, instead. Although, of course, a lot if it was to conduct business activities that weren't exactly legal. Also, many of the Chinese citizens were not living legally in Mexico, so they also lived underground. With time, that whole area became known as *La Chinesca*, which is basically the city's Chinatown, similar to other cities around the world. And even though most the Chinese population didn't all live there, it's where most of the Chinese-owned businesses remained."

Gigi jot down a few notes while nodding. "And how does all of this play a factor into the tunnels?"

"Ah, yes. Well, fast forward half a century," Mr. Lorenz continued. "When prohibition started in the US, these tunnels started to be used to smuggle liquor to Calexico. They were so popular, that many people even connected these tunnels and that practice to Al Capone. He was seen in the area many times, apparently."

"You're saying that Al Capone used these tunnels?"

"Oh, yes! Among others in other border cities."

"I did not know that."

"We learn something new every day, Miss Gill. And well, after prohibition ended, so did the need for many of these tunnels. At some point, there was a big fire in the area, and many of the Chinese people living underground died. Many businesses were closed after that, and the government sealed the tunnels. People never lived there anymore after that. But, of course, some tunnels survived. Many of the business owners kept them and utilized them for storage or whatnot."

Gigi kept taking notes. "Sure, that makes sense."

"But let's move forward in time once again. In the early 1980s, there was a huge rise in drug consumption in the US. And some Mexican farmers mostly from the jungles of Sinaloa jumped the gun and took this as a business opportunity. And the cartels were created. Supply and demand, Miss Gill. They had the product and the client; they just needed a passageway to get it to them. In the late 80s and early 1990s the Colombians brought a new product that took weed off the shelfs. And the Mexican cartels wanted a piece of that. When the DEA stopped all the embarks in the Caribbean going to Florida, the Colombians had no choice but to rely on the Mexican cartels to smuggle their product through the Mexican-American border. With time, the Mexican cartels took control and broke into factions. By this time, Miss Gill, the tunnels were brought up again. But with capital and unlimited funding, these tunnels were taken to the next level. These tunnels now had electricity, running air, and were wide enough for large trucks to go through."

"So, even today these tunnels under Mexicali are being used to smuggle drugs across the US?"

"What do you think? I am talking drugs, people. But also, to smuggle weapons going south. It goes both ways. I am not sure if you know this, Miss Gill, but firearms are illegal in Mexico. And once again, we have the issue of supply and demand. And that's how cartels have gotten so powerful."

Gigi wasn't expecting any of this. This is not the direction she'd thought her story would go, but she found it fascinating. Maybe she could cover this, but still stay true to the humanistic approach that Mr. Macy had asked for. It'd be a challenge, but she'd make it work, one way or another.

"Thank you, Mr. Lorenz. This is all very valuable information. I'll look deeper into this."

"Don't!" Mr. Lorenz said. "You promised you wouldn't look too much into it. At least, don't pursue this while you are down here."

Gigi though about it for a moment. "Okay. I'll see what I can do. But I'll let the story guide me. It's what we do."

Mr. Lorenz's phone rang and he told her he had to go. Gigi nodded and stood up. She thanked him and walked away back to her car.

Arriving at the Hotel Lucero not much later, she parked and got out of her car, entering the dead heat of the afternoon. The sun was so bright that even wearing dark sunglasses, Genesis struggled to look around without squinting. She walked toward the lobby where a man wearing a flat cap welcomed her. He wasn't one of the bell boys.

"Miss Gill?" the handsome, dark-skinned man called to her, his smile bright. "Do you need help with your luggage? I recognize you from the picture Jay sent me."

He had a pleasant expression under a grayish beard, and kind eyes. Genesis was quick to notice that, even though he wore a loose, light-green button-up shirt, his muscles were clearly defined, pulling against the fabric at his biceps.

Genesis nodded. "Thank you. Nice to meet you," she said, extending her hand.

This prompted him to come forward, shake her hand, and take the rolling suitcase from her. "I am so sorry that you got detained at the crossing. I hope everything was okay."

"Oh, actually, it all worked out great. And I got to interview someone there, so I take it as a win, actually."

"I see." The man picked up the suitcase. "Jay told me you didn't know how long you'd be here, but this doesn't seem like what you would pack for a lengthy stay."

"I always pack light. Makes it easier to move around."

"I see. Play by your own rules," he said. "Well, as I said, welcome to Mexico. I am Alejandro Dasani, but you can call me *Das*, just like everyone else."

"Thank you, Das," Genesis said with a smile.

"Let's check you in and get you settled. By the way, you are way prettier in person."

As usual, when it came to compliments on her appearance, Genesis didn't know what to say and simply smiled.

Together, they walked toward the lobby where a lean, young bell boy collected Gigi's bag from Das. Das spoke in Spanish to him in a quick manner, too fast for Genesis to understand. The bell boy turned to Genesis, gave her a bright smile, and welcomed her in an accented English.

As they walked toward the tower in which her room was, they passed a few inviting pools. She would certainly make use of them later, especially with this heat. Especially now that she could, since it had been three weeks since getting her tattoo.

When they got to her room on the fourth floor, Das opened the door for her and the bell boy placed Gigi's suitcase by the desk. The room was nice and clean, but most importantly, the temperature was cool.

Das leaned against the door frame while Genesis familiarized herself with the room. "Nice place. You'll be comfortable here. Oh, by the way—" His change in tone brought Gigi's eyes to him. He reached into his pocket and pulled out a slip of card. "Use this while you're here. Even though I'm sure you can use your phone, it will be easier to communicate with you if you have a local number."

Genesis took the SIM card. "Thanks. What do I owe you?"

"Nothing," he said firmly. "I just want to help you, that's all. Besides, the Rodriguez's are like family, and soon you'll be too. Jules is like my sister, and Jay will always be Little J to me, no matter how big he is."

Genesis laughed. "Thank you, I appreciate that. I'll be sure to tell Jay how kind you were. He'll be happy to hear you're doing well."

Das winked and said, "You got it, girl. Get some rest. Today, just acclimate yourself. Relax and enjoy your stay. I'll pick you up tomorrow morning to begin."

As he turned to leave, Gigi stopped him. "You know..." He turned back to face her, and she continued, "I meant to tell you, you really don't have to come with me," she said. "I don't like being a burden, and this trip is... well, it's kind of personal to me. I wanted to come here alone, and I only agreed to let you help me to give Jay peace of mind. Can you just tell him that you helped me and we can go our separate ways?"

Das laughed. "Jay said you might try to cut me out. He also told me that I must insist on coming with you. Apparently, your boss is on board too."

"Ugh, of course."

"Look, trust me. It'll be useful to have a local on your side, especially when you're not familiar with the area. Journalist or not, you need my help. And if anything, I'll be good for the company. I can be a charming man when I really want to be."

Genesis rolled her eyes. "Okay, if it means that much to Jay *and* Macy, I guess I'll let you come along. Just don't ask too many questions."

Das grinned. "Sounds good," he said, letting the door close. "*Adios!*"

When he was gone, Genesis groaned and flopped onto the bed.

Of course, Jay would get Macy involved. She appreciated their concern, but on such a personal trip, it wasn't entirely welcome.

She thought it would be good to wind down after a tiresome drive, so she spent the rest of the day swimming and reading by the pool, but not before checking in with Mr. Macy and Jay, as she had promised.

In the nighttime, Gigi went to the hotel's bar. While there, she overheard some of the bell boys talking to a guest. Though her Spanish wasn't the best, it was good enough to understand. The guest had asked one of them where he was from, as he'd heard an accent, and the young service worker was telling him that he'd come from El Salvador. He'd been here for a couple of years already and was saving enough to eventually cross the border to be with his family in Los Angeles.

She casually approached the two young workers once the other guest left and asked them, "Hi! I don't mean to intrude, but I just overheard you, so I wanted to ask you a couple of questions, if you don't mind." She was always on the job, even when she wasn't.

The two workers looked at each other and upon realizing she was struggling with some Spanish, one of them answered in English. "Sure. How can we help you?"

"Oh, you speak English. Great! That'll certainly be easier," she replied. "I'm actually staying here. And I don't actually need anything; I was just wondering if I could ask you guys a couple of quick questions."

"Sure. About what? We know the city well, so we'd gladly point you in any direction. I know the best places to eat. If you want to party, this guy over here is the expert." The two boys laughed.

"I see." She smiled. "Well, I'm not here to party, unfortunately. I am actually a reporter for the *LA Chronicle* and I am here on business." She extended her arm to introduce herself. "My name is Genesis Gill, and I'm doing a story on..." She stopped. She sighed. "I'm doing a story on the tunnels that cartels use to smuggle drugs and people across the border. I heard that you are here temporarily and want to cross eventually to be with your family."

One of the young men smiled and said he had to go in Spanish. He said he was needed somewhere. The other one who'd spoken with the other guest remained and nodded.

"I'm sorry Missis Genesis," he said. "I don't know how much I can help you with that. I don't know anything about that. And I really have to get back to work."

"Oh, I see." She cleared her throat. "I understand. Well, thank you for your time, then."

She took a heavy sigh as the young man stared at her from a distance and eventually started to interact with new guests arriving. She figured she'd just start tomorrow, then.

Alright, I guess we'll pick it up tomorrow.

THE FLIGHT OF THE BUTTERFLY

CHAPTER FIVE

Mexicali, Baja California
June 2019

Taking the notepad from her purse, Genesis leaned against the headboard of the bed and marked the date. The bright morning had come quickly after a restful night, and Genesis had woken with firm resolve. All she wanted was to go outside and start searching, but experience told her she had to draw up a detailed list to prepare for her day.

First, she had a job to do—an article to write for her boss. That would involve some digging. She would need to talk to both locals and foreigners residing here to see a full picture. There were multiple angles involved in this, along with immigration, drugs, international relations, and so on.

Secondly, she couldn't forget about her own personal mission here. It was this quest that mattered most to her.

But where to even begin?

And then there was Das, who had stopped by the hotel again last night after her bath, supposedly to check on her. She wondered if he would soon become an impediment to her.

Genesis chewed on her pen, brows knitted and lost in thought, when her phone rang.

"*Bonjour, belle.* I trust you slept well," Das's charming voice came through the phone.

"Yes, I slept well. Thank you. Good morning to you, Das. I didn't know that in addition to Spanish and English, you also speak French," she replied.

"That's because I am versed in multiple languages. I also speak Portuguese, in case you were wondering."

"No, I wasn't," she replied with a laugh, "but that's good to know, I guess. I can see you're also very modest," she teased sarcastically, prompting a laugh out of him.

"So, I've been told before. Modesty is one of my millions of enticing qualities." A snort matched hers from the other end of the line. "Anyway, Gigi, what are you up to this morning? Do you wanna go drug busting today, or what?"

Genesis heard the excitement in Das's voice, but wasn't sure if he was still being sarcastic. She didn't know him well enough. She simply gave another hearty laugh. Drug chasing and busting was way off from her agenda—at least for now. If she was going to do anything besides research for her article, then her first call would have to be to find the orphanage from where she had been adopted. Genesis knew she could get most, if not all, of the answers she sought from the orphanage, assuming they still had all the proper records.

"Drug busting is not my thing, Das. Thanks. But I could use your help; I need a guide and a translator." The words came out of her mouth as she doodled flowers on her notepad. "My Spanish is kinda... rusty."

"Sounds good. Besides, that is the right answer. Remember... as long as you don't go searching for something that isn't there, your wish is always my command," Das replied.

"You sound just like Jay making sure I don't go down a dangerous road."

"I will be there at 9 am. Please go eat breakfast at the hotel buffet. It is amazing! You won't want to miss it." He added a quick goodbye before dropping the call.

Genesis smiled and placed the phone down. As she walked over to the desk and sat in the padded chair, the name of the orphanage her father had told her rang in her head. She found her notes and confirmed the name. That was exactly where she was going to start.

Casa Hogar San Jose.

Das hadn't lied; the breakfast buffet had been nothing short of divine. Gigi was stuffed and would be good for most of the day. Das had said he would pick her up at 9 am, and to be ready on time. She still had some time.

While getting ready, Genesis checked in with Macy. "Good morning, sir."

"Morning, Gill. Everything good?"

"Yes, sir. Just checking in, once again, as promised. I just wanted to let you know that I've contacted my fixer. He will be my guide and translator as he shows me around. Of course, as you already know, he is a friend of Jay's."

"Oh, good. I am glad things worked out in that sense. Still, Gill, you know my usual speech. Be careful. Whatever you do, wherever you go, keep an eye open. Always be prepared for the unexpected. And again, be extra careful. Don't go chasing rabbit holes unless you're prepared to face what's in there. And in your case, just don't."

"Yes, sir. I know, I know! Be extra careful. Be prepared. *Et cetera.* Always, sir."

"Good. I'm just making sure."

"Thank you, Mr. Macy. I'll talk to you later." With that, she hung up as she got a text.

"I'll be there in 5." It was Das. 8:45 am. This guy was on military time.

Gigi noticed that she hadn't charged her phone the night before, staying on it until late, and the battery was about to die. She quickly plugged her phone and hurried to finish getting ready.

A few moments later, Genesis rushed outside to the hotel entrance. The sound of a rumbling engine echoed through the parking lot. She looked over and saw a dark-green convertible Mustang kicking up dust; her ride for her trip. Right on time, as he has said. But she winced. The sun would be on her skin all through the journey. While she appreciated a nice tan, she was not in the mood for constant scorching heat enveloping her body.

"Nice ride!" she called out, but Das couldn't hear her until he turned off the engine.

He got out of his car and walked to the passenger's side to open the door for her. "*Buenos días*, beautiful lady. Your chariot awaits."

"I can open my own door, thank you," she said with a smile.

"You need a hat first," he said quickly, then grabbed a women's wide brim straw hat from the backseat.

"I do? What for?"

"Just trust me. You'll thank me later, my lady. The adventure begins now."

"I mean, I guess... Well then, thank you, my knight," she said sarcastically, and performed a slight curtsy in her plum dress. She put on the hat and settled into her seat. When she was buckled in, she asked, "By the way, is there any chance I could drive this beast at some point?"

"Not a chance," he said firmly, closing the door on his side. "Only I can tame the beast. She requires a special touch, if you know what I mean."

"If you say so!" Gigi smirked.

"Nice dress, by the way."

"Thanks. It has pockets!"

Das laughed as he revved the engine. "That's cool, I guess."

Gigi joined him in laughter. Das engaged the reverse gear, then backed out of the parking lot before re-engaging and proceeding on their journey. A light wind blew dust on the road, providing brief relief from the burning sun.

"Did you know that I follow your career back in the States?"

"Oh, really?" Gigi raised a bemused eyebrow in Das's direction. "Thank you. I mean, that's random, but okay. What do you think?"

"Yeah! I'm a fan. I'm, like, totally fangirling right now."

She chuckled. "You're ridiculous."

He smirked and shook his head, eyes still on the road. "In all honesty, I do like your pieces. I like your style. I enjoyed your piece about the trafficked children. It really got to me."

Gigi nodded. "Yeah, that one got to me too." After a moment of silence, she asked, "By the way, I noticed your English sounds pure American. No tinge of accent attached like some other people here," Genesis observed. "Not that I've dealt with many people yet, but I know what a person born in Mexico should sound like."

"Okay, one, that's racist *and* ignorant," Das pointed, and Gigi smiled awkwardly, "but I'll let it pass. And two, that's because I studied most of my years in Calexico, on the other side of the fence. I grew up on both sides of the border; it's a common thing around here. I did the last chunk of elementary, junior high, and part of high school over there at a private school. My parents wanted my siblings and I to learn English, so they made sure we did. I met your soon-to-be sister-in-law Jules and also Jay back in high school when they used to live by the border with their dad," Das replied. "Jules and I were in the same grade, and Jay must've been in junior high then."

"Oh, I see. That's interesting."

"I'm not sure if you're being sarcastic with me right now."

"What? No, I mean it!" Gigi exclaimed. "To be honest, the idea of growing up binational and bicultural fascinates me. I've read plenty on Third Culture Kids, especially since I am engaged to one. I love meeting people that break the mold of stereotypes. And I've got to admit, throughout my years in journalism, I've met a lot of people who break stereotypes."

"You shouldn't have stereotypes to begin with," he said while shifting gears to pass a slower car.

"Yeah, you're probably right." Gigi looked out the window, staring at the endless stores.

"Speaking of journalism, how do you intend to tackle the issues of cartels, tunnels, and all that mumbo jumbo without getting into trouble?"

"What do you mean?"

Das gave her a look of surprise. "Well, some may that think you're an undercover agent, leading an investigation on *narcos* or something. It's happened before. And, you know, there are powerful people here linked to cartels who also have ties to the government and have people feeding them information. It may seem weird, but the moment you start asking too many questions, a tail may be attached to you. It's basically inviting trouble."

Gigi shrugged. She took out a piece of gum and offered one to Das. "That's the price we pay for being reporters. Our lives are connected to several people at once. The moment we tell people who we are, the suspicion creeps in. But don't worry, Das, I won't be snooping around enough to catch the attention of any people that could cause us harm. I hope..." she replied using her hands to make a praying motion. "My gut usually leads me in the right direction. But if I do get into trouble, don't worry; I know how to get out of it."

"If you say so. You know, I've looked into the tunnels myself in the past." Das cleaned the sweat on his forehead running from under his hat.

"You have? Why? Like, out of personal curiosity or some conviction?"

"You could say that. In fact, I'm actually working on finding out how human trafficking and prostitution rings operate in this part of the world. Many of the people are coming down from the south or from giant ships ferried in through Asia. The young girls brought in are forcibly converted to call-girls. Some people are even used as baggage to transport all kinds of narcotics to the States. Almost all of them are taken there through the narco-tunnels. Some they've found recently are quite sophisticated, with paving, ventilation, and electricity." Das honked at a slow pickup truck crossing the intersection. Then maneuvered a bend to bring the car to a stop at a red light.

He had piqued her interest, though. Prostitution? Human trafficking? Narco-tunnels? These were all things she cared about reporting. She yearned to highlight the truth behind these operations, which were sadly glorified in television shows and other forms of media. Her eyes sparkled with curiosity.

"Anyway," Das continued, "I didn't get too far myself, but perhaps you'll find out more than I could. Just promise me one thing: please don't go around asking about the tunnels just anywhere. If you don't have a reliable source out here already, don't try to find someone new. I'm taking you to a few good starting points, but do your best to be subtle. Extremely subtle. I can't stress that enough."

"I heard that before already. Okay, so, what if I actually came here to find someone or something from the past that had nothing to do with what I told you?" Genesis asked abruptly as she removed her dark shades from her eyes, her right hand resting on her waist.

Das looked at her. "What do you mean?"

"Don't get mad, but what if I've already been asking around about... well, what you just mentioned?"

Das let out a heavy sigh and fixed his hat. "You have?"

"Don't worry, Das. I only asked some hotel workers about their thoughts on this, and on the recent news stories," she replied. "I just wanted to know what they knew, but I didn't get very far. Besides, they barely spoke English, and I barely speak Spanish."

"Well…" Das said as he shifted gears and raced through the green light. "Let's just hope it doesn't lead to anything bad, then."

"Are you sure she's in there?" Beto said.

"Yes!" replied the bell boy. "I helped her and another guy take her luggage up to her room myself, and she tipped me with a ten-dollar bill. I think she's loaded. She was at the pool yesterday for a while; she's pretty hot. Anyway, later in the night she started asking questions."

Beto looked at the hotel tower on the left one last time before dipping his hand into his back pocket and bringing out his wallet while he said, "The boss appreciates you calling." He took out a coral-colored five-hundred-pesos bill and handed it to the boy. "We will take it from here. Leave now."

The boy took the bill and ran back to work.

A wicked smile crossed Beto's lip's, but he cursed under his breath as he became aware of the heat radiating from a van to his side, concealing him from view. He took off his sunglasses and wiped his face with a handkerchief pulled from his jacket. He stared at his hands with his good eye, feeling the condensation on his skin. A deep socket with an equally deeper gash took the position of his other eye; a scar streaking down his left cheek ensured any smile came out as a sneer.

At that moment, a dark-green convertible Mustang made the bend and noisily drove into the parking lot of the hotel. It stopped, and a man wearing a funky flat cap jumped out of the driver's seat. This was the man Andres had told him about. He smiled.

Strong. But still an easy target.

A young woman approached the car. Thin, but fit, most likely in her late twenties. They spoke briefly, then both entered the vehicle.

As the sound and smoke from the exhaust pipe faded into the distance on the busy Justo Sierra Boulevard, the man with dark shades dipped his hand into his pocket and drew out a phone. He dialed a number and said, "I'm texting you a plate number. You know what to do."

Before the person on the other line could respond, he hung up. Satisfied that his orders would be followed, he returned the phone back into his pocket and walked over to a crimson Chevrolet truck parked a few steps away from the van, where two other men waited for him. He got inside.

"Let's go," he told them, and they sped out of the parking lot in pursuit of the Mustang.

CHAPTER SIX

Looking out at the passing city, Gigi couldn't help feeling a sense of familiarity. They could easily be in any neighborhood in Los Angeles. They passed a couple of overpasses and a tunnel, and Das kept driving. Soon, the traffic lessened, and the urban became rural. Gigi began to feel concerned.

"Hey, where are you taking me? I thought we were starting at Refugio San Jose in Avenida Maderos?" Genesis asked as the car kept going west on the highway. "San Jose is the same orphanage my father picked me up from. He's told me everything he knows about it."

"I understand," Das said solemnly, giving her a sideways glance. "But listen to me, you don't come to Mexico and leave in a hurry without experiencing local life. I wouldn't be a very good tour guide if I didn't take you to the true Mexico."

"Oh, really? You don't say. And experiencing true Mexico means to adorn myself with a pretty straw hat and start driving down an endless road?" Genesis pouted. The wind created by their speed felt good, nonetheless.

"Yes; that *is* part of it. Sun, good company, and an endless road to freedom."

Genesis laughed and let out an excited "Woo!" across the land. The desert view with the mountain backdrop was beautiful, so she couldn't complain, not really. There was time, after all. She hadn't told anyone a projected return date. If John asked anything when she checked in with him this evening, she would just tell him she found a good lead that she couldn't pass up. *Work hard, play hard* was his philosophy, and she liked it. Das smiled at her unexpected whimsical outburst.

He pushed a button to close the roof of the car, and they continued driving outside the western suburbs. The vast sandy flatland outside the city was completely isolated. One could die here alone and never be found, that's for sure.

"Is this the part where you throw me out of the car and tell me to fend for myself? We've driven a pretty straight route, so I should have no problem navigating back to the city."

Das showed a weak smile. "I would never abandon a pretty lady in the desert. Shoot, I'd never leave anyone here, period. Trust me; this is no place to camp, anyway. The heat would kill you before dehydration did."

Soon, they were driving up the mountains, and no matter how many times she asked, he still wouldn't tell her where they were going. But she picked up his idea fairly quickly once she saw the signs. Within an hour they'd passed the city of Tecate. Gigi knew Tijuana wasn't far after that. Turning to Das, she grinned. "I thought we weren't going to look for trouble."

"True, but this is the fun kind of trouble," he said with a wink.

After about an hour and a half of driving, Gigi finally caught sight of the sea that was quickly approaching as they drove down the city heavily populated by hills. She threw Das a look of delight. "This is what you call investigative journalism, huh? Going to the beach and every other city in this state?"

"No. I'm off duty today, and I believe that you are as well," Das replied with a laugh. "I'm still saving the best for last. When we get back to Mexicali, I'll take you to a place that serves the *best* tacos anywhere in the world!"

"I'm always down for tacos. But... off duty, huh? What do you do for a living? I mean, how can you just take off in the middle of a weekday?"

"I'm in sales. I'm a rep. In fact, I have some business to attend to up here in TJ, which is why I had to come and couldn't wait. I figured I might as well bring you along."

"So much for being off duty," Gigi shot him a sly grin. "What do you sell?"

"All kinds of stuff. I'm more of a middleman, actually. But enough about my work. Let's enjoy the moment!" Das turned the radio volume up.

The stereo in the car blasted Mexican ska. Genesis enjoyed the music throughout the trip, even though she wasn't familiar with it and didn't understand half of the lyrics. Das had good taste, and she found herself moving along to the rhythm in her seat.

After a few songs, Genesis lowered the music. "Das, I've been thinking. I happen to have my Dictaphone right here with me. Why not make a start?"

"I thought this was a break—"

"I am starting with you," Genesis countered. "Right here, right now. After listening to you so far, and as my fixer, I actually think you can help me out a lot."

She dipped her hand into her bag and retrieved the recording device, which she clicked and held to her mouth. She said some words and put it on replay to see if the effect of the wind outside the car was going to affect the quality of the recording. There was no interference at all, so she pushed the recorder toward Das.

"Now, Mr. Dasani, please state your full name."

He cleared his throat. "Um... Alejandro Dasani. What are you going to ask me?"

"Don't worry about it. Just go along with it."

"Okay...?"

"Anyway, Mr. Dasani, as a local of this beautiful state, what do you have to say about all these immigrants coming daily into the border cities of Mexicali and Tijuana? Also, how do you feel about these underground tunnels used to traffic drugs and humans to the United States?"

"Nothing. I'm not an immigration officer, so I don't know anything," Das replied giving Genesis a dubious look. "Besides, if these people don't bother me, then I won't bother them. I have no issues with people simply wanting a better life. Some come here from other southern states or even other countries and stay. In the same way, many others, including, as you know, some of my fellow *paisanos*, go north of the fence for a better life too. It's simply a fact of life."

"You mentioned to me that you had personally seen giant container ships in the Ensenada harbors that had a large number of Asian immigrants within them. You also mentioned the thousands of people coming from Central America and southern Mexico. And now, we see the recent influx of Haitians and people from the Congo who came to ask for political asylum in the U.S., but got stuck on the Mexican side of the border. How do you feel the local economy is affected by all of these groups?" Genesis could have asked more questions, but she was running out of breath.

Das looked at the recorder held by Gigi close to his face as he drove. He cleared his throat once again. "Look, what I said I mostly watched on the news. I don't think I can tell you anything that everybody else doesn't already know."

It was evident he was uncomfortable by the way he shifted in his seat, so she would have to try something else. Gigi turned off the device and said, "Okay, if you're not willing to be interviewed, I can't force you. What if you remain an anonymous source?"

Das gave her a look, so she put the recorder back in her purse, defeated.

They sat in awkward silence for a short while. Trying to lighten the mood, Genesis grabbed a pen from her purse and pretended to hold the recorder in her hands. "So, Mr. Dasani, why exactly do you wear golf hats on a daily basis?"

Das looked at her with one brow raised, then burst out laughing. Genesis joined in.

"Well, my dear, if you really want to know, I don't mind answering *that*. Here, take a peek." Das took off his flat cap and revealed a deep receding hair line. "I'm not even forty, and I'm going bald. It's hereditary. I thought about shaving it all off, but I don't have the courage just yet. Besides, I've always been a hat type of guy."

"Well, if you ask me... I think hats suit you well."

"*Gracias, señorita*. I'm glad you approve of the look. I have a huge collection by now. It's pretty much the only thing I ever get for birthdays and Christmases. Of course, I don't mind."

A few songs later, the car reached the coast; a magnificent beach that was also a tourist attraction. The infinite blue of the Pacific Ocean served as a backdrop to different people, both local and foreign, that could be seen walking around, some armed with cameras, while others splashed in the waves. Girls dressed in bikinis were playing volleyball against a group of lads having fun spiking the ball far away to make the girls walk a distance to bend and retrieve it.

"Welcome to Playas de Tijuana, Ms. Gill," Das said to Genesis as he powered off the engine in a dirt parking lot a block away from the beach. "That's why I brought my sister's straw hat—so that you could use it to shade yourself from the sun while here."

"The sun is everywhere, not just at the beach," she laughed.

"Well, now you can blend in with the others, local and tourists. You can walk around and do your thing. This breeze will be a nice break from the Mexicali heat. I would've taken you to Rosarito, since the beach there is better, but like I said, I have to meet some people here in the area. You can ask questions about the immigrants if you so wish. You'll find plenty of them here, working in all the service areas. Just don't ask about drugs. If you need anything, call me, and I'll be back in a jiffy."

As the two of them exited the car, a red Chevy truck with tinted windows came in behind them and parked a few spaces away.

"Let's meet back here... say, in two hours," Das didn't give Genesis the time to reply before walking off into the crowd, the opposite direction to the beach. Genesis watched him walk away until she could no longer see his flat cap above the sea of heads, and she shrugged. She was an adult and was used to doing things on her own, anyway. She would pull this off herself.

Turning her gaze from the hill, she looked around and leaned against the car to admire the beach. On the right end, she could see the international fence going all the way into the water, separating these two nations. In the distance, behind that fence, she perceived what seemed to be downtown San Diego. She began to walk the boardwalk south, toward the busier side of the beach.

The question she kept asking herself over and over in her head was where exactly was she going to start? She hadn't envisaged it to be this difficult, but there was so much going on at the beach and too many people to question. She struck up conversations with a few Americans, but most of them had no information. She had to find someone who she knew was local.

Readjusting her straw hat, she started walking toward the first food cart she saw. The young man standing beside it looked Chinese.

"Excuse me, how much for a coconut?" Genesis asked in broken Spanish to the young man.

He raised his head, with a quizzical gaze. When he saw her, his face broke into a smile. The sweat that was finding its way down the side of his head plastered his hair to both sides of his face.

"*Hola, señorita.* Just pick your choice, and I will prepare it for you." His Spanish was flawless, as it if was his first language. This surprised Gigi. She wasn't used to hearing Asians speaking Spanish. In fact, this was the first time she'd experienced it.

"Please, you choose one for me yourself. I am a stranger in these parts; I just arrived yesterday," Genesis replied, smiling. "They all look the same to me, to be honest," she remarked, this time with a laugh.

The young man looked at her closely, from her hat, all the way down to her wedges. This made Genesis uneasy, but she didn't stop smiling. The boy said something in Cantonese. Gigi had no idea what he was saying and simply looked puzzled.

"*Lo siento.* I don't speak Chinese," she said.

"Oh, *perdón.*"

"*Yo soy de California,*" she continued in Spanish.

"Ah, American. I assumed you had just arrived from China when you said you just got here," the man said in English. Gigi was relieved to find he spoke her language better than she spoke Spanish... or Cantonese.

"I apologize for the mix-up," Gigi said. "I'm actually here working." After seeing how the young man ogled at her with a confused, judging look, she continued, "My name's Genesis. I'm a reporter for the *L.A. Chronicle.* I'm doing a piece on... well, on a lot of things. I'm not entirely sure how it's going to turn out. But I'm basically trying to share the human side of people on the border. Locals and foreigners."

"Ah, that is interesting."

"Would you like to contribute? I mean, I find it fascinating that there is such a large Chinese community here who have adapted to Mexican culture, but also keep their own traditions. Especially since I am Chinese-American myself... or... *I think I am.*" That last part was more of a whisper.

"Sure!" The eager young man put down his cutting knife and sat next to some wooden planks that outlined the wooden boardwalk. "Come, join me here under the umbrella," he said to Gigi.

As she sat down next to him, she took out her recorder. "Would you mind if I record you? It's just to help me later as I find it easier and faster than simple note-taking."

"That's okay. As long as I can remain anonymous."

"No problem. So, before I ask you anything else, tell me what you said to me in Chinese, but first start with your name. Don't worry, I promise you'll remain anonymous. I just want to know what to call you."

The coconut vendor took a deep breath, looked in all directions to make sure no one was around, and played with his hair as he said, "They call me Paco. And I said that you shouldn't be walking around carelessly if you had just arrived yesterday."

Gigi tilted her head. "And why is that?"

"Well, I thought you were... Well, it doesn't matter."

"No, it does. Why wouldn't a person who just came from China be free to walk around like... well, like I am?"

"Because of the *policias*," Paco said, his voice lowered. "They are everywhere."

"I see..." Genesis said as it dawned on her what he meant. "Do you see many...?" She trailed off and let her question hang in the air.

Paco shook his head. "Not here specifically," he said. "But just yesterday, there was a heist at the Red Dragon pub in *el centro*. I guess some pissed off customer told the *policias* that they employed and harbored *Chinos ilegales* in their basement—so they came around snooping. And because, apparently, whoever this guy is has some influence, Mexican customs shut down the pub and have since been looking for *Chinos* all over the city." The young man stood up. "Let me work on your order, miss." He selected a big coconut, then used a large machete, which he drew out from beneath the cart, to hack a clean hole at the top of the fruit with one clean swipe.

"If I may ask, then, what are *you* doing here out in the open then?" Genesis asked empathetic for the man. "Don't you feel uncomfortable exposing yourself this way? What if the *policias* come for you too?" Genesis looked around her for any sign of trouble. She saw uniformed men walking around in pairs everywhere, but the young man seemed unfazed.

"*Me*? No, I am the least of their worries. I became a national a very long time ago. I even have two little ones who were born here."

"I see. And did it take long to become a national?"

Instead of answering her question, the man said, "But... even if I wasn't a Mexican yet, they wouldn't touch me."

Confused, Gigi asked the obvious question: "And why is that?"

"Well, because they would have to go through Wong if they did." The young man dropped a straw and a miniature umbrella into the drink. "Here, *señorita*; it will make your day come alive," he said handing over the prepared fruit to her.

Gigi stood up and collected it to take a small sip. The juice of the coconut hit her tongue and tickled her taste buds. She took a longer sip, closing her eyes. True to the words of the young man, she really did feel alive. It was refreshing and tasty.

"This is amazing!" Before the vendor could say anything, she continued, "So... who is *Wong*?" The words came out of her mouth smoothly as she sipped some more of the cool coconut water.

The man put the machete away after cleaning it and took a few moments looking around once again. He sat down on the planks once more and motioned for Gigi to lean closer to him. Her eyes widened, her hands trembled. Excitement flowing through her veins, uncertain of what the man would share.

"Wong is... Let's just say, Wong is a very powerful man. He controls this area."

Gigi pulled back a little to look Paco in the eye. "What do you mean he controls this area? What area? What exactly does he control?"

"Look, I am telling you because I feel that anyone who comes here needs to know who is who in these parts. I am not sure if this will help you for your article or not. But as long as no one knows it came from me, then it's all good. His full name is Carlos Wong. Some call him the Dragon. He lives in Mexicali, but owns properties all over the state. He owns and runs a bunch of businesses in the state of Baja California—casinos, night clubs, restaurants, massage parlors, spas, brothels, you name it. He is part owner of some local sports teams too. The man has his hands in everything."

"I see. And why *Dragon?*"

"I don't know. Probably because he will burn you if you cross him."

Gigi hummed thoughtfully. "And are these businesses all legit? I mean, brothels? Is prostitution even legal here?"

Paco chucked. "Of course not. But that won't stop it from being a lucrative business. All these things happen right under the noses of the politicians, but of course they won't do anything. There are a couple of brothels, one here and one down in Mexicali, that people consider the best in northern Mexico. I've heard that you can find whatever you want in them. I also hear that there are young girls too, some as young as eleven or twelve.

Genesis's heart nearly stopped beating, and she almost choked on her drink. She knew Das wasn't kidding when he made mention of human trafficking and illegal prostitution rings, but she didn't expect to be discovering so much about this topic so fast. She'd dealt with many horrific topics before, but hearing the reality of the situation with her own ears always got to her. The thought of children being kept as sex slaves made her skin crawl.

"Girls from all over the world," Paco continued. "But you think anyone is gonna cross the Dragon? Hell no."

Gigi nodded. "I see. And what do you mean by that to 'touch you they would have to get through him'?"

Before the young man could answer, a voice called behind them. "Paco, you know boss doesn't like it when you talk too much to costumers." The speaker spoke in Spanish, but Gigi understood him well enough.

Genesis hadn't seen the man creep up behind them. And neither had Paco, judging by the surprise he quickly wiped from his face and replaced with a scowl. Both Paco and Genesis turned to face the newcomer.

"Chow, the next time you creep up on me, your head will rest beside your legs before you know it, *pendejo,*" Paco said.

Chow laughed at the vendor's threat. "Relax, man. You get angry so quickly. I was only trying to look out for you." He then spoke something to Paco in Cantonese, eyeing Genesis suspiciously.

Genesis slipped the recorder into her dress pocket before the new mysterious man spotted it.

The two men shared a brief exchange between in Cantonese. As the new guy continued to stare, Genesis knew it was time for her to leave; things had turned awkward way too fast. Glancing at her watch, she discovered that over an hour had passed since Das left.

She patted the young vendor's shoulder, "I'll see you some other time, Paco," and walked away with the coconut held against her chest.

"You told her your name? You really have to be careful, Paco. She could be police," Chow warned.

"I know, you idiot. I was only moved by her... um... sweetness."

"Yeah, sure. *Pendejo!*" Chow answered as they watched Genesis's backside retreat. They both laughed as they enjoyed the view for a moment.

"So, who is she?" Chow asked.

"I don't know. I just met her. She was just buying a coconut," Paco replied, turning back to his cart to tidy up. "She's just an American tourist," he lied. "She's nobody; don't worry. She barely speaks Spanish, much less Chinese."

He watched Genesis disappear among a crowd of dancers for a moment, then went back to sweeping broken coconut shards into a trash bag.

Chow leaned on the cart by Paco's side, squinting into the crowd. "Well, what the hell does she want? What was she asking?" he asked.

"*No sé. Tu pregúntale.*" The reply was brief, but this time in Spanish. *I don't know. Ask her yourself.*

Under Chow's suspicious gaze, Paco swallowed uncomfortably but managed to bring his eyes up to meet Chow's, feigning confidence. "Anyway... What brings you to Tijuana? Escaping the Mexicali heat? Did you come for good tacos?"

"Dumb! You know ours are way better. Actually," Chow dipped and drew the Paco's machete from the stall, then grabbed a coconut, "it's that girl you were talking to. *She* brings me to Tijuana. We came down with Beto." He brought the blade down hard.

CHAPTER SEVEN

Das had lied to Gigi. He was nowhere near the beach. He had taken a taxi to the old part of the city close to the border crossing, *El Centro*, about twenty minutes away. He wanted to keep Genesis as far away as possible. He knew Genesis would never give up on what brought her here until she got something tangible to hold unto. At least, that's what Jay had told him.

As he made his way through the busy streets, he wondered why Genesis was suddenly so interested in immigration in Mexico. For the most part, he knew her articles were mostly harmless ones, nothing that would cause much political uproar—this could be a big story for her.

Das stopped in front of a candy store and walked in. There were a few customers looking through the inventory, and a young man who worked there was helping them. Das saluted him and showed him something hidden in his palm before making his way toward the back door, past the counter. The working man nodded and didn't say a word.

Das walked into an adjoining room, where an older Asian man was watching cartoons loudly on a couch. He laughed while eating a bowl of noodles. Das walked right behind the gray-haired man, trying to scare him, but he hit a tin can and the man looked back. The old man grunted. Without saying anything, he turned the TV off and stood up from the couch. He walked with a limp and used a cane to help him. His eyes didn't connect with Das's for a long time until he reached a table and set two glasses with water on them.

"What do *you* want?" the man asked with a shaky voice as they both sat down.

"Nice to see you too, Jin," Das replied while taking a seat by the table.

"Cut the crap, Das. I thought I told you everything you wanted to know already. I can't even come to Tijuana in peace." The old man took a sip from his water.

"Oh, you did, Jin. This is about something else. Something very sensitive and important," Das replied with a smile. "Otherwise I wouldn't have come all the way here."

The man looked at him with obvious hatred. "How did you find me?"

"That's not important. You know it was only a matter of time." Das took a sip of his water.

Jin clutched his glass in his fist. "Will you guys ever just leave me alone? You know what? Don't answer that." He scratched his balding head. "I know I shouldn't have done it, I know. If I hadn't forced myself on her, you—"

"Easy, *amigo*. I am not here to ask you questions about your life. Not this time, anyway. I need your help."

Jin glanced at Das and crossed his arms. "I see. Help, you say. Of course. Does this mean all of your other friends have exhausted their resources? What kind of help could I offer you that you can't find elsewhere?"

"The kind of help that might just make me forget that you tried to force a law-abiding citizen of the Mexican State into becoming your personal sex slave... Emphasis on the *might*."

Jin bared his teeth. "First of all, I served my time and paid the price. And second, that was a long time ago. I'm a changed man; you know that. And third... you wouldn't understand. I know you're not into women."

Das laughed. "Sure, old man. But I am also not forgetting that it *did* happen. And just because you can't get a boner anymore doesn't mean that—"

"Shut up, you, ignorant fool," Jin snarled. His clawed fingers curled tighter around his glass as if to keep him from lashing out. "And mind your manners. I may be an old man, but I can still beat your ass."

Das laughed again, this time a little longer. "You're a funny man. Look, just cooperate with me, Jin." He unwrapped a spicy tamarind candy that he had taken from the other side of the counter as he said, "You know well that helping us has its perks."

Jin shook his head and sighed. He took a drink from his glass, emptying the contents in his mouth. "Fine. What do you want to know?" Jin asked hesitantly as he stood up. He picked up a teapot and started polishing it. "I probably won't know anything, anyway."

"Don't be paranoid," Das grumbled. "No one is recording us or watching us. It took me a while to find you, so I doubt those amateurs could do the same. I came up with an excuse to make the drive all the way to Tijuana. I'm here because I need to talk to you about Carlos. You know we'll protect you."

Jin froze. "Carlos? You gotta be shitting me! His last name better not be Wong."

"Of course, it's Wong. What other *Carlos* would I come and talk to you about? I know what he's gotten himself into, but with all his connections, there's no way I could touch him. I always hated politics, and this guy knows how to play the system. I know he's dirty, despite what everyone else might say, but we don't have viable proof yet that will hold in court."

Jin lifted the teapot onto a shelf, then brought down a few containers of spices. He poured them into a stone bowl and mixed them together. "What makes you think I can help?"

Das rubbed his forehead. "Don't play games, okay? I'm not in the mood today. You made come all this way."

"Das, they took my sons once, and I'm not letting you do that to me or my family again," he said firmly.

Das leaned against the table and flashed him a charming smile. "We got them out, though, didn't we? Besides, that wasn't even Wong's main crew. That was just a scare tactic from his minions."

"Well, it worked!" Jin slammed his fist on the table, making the glasses jump. "I'm scared. I don't want to be an informant anymore. Rats get killed in this business. And I'm an old man who simply wants to live life and enjoy the last few good years I have left with my grandkids."

"You know you don't need to be scared when you have me to protect you."

"A lot of good that did me. My family is important to me; I won't put them in any more danger."

"No one will ever find out you're helping us."

Jin huffed, then started walking around the room, reorganizing the dusty shelves. Das followed him around, trying to make eye contact.

"Leave my store," the old man said without looking at Das. "I can't help. Not this time. Not if it has to do with the Dragon."

"Jin," he said, grabbing his arm, "Wong is running a prostitution ring. You know it, I know it, and the people know it. But we need something tangible to nail the bastard. He treats little children like property and sells them like goods and services. He uses his tunnels to cross people to the States. *People*, Jin. Kids. Little kids like your granddaughters. Think of them. The drugs are one thing, but *children*? Even thieves draw a line. Everyone knows what he's capable of, yet they're so afraid of him that they're covering it up."

"It's not my problem," Jin said, walking back to the table. "If it doesn't affect me, then I don't need to get involved. Besides, if it's not him, someone else like him will continue."

"Really? That's your excuse to not help, Jin? I'm disappointed in you. Think about it. You're the best informant in the business. You know what everyone is doing before they even think about doing it. You have connections that I couldn't even begin to fathom. You have *friends* all over this state, people that wouldn't dare talk to me. Please, Jin. I know you said it doesn't affect you, but what if it was your granddaughter being sold as a sex slave?"

"Do not talk about my family!" Jin shouted, weakly reaching for Das's throat.

Das stepped back with his hands raised, easily maneuvering away from the older man. "I'm just trying to get you to empathize. I'm sorry, Jin, but it's important I take the Dragon down. You should understand that. And right now, only you can help."

Jin moaned and took more spices off the shelves. "Okay, I'll see what I can do; but it won't happen overnight. The rumors have been quiet lately, and I don't know if anyone will have something new."

"I'll take anything," Das said. "I'll come visit you at your Mexicali store in a couple of days. That should be enough time for you to put something together. Maybe I'll bring you a beautiful lady to lay your eyes on?"

Jin raised his eyebrows and grinned. "Sure, I'll be there the day after tomorrow and for the rest of the week. But do I get to keep her?" He winked.

"Jin," he scolded, "I'm talking about a friend of mine. She might like to meet you for some questions of her own, but nothing else. And no touching, you old perv. Do you understand?"

Jin exhaled and ground more spices. "Fine, but one day, when I become the most powerful man in the world, you'll be the first one I punish. You make my life hell, Das. People talk around here, and if you keep coming around, I'll have to go into the shadows again."

Das chuckled. "Oh, you're such a flatterer."

He grabbed the old man's hand before he could pull it back and gently kissed the back of it. Jin pulled it back, disgusted, and wiped it on a cloth.

"Get out of here," the old Asian man grumbled, "before I call some real cops."

As the day wore on, Genesis covered considerable ground. Das hadn't returned to the car, so she figured that was his way of telling her to continue her investigation. She was surprised that almost every person she talked to spoke decent English and was eager to help a foreigner. The people on the beach proved themselves to be of tremendous help; some even volunteered to take her around the city. She didn't accept their offer, of course.

She flirted information out of a few men; this was something she was good at. Her greatest informants had been the coconut vendor, a young Haitian girl that walked around scouting for potential clients, and a couple of young boys playing soccer on the sand who had made their way up north from Honduras.

Even though she hadn't yet uncovered any information about the orphanage where she'd been left, she had collected enough information to add volume to her article. Soon, she would have something to present to Macy. Now she could spend her remaining days focusing on her origin.

Almost three-and-a-half-hours had passed, and after checking on the car for the umpteenth time, she again found Das absent. Das's mustang was still there, of course. So was the shiny crimson Chevy truck with the tinted windows. Most other cars in the parking lot had come and gone.

Gigi removed her hat and swung it about. The wind from the sea brushed through her hair, causing it to tickle her ears. Calling Das wasn't an option. For some stupid reason, she had forgotten her phone on the bed back at the hotel after leaving in a hurry. Halfway through the journey up the mountains, she'd realize the phone was left charging at the hotel after receiving Das's text. But it was too late to turn around then, so she didn't mention anything to him. Of course, it could've come in handy now.

Where are you, Das?

For a moment, Gigi started questioning what Das was into. Where had he gone? Why had he left her for so long? Was he up to no good?

But she chose to dismiss the thought.

Though she had no reason to believe he would abandon her there with his car, she was supposed to check in with Macy—she would need to come up with a good excuse.

As she perched herself upon his bonnet, Genesis saw an older, indigenous lady selling artwork on the boardwalk. The vibrant reds and oranges in her paintings fascinated her, and she ended up making her way over to inspect the artwork. After finding out how cheap they were, she even bought a few; they would look great in her living room once they were nicely framed.

"I see you're enjoying your time."

Genesis whirled around to see Das standing, arms crossed and looking at her with a wide smile. She didn't know whether to be angry or not, so she just shook her head.

"So much for two hours, you jackass. It's been almost four! What if someone else had come to get me?" She rolled her eyes.

"I'd have had to fight a duel with that person. You know, I can't risk losing you. Jay would have my head," Das replied jokingly, moving toward her.

"He sure would. I'll be sure to let him know you left me on a crowded beach and went off in search of a castle you had built in the sand."

In reality, Gigi knew her Blue Jay would never hurt a fly, even if it was to defend her, but she enjoyed the fantasy she could envision at the prospect.

"The dancing butterfly would be a good term to describe you. I've been here all day watching you from a distance as you asked people questions, zigzagging from one person to another, dancing along the way. I wonder the kind of charm you used on them..." Das said spreading his arms out.

Genesis walked toward him with sure steps. As she got closer, she clenched her fists, and Das turned and ran toward the car, chuckling all the way. Gigi gave chase.

"Come back here!"

"Don't drop your souvenirs!" Das called back.

Irvine, California

It was 9:25 pm. People throughout Orange County impatiently rushed to their various destinations with no regard for other cars or pedestrians. Jay stood by his living room window, looking out onto the array of trendy condos and modern apartments full of high-income, professional millennials on Jamboree Road. Gigi's place was nearby.

He took a sip of his drink as he raised his gaze and stared into the darkness that reached farther than his eyes could see. He kept scuffing his toe into the soft carpet. He had come home from work a little disturbed. The weight of the long day and the worry he felt for his fiancée pushed down on him. He had been calling her for the past few hours, but every call would simply ring and then to voicemail. He'd stopped leaving messages by now.

Was she okay? What happened to checking in throughout the day? And now, Das wasn't answering either.

Jay scolded himself under his breath. Why was he endlessly waiting for an update when she had barely been gone for a few days? She would contact him when she had something worth sharing. He told himself she was just busy and wrapped up in her work, as usual.

And just as he thought this, the gentle vibration of his phone on the table made him turn, his quick movement one filled with hope. He picked it up.

It was Richard Gill.

He tried not to sound disappointed as he answered, "Good evening, Rick."

He held his breath. Mr. Gill, and even the late Mrs. Gill, always called on him once in a while to check up on how he or his mother was doing. He knew how caring they were, but this was the first time since the funeral that Mr. Gill had called him instead of sending a quick text.

"Good evening, son. How are you doing?" came Mr. Gill's voice.

"I'm fine. Have you received any word from Gigi today by any chance?" Jay asked. He tried not to let his fear creep into his voice.

"I did," Richard replied. "Just this morning, though. She hasn't answered any of my calls, though. I'm sure she's fine, just busy. But that's why I was calling you."

"Yeah, same here. And I'm sure she's all right too. Like you say, probably just really busy. I'll buzz you if I get any messages from her. I promise."

"Sounds good. Thank you, Jay. I'll do the same. Please say hello to your mother. Have a goodnight."

"I will. Goodnight, Rick."

Jay put the phone in his pocket and balled his hands into fists in exasperation. What could be keeping Genesis from sending at least a text? Even if she didn't have news about her investigation, he thought she would have sent a quick hello.

He was about to turn back to the window when his phone vibrated a second time. He quickly took it out, looked at it, and saw Das's name displayed on the screen.

"Finally," he muttered as he reached pressed answer. Das was the second-best choice for an update.

"Hello?"

"Jay, I'm so sorry."

"Das?" The tone of his friend's voice had a strange effect on Jay's knees, and he clutched the table as he said, "What's wrong? What do you mean? Where have you guys been?"

"We were jumped while driving back to Mexicali. They took Gigi!"

Laguna Salada, Baja California
20 miles west of Mexicali

It had happened so quickly. The crimson Chevy truck had cut them off as Das and Gigi began on their way back to Mexicali. Das stepped hard on the brakes, jolting them both in their seats. While Gigi's first impression was that the incident was an accident, Das let out an aggressive curse and reached under his seat.

Just like in one of the many action movies Genesis had watched in the theaters with Jay, the two rear doors of the truck flung open and two masked men, one armed with an AK-47 and the other with a pistol, approach the convertible rapidly.

Gigi froze at the sight of the two weapons and only moved when a loud crack next to her sent Das falling face-first into the steering wheel. A gun fell next to his feet in the foot well.

Gigi didn't have time to gawk at it, because the masked man with the pistol yanked open the passenger door. He pointed his pistol at Genesis and, without speaking, turned to point it toward the truck. Genesis quickly held her hands up, her heart beating rapidly in her ears. She breathed heavily, staring down the barrel of the gun.

"Bring your purse with you," the abductor said.

They had been so close to returning to the urban sprawl of Mexicali when the men attacked, passing through the deserted flatland area known as *Laguna Salada*; a vast dry lake, thirty feet below sea level. It reminded her of Death Valley in California on the road to Las Vegas.

Gigi knew help wasn't an option, as evidently this route was rarely traveled by anyone at this time.

They were alone.

Genesis disembarked from the car, grabbed her purse, and walked to the waiting truck without as much as a struggle. She looked back, but Das was out cold. She thought about running, but what if they shot her? And there was nowhere to run in this vast desert.

Her entire body shook, and her knees were about to buckle under her. Genesis had barely sat down before the truck sped off. As it raced away, she turned and looked at the dark-green Mustang parked on the side of the road and prayed that poor Das was okay.

"We are not here to hurt you," one of the masked men told her. "We just need you to call your people and tell them that we have you."

He was sitting to her left in the back seat, looking straight ahead, holding his gun between his knees. The silent driver didn't turn around to look at her as he concentrated on the road before him.

Genesis was rattled. Her stomach clenched with anxiety. Her heart raced. She opened her mouth, but no sound dared come out. Sweat was pouring down her face. Everything happened so fast!

She closed her eyes, pretending she was with Jay back in her cozy apartment. Even in her wildest dreams, she had never imagined herself being kidnapped, let alone at gun point.

"Hey, Miss... he is talking to you," the masked man at her right nudged her, bringing her back to reality.

It was futile screaming, not that she could muster up enough strength to do so. Genesis swallowed hard, trying to get any moisture into her dry throat. "I have nobody here," she managed to say. Her voice was cracked and shaky. "It's just me. There is no one to call."

She didn't expect the slap. It landed on her cheek, pushing her into the body of the captor on her other side. When she raised her head, she tasted blood in her mouth. The men laughed and tucked the rifles they held into cases at their feet; maybe because they felt she was of little threat to them.

"*¡Mentirosa!*"

"I'm *not* lying," she whispered back.

"*Cuidado. Recuerda que el jefe no la quiere lastimada,*" the driver said.

Remember that the boss doesn't want her hurt? What boss? Gigi was even more confused now. And concerned. *This was planned. How long have they been following me?*

"Where is your cell phone?" the one on her right asked her.

"I… forgot it at the hotel. I swear." She wasn't lying. She'd left her phone by accident, and the camera on purpose. But now she wished she hadn't left any of it behind.

"Give me your purse."

Genesis gave it to the man as she slowly turned her head to study their features without prompting another slap. One of them wore an eye patch. She searched her brain, trying to figure out the right move, the right thing to say to come out of this situation alive, but her rationality was foggy. She braced herself for another blow. It did not come.

"I am not going to hit you again," the violent one said. "Just give us what we want, and we will let you go without a scratch on your body."

The driver slowed down a little and turned left off the main road. He drove a couple hundred feet deep along a dirt road next to an old cemetery. When he got a suitable spot, he stopped the truck and killed the engine.

"She could be DEA," the driver stated, still not turning around to face the others. His voice was familiar. Genesis was silent and took slow breaths to avoid any sudden movements. The driver quickly turned around, and Genesis knew who he was: it was Chow, Paco's friend. Though he was masked, his eyes and mouth gave him away.

"I am NOT *policia*, or DEA, or anything like that," Genesis said firmly, glad to have found her voice. "I am just a tourist. And I am an American citizen."

Genesis had never been so scared in all her life. Her chest felt tight. She wanted to punch the men and escape on foot like in the movies. Unfortunately, she didn't feel like much of an action hero at that moment.

Suddenly, everything came back to her in a flash. She had noticed the super-clean red Chevrolet truck from her hotel window when she had been working on the list that morning. She had also seen the bell boy walk up to a man with dark shades in the parking lot and point toward the tower where she was staying. She had seen the truck in the distance when Das drove toward the beach on the road that had no end. The truck appeared again, pulling into the same parking lot as Das and had parked some spaces away from them. How she didn't pick up on that sooner to warn Das, she would never understand. She was never this distracted during an investigation.

The voice of Macy echoed in her mind: *Always be extra careful. Don't get distracted. Be professional. Be aware of your surroundings.*

How could I be so careless?

"You are *not* a tourist. You are a reporter, *señorita*. And if you are not, then tell me, what is this notepad doing here? Probable questions are even written on it." He pulled the notepad out of the bag as he looked through it and waved it in her face. "You know, we don't really like journalists like you snooping around our business here."

Genesis held onto her pen, tight, shoving it under her thigh, hiding it from her captors. She had brought it out of her purse when she was shoved into the back of the truck by one of her abductors. She fixed her dress to cover her exposed trembling knees. Then she felt her right pocket, the small recording device was still there. Subtly, she turned it on.

"That's nothing. It's just my sketches that I do. I like to draw, as you can see. And other pages are just random things, like a list of items I intend to buy from the market while staying here," she replied. "Souvenirs."

"Lies! You can't bullshit a bullshitter. You really think—" The eye-patch man didn't have the chance to finish his sentence when a quick jab to his throat by Genesis made him choke.

What the captors didn't know was that this petite woman could defend herself. Genesis had taken Krav Maga for fifteen years, and she had picked up Jujitsu as a hobby during college. Her training had started early in elementary, after being bullied because of her size. She had only used it once, in sixth grade, to defend herself against a pair of larger girls who would bully her and her friend after school. It all stopped that day. One of the girls had to go to the hospital for a broken arm and a bruised rib.

Her movement was so swift, that before the other captor on her left had time to react, she stabbed him in the leg with the pen, immediately pushing the door open and scrambling over the choking man.

The reporter had used the pen as a weapon. A literal one.

Their boss doesn't want them to hurt me. I can use that. It was an instinctual move.

The second man stretched himself, but could only get as far as ripping the cloth on the back of her dress.

Gigi ran as she had never run before toward where she perceived was the highway. She took off her wedges and held them in her hands to run faster, feeling the adrenaline pump through her veins. She didn't even feel pain in the soles of her feet. Fear had taken over.

A car was coming fast down the road, its lights increasing in intensity and size, and she began to scream as she ran to flag it down. It was dark, and the car's lights blinded her. The car stopped next to her, and immediately, two uniformed men jumped out and ran toward her with .9 mm's drawn. One of them grabbed Genesis's arm, while the other stood a distance away, pointing his gun at her.

"Please, don't hurt me," she said, "I need help! *Ayuda!*"

The police rushed her to the car and sat her in the backseat, leaving the door open. In the distance, the crimson truck sped onto the main road, going toward the city.

"There!" she shouted, pointing at the truck. "Get them! *They kidnapped me!*"

"Are you all right, Miss?" one kept asking her repeatedly, in English and Spanish, as the other radioed dispatch with a description of the truck. He then turned on the red and blue lights.

Genesis wept, her words barely understandable to the officers. The adrenaline coursing through her had not yet worn off, so she got out of the car and paced, trying to slow her breathing. Then, Genesis heard the rumbling engine of the Mustang which came to an abrupt stop beside the police car.

Das jumped over the door, without bothering to open it and made for where Genesis paced a line across the dirt. The two police officers saluted Das.

"Are you okay?" Das asked, pulling her into his arms, but she pushed him away.

Only one question came out of Genesis's mouth: "So, you're a cop, huh, Das? Sales rep my ass."

Das laughed and returned the officers' salute. "What would give you that idea?"

THE FLIGHT OF THE BUTTERFLY

CHAPTER EIGHT

Mexicali, Baja California
June 2019

"She has a tattoo on her back, boss," Beto said while gripping a piece of the woman's purple dress in his fist and placing it on the large desk separating him and the boss.

The older Chinese man with a gray mustache sat on a leather chair opposite the desk, hidden behind a cloud of cigar smoke. Even though Beto was much larger than himself, he knew that Beto would never dare cross him. No one would dare cross the boss.

"Let me get this straight. You are saying that you allowed her—a five-feet-two-inches-tall, one-hundred-fifteen-pound girl—to get away from you?" the older man rasped. "And all you can say is that she has a tattoo? How does that help me?" There was a thick cough, one that exposed years of chain smoking.

"Well, we got her purse, and the pictures. At least we know who she is, sir."

The boss looked at the five pictures of the journalist outside Hotel Lucero laying on his desk. The girl was cute; she reminded him of someone from his past. Someone that still haunted him in his sleep. A ghost of his former life. The resemblance was too much. Perhaps a coincidence. Still, his curiosity about this woman—who had been asking about the tunnels, his tunnels, and about his shady businesses—only grew more intense with each moment that passed.

Beto was right; now they had the woman's purse, which contained her California driver's license. Her name was Genesis Gill, she lived in Irvine, and from a quick search, they found out she was a reporter for the *L.A. Chronicle*. She wasn't the first journalist to be caught meddling in his business. Of course, none of them ever lived long enough to publish.

"So, tell me again, Beto... Why did you lose her?"

"Well, sir... the thing is," Beto said, his voice shaky, "we... I mean, I could have shot her, easily. But then I remembered that you clearly stated you wanted her alive. You said you didn't want any harm done to her, remember? Not one mark. Those were your words, boss." Beto stopped, as if hoping for encouragement from the boss. He received none. He looked around at the armed guards standing on each side before continuing, "I... well, I didn't want to hurt her when she fought us, because of what you'd said. And since we knew the police were close behind us, we figured that we would just let her go this time, and then we—"

"You were not told to harm her or kill anybody," the boss interrupted, "that is true. But you were also asked to bring her here, alive. I wanted... I need to ask her a few questions."

"Yes, Mr. Dragon. I understand. But..."

"I am not done." The man placed his cigar on a fancy ash tray adorned with Chinese calligraphy.

"Yes. Sorry, sir." Beto looked down towards his feet.

The Dragon stood up from his chair and walked around the large desk. "You see, the fact is that you failed to bring her to me. And that is a problem. She could bring a lot of attention to my operations, and attention brings trouble." There was a pause as Dragon reached for the cigar, letting the anticipation build. He inhaled deep on the Cohiba cigar, letting the savor take root on his mouth, before finally releasing the smoke on Beto.

Beto didn't flinch. "I am aware of that, sir."

After a cough, the Dragon continued. "Then I trust that you also understand how you have ruined things by allowing her to get away. So, what should I do with you, Beto?"

Beto didn't say anything, still looking down while sitting.

The Dragon put his cigar back on his desk and walked to a small indoor putting green next to the desk. He pulled out a golf club iron from a golf stand bag that was standing by the window. "I mean, you still have one eye left. That gives me some ideas."

Beto got up from the chair and dropped to his knees while folding his hands in a prayer motion. "No, Dragon. Please! You know that I've never failed you before this incident. Please, just... give me another chance, and I will make it right. I promise!"

Dragon leaned over to scowl at the cowering man on the floor. "You failed this time, Beto; and I don't give people second chances." Dragon swung his club in the air, and Beto flinched. "But with you, I will make an exception," he added, a sly grin crossing his face.

Beto sank farther into the floor, obviously relieved. "Thank you! Thank you, *jefe*! I owe you my life," Beto exclaimed, placing his head on the ground in front of his shiny shoes.

"Not only your life, Beto; your very existence," Dragon replied while moving his shoes away from the begging man. "Don't you forget that. Now, get up."

Beto did as told and remained standing behind the chair. The Dragon went back and sat on his throne, still holding the golf club. A gentle cough pushed smoke in different directions. Dragon had not asked about the woman's tattoo, though it piqued his interest. Nonetheless, his first order of business was to figure out how to punish Beto. He would spare his life, but no one crossed the *jefe* without sacrificing something in return.

"So, tell me about her tattoo."

Genesis didn't leave her hotel room for a full day, ignoring calls from Jay and her father. She knew Das had told Jay everything that was going on, but she wasn't ready to talk about her abduction. Her dad would be petrified if Jay told him. She hoped that he hadn't. She hoped Macy didn't know either, or he'd pull her back right away.

The twenty-first day of June came with its introduction into the summer. But here, the summer had started months ago. The wind was dusty in the afternoons, and the days remained hotter than ever.

Dry. Scorching hot.

She sat at her table, staring at the computer, angry at the men in her life, always interfering. She was slowly coming to terms with the fact that Jay attached a police officer to her without her knowledge and consent. She thought it was strange that a police car so easily and quickly found her on the road.

At first, it had been too much to take in, but as she settled down that night in the new hotel where they had moved her, she understood it was for the best. Jay was just trying to show his love and support, and she had to respect that. She was tempted to call him and fight with him, but she knew as soon as she heard his soothing voice, she wouldn't be able to stay mad. And sometimes she needed anger to help her focus on the task at hand.

She shook thoughts of the police officers out of her mind, as her mission here was not to interview government officials or to follow up corporate organizations that were losing heavily in the stock markets. These organizations always provided her with one form of security detail or another when she worked on stories for them. She also did not get to mingle with people on the streets in those situations. In those circumstances, she was always in her hotel room and a driver was always at hand to take her wherever she needed to go. But that wasn't the case this time, and while Jay had acted in her interest, he should have at least told her. She would have fought him on it, but at least she would've been aware. In her experience, ignorance was *not* bliss. Though, in due time, she would ask him, and he would explain his reasons.

When Genesis and Das returned to Hotel Lucero two nights ago, the bell boy was nowhere to be seen. The receptionist said the bell boy had disappeared that afternoon. Das left her at the reception with the two police officers, went up to her room, and retrieved all her items himself. He came down without saying much and walked outside, signaling the officers to bring Gigi along. And now, Gigi found herself in another hotel in a different part of the city, closer to the border crossing. Hotel Califas was still very nice, but a lot more discreet. But even though her location had been changed, her mission still remained, and her resolute was as firm as ever.

The new hotel room was bigger than the other one, although not quite as luxurious. A police officer was now always stationed at her door. It took away some of her privacy, but she couldn't deny the fact that it felt superb. She felt like she was an American Ambassador, or someone important like that. But most importantly, she felt safe, and she never wanted to put herself in danger like that ever again.

As Genesis scrolled through the lists of the orphanages located within the area that she was in, a text popped up on her phone. She had gone through the names over and over again, but she still couldn't find *Casa Hogar San Jose* among the ones listed.

Sighing, she sat back and opened the message from Das. It was short and concise: "I've found the orphanage. I will be in the hotel to pick you up in twenty minutes. Get ready."

Gigi's heart leaped out of her chest, and she wondered if this was just a trick to get her to call him. She'd had to inform Das about what brought her to Mexico that night at the bar of the new hotel. She couldn't spend any more time investigating the wrong thing, and she needed Das's help. The playfulness of Das was gone as he sat at the bar with a stiff drink in hand, replaced by a seriousness that she had not noticed before. He looked like a man who had a job to do, who would do the job, and who would do it undeniably well.

"I came here under the guise of doing research for an article, Das. But in all truth, I'm only here to trace my origin." Genesis sipped from the glass of lemonade placed before her. Her eyes still appeared dazed and her hair a little disheveled, even though she had run a comb through it. She felt like she'd been hit by a truck and was exhausted.

"You should have just called the ministry in charge here, or at least told me what was going on," Das retorted. He was drinking whisky with ice dangling at the bottom of the glass. He had told her he wasn't much of a drinker, but he was off duty.

But then again, he was never really off duty, was he?

"To be honest, I don't see how telling you about my true intentions would have changed anything. I mean, you would've still taken me out, and the men following us would still most likely... well, you know."

"I guess."

"Besides, I told Jay not to say anything. I still had to research for my article, so my boss wouldn't find out that he was funding a trip for my own personal needs. I thought about telling everyone the truth from the get-go. Believe me! But I felt I should be here myself, even if no one thought it was a good idea."

Das shook his head and looked Genesis straight in the eyes. "You are one determined gal, aren't you?"

"Jay calls it stubborn." She smirked, looking down, choosing not to make eye contact.

Das laughed. "Yeah, that too. I just still can't believe it."

"You can't believe what?" she retorted looking up at him.

"Well, let's see; you escaped from three armed men—that still baffles me. And now, you're sitting calmly in this bar like nothing even happened. It just amazes me. But even more, hearing you now, reiterating your commitment to seek your roots out."

Gigi smiled, not knowing what to say.

"Well, what do you know about your origins?"

The question caught Genesis by surprise. She hadn't really thought about it since she arrived in Mexico. She knew practically nothing. Her mission seemed pretty bleak at that moment. She looked at Das to find him staring at her intently.

The pain of the night of her parent's admission seemed to be birthing up in her soul again. She exhaled deeply and pointed at her cup. It was almost empty. It looked like she was going to breakdown at any moment, but as she gulped the last of the drink, she pulled herself together.

"I was adopted by a well-to-do couple. My father is a white American... you know, a typical *gringo*. My mom toggled between American and Chinese. Her parents were from Hawaii, Chinese-American, but she was born and raised in California, as was my dad. They met at church when they were both adults. I came into their life when I was two years old. I basically came at a time when they'd lost all hope of having children of their own. My childhood was filled with bout after bout of sickness. I guess that's why I'm small."

Das stared at her in silence with utmost attention. She ate an ice cube from her glass before continuing her story.

"I was raised as a very devout Christian. As a teenager, I was very active in church. My upbringing was a little too conservative for my liking, to be honest. But it was fine for a while. However, I began having doubts after college. It got even worse when I became a journalist and started traveling around to interview all kinds of people, from the victims of war to those in impoverished regions of the world."

Gigi took one more sip and let the silence linger for a few seconds. After a thoughtful pause, she continued. "I thought, if God was real, He wouldn't have allowed those whom He had created in His image and likeness to go through all this suffering. I started questioning the very existence of this Supreme Being. And as it stands now, I honestly just don't know what to believe anymore."

Genesis paused to have her glass refilled by the bartender, but this time she did not raise the drink to her lips. She stared into it while stirring it repeatedly, looking at the brilliant sparkle of the drink inside the cup.

"Go on," Das encouraged, placing his hat on the table.

Gigi sighed. "I was born in the year 1990. Well, at least that was what I was told by my parents. I don't even know what my real birth date is. We celebrate the day when I was adopted; although, I didn't learn that fact until years later. My parents said they adopted me from an agency that brought kids from Latin America. I was two years old when they adopted me, and I don't even know the details of my stay in the orphanage.

"But you know what's crazy? All my life, before I found out I was adopted, I had always believed that Richard and Michelle Gill were my biological parents. I never questioned it. The funny thing is that I bear a striking resemblance to my mother. Shoot, I even inherited some traits! My love for art and painting. Even my fashion sense. I guess not everything is genetic. Of course, I also got some things from Dad..."

Genesis twirled her hair and looked past Das, staring into nothing. "Obviously, I don't speak any Chinese. In fact, my mom could barely speak Mandarin herself, being born in the US too. The only foreign language I can speak is Spanish, but even then, I'm not that great, as you already noticed. This I picked up from school and friends, and then eventually improved it through my travels. Jay helps me with Spanish as well. His mom, whom you know, doesn't speak English that well, so I get to practice with her." She took a break to finally sip her drink.

Das remained invested in her story. "And how did you take it when you found out you were adopted?"

Gigi snorted. "Imagine my horror. I know for many people it's not that big of a deal, but for me... well, it took me years to put it behind me. I don't even know why, to be honest. But my mom made my dad promise on her death bed to make me seek my origin before I settled down in marriage. He doesn't know I know, but I overheard them talking one night. She knew this is important to me and didn't want me to give up. She also said it would help my children know their roots too. The only information that I know, though, is that a teenage boy brought me to the orphanage and disappeared thereafter."

"A boy?"

"Yup," Gigi shrugged. "The orphanage, *Casa Hogar San Jose*, claimed they hadn't seen him since. And that's the only thing I know. So that's why I am here. I need to find out more about this boy. Was he my father? Why did he abandon me? I am just full of questions. And these questions need answering, for my peace of mind."

Das handed a white handkerchief to Genesis, who wiped off the single tear she hadn't realized was snaking its way down her petite face. Das beheld her with pity.

"My respect for you has just soared. You are a *chiltepin*, G."

"Excuse me?"

Das laughed. "A *chiltepin*. *Chiquita pero picosa*."

"I don't follow."

"Nothing. Forget about it."

"Um, I don't think so. Here I am opening my floodgates and pouring out my deepest thoughts, and you just called me a... a *what* exactly?"

"A *chiltepin*. It is a very small, but extremely spicy chili from the northern Mexican deserts. *Chiquita pero picosa*: tiny but spicy."

"Are you saying that I'm hot?"

Das blushed.

"I'm kidding," she added.

Das put his hat on again. "No! I mean... well... yeah, but no!" He cleared his throat before continuing, "I, um... I don't swing that way. If you know what I mean."

"Oh!" Gigi said. "I'm sorry, I didn't know."

"It's okay. I thought you knew. I figured Jay would've told you."

"No! I had no idea. And honestly, I would've never guessed."

"Really? Why is that? I don't fit your stereotype of a gay guy, is that it?"

"Well… yeah. I mean… No! Ugh. I'm so sorry. I'm a horrible person, I know!" She put her hands on her face. "I really suck, huh?"

"Look, I am glad to continue to break your idea and mold of a person should be like. But no, you're not a horrible person. And yes, dear. You are hot! But that's not at all what I meant. By calling you a *chiltepin*, I meant that you might be small, but you sure pack a hard punch. You're spunky. And I like that. I mean, you escaped some bad dudes, and here you are telling me about your life and your story! That's so bad ass."

Gigi smiled. "I guess."

"Don't guess. Know that you are awesome. Not everyone has been able to do what you did. And you know what, Ms. Gill?" He took both her hands in his. "I'm going to do my best to help you. I'll make your mission my own—and I know just where to start. Jin!"

Genesis raised an eyebrow. "*Gin?* I told you I'm not drinking."

"No, not Gin. Trust me, I don't need another drink either." He laughed. "Jin, with a J!"

"Oh. Who's Jin?"

"Let me tell you about this guy. Jin was in Mexicali for a very long time before relocating to Tijuana. Well, he goes back and forth now. But what's important is that he was well-connected back in the day. And when I say he was well-connected, I don't mean with good people. He's been around for a long time, and he used to be involved with questionable characters from the city back in the day. An insider. He did some time in prison and he's out now, just running his businesses. But this might be beneficial to us. I was going to take you to meet him regardless, because I think he can help you with your article. But now, I know he can help you with this other mission of yours too. Trust me, this guy may know a thing or two."

"Nice. And when do we meet this Jin?"

"Well, for now, you need to go get some rest. I'll get in touch with you when I have something concrete. I need to make sure he's around here first. See you *mañana, Chiltepin!*"

With that, Das stood up, kissed her hand, and left the bar. One of the two uniformed police officers sitting close by stood and left behind him. The other one remained, as he would stick around to make sure Gigi was fine through the night.

Gigi only hoped one guard would be enough.

CHAPTER NINE

When the gentle knock came at her door, Genesis was ready. She had barely slept, and she was eager to begin her mission for the day. Anything to keep her mind busy from the nightmares she had during the night. Images of guns pointed at her, thoughts of what could've been, the idea of not seeing Jay ever again. So, she was eager to continue her search.

She wore a white cotton dress and a red baseball cap adorned with a green and white *M* that she'd bought at the boutique in the hotel lobby. According to the guy at the store, it represented the Mexican national baseball team. It'd make a nice souvenir, she thought.

Gigi grabbed her new purse, also purchased from the store which, besides some personal items, contained her recorder and a new notepad. She grabbed the camera, as well. According to Das, they would be killing two birds with one stone today. She liked that.

Genesis opened the door to find Das standing, waiting, his wool cap in place. She hadn't seen this one. It was nice. He tilted the hat to indicate good morning. "Top of the mornin' to ya, mate," Das said in a failed Australian accent.

Genesis laughed. "*Buenos días,*" she said.

Together, they walked down the hall, making their way toward the parking lot, with two police officers trailing some feet behind. Genesis turned to wave hello, and both greeted her with a smile.

"*Casa Hogar San Jose* isn't the same place as it was in the 90s. I think that's why they weren't listed as an orphanage when you ran them through the search engine," Das explained to her as he pressed the clutch and engaged the gear of the Mustang.

This information didn't surprise Genesis. She had expected something like this. With the transformation that the country had gone through over the last couple of decades, there was bound to be a few changes here and there.

"What is it now?" Gigi asked.

"A shelter for the homeless, the destitute, and those that have been denied entry into the States..." He kept his answer short and looked through the rear mirror, prompting Genesis to do the same.

She saw the police truck trailing them. Since the incident, Das had been understandably cautious; they didn't want a repetition of that night. And she was grateful. All she wanted was to finish her mission here soon and return to the United States fulfilled and in one piece.

The drive was quiet. There wasn't much to be said at this point.

"We should be there any moment from now," Das said as he negotiated a bend from the wide boulevard to a narrower street just a few minutes from their origin.

They drove between trees until he came to a cleared space. An open fence created a perimeter that housed an expansive building. Within the fence, people moved about. Some chatted, while others prepared food and stacked clean plates on the tables. At what seemed to be an outside kitchen, a chef scooped food from one big pot onto the plates held by the line of people filing past him.

"We're here," Das stated the obvious as he parked the car.

An older man with a gray beard, maybe in his late sixties or early seventies, saw them and waved. At his neck, a clerical collar peeked out from behind his collar. His face seemed to be made from reddish leather, as if he'd spent years in the open sun. He rushed toward where the car was parked and stepped forward to open the door for Gigi, who stepped out of the car. She shook his extended hand warmly.

"Welcome to Refugio Santa Maria, Miss Gill," the man said in a broken English. "I am Padre Diego, at your service. I manage this shelter. Señor Alejandro told me yesterday that you would be coming today."

"Father, it's so nice to meet you. Thank you for seeing us," she replied.

"Let's go to my office." The man gestured for them to follow him.

Genesis glanced around as they moved toward the building. Strangely, she felt a strong attachment to the refuge, even though she couldn't remember anything about what had transpired when she was brought here almost three decades ago. It felt safe. She waited for some sort of memory to cross her mind as she gazed around, but nothing came.

There was a rusty playground near the patio and ancient trees with old swings hanging from the branches. Even though it seemed overcrowded, the people here were nice, welcoming. Everyone smiled and waved at them. For some reason, she had a strong sense that she had enjoyed her short time here as an infant.

Father Diego ushered them through the main doors and into a passage that extended farther into the building. Doors left and right lead dormitories, common areas, and offices. It was dim, with only a few small, dirt-encrusted windows to provide light. An aging portrait of the Virgin Mary surrounded by a Mexican flag hung at the far end of the passage. Hanging on the right wall beside her, there was another smaller, more modern painting of the Virgin Mary tending to a bleeding Jesus on her lap. As they approached it, Father Diego dipped his head and crossed himself, then he pushed the door to his left open and signaled for Gigi and Das to enter.

Inside Father Diego's office was a huge mahogany table that served as a desk, on which sat a giant, cream Catholic Bible. An incense burner hung from the wall with a wooden cross nailed firmly beside it.

"Please, do have a seat," Father Diego said pointing to the only two chairs on the other side of his table.

He slowly lowered himself into his seat. Sweat dripped from his brow, and he used a handkerchief to wipe it away. He picked up a file from the drawer on his table, flipped it open, put on his glasses, and started going through the contents. His finger traveled down each line, as he muttered names. He paused when he got to a specific one.

"Das told me everything. The documents in the orphanage were handed over to me years ago, when it closed down due to financial constraints. I never thought I'd need them for anything, but now I'm glad we kept them around," he told them, looking over his glasses.

Taking out her notepad and pen, Gigi asked, "What happened to the orphanage?"

"There was immense pressure from the state for the orphanage to be shut down."

Gigi frowned. "Closed? Why?"

"It just wasn't built for kids," Father Diego sighed. "When it was handed over, there was very little that I could do for the children. Social workers were here daily to transfer the children to better institutions around the city and throughout the state. I did not budge, though. I had seen the suffering of the ordinary people on the streets, and I knew something needed to be done to alleviate the suffering." He wiped away more sweat from his brow.

"What did you do?" Das asked.

"I put this plan together and presented to the local dioceses to transform this place into a shelter. I knew that the kids would be safe and well-taken care of at the other facilities. Besides, this place was not fit for *los niños*."

"Were there a lot of kids here at that time, *Padre*?" Das enquired again.

"Yes, many!" He waved his hands. "And although the place wasn't fit for little ones, I knew that adults could benefit from it. It was difficult at first to convince the Church, but by the grace of God and our mother María, I was able to persuade the cardinal to give the okay."

Genesis was taking notes.

Das asked, "What happened next?"

The priest cleared his throat and continued. "I put everything together. I went out and looked for helping hands and those with beliefs similar to my own. It turned that there were many who believed in the cause and wanted to help. Ironically, most helpers and donors came from the Protestant churches in the area—not the Catholic Church. Very soon, this became more than a ministry; it became our lives, our inter-denominational mission. Together we've worked until this day."

The task sounded harsh, but worthy. Genesis's eyes grew misty from the emotion bursting from his selfless acts of service. From his silence, Das seemed moved as well.

Father Diego stood up and walked over to a cabinet with a bucket of ice and a water jug. He poured each of them a glass, then flicked on a fan to grace them with a little relief from the heat. When he sat down again, he cleared his throat, then continued.

"And here is where I think you come into this picture, Miss. You see, there was a girl by the name of Addy who lived here many years ago. Unfortunately, the streets swallowed her up again. But she was raised right here, in this very same building, until she was thirteen years old. But then one day she ran away. We looked for her, but couldn't find her."

"Addy? And who was she?" Gigi asked.

"Well, here's the thing. A boy came here two years later and said Addy had told him about this place. He said Addy had been raised here, and that the people were good to her here. But that's not all. This boy had a little baby with him who had caught a cold. The baby was about a year old, small, very fragile, and suffering from early-stage pneumonia."

Genesis's eyes lit up at that revelation. A boy with a baby! This couldn't be a coincidence. She sat up straighter and intertwined her fingers to stop them from fidgeting. A million questions raced through her mind, but she had to be patient in order to not interrupt his story.

"I remember that day so clearly." The priest scratched the top of his gray, balding, head, as if reminiscing. "We had just celebrated with a young girl who was thirty days clean of drugs." He paused to take a sip of water, then continued, "He left the child here. The only name he gave was *Lucho*. The look in his eyes was devastating. He was so lost and alone. I pray for him every day, hoping he found a home more comforting than the rough streets. I begged him to stay, but he kept shaking his head. He wasn't much of a talker. I could sense he was holding something back, and I wish I could have helped that boy find God."

"Padre Diego..." Genesis interrupted. She couldn't take it anymore. Curiosity was burning her insides; story time was over. "Is that the name of the child who was brought by the boy?"

Father Diego looked at her, shaking his head from side to side, his eyes filled with sorrow. "No. That's the name of the boy who brought the child—*Lucho*. Addy, years later, told me his name was Luis Fuentes, but that everyone knew him as Lucho. They were close friends. They tried to raise this baby on their own, but couldn't do it anymore. Addy suggested the orphanage where she had been raised as a better option for this baby. But Lucho brought the baby girl on his own."

"A baby *girl*?" Gigi asked with excitement.

"Indeed. At first, we thought it was Addy's baby. But he said it wasn't theirs. He was not the father and Addy was not the mother. When questioned, he said he had found the newborn with a young Chinese girl that was dying in an alley. She had given birth to the child and had used her clothes to wrap the child up to shield it from the cold. I am assuming the same cold killed her. He stated that the mother had whispered something to him before passing on: *Woo Deep*. And that was to be the name of the baby girl."

The priest took a sip of water and then chuckled. "You know, we eventually found out that when roughly translated, it means something like *little butterfly*. So Lucho and Addy named the baby Woo Deep, and that was the name that we used to register her in the orphanage. It's a miracle a baby so small and young could have survived a cold night like that. It was one of the coldest nights ever recorded here, which may not seem so bad considering how hot it gets, but Mexicali weather can be very extreme."

"*Padre*, do you think that baby could be me?"

Father Diego leaned forward, folding his hands on the desk. "Now, Miss, I don't know for certain if that same child is you or not, but everything points toward it from what Das had told me. To my knowledge, there has been no other instance of a boy bringing a baby here and then leaving in that timeframe. I don't think it's a coincidence."

Genesis couldn't talk. There was a knot in her throat and a tear on her cheek. Was she finally getting the answers she'd been looking for? The priest was right; it seemed unlikely this was a coincidence. Genesis's heart pounded and her hand shook as she raised her water to her lips.

"And what of Addy?" It was Das who asked the question.

Father Diego mopped up the sweat that had once again gathered on his brow and was making its way in droplets down his neck, dripping onto his clothes. He adjusted his shirt to cover his round belly and sighed deeply. He looked at Das and then Gigi, his gaze unable to inspire confidence in either of them.

"She may be of very little help to you," he said despondently.

"Oh, no, Father! Is she dead?" Her words shot out of her mouth as if she had no control over them. Genesis rose from her seat, alarmed. She rested her palms on the top of the desk, and Das tried to pull her back to sit. She shrugged him off and tried to look at the priest, who was now avoiding eye contact.

"No, she isn't. But she is... how can I say this? She is not exactly in the best state of mind. Addy is schizophrenic. *Está enfermita, mi Addy.*"

"Oh! I see," she replied readjusting herself in the chair.

Gigi and Das exchanged looks.

"I have sent for her," Father Diego said, "She should have been here hours ago, but I think it's safe to assume she is on her way. We've grown close over the years, and though she doesn't always remember me, she always feels calmer around me. We find her roaming in the streets around here almost every day. But she refuses to come home or go to a place where she can get help. All the years of drug use messed her up badly. She has her ups and downs. Sometimes she is very articulate and remembers everything. But on other days, her hallucinations take precedence. So, please don't be scared if she starts acting out. She sees things that are not there and imagines things that never happened. But we have nothing to lose, right?"

"No, we don't, I guess," Genesis replied slowly. "Will I be able to talk to her?"

"Yes, of course. That is why I called for her. But there is something else you need to know. On two different occasions that Addy was here, she caused a scene."

"What do you mean," Das asked.

"Well, once we had a family member visiting someone, and she went to her and said she was her Woo Deep. She swore she was that baby from many years ago."

"You mean, me?" Gigi said without really expecting an answer.

Father Diego simply continued, "We had to literally subdue her that time. She was adamant that it was her. And on another occasion, she threw a fit because she swore people here were drugging her on purpose. She claimed aliens had told her this. What I am trying to say is, don't expect much. And she might do something... unexpected, to say the least."

Almost as if on cue, the door opened, and a lady came in. "*Padre, aquí está Addy.*"

Father Diego then looked to Genesis, "She is here," and spoke to the woman at the door, "*Que pase, por favor.*"

The woman nodded and went back outside. A few seconds later, the door reopened, and two men with another woman in her mid to late forties entered the room. She was dressed in old, dirty clothes, and her hair was tied in a bun. She stunk of garbage and feces, which made Genesis's stomach turn. She stared at the woman, trying to decide if she was a familiar face.

"*Hola, Padre,*" Addy stated as she stood a considerable distance from the table and very close to the entrance.

The two gentlemen who had brought her remained close to the door, unmoving.

"Hello, dear. *Ven aquí, mija.* I want you to meet these people." Diego told her in Spanish as he gestured across the table, and Das stood to greet her properly.

When Addy's gaze fell on Genesis, she broke into a smile. "Oh, my child. *Mi niña!* You have returned home!" She was speaking Spanish, but Genesis understood her clearly.

Addy gently pushed Das out of the way to get a better look at Genesis. Das played along and whispered in English, "*Here we go.*"

Genesis stood to face the woman, confused, with her chair between them. Gigi had never seen the woman before in her life and had no recollection of her sad eyes and yellow teeth. How did Addy know that Gigi was *her* kid, if that was even the case? There was no way this was even possible. This must have been what the priest talked about. The woman had to be mistaken, imagining things.

Yet Addy continued as if they'd seen each other just the other day. Before Genesis could protest, the woman walked up to her and grabbed both of her hands, holding them together. She drew them to her face and kissed them before placing them tenderly on each cheek. Addy's eyes became misty.

"*Um, hola. Mucho gusto,*" Genesis said, letting her know it was a pleasure to meet her. The two men simply allowed the exchange to continue.

"Lucho said you would return some day," Addy said. They were the same height, and Addy's breath smelled vile as her words formed slowly on her lips. "He promised me you would come back here. I did not believe him. I am so sorry, baby girl!" The woman hugged Gigi tightly and continued to mutter, too quickly for Gigi to understand.

Gigi only looked over Addy's shoulder to Das, alarmed, and mouthed "*What is she saying?*"

"She said that she didn't want to bring you here, but Lucho insisted," he said quietly. "She wanted him to keep you so she could nurture you back to health. You were *their* baby. Pato's, Lucho's, and hers." Das continued to translate as Addy let Genesis go.

"She's saying she couldn't do it. They were too young and too poor... and..." Das smirked, then said, "too high. They didn't know what they were doing. It was for the best to bring you here to them."

"I'm so sorry, my baby girl!" Addy said, speaking again at a speed Gigi could comprehend.

Gigi was speechless. Confused. She looked at both men as if to ask for guidance; Father Diego's mouth was hanging open. Das simply shrugged his shoulders.

She cleared her throat and asked the woman if she knew who she was, "*¿Sabes quién soy yo?*"

She stared into the woman's eyes, looking for a sense of familiarity or some clarity as to why Addy felt such a strong bond to her. She had more questions too: Who was this Pato and Lucho she referred to? A duck? She knew *pato* meant duck, but she had no idea what Lucho meant. Most importantly, who was *she*, this woman in front of her, right here and right now? And what did she mean that Genesis was *theirs*?

"*Eres Woo Deep, ¡mi niña!*"

Father Diego stepped forward and put his arm around Addy. "Now, Addy, remember what happened last time. This is not the first time you've thought you saw that girl from your childhood. What makes you think this is her this time?"

But Addy ignored the priest and removed his arm from her. Instead, she pushed a strand of hair from Gigi's face and gazed into her eyes, speaking slowly, "You have grown so big... and so beautiful. If Lucho had not crossed over the fence to the other side, to the states, he would have been so proud to watch you grow up. And if only we hadn't lost Pato to the streets many years ago."

Tears began to collect in Genesis's eyes, though she didn't know the exact reason why. Was it just because the woman was crying, or did she feel a connection? Here was a woman who was sick to the core, but still hadn't forgotten her after almost three decades. Or was she imagining things? How was Addy able to remember her? Recognize her?

Gigi was aware that schizophrenia was a mental disorder that generally appeared in late childhood, and that delusions, hallucinations, and other cognitive difficulties characterized it. This was a disease that spanned the entirety of one's life. How Addy had been able to overcome the cognitive difficulty just by looking at her was a miracle. No doubt about that. Or was this simply another episode of hallucinations?

Addy opened her arms and pulled Genesis into another big hug. This time, Genesis hugged her back, feeling awkward as the men stared at them. The women cried, unafraid of their emotions, even if Genesis couldn't pinpoint exactly why she felt this way.

Das stood and rubbed Genesis's back to comfort her. Tears formed in his eyes, and the same was true of Father Diego. All four of them shared a moment of raw emotion, none of them knowing the right words to say.

"I think I *am* your Woo Deep, Addy," Gigi finally said in between sobs.

CHAPTER TEN

"Addy, can you tell us more about Lucho?" Father Diego asked.

"What Lucho? Who are you? It's you, again, isn't it! I know what you want. You've come for me again, haven't you? But I won't let you take me this time." Addy started punching the air viciously and voicing noises.

What in the world? Is she tripping?

Das and Gigi exchanged looks, then Gigi turned toward Addy, "Addy, what is the last thing you remember of me?"

"Who are you?!" the woman yelled back. "What do you want from me, woman?"

Genesis reared back from Addy's sudden aggression, but her fright was quickly replaced by fear of another kind. *Did we lose you already? No! Please come. I still have so many questions.*

Genesis asked Addy again, but the woman wasn't coherent. Addy was hallucinating.

"Pato!" Addy turned to Das, pointing her finger accusingly. "Pato, why did you go?!"

Das back away slowly, casting a glance to Father Diego, who subtly motioned for the two men accompanying Addy to take her outside before things escalated.

"I'm sorry, but Addy will no longer be able to help you. I was afraid this would happen."

"It's okay, Padre. It was too good to be true. I truly appreciate all of your help. And while I don't remember her, or this Pato or Lucho, I at least have something to look into."

The priest walked the duo back to the Mustang. As Gigi and Das left the premises, Gigi shed a tear.

"Well, that was... interesting," Das observed as they drove away from the shelter, Father Diego waving in the distance. "Who would've thought she would still recognize you after so many years?"

"Yeah, I don't really know what to make of what just happened."

"But you do think you are that girl, right?" he asked while signaling the officers to follow them.

Gigi took a moment to think about what to answer. She ran a hand through her hair as she sighed. "I *know* I am, Das. It's just that I wish I could've asked more things. Like, who is my mom? She mentioned Lucho brought me after he found me. So, he isn't my father, and she isn't my mother. So where did Lucho find me?"

"Yeah, I have questions of my own too," Das replied.

"So *many* questions! Like, how were they able to raise me in their condition, even if it was for a short while, for example." Gigi rested her arm on the open window and looked outside. "So many unanswered questions."

"I know, *Chiltepin*. But hey, at least you have Lucho's full name now. You also know that he went to the States and when."

"Yes, that's a start. I guess it is true, after all." Genesis sighed, admittedly rather lost. "So, what now?" She turned to Das.

He paused to indicate as they turned back onto the main road. "Now, we go to Jin. He'll be able to help you out too."

When the number of Chinese people walking and conducting business on the road increased, Genesis knew they were close. She looked around for a sign to tell her which part of town they were in, but all she saw were Chinese characters posted on the buildings. The roads became thinner, the noise louder, and the smell of food stronger. There were trinket stores all around, and a lot of busses parking and leaving.

"Where are we?" Genesis yelled over the din of the street.

"*La Chinesca*," Das replied, matching her volume.

He parked the car on a narrow alley against an old brick wall and jumped out without opening the door. He walked around the front of the car as Genesis stepped out. The dull melodies of Chinese music, coupled with the lights displayed across every shop front gave the evening life. Some of the buildings bore portraits of naked women, dancing under disco lights; brothels of some sort.

A gentle tap from Das brought her back. "*Chiltepin*, follow me."

Genesis and Das walked together, side by side, through winding streets and turns. They came across different sights, from acrobatic displays in the middle of streets to an open-air opera, presented by a drunk, homeless man. Genesis would stall at times to take pictures, Das standing patiently by her side. These would be great for her article.

Soon, they moved to a part of town that was quiet. It was occupied by older shops and buildings that looked like they would topple over at any moment. Genesis shot Das a quizzical look. He squeezed her shoulder gently, reassuring her.

"We're almost at Jin's place," he said as he crossed over to an adjoining street.

Many of the shops here appeared abandoned. This one, though, had different spices exhibited in the display window. Powders, teas, and several other interesting items like that. There was a large variety of Mexican candy and Chinese spices on display as well. It smelled good. Her appetite was awakened.

Das pushed open the door and entered. An older man, who Genesis assumed to be Jin, was at the counter, polishing it with a piece of rag. He lifted his head to look at Das, then gave a slight nod to Genesis.

"What's up, Jin. Miss me?" Das greeted in English. Jin simply shook his head. "This is Genesis, whom I told you about. Ready to be interviewed?" Das tapped lightly on the counter with his fingers.

Jin smiled slyly upon eyeing her from head to toe and nodded his head in agreement. "Let's do it," he affirmed. "Nice to meet you, Miss. So please, tell me, how can I help you, *señorita bonita?*"

"I don't know," Genesis laughed, "I guess we'll find out."

"She's from the *L.A. Chronicle*, so this is a big deal," Das said quickly. "She's here writing an article about life on the Mexican-American border. One of the things she's interested in particular has to do with foreigners that live here. Why don't you start with that?"

"Um, excuse me, Das. I'm the journalist here. I ask the questions," Genesis teased.

Jin chuckled. "Okay, I will share anything with her, if she asks nicely over a cup of tea," he said, staring at her longingly. Jin then changed his gaze to Das. "By the way, I put your order together, Das."

"Order?"

"You know, the info you wanted in Tijuana. You'll find an envelope in the back. I'll stay here with our journalist friend."

"Oh, wow. You actually have something already?" Das asked excitedly, drawing a curious look from Genesis. "That was quick."

"Maybe it'll help," he replied. "So, tell me, princess, what specifically do you want to ask me? I'm an open book," he said turning back toward Genesis. "No more interruptions, Das. Let the lady and I talk in peace." Jin reached across the counter and placed his hand on top of Genesis's. She tried not to recoil; she was used to the sleazy type and would grin and bear it for a good story. Part of her wanted to punch the old man in the face, though.

But Das glared at the old man and swatted his hand away. "Don't start, Jin!"

"Das! Don't be so rude," Genesis said. "He's a sweet old man who'll help me with my piece. Right?"

"That's right," Jin said, beaming with pride. "I'm a sweet, old, innocent man. A man who is helping *both* of you, if you recall."

Das walked around the counter and stood beside Jin. Genesis watched them out of the corner of her eye as she inspected some of the candy on display. Das gripped Jin by his arm and whispered in his ear, "I'm going to check on the stuff back there. If I find out you tried anything inappropriate, I'm going to break your arm. I don't care how old you are. This is my friend. Stop being a creep. Understood?"

Genesis rolled her eyes subtly as Jin exclaimed, "Any friend of Das's is a friend of mine!"

Then Das turned to Gigi. "You sure you'll be alright? I'm telling you... You gotta watch out for this old man, here."

"Don't worry about me," she replied with a smile. She'd already managed to escape one set of abductors; what was more? she thought sarcastically. Besides, this poor man looked fragile.

Das nodded, lips pursed, then rushed to the back room.

Genesis lifted a few containers of spices and Mexican candy onto the counter. "Before I start, how much for all this?" she asked.

Jin eyed the product, then looked up at Genesis's chest. "For you, princess? It's free."

"What?" Genesis gasped. "No, I have to pay you. No offense, but I don't see a lot of customers coming in and out of those doors." She pointed her thumb at the entrance and placed a few bills on the counter. "Please, take it."

"I couldn't possibly," he said, pushing the bills back across the counter. "Das is your friend, so you get free items. That's how it works."

"Well," she said with a smile, "this is turning out to be a pretty amazing day. You don't even know the half it." Genesis put the items in her purse and rested her elbows on the counter. "What's Das looking at back there, anyway?"

"Private information," Jin said. "Honestly, I would tell you more, but that might make Das angry."

"Angry?" Genesis asked, "That's hard to picture. He's usually so sensitive."

"Toward a beautiful lady, yes," Jin said, tilting his head slightly to look down at Gigi's backside.

Even though it was fast, Genesis noticed it. Goosebumps broke out across her skin, and she clenched her hands into fists. The things she would endure to get information. Though she was used to being ogled by men, young and old, it didn't mean she was comfortable with it. Whatever it took to get a story, she would remind herself.

She gave him a fake smile as the memory of growing up as an insecure girl came to mind. In elementary school, kids would make fun of her calling her an ugly caterpillar. Her mother had reminded her that caterpillars turn into beautiful butterflies, and she always looked forward to one day going through some sort of metamorphosis herself and turning into something beautiful. By the time she was in high school, however, everywhere she went, everyone stared at her.

Just then, Das returned from the back room with an envelope in hand. "How were you able to get these? And do you have any more?"

"That's everything. You'll have to follow the trail to get anything tangible," Jin replied. "Don't worry about how I got them. Just know they'll help."

"Okay," Das said. "Let's get going, *Chiltepin*. We can come back later for your questions."

"What? I haven't gotten anything for my piece yet. I was about to ask him how you two know each other."

"Now *that* is a fun story," Jin said, raising his eyebrows.

"Another time," Das said, pulling Genesis away.

"Oh, sure! Because I'm in Mexico so often," she grumbled, pulling her arm back. "I want to stay. I really think his input would be good for my piece."

"It's settled. Tea for everyone!" Jin cheered and ran into the back room. Behind the door, Gigi could hear the clattering of cups and metal canisters.

"You brought me here," Genesis whispered to Das, keeping one eye on the door. "You can't just drag me away now. You told me we came here because he could help me. But now I know we came here for you."

"You're right," he replied, "I'm sorry. It's just that... well, don't worry about it. I guess this can wait. And yes, Jin might not the friendliest guy, but he's very knowledgeable about the city, and he can help you too."

"He's not friendly to you, you mean," Genesis teased, "I think he's being a little too friendly with me right now."

Das grimaced. "Ugh, I hate this guy."

"It's okay, Das. Look, I won't be staying around much longer, so I want to make the most of it. Let's just stay for tea, I'll ask my questions and then we'll be on our way. Okay?"

"Fine," he said with a forced a smile when Jin returned with tea.

Gigi learned a lot from Jin. The old man had been eager to share his story. He even overshared a little about his run-ins with the law. Jin also talked about the struggles and opportunities associated with being a foreign businessman, stuck between two lands, neither of which was his native one. It was good stuff. He even talked about the local economics, politics, and how each side of the fence depended on the other.

However, when she pushed about illegal activities and mentioned Carlos Wong, Jin simply looked at Das and backed out. He was done talking for the night. He said he was tired and needed to close the shop and go home. Gigi knew there was more to tell there, but was thankful to have gotten what she had. She decided not to push.

During the drive back to the hotel, Das asked her, "Why are you so pensive?"

Gigi had been sat silently, staring out across the land, but not really seeing anything. Upon hearing Das's question, she turned back to face the front. "I just need to know more about this shady Carlos character. Why is it that people are so scared of him? What is his deal? What's his story? Maybe I can expose him. I could help, you know?"

With an exaggerated sigh, Das signaled right and turned into the parking lot of a large shopping center. He parked the car and closed the top. Genesis looked at him, wondering what was happening.

"Where are we, and why are we stopping here? I thought we were done for the night."

"We're not going anywhere. I just want to talk about this, and I'd rather do it in a safe space."

"Okay...?" Gigi looked at him, apprehensive.

"Look, *Chiltepin*. Going around asking questions about people like Wong will only get you in trouble. I don't want anything happening to you. Again, that is. Consider yourself lucky. Things could've been a lot worse."

"What? It's obvious those men that grabbed me work for him! I've been thinking about it a lot now, and I believe that exposing him is the least I can do! I couldn't even sleep at night because of him, Das!"

Das signaled the cops who had just parked next to them to wait there. He then turned to Gigi. "I thought your boss wanted you back right away after hearing what happened to you. And I was under the impression that you had enough for your article too."

"Yes; but I'm not satisfied. Besides, it wasn't me who told my boss about what happened." She looked outside and rolled her window down to let some air in since the roof was closed now. "Also, this is just wrong, and you know it! Someone has to say something about what's happening here. About Wong, the Dragon, or whatever he goes by. About the human trafficking. The modern-day slavery. I want to write more on that! Maybe exposure is what needs to happen. Like I said, I'm sure it was his man who took me. And who knows what would've happened to me if—"

"Of course, it was his men," Das interrupted, turning off the engine. He took his hat off and, with a handkerchief, wiped the sweat from his forehead. "And that's why this is dangerous. Look, G, Wong is untouchable, both legally and politically speaking. It's not as easy as it sounds. Trust me; I've been doing my own investigations. In fact, that's why we went to Jin. That's why we drove to Tijuana! He's helping me gather evidence against him. But to take a man like him down will take a lot more than just an article. No offense. Besides, I worry about what could happen to you if you expose him. Others have tried before, and it never ends well."

"I get that. But why didn't you tell me that you were working on this and that Jin was helping you with this too?"

"I wanted to protect you. I feel guilty for what happened to you!" He hit the steering wheel with both his hands.

"*Nothing* happened to me, Das. I'm fine!" Gigi crossed her arms.

"Yes, you're fine *now*. But like I said before, it could've been much worse! You know that. And besides, he knows who you are now. He has your ID. That means he knows your name and where you live. This man is dangerous! Besides, your name and picture are easy to find online with your articles." Das cleaned his sweat off again.

Genesis nodded. "Yes, I know." She unfolded her arms and looked out the window, toward the evening shoppers entering and leaving the busy mall. She placed her right elbow on the window. "Jay already knows. We're going to move in together as soon I return, and the address on my license is old, anyway. Jay is getting the keys to our new place soon."

"Good. But that's not the point. Look, *Chiltepin*, you have to understand a few things about Wong and about how things work here. This is Mexico, after all. Besides, Wong is one of the largest job producers in the state of Baja California. The man owns casinos, restaurants, stores, and a bunch of other stuff." Das adjusted his hat and looked himself at the mirror to make sure it was fine.

"So, I've heard," Gigi said while opening her purse to retrieve some gum. She offered some to Das, but he shook his head.

"It's not just that, though. Wong is a smart man. He donates a lot of money every year to the three major and most powerful political parties in the state. This is his way of protecting his assets, because it doesn't matter which party takes control of the government, he knows he will always be protected. He puts people in positions of power, and they pay him back with favors and protection. Politicians here control everything. And he controls those politicians. So, imagine the power this man has!"

"Ugh! But don't people know about his sketchy side businesses? I mean, it seems to me like people are aware, but they just don't want to do anything about it. It pisses me off!" She kicked down on the floorboard.

"Well, yeah! That's true. But it's more complicated than that. Wong also runs fundraiser balls for the police, both municipal and state, and is close to the guys in charge. The police, Gigi! He is smart *and* careful. Some time ago, we even looked at tax evasion, but the man is clean on paper. He dots his i's and crosses his t's," Das said while turning the engine on again and blasting the AC all the way up. "Close the window, I'm gonna put the air on."

Gigi did as she was told. "I see. So that's how he does it. And I do get it, Das. I do. It's just frustrating. How much evidence do you have on him? I mean, like, are you guys getting close to busting him or something? Can you link him to the drug trade? Human trafficking? Extortion? Anything!"

"We know some things for certain, about all of these things and others. Some people are finally willing to talk anonymously too, which helps. Including Jin. But the thing is, I have to be careful. You never know who in the force is on his payroll. My boss assigned me this task some time ago, but I can't be sharing stuff with everyone in the department. Only a few of us know about it. And when we're ready, we'll get him. Trust me on this."

"This is all so crazy!"

"Yup. No one truly knows how deep his pockets go and who he owns and whom he has put in positions of power. That's why you going around and asking about him will not help. So, please, do me a favor and just stick to writing about what you got so far. Focus on your roots. That should keep you busy. Let *me* worry about Wong. Please?"

"Okay. I understand, Das. Thank you. And I *will* stop. I promise—for now."

Das didn't appear to be convinced. "What do you mean, 'for now'?"

"Well... what bothers me is that this Wong guy continues to partake in illegal business, when he obviously already makes a lot of money through his legit sources. I mean, what need does he have to traffic people, drugs, and who knows what else? I've Googled the guy and done some research, and he is obviously loaded. Why the heck would he have a need for this stuff?"

"Oh, my goodness! Leave it, *Chiltepin*! *Eres terca.*"

"I'm what?"

Das laughed. "*Terca*. Stubborn!" He signaled to the cops to go.

"Well, yes." Gigi smiled. "We already knew that. But I'm serious. I just don't understand it."

Das chuckled as he started the car back up and reversed out of the parking spot. "Look, that's how greedy people are. They simply want more and more. There's a reason why people refer to him as 'Dragon.' For him it's all about control. It's about power over people, not about the money itself. I think at this point he cares more about his reputation than anything else. People like him get satisfaction from controlling people, by owning them."

Gigi looked at a group of young pretty girls walking through the parking lot towards the shopping mall. "How does he bring in the girls that he prostitutes? I heard there are girls from all over the world. How does he get away with it? And where are they coming from and how?"

"Well, it varies," Das replied as he signaled to turn and exit. "Some are lured onto airplanes with promises of jobs as waitresses, models, nannies, dishwashers, maids, and dancers. You know, being on the border with the US is enticing for foreigners. It provides hope that perhaps they'll make it there some day, but it's easier to migrate here for now. But when they arrive here, they're stripped of their identity, and their nightmare begins. They're kept enslaved and prostituted. Those who resist are beaten, raped, and sometimes killed as examples for the others."

Gigi shed a tear as she listened intently.

Das continued while focused on the road, "Unfortunately, they don't have anywhere to turn. In many cases, the men who should be rescuing them, from immigration officials to police officers and international peacekeepers, are among their aggressors. And again, being on the border creates a unique opportunity."

"What do you mean?"

"Well, Americans love captive pussy."

"Excuse me?" Gigi was confused by the statement. Even hurt.

"Sorry. What I meant to say is, most of the Johns are from the other side. Your people, G. They are the ones that are addicted to the drugs and girls that flow north. But in turn, they push guns illegally down here as forms of payment. The dollar goes far here too. And because of that, we are in the situation that we are."

"And how is that?"

"Believe it or not, this was a safe place not that long ago. Guns are illegal in Mexico. But with so many guns around, gangs are empowered, and with this supply and demand of drugs and sex, it's a lucrative business. That's why cartels exist in the first place. That's why people like Wong are almost untouchable. Supply and demand."

"And the demand is big. Ugh!"

"Exactly." Das looked in the mirror to make sure the officers were still following them.

"See! It's exactly injustices like this that got me into this vocation. I figured if I helped expose wrongs like that, I'd be helping the world become a better place. I've always believed that to be a moral witness is the highest calling of journalism! And it's been my mission to tell stories that need to be heard. To expose evil by its name. That's why I need to do something about it, Das!"

Das smiled. "Don't be naïve, Genesis."

Genesis thought for a moment, preparing to retort. But then deflated back into her seat. "Ugh, you're right, Das. Who am I kidding? I can't do shit to help! I'm just a freaking journalist who doesn't even know who she is or where she comes from." Genesis hit the window with her elbow, evidently upset.

"What? No, I didn't say that. What you do *does* matter! And who you are matters too. I admire your passion and feel your desire for justice. I really do. It's just that I've learned there's a time and place for exposing people like this."

"I guess...?"

"And like I told you, people like Wong have killed and disappeared journalists before. Several!"

Gigi was quiet, looking outside the window.

"Look, I promise you that when we're ready, I'll contact you and you can help us expose this evil monster of a man internationally. The *Chronicle* reaches literally millions of people, and it would help. But, like I said, we aren't ready yet. I know how things work. Also, careful, by the way. Don't break my window, please."

Genesis laughed. "Sorry."

They stopped at a red light. "Unfortunately, this is the way it works in Mexico. Like I said, people like him here are untouchable."

After a few pensive moments, Gigi replied, "It's not just here, Das. It's the same way in the good ol' United States of America too. It's just that over there, we might hide it better, that's all."

Das nodded, "I guess you're right."

They drove in silence for a few blocks.

"Actually, come to think of it, that is how it is everywhere," Gigi added.

"Indeed," Das replied as he turned into the hotel parking lot. "Indeed, it is, my friend." He parked the car to let Genesis out as one of the officers charged to protect her came to open her door. "Don't worry, though. I promise you. We're close to nailing this guy. You, just stay safe for now."

CHAPTER ELEVEN

Irvine, California
July 2019

Jay and Richard waited outside Gigi's apartment, ready to welcome her home. The kidnapping incident had rattled Jay, but he hadn't informed Mr. Gill about it immediately. He knew it would crush him, so he decided to wait. Thankfully, Das had called him back within an hour to inform him that Genesis was safe and in their hands.

He had also learned that she would be accompanied by police escorts for the remainder of her stay there. This had brought him peace. Of course, now they had to move as soon as possible, but he didn't mind that at all, as long as she was home safe.

And thankfully, Gigi remained in touch with him constantly for the rest of her trip.

Jay glanced at his phone again. This was the seventh time that he'd checked for any messages from her since they had last spoken. Time crawled by slowly.

Gigi had asked Jay the day before asking him to help her check the name Luis Fuentes in as many databases as he could think of. He was good at that, so he did just as she had requested without asking questions. Computer searches for the state of California had given him eighty-nine matches. DMV listings for the age bracket she had given him brought up seven potential matches. He took down each of the respective addresses and emailed them to Genesis.

A few phone calls later, Jay and Genesis had narrowed the seven down to two. One was on the East Coast, and the other was close by, in Corona, California. And she planned to check him out upon returning.

Richard leaned over to Jay. "I swear you're acting like she's been gone forever. It's just been a week. Cheer up, son. She'll soon drive through that gate."

Jay smiled. "I know." He was acting like a teenager in high school, eager to leave for his first prom night. "Ah! There she is!" he said in excitement.

True to his word, Genesis's car appeared with a few other cars coming in through the apartment gate. Her eyes were covered with dark sunglasses, and her hair was down. Her complexion was a bit tanned.

Jay waved at her from where he stood with Richard; Gigi waved back and smiled.

Some minutes later, they were inside her apartment, eating grapes, cheese, and crackers. She had brought Jay some of the Mexican candy he liked so much, and her dad, some spices. Both, courtesy of a man she referred to as "Jin."

Jay, who was dying to ask Genesis more details on how she had managed to escape her abductors and other details about her trip, had to bite his tongue because of Rick. He knew he would get his opportunity once they were alone.

After her father left, only Jay remained. Genesis was tired, but ecstatic to be home with the man she loved. How she had missed him.

As Jay helped clean up the kitchen, Gigi's phone vibrated. An email had come in. It was from their boss. She tapped on the message.

The message started with Mr. Macy asking about her trip and went on—to Gigi's disappointment—to explain how the article she had mailed him was not up to his expectations. She needed to fix some things. He ended with asking her to rest over the weekend and report back to work on Monday. He did enjoy the pictures, though, and wanted her to find a way to incorporate them better into the article.

Gigi sighed and dropped her phone down. She had only two days to make it up to her boss and figure out a reason why her article wasn't up to par. She would swing into action after resting, she thought to herself.

Jay followed her into the bedroom and sat on the stool by her vanity. Genesis walked up to him and gave him a tight embrace as she sat on his lap. Even though she was tired from the journey, she was still pleasantly happy to see her Blue Jay.

"I missed you so much, babe," she said in between kisses as she pushed her fingers through his hair.

Jay held her, one arm around her waist and the other on her leg. "I missed you too," he whispered against her lips, sliding his hand farther up her thigh.

Gigi smirked and lowered her mouth to his ear. "All I wanted was to be home, here with you." she said.

Before Jay could move his hand any higher, Gigi stood up, kicked her sandals off, and in one swift move, removed her dress. She then extended her hand to Jay, as he stood up and began to unbutton his shirt. There he was, tall, tanned, and more handsome than ever. Her Blue Jay. With all her flaws, he loved her unconditionally. With all his flaws, he was still her favorite creation in the universe. He was hers and she was his.

As he finished taking his clothes off, she pulled him to the bed behind her.

"I was scared I was never going to see you again," Genesis whispered as she lay on Jay's chest with his arms around her.

He stroked her hair and kissed the top of her head. "I was scared too. I didn't know what to do!"

"I can only imagine. But thank God I'm home now." Gigi shook her head. "It all happened so fast."

"This is one story you'll have to write about some day."

"Yeah, someday..." She remembered the recording. She also remembered how close she had been to potential death.

"It would be an awesome piece!" Jay said. "I can imagine it already."

"Yeah, maybe. But, unfortunately, that piece will have to wait. One thing at a time. I've so much work to do for now, I'm afraid I may stay up all night," Genesis stood and walked toward her bathroom. "I gotta fix this article for Macy. And then I gotta follow through with this lead I got from the orphanage too."

Jay sat on the edge of the bed and pulled his shirt back on. "I can imagine. Oh, and speaking of which, what else happened at the orphanage? You didn't tell me if you found much else after that."

Addy's face flashed across Gigi's mind as she leaned against the doorframe. "Honestly, this Luis Fuentes guy is my best lead right now. Thanks for helping me with it, by the way. I have a strong feeling that he's the boy that rescued me. I'm going to look him up as soon as I finish this project for Macy."

"I'm sure all your hard work will pay off, babe."

"I hope so. I am just so tired right now."

"Okay, I tell you what. I'll let you rest up. I gotta check on Mom, anyway. But I'll bring breakfast in the morning."

"Sounds great."

"Welcome home, Gigi. *¡Te amo, mi mariposita!*"

"*Gracias*, Blue Jay. I'll see you in the morning."

Genesis smiled and opened the bathroom door. As she shut it behind her, she heard Jay getting up and walking out of her room. She shook her head, still with a smile. Soon, very soon, she would be walking down the aisle with this man, and she would say *I do*. The thought itself brought a smile to her face.

For now, she needed to hurry up and finish fixing the piece so she could focus on what was heavy on her mind. She needed to find this Luis Fuentes that lived in Corona, only about forty minutes away. The other six Luis Fuentes they had found didn't match the bio. She had a good feeling about this one.

Is this you, Lucho?

According to her intel, he was a store manager at a Bullseye, a high-end general merchandise retail store. She would check him out there.

PART 2

Lin

CHAPTER TWELVE

Guangzhou, China
1988

It was twilight in the urban slums of Guangzhou, once called Canton City. Men and women trudged to their various homes after a grueling day. The air was fetid with the stench of a decomposing dog lying on the road. The bins at the side of the road were overflowing with putrescent garbage, and a ragged man dressed in worn clothing rummaged around in them, hoping to find something to eat.

Cheuk Wu's bar, YinYang, was filled to the brim with men who sought to drown their worries in drink. Children at various stages of development played loudly in the spaces between the hovels that lined the streets while their exhausted mothers racked their brains as to what to prepare for dinner.

Zhang Wong sighed as he passed YinYang. It would be so easy for him to lose himself in drink. All he had to do was slow down, go into the bar, and order one or two glasses of Cheuk's potent brew. Once he did that, he would be oblivious to the aches and pains in his bones after his hard day. He could forget about his thankless job as a laborer in the manufacturing plant and could drink himself into a state of blessed oblivion.

Zhang smiled remorsefully and shook his head. *Not today, my friend.*

There were two big problems he had with drinking his troubles away. First, in his bid to forget about what was wrong with his world, he would also forget all the things that were right in it. He would forget his wife, who was still the most beautiful woman in the world to him, and he would disregard his teenage daughter and his little boy; the two lights of his life. Second, he was a recovering alcoholic, and he intended to keep the promise he had made to his wife. His family was the only reason he relented to face the same merciless grind every day. But the temptation to give in was gaining momentum.

He opened the door of his house and let himself in.

"Papa!" his eight-year-old son, Liu, rushed toward him, hugged him tightly, and took his bag.

Warmth bubbled in Zhang's heart, and he was suddenly grateful he hadn't given in to the urge to drown himself in drink. One more day clean. Besides, this was one of the highlights of his day—coming home to an enthusiastic welcome from his son.

On hearing the commotion, his wife glided into the room—at least that was how he saw it—and smiled at him. Cheng was a small woman with lush dark hair gently streaked with touches of gray. She stepped up to him with a cup of water in her hand and bowed briefly in greeting.

"Welcome home," she said, offering the water to him.

"Thank you." He took a long swallow, grateful for its soothing feeling over his parched throat. For a split second, he imagined it was stiff alcohol.

"He threw up a lot again today, Zhang," she whispered. "I don't know what to do anymore."

"He seems fine right now," he replied.

"Right now. But you weren't here earlier."

"We'll figure something out, woman. Don't worry. Where is Lin?" he asked, looking around for his daughter. The small, but crowded space felt hollow without her laughter.

His wife smiled as she collected the now-empty cup from him. "She is with Jing, who has a fever. Again."

Zhang grunted but didn't say anything.

His wife sighed. "Zhang, our girl is helping take care of Jing's son— she has no strength to do so. She will be here soon, don't worry."

Zhang gently cupped his wife's chin. "She is our Wu-Dip," he said with a smile. "Our butterfly. Once more spreading some cheer in her unique way." He stepped away, moving to the next room. "I will be out for dinner soon. I need to wash off the dirt from today."

Cheng nodded in understanding and went back the shed at the back of the house that served as a kitchen, while Zhang moved into the next room to change. Truthfully, he was torn upon hearing the news. On one side, he could not help the feeling of pride and affection he felt for his daughter. On the other hand, he despised the fact that his daughter was spending so much time with this sketchy "Jing" woman.

But he was determined not to fight with his wife today. Not like yesterday. He was too tired for it all. At least his son looked better.

In a dilapidated high-rise building, three blocks away from the Wong's home, Lin—or Wu-Dip, as her parents fondly called her—placed a wet rag on a feverish woman's brow. The woman shivered uncontrollably and had to fight to keep her teeth from chattering, yet her skin felt like a furnace had been set up just under it, slowly roasting her from within.

As the woman shook, Lin murmured reassuring words, "You'll be okay, Jing. You will be fine."

"My boy?" the woman managed to gasp out. "Where is he?"

She attempted to sit up, fevered eyes darting around the room.

"He is right here," Lin replied calmly, gently pressing the woman back into the straw cot. "He is asleep."

"I want to see him," the woman sent a pleading look to her. "Please help me up. I want to see my son."

The young girl conceded and helped the older woman into a sitting position so she could see her son asleep on a bundle of rags a little distance from her.

She exhaled, relieved, then took another deep breath—sitting up had exhausted her—and said, "Please... He needs to eat."

"That has been taken care of," Lin said. "He had some noodles for dinner that my mom made. Rest now, Jing. You need to rest."

Jing focused bloodshot eyes on her.

"Lin, you should go home. These streets are not safe to walk at night."

"I know. I'll leave soon, once you settle down to rest. My mother made you a potion." She walked to the table and picked up a covered bowl as she spoke. "She says it's very potent. She would be here, but she's seeing to my father and brother."

Sitting beside the sick woman once more, Lin lifted the lid from the bowl. The room was immediately filled with the overwhelming smell of mixed herbs. The other woman, despite her illness, had the presence of mind to shuffle a little farther away on the narrow cot.

"What is *that?*"

"It's my mother's concoction," Lin replied. "She makes it for us whenever we get sick, and it always works." She poured some into a cup and held it out to the sick woman. "Have some."

The woman looked doubtfully at the cup at first, but took it and drank every drop of it nonetheless. Then she she grabbed the girl's hands in hers. "Thank you, Lin. You took care of my boy. You took care of me. Thank you."

Her eyes were already beginning to droop.

"Thank... you," she said once more. And soon, she was asleep.

Lin smiled, got up, and looked around to make sure everything was in place. Seeing that the baby was also asleep, she left the apartment.

The dinner dishes were just being cleared when Lin arrived home. "*Néih hóu*, Papa!" she said, curtsying in front of her father.

Zhang smiled and nodded in reply from his sit, his eyes taking in her threadbare appearance: clothes stitched in so many places the patches were almost overlapping, sandals that had been rescued from the refuse heap when she outgrew her old ones, her long, black, shiny hair held back with a strip of old clothing, and her skin baring numerous scars left by insects. In contrast to her general appearance, her eyes twinkled with laughter and sincere joy, and her smile was warm and welcoming. He took a deep breath. Lin—his *Wu-Dip*, his little butterfly—deserved so much more than what she got, so much more than he could afford.

"How is Jing faring tonight?" Cheng asked.

"She seems to be getting better," Lin replied with a smile as she played with her long ponytail. "Your potion did wonders, Mama. She fell asleep almost immediately after she drank it."

"That's good to know," Cheng said, turning for the kitchen, arms laden with dishes.

"Let me do that, Mama." Lin collected the dishes from her mother. "You need to rest. I'll take care of these." With her arms full of plates and bowls, she headed to the back of the house.

Cheng exhaled loudly and sank onto the old chair beside her husband. "She's such a sweet girl, our Wu-Dip. We are indeed blessed to have her."

Zhang nodded in agreement as he blew into his cup of tea. "She is too good for this place. She deserves better than I can give her," he replied.

"So you say, and I completely agree. Our girl has so much light inside her. I wish it didn't have to be restricted to this place. But what can we do?"

"I don't know yet; but there must be something." Zhang took a sip of his tea holding the hot cup with both hands. As he put it down he continued, "She has wings; she needs to fly. I will figure out something."

"You always say that." Cheng stood up to fix the table mantle for the other side. "Lift your cup."

"No, I'm serious. I'm done with this life," he added as he did as told. "If we can't improve our quality of life, I will at least make sure something is done for our kids. I already have an idea. But I don't think you're going to like it."

The next day, Lin went with her mother to the lavish homes where she worked as a cleaning lady. These homes were in Liwan, on the other side of the Zhujiang River in Guangzhou, away from the slums of the Yangji Cun village where they resided. Here, the streets were well-kept and clean. A far cry from the vermin-infested, garbage-filled streets of Yangji. The air was fresh and clean, completely free of the offensive odor of rotting carcasses and putrefying trash coming from the disease-ridden river. The houses were grand, with sprawling compounds that appeared to go on for miles.

While the infrastructure of the city of Guangzhou was changing to reflect the coming of the new millennium, replacing slums with modern high rises as far as the eye could see, this area seemed to remain intact and unharmed by the rapid change.

Lin had been overcome by awe when she went with her mother for the first time. It had now become a regular routine; she would go with her mother to work and help with whatever needed to be done, be it scrubbing floors, baths, or ironing clothes. Her mother's employers liked her because she was a hard worker and always left her mark on anything she tackled. If it were floors, they'd be sparkling clean by the time she was done scrubbing. The same went for the bathrooms. Her sunny personality ensured she was always welcome wherever she went with her mother, and she was grateful for the chance to help reduce the older woman's workload.

Though she longed for the pretty clothes and beautiful hairdos worn by the daughters of the people she worked for, she hid it well. She constantly reminded herself there was no point longing for something that would most likely never be hers—she needed to focus on helping her family out in any way she could.

This is my reality. Some are born lucky. We weren't. Lin scrubbed the crusted vomit from guest bathroom floor—remnants of the lavish party the night before. *This is simply my part in helping the family.*

While Lin worked with her mother, her younger brother was supposed to be in elementary school. But most of the time, he would join other boys of his age roaming the streets, searching the large garbage containers for anything they could scavenge. Liu had found many helpful things this way. Sometimes he got lucky and found barely-used items thrown away by the rich, such as the sandals his sister now wore. Other times, he found food items which were still relatively edible. He would take them to his mother, who would wash them, cut off the rotting parts, and make a meal from them.

Everyone does their part. Today I clean barf. Tomorrow, who knows? At least I get to eat.

After a long and hard day, the ladies made their way home taking two buses and several long walks. Lin's mother had been more quiet than usual, and it didn't go unnoticed.

"Mama, what's wrong? This whole day you've been... different," Lin asked her mother while walking through a muddy road.

"What do you mean different?" she replied without looking back at her, trying to evade a murky puddle.

"I don't know, just more quiet than usual. What's wrong?" Lin stopped and held her mother's arm to make sure she stopped as well.

Her mom turned to her and let out a heavy sigh as they made eye contact. "What's wrong? Lin, *everything* is wrong!" She dropped her bag on the ground. A few brown drops splashed both their legs. "I am just tired, that's all. And your father has these crazy ideas. I just don't know what to do anymore."

Lin ignored the mess the splash had done on her feet, but focused instead on her mother's teary eyes. Immediately, hers dampened as well mirroring those of her mother's. "Is there something I can do to help? I don't like seeing you like this, Mama."

"Oh, Wu-Dip. If only you knew." Her mother dried her tears with her wrist and picked up the soggy bag from the ground. "Come on, let's go home. Don't worry, baby girl. We will figure things out. You just continue being you."

That evening, after dinner, Lin asked for permission to visit Jing. Her mother accepted, and she left, taking a small bowl of food with her.

Standing outside the apartment door, Lin heard the woman singing softly to her son. She knocked and waited. The singing stopped, then footsteps preceded the click of the rusted latch.

"Lin... You came here early this morning. I didn't think you'd come again," said the fragile woman welcoming her in. Lin looked quickly around the small home and spotted the young boy sleeping soundly on the cot.

"My mother told me to bring you some dinner." She offered her the bowl. "It's just rice. I'm sorry, but that's all we have."

Jing's eyes filled with tears as she placed her hand over her heart. "Little Miss Wong, you and your mother are too good to me. But you really shouldn't come around so often. It's true what they say: those who have the least are the most generous." She accepted the bowl. "My fever broke this afternoon, and I can already feel my strength returning to me. You should go home."

Lin frowned as she nervously grabbed her pony tail. "You want me to leave? Why? Have I done something wrong?"

Jing had never turned her away so quickly before. She just wanted to be helpful, and it pained her to be pushed away.

"Of course not, you silly girl!" The middle-aged woman shuffled across the room to her rickety table and put the bowl of food on top of it. "You have been so good to me, and I wish to return the favor. You and your parents are good people. I do not want to spoil your name. Besides, I don't think your dad is very fond of me."

"I don't understand." She continued to run her fingers through her raven hair.

A sad smile spread across Jing's face, mirroring Lin's. "I know you know, Lin. You must have heard the whispers about me. I do not wish for the names of yourself and your family to join mine in the mouths of those cowardly gossips."

"I don't care about any of that..." Lin stood up and looked out the window.

"Oh, but you should!" Jing came and stood next to Lin. She put a hand on her shoulder. "Like I said, you and your mother have been so good to me. I only wish to return the favor. What will people say about your suddenly increased visits to a woman like me? You're a good girl, Lin. Sweet and innocent. I don't want your reputation ruined simply because you became too close to me for the public's liking. You are young and beautiful, with so much life ahead of you."

Lin turn around and faced Jing. "What people think or say does not matter. At least, it doesn't matter to me."

"Oh, but it does. And it should! Come sit with me." Jing pull both her chairs and placed them facing each other. She sat on one and motioned for Lin to do the same, which she did. "I am a prostitute, and people hate me for it. The men look at me and are ashamed of their weakness. The women hate me because I give their husbands the kind of sexual succor they cannot." She shook her head. "If only they understood that I'm only trying to survive. I've been alone on the streets since I was a child. How else am I supposed to survive? If only they understood that I have no other choice, that I'm doomed to this life. This is all I know. I have a child to take care of!" She buried her head in her hands as anguish seeped into her voice.

Lin reached out and move her chair closer bridging the gap between them. She now put her hands on Jing's shoulders.

"This is all I know..." Jing continued. Her body shook as she began to sob.

On the couch next to them, the boy stirred, jarred from his sleep by his mother's distress. He then turned and continued to sleep.

Lin stood up and put her arms around Jing. She whispered, "Don't cry. Everything will be fine." She held her tightly while Jing sat, like her mother always did for her when she was upset.

Jing pulled back to look at her. "Your parents call you *Wu-Dip*, right?"

The petite girl smiled while looking down at the older woman. "Yes. You know this."

"Butterfly. A beautiful creature spreading beauty, making the world a better place. But also, fragile. Be careful, little girl. There are people out there whose only delight is ruining a butterfly's beauty." She leaned back further, easing out of the hug. The child grunted in his sleep. "It's getting late, and these streets are dangerous. You should leave now." Jing stood up and smoothed out Lin's pony tail and planted a gentle kiss on the top of her head.

"Okay. Goodnight, Jing."

"Sleep well, little Miss Wong. And thank you, again."

As Lin left, she looked back at Jing, who now cradled her son and sang him a lullaby while rubbing at her moist eyes with the back of her hand. Lin smiled and walked out into the lonely streets.

It was a murky night, the moon hiding behind a thick, gray celestial curtain which prohibited its light from reaching the earth below. Though it wasn't cold, chills ran over Lin's skin. She hurried her steps.

"Let's just get home safe, Lin..." she told herself.

Having spent all her life there, Lin knew the streets of this part of Guangzhou as intimately as the palm of her hand. She knew how to navigate the narrow canals to go around the neighborhoods faster than one would using the swarming, and often, dangerous streets. But she had no canoe or boat this time.

Lin turned right onto an alley toward home when she saw a group of young men smoking and lounging in the street. Wary, she decided to go the opposite way. It would take longer, *but better safe than sorry.*

Her weary feet picked their way through the debris that littered the streets. Ignoring the distant sirens, she went over what Jing had said. She remembered the pain in Jing's voice as she spoke of the way other people viewed her. Lin had heard other women from the neighborhood whispering about the woman and her son, but had paid no attention to them. Cheng had taught her not to take the words of gossips to heart. And Jing had been there for them before. It was time they returned the support.

A shadow stretching across the ground from behind her was the only warning Lin had before strong hands clamped hard over her mouth and wrapped around her shoulders. She shrieked and struggled as she was pulled easily into the darkness of the alley. Kicking her legs and clawing at his arms, she sensed her efforts would go unnoticed when he didn't let out so much of a groan.

"Let me go!" she screamed, but her words were muffled against the man's hands.

She tried to pull his arms off her, but he wouldn't budge. He was too strong, and for a moment, all she could focus on was the smell of garbage coming off his hand, burning her nostrils. The smells that seeped off his skin nearly rendered her unconscious. He reeked like someone had dumped an entire garbage bin over him, then soaked him in alcohol in the blazing sun while he smoked packs of cheap cigarettes.

Her heart threatened to burst right out of her chest. The man was evidently drunk by the way he stumbled and kicked empty bottles on the ground. There would be no reasoning with him, even though she had no idea what he truly wanted from her.

But then her nose picked up something else—a familiar, pungent stench. Her feet kicked aside various loose items on the floor, and she understood. He was drawing her to one of the several trash mounts that dotted the street, most likely hidden between two buildings.

Eventually, she was spun around, and her back hit a wall, cracking her head against the bricks. His large hands pushed into her shoulders.

She tried to kick him in her delerium, but her knees buckled, and she was too short to reach anywhere that would actually hurt him. She recoiled as her attacker's free hand ran down her arm and torso, then back up again.

She had heard about incidents like this but had never imagined she would experience it firsthand. One of her neighbors who was her age had been taken to Hong Kong where she was never heard from ever again.

Her eyes misted over with tears. The man's hands roamed all over her body, and she couldn't stop the whimpers of terror from escaping her mouth.

"Ah, you like that?" he whispered close to her ear. The fumes of whatever distilled spirits this man had drank made her dizzy. "There's more where that came from."

Suddenly, something snapped in her. She felt the fear give way to overwhelming amounts of anger. The anger spread through every part of her, chasing away the fear and allowing her mind to assume a measure of clarity. An idea came to her.

Without contemplating it, she gently moved her assailant's hand back to her mouth and chomped down on it as hard as she could. The man yelled and pulled his hand away, but still didn't release his forearm from her chest, barring her against the wall. And yet her confidence returned, and she took a deep bloody breath to scream with everything she had.

"Help! Somebody, help me!"

"Shut up, you stupid fool!" the man growled. His hand came swinging next, a blur through the darkness. The slap sent her head back against the wall once again, and she tasted blood; hers mixed with his. Her ears rang, but she heard him say, "I am going to kill you if you keep making noise, stupid girl!"

Lin's tears streamed down her cheeks, and she continued to scream and kick her legs, ignoring his threat. Nobody heard her. Or nobody cared. Still, she refused to go down without a fight. She managed to get out another scream before her mouth was covered again, as the man, breathing threats and profanities, dragged her even farther into the darkness of the alley.

THE FLIGHT OF THE BUTTERFLY

CHAPTER THIRTEEN

On the street, two men, a young one and an older one, were walking by the alley after work. The younger one stopped and listened. "I thought I heard a scream," he said.

"I did too," replied his older partner.

They entered the alley between two buildings and peered into the shadows. They heard muffled voices and proceeded closer. The darkness slowly gave way to a man grumbling profanities while a young woman cried.

Suspicious, they ran deeper into the alley, treading carefully until they clearly saw a drunk fighting to subdue a struggling young girl.

"Hey!" the younger man shouted while his partner lunged without hesitation. The shout distracted the drunk's attention from the girl, and he whirled around.

The older man grabbed the drunk by the collar and dragged him away from the girl. The stinking drunk turned around and tried to fight, holding up his fists, ready to get into it, when the older man knocked him out with a single blow to the face.

"Stupid drunk," he muttered shaking off he pain on his knuckles.

Meanwhile, the girl sank to the ground and huddled against the wall. She made sure her tattered clothing was wrapped tightly around her body, then shivered as a gust of wind passed over the area.

The young guy crouched near her and regarded her with concern while his partner ensured the drunk was out cold a few feet away. "Are you okay?" he asked.

She nodded, though all other parts of her body remained paralyzed. Her mouth was full of blood, and she stared at her unconscious attacker lying on the ground.

"Can you move?" he asked again with concern.

The girl hesitated, then nodded once more. Trembling, she managed to stand, and the helpful man stood with her, ready to support her if she fell.

"Th-thank you..." She couldn't stop shaking. "Thank you."

"Wait a minute," the older gentleman said as he came closer to her, squinting in the darkness to see her better. She shrank against the wall once again, so he stopped and said, "I think I know her. Zhang Wong's girl? Is that you?"

Again, she nodded and let out a shaky, "Yes."

"Lin, right? What are you doing out here all by yourself?" he asked. "Do your parents know where you are?"

"I was... visiting a friend," she replied, hanging her head. "I need to go home."

Without another word, Lin started walking down the alley to the street, her legs barely supporting her movements, and the two men followed behind.

"Let us take you," the young guy said. "We can't let you travel alone after what you've just experienced."

Lin nodded once again, and the men walked with her, one on each side. The older of the two took out a handkerchief and handed it to her. "Clean your blood with this."

"Thank you. I don't think it's my blood," the frightened girl replied.

When they reached Lin's home, they knocked on the door and delivered her safely into the arms of her mother and brother, who were overcome with worry. Her father had gone out to search for her, worried about why she hadn't returned from Jing's yet.

"Thank you so much for bringing her home," her mother said, hugging her tightly. "We were so worried!" She looked down at her daughter and said, "What happened?"

Lin pursed her lips, not yet having the courage to tell her mother the truth. She smiled at the men, thanking them with her eyes.

"You must come in for tea," Cheng said, "and I can cook you something hot to eat."

"That's very kind," the young man said, "but I'm afraid we must decline. We have our own family to get home to, now that your daughter is safe."

"Yes," the other added. "We don't want to worry them, either; it's already late."

With that, they exchanged goodbyes and walked away from the house. Though before they could get far, Lin called out to them: "Your handkerchief, sir."

"Keep it. I have more."

Immediately after they left, Cheng closed the door and turned her attention to her trembling daughter, knowing full well there was something she wasn't telling her. The young girl sat in silence at the dining table, staring down at the handkerchief she fiddled with. Cheng frowned when she noticed the red stains and sat in the chair beside her daughter. Now close, she saw how miserable Lin looked, shivering as if she could never get warm again. It wasn't even cold.

"Oh, my child," she breathed.

Cheng ordered her son to brew herbal tea to warm and soothe his sister while she hustled Lin into the bathroom. Lin spent a long time in the hot bath, with her mother checking in on her every few minutes. When she came out, her skin was raw and red, as if she had tried to wash off every memory of whatever it was she had experienced. Cheng looked at her, highly concerned, then guided her back to the bedroom.

Lin sat up on the edge of the makeshift bed while her brother brought her some food. She was being fed cabbage soup by her attentive brother when their father stormed in, his face burning with anger.

"Cheng!" he screamed. "Do you know what almost happened to our daughter?"

Cheng rushed over to him, placing her hands on his chest. "Clam down, Zhang. She's still shaking. Let her tell us. Don't go in with her like this. Come, stay here with me." She attempted to guide him back to the dining area, but he resisted.

"She was in danger!" he shouted, waving his fists in the air. "I ran into a couple of my coworkers on my way home, and they told me she was attacked by some drunk in an alley. She could have been raped, Cheng. Or worse!"

"Zhang!"

A soft hiccup came from behind the mother and father, and they both looked back to see Lin, her face buried in her kneecaps and her damp black hair falling around her legs. Her brother lay a comforting hand on top of her head and looked back at his parents with glassy eyes.

Zhang spoke to Cheng again, this time more quietly. "What if my coworkers hadn't been passing by? We might've never seen her again. Could you even imagine what that would feel like?"

Though this news was harrowing to Cheng, she swallowed the fear his words had instilled in her. "Zhang, please calm down. You're going to scare the kids even more."

"I am angry, Cheng. I am mad at myself for not doing more to protect her," he replied as the first tears escaped his eyes.

Cheng pulled a chair from the dining area and set it next to hers beside the bed. One simple smile, which at that point was forced, calmed him, and his entire demeanor changed. He closed his eyes and took deep breaths, as if trying hard to fight down the rage boiling within. He sat down.

"Zhang, she is fine now. That is all that matters."

"Yes, but... you don't understand, Cheng. I have this urge to go out and find the man that dared to touch her."

"I know. But that can be dealt with later. We have to be here with the whole family now. Give her time."

After several long minutes of peace, Zhang moved deliberately slowly to where his daughter sat, looking up at he and his wife with troubled eyes. This was their baby girl. Their butterfly. So fragile, so delicate. Looking at the fear in her eyes caused Zhang's heart to shatter into a million pieces. He wanted to wrap her up in a hug and never let her leave home again.

"Wu-Dip..." he said softly as he approached her. He reached out to touch her, but she flinched away. The small movement cut him deeply. He took a deep breath to soothe the sharp pain and tried again, being careful not to get too close. He sat by her and took the bowl of soup from his son, which was nearly empty, and handed it to Cheng. "Wu-Dip, how are you?"

"Fine," she replied, though her eyes told another story. "I'm *fine*. I just want to sleep now." She laid back and watched her brother get up and embrace their mother.

Zhang took in the rigid way she held herself in those rags, as if she was afraid she would fall to pieces if she dared to relax even for a second. Seeing her so wounded made him feel that same pain. His muscles tightened, and for a moment, Zhang watched after his wife, who took Liu back to the dining area with the dirtied bowl. It was only he and Lin in the bedroom now. The look in her eyes was like that of an alert animal, conscious about the proximity of a predator and poised to flee at any second—or fight back.

"That's good," Zhang said, feeling helpless in the face of his daughter's pain. "Rest, baby girl." He kissed the top of her head as she lay. "We'll talk more tomorrow."

He got up and turned toward the other room. Cheng sent a sleepy Liu in as Zhang left, and the boy cuddled close to his sister, laying a small hand over hers. Zhang watched them for a moment more before joining his wife at the dining table.

Zhang's face once again glowed with anger.

"What is it?" Cheng asked warily.

"I know who it was."

Cheng's eyes widened slightly. "Already?"

"It was Chan." He balled his hands into fists again, trying to keep his voice low. "By the description my coworkers gave me, I have no doubt in my mind. I saw him earlier too. That idiot was dead drunk." He shook his head and turned for the flimsy front door. "When I lay my hands on him..."

"Zhang Wong!" his wife interrupted, making a grab for his hand. She held it firmly as she said, "He's not worth it. What matters is that she is home now, safe and unharmed."

"Unharmed? Look at her! Look at our butterfly, looking as if someone just tore off her wings. I swear to you, Cheng... I swear, when I get my hands around Chan's neck, he will learn to never to touch my girl—or any other girl—ever again."

"Zhang, please... don't do anything you'll regret later. We need to report the incident to the police."

Zhang scoffed. "The police? The police don't care about people like us. They won't bother with anyone from here. You can't talk me out of this, Cheng. It doesn't get worse than this. Don't you get it? No one traumatizes my family like that and gets away with it. No one." With that, he strode out into the night again, leaving his wife staring anxiously after him.

Lin curled up in a fetal position on the bundle of rags that served as her bed. Try as she might, she couldn't shake the memory of the attack. She could still smell the man's foul breath and could still hear the lewd things his raspy voice whispered in her ear as she struggled to escape.

She had heard of similar incidents involving other girls, some of whom she knew, but she had somehow convinced herself this would never happen to her. She thought she knew how to protect herself and that if she kept to herself, no one would bother her. Lin learned the hard way that bad things did indeed happen to good people.

I hate my life.

Her faith in humanity had been shattered. A little bit of her innocence died in that alley. She curled deeper into her bed and tried to banish the chill that remained in her bones. The man's taunts still rang loudly in her ears as she drifted into an uneasy sleep, wondering if she would ever forget her attacker's face. Or his smell.

In the other room she heard her mother and father arguing, then the door banged and all that was left was the sound of her mother's cries.

While his family attempted to sleep their problems away, Zhang walked the streets with fire in his eyes and murder in his heart.

Chan! That worthless drunk, he thought to himself. *He will pay for this!*

The man was a menace when sober. Drunk, he was a danger to himself and the community. Some men became amiable and talkative when drunk. Others would simply fall into a drunken stupor, sometimes in the middle of their own vomit.

But everyone in the neighborhood knew about Chan's weakness for drink and young women; a weakness made even more dangerous by his violent streak. He had already left a trail of broken girls in his wake, and Zhang was tired of no one teaching him a lesson.

Zhang uttered a low oath as Lin's broken and beautiful face appeared in his mind. Her eyes had already lost their sparkle. The memory of how she flinched away from him tore at his heart. He could only imagine what Lin saw when she looked at him. Her mind could have been playing tricks on her, making her believe that her attacker had infiltrated their home.

I should have been there for her. The thought beat at him, pummeling his mind until he wanted to pull out his hair and roar with rage and frustration.

He *should* have been there for her. Fathers were supposed to protect their children, but he hadn't been there for his daughter when she needed him the most. How disappointed she must have been in him.

A part of his mind, a small part, told him that he was being irrational, but he was unwilling to listen. His hands balled into fists. Maybe it was too late to protect his daughter, but it wasn't too late to send a message—and it was not too late to avenge her innocence.

As rage filled his mind, Zhang continued with determined steps. He grunted as he clunched his teeth. "Chan!" he shouted. "Where are you, Chan?" He continued through the dark streets.

And then he saw the drunk man's silohuette in the distance.

Late that night he arrived home expecting everyone to be sleeping, but his wife was waiting up for him. She turned on the oil-lamp and gasped when the light fell on his face. He had a split lip, and one eye was swollen closed.

"Zhang! What did you *do*?" she whispered, unable to move out of her chair.

"What had to be done." His voice was hoarse, a consequence of having Chan's desperate hands around his neck. "It's done." He stumbled into the chair beside his wife and hung his head.

Without another word, his wife bustled about the room, getting everything she needed to tend to his wounds. A few minutes later, she knelt in front of him with water and a clean rag.

"My love..." she began as she leaned forward to dab the worst of his scrapes, "was this really necessary?"

"Yes." He winced, as even the gentle contact stung. "Nobody harms what's mine, Cheng. I need people to know that."

"But your reputation! Everybody knows you for your gentle and easygoing ways. What are people going to say? How could you let people see your anger evolve like this?"

"People are going to call me the kind of father who avenges his daughter's honor. I might be gentle, but I am not stupid. People will realize that."

"We both know Chan is a no-good drunk..."

"Even more reason for him to be taught a lesson." Zhang's voice was hard and emotionless. His wife looked him in the eyes, and he began to tear up. He reeked of remorse. Regret pounding his mind. "I'm sorry," he said.

"It wasn't your fault, Zhang," she said gently, placing her hand on top of his. But he pulled back and turned his face away from her. "You didn't know this was going to happen," she continued and finished washing out his wounds.

"Well, I should have..." he said firmly, leaning forward to rest his arms on his thighs. "I should have been more insistent in my warnings to Lin about the dangers of the night and hanging out with shady people. The truth is that I should've followed my instincts and shouldn't have given her the permission to spend so much time with Jing."

"Zhang."

"Yeah, I know. Everyone says that woman is a bad influence on Lin, but I know her as a kind woman." He grunted as he walked and took a sit on the chair he always sat on. "Maybe I should have known that Chan would go on a drinking spree tonight. I mean, we got paid today. I should have..."

"Shhh..." His wife held her finger to his lips. "You're going to wake the kids. Besides, blaming yourself won't undo what's done. Beating Chan to a bloody pulp won't either. I'm just as angry as you are about what happened, but we need to focus on helping our daughter through this."

Cheng walked to the old, small, and barely working fridge they owned and pulled out a bag of frozen vegetables.

"I should've... I mean... I could've killed him, Cheng."

She came back to him and sat next to him. She kissed his bruised knuckles before placing the ice-cold bag on them. "I am glad you didn't. But I do thank you for going to fight for our daughter's honor, Zhang. You're a good man. You care about your family, and I know that Lin will be grateful for your actions."

He smiled his thanks to his wife, then his glazed eyes fully erupted into sobs. "I'm just thinking about all the things that could have happened..."

"Don't dwell on that. You're a good father. What happened does not make that fact any less true."

"I couldn't protect her, Cheng!"

"*Stop* blaming yourself. You can't be everywhere at once. Besides, Jing's place is only a few blocks away. We couldn't have known."

He was quiet for a moment. Cheng got up and put various items away, then came back to sit beside him again, saying nothing.

"She deserves better," he finally said. "Lin does not belong here, wearing rags and scrubbing rich people's floors. She deserves better."

His wife nodded her agreement. "I know."

"I want to go forward with my idea."

Cheng didn't say anything. He knew she didn't like it.

Zhang fell silent again while the wheels in his head turned rapidly. He stood up and peeked into the room, looking at his sleeping kids. Even though it was hot, Lin had wrapped her blankets around her as if for protection. The light of the oil lamp fell on her face, and her expression was disturbed, even in a deep sleep. It was like she was wrapped in a constant state of fear now. His heart constricted with love and protection. She was his butterfly. Too delicate for this place.

His gaze turned where Liu lay asleep beside her. His little boy was already becoming a man. He wished his son didn't have to hunt for the leftovers of the more fortunate to contribute his own quota to the family's upkeep, but there was nothing he could do about it. Already, his son was settling into his role as the other man of the house.

He was a playful, happy boy, but would often choose to stay home with his mother, rather than go out to play with his friends. He was helpful and responsible. Very mature for his young age. Just like Zhang and his father before him, Liu was being forced to grow up due to their circumstances—he didn't have much chance to be a real kid.

Zhang recognized that Liu watched over his mother and sister as best an eight-year-old could, and his resourcefulness had helped them through difficult times. Zhang's frown turned into a smile knowing that, while Liu's friends chose toys and other items they could use for their amusement, Liu always ensured he brought home something that would benefit his whole family. He was selfless.

At his tender age, he was already well-versed in the way of the streets. He could even hold his own in a street fight. Yes, Liu might be little, but he was fully capable of taking care of himself. He could certainly survive here. He *would* survive here, no matter what life threw his way.

Zhang's forehead crinkled. Unfortunately, he couldn't say the same for his Wu-Dip. She was too sweet for this sour world, and that thought made him miserable. She was also a selfless soul and had a strength of her own, but she thought the best of everybody around her. Optimism and self-sacrifice were dangerous qualities to have in a place where a certain set of people prowled the land, searching for unsuspecting prey.

His little girl had so much light inside her, and he was afraid her light would be snuffed out if she stayed here.

As Cheng came to stand next to Zhang in the doorway, he whispered, "We need to give Wu-Dip a better chance. And it's not here."

THE FLIGHT OF THE BUTTERFLY

CHAPTER FOURTEEN

Mexicali, Mexico
1988

The air was heavy with tension. The men in the room had to work hard to keep themselves from fidgeting. Fidgeting was a sign of weakness, and they had to keep up an appearance of strength, even if they were nearly senseless with fear. One of them, a big man with a prominent scar on his neck, scowled at the floor. He clenched and unclenched his fists—a sure sign of his inner turmoil. The other men, all seasoned and hardened criminals, were equally preoccupied.

They had messed up.

Everybody knew the boss hated botched jobs and showed no mercy in punishing those responsible. Stories of men tortured to death filled their heads and made their hearts quake with fear. Escape was out of the question. The house was heavily guarded; they'd be dead before they even got to the door.

The men looked up at the same time when the source of their fear strode into the room. Without sparing a glance at them, he walked straight to his plush leather chair behind his vast, polished table and sat down. He then leaned his elbows on the table, made a steeple with his fingers, and sent each of the men around the table a hard glare.

The man exuded power and money. He carried himself with an arrogance that nobody dared question. His suit was exquisitely tailored to fit his frame—a far cry from the off-the-rack suits worn by the other men in the room. His immaculate appearance and the aura of power that surrounded him combined to create a commanding air. Even though he wasn't as big as most of his hired muscle, he was feared by both his business associates and those on his payroll.

"What happened?" he asked in a hoarse voice, a result of barely surviving getting strangled to death during a fight years before; his voice box had come close to being crushed.

Initially, he had hated the new raspy timbre of his voice. Every time he spoke, he sounded like a chain-smoker—though he detested cigarettes, preferring Cuban cigars. After a while, however, he had learned to use the rasp to his advantage; it became a tool to strike fear into the hearts of his employees.

He fixed his gaze on the big guy, the leader of the gang, who fought the urge to squirm. "Mario, you told me everything was settled. What happened?"

"I don't understand, boss," Mario replied. "Everything went as planned, initially. We'd gotten the merchandise and were just about to move when the police appeared out of nowhere. We managed to escape. But..." he swallowed, "we lost the merchandise, boss. All of it."

"And, where is it?" asked the boss without missing a beat.

"*La policia* has it, boss."

The man leaned back in his chair, thoughtfully stroking his carefully groomed mustache. On the outside, he looked like a regular wealthy man with a string of successful businesses. Indeed, that was the image he projected to the world. Many times, he had made the news for his huge donations to charity—especially to organizations that helped destitute women and children.

He was highly respected in society and regularly rubbed shoulders with the high and mighty of the land. He owned multiple restaurants, casinos, department stores, a few hotels, massage parlors, warehouses, apartment complexes, and a couple of money exchange offices throughout the state. His empire in Northern Mexico made him a powerful man with political connections, both locally and internationally.

The public liked him and constantly praised him for his generosity. The state businessmen appreciated his sharp business acumen and readiness to take on an almost hopeless enterprise and turn it around. The media venerated him. At least, the part of him that they could see. Yes, he was a force to be reckoned with.

One side of his lip turned up in what looked more like a sneer than a smile. His employees saw the half-grin and fought the urge to shudder. This man's grin could either mean a bountiful reward or merciless punishment.

"Mario..." he began softly, directing his words once again to the big man seated in front of him. "You told me that everything had been taken care of and that all I had to do was relax and wait for the delivery. Yet, here we are, with my merchandise under police custody. So, please," he lit a long, dark Cuban cigar, "explain it clearly to me. Exactly how did it all happen?"

"Bossman," said the scared man.

"Call me Dragon," replied the boss as he admired with his cufflinks under the glow of his lighter. They were custom-made with a dragon engraved on each of them, imported from Hong Kong. The dragon was his only link to his native land, which he had no memory of, having been brought to Baja California by his parents when he was a baby. Beyond that, he liked to think of the dragon as his personal totem: fierce, ferocious, fire-breathing.

"Yes, sorry, Mr. Dragon bossman. So, we talked to our friends in the police. I swear, *jefe*. We told them we were going to be busy that night and that maybe they'd wanna be busy *somewhere else*. They said, 'yeah, okay, no problem.' But when got to the warehouse, there were cops all over the place. Our friends swear they didn't know anything was going to happen—someone must've ratted."

Dragon frowned. He had paid a lot of money for this new batch of cocaine from Medellin, and he had planned to exponentially grow his capital by crossing it to California to distribute there. And while the money meant nothing to him, he had a reputation to protect. Whoever had led that police operation would pay dearly. No one crossed a dragon and got away with it.

"I don't like this, Mario. So tell me, what are we going to do about it?"

Mario didn't know what to say. His eyes gave way to the fear within. What made the bossman, Carlos Wong—aka The Dragon—dangerous and feared was not his connections with both sides of the law on both sides of the border, but rather his own merciless existence. He was a *sicario.* A heartless assassin. And those in the narco business knew this. While other bosses sent their killers to take care of business, the Dragon liked handling killings himself.

Mario trembled. "Please sir, understand that this wasn't really my fault. I know that someone must pay, but..."

"Oh, Mario, Mario," Wong interrupted. He looked up then at the man sitting opposite him, quietly enjoying the look of terror and uncertainty in his eyes. He blew smoke from the cigar in his hand. "I don't like excuses. *You* messed up, Mario. *You* and your boys. And you know how much I detest mess-ups." He fell silent, knowing this action was feared more than his speech. After a while, he spoke again.

"I'll tell you what. I will give you a second chance. But you have to do two things for me. First, bring me two of your men. Their blood will be on you. And second, find this fool who dared to oppose me. And maybe... just maybe... I'll let you live."

"Yes, sir," Mario said swiftly, hoping his voice showed none of the dizzying relief he felt. "Right away, Bossman... I mean, Mr. Dragon, sir."

Mario turned and left the office, followed by his men who weren't as relieved.

Wong got up and walked to his home office's open window. The panoramic view his mansion gave of his ranch outside the city never failed to thrill him. His mind strayed into the past, to the days when he roamed the streets hungry and worked as a server at a Chinese restaurant while studying Business Administration at UABC, the local university. Oh, the rage he felt then, when he saw those local rich men and women wearing clothes of the highest quality. When they looked down their noses at him as if he were equal to the vermin he slept among.

He looked at his stables and remembered the days when it had been his job to clean out the bathrooms at the restaurant. The smells there sometimes were worse than all the horse crap in the world.

A gentle breeze, permeated with the sweet smell of flowers from his lush gardens, caressed his face, and for a moment, he was transported to another place and time...

"*Jefe?*" The voice of his head henchman brought him back to the present.

He looked with contentment across his vast property. *I made it. I got myself out of that hell hole.* A smile formed on his face as he stared through the floor-to-ceiling window. "Talk to me," he said without turning around.

"You have a meeting with the mayor at 3 p.m."

He exhaled deeply and placed his cigar on a plate. Wong despised the mayor—a sniveling, corrupt character with an ingratiating attitude. The man was a weakling, mere putty to be molded as he saw fit. While the mayor's weakness of character served Wong well, it also repulsed him. He just could not stand weak men. Still, he decided, as he straightened his back and inspected his cufflinks, men like him had their uses.

"Also," the henchman continued. "Mario has two men ready outside for... um... well, for you."

Wong took a deep breath, then turned and took his coat off, setting it on top of the desk. He removed his cufflinks and leisurely rolled up his sleeves, then retrieved a large knife with Chinese characters engraved in jade from his desk and walked out of the office.

Guangzhou, China
1988

It was a hot and humid afternoon in the slums of Guangzhou, a month after the incident on that dark night. For a while, Lin had been too ashamed to go with her mother to work, fearful of what people would say about her. One thing she knew for certain about everyone was that they loved their gossip. Even though she told Jing she didn't care what people thought of her, the disgrace of her attack festered.

She took long baths, mercilessly scrubbing her skin to wash away the shame and dirt that she felt clinging to her. Lin struggled to comprehend all the emotions that flowed through her. She couldn't figure out why she was upset one minute, then angry the next, and who the anger was directed toward.

One thing for sure was that Lin blamed herself for what had happened, torturing herself with various what-ifs, ignoring that small, rational part of her mind that insisted it was not her fault. She should have known better than to travel alone at night. She shouldn't have been so naïve to think that she was safe. This neighborhood was flooded with crime and indecent people—and that was putting it lightly. She had been careless, and for a split second, she thought that she deserved it.

Eventually, she started to emerge from the protective shell she had wrapped herself in. She wanted to move forward with her life and get rid of the pity in her family's eyes. She resumed going to work with her mother, grateful that the older woman had not forced her to, despite the extra income they could have made from her presence.

But Lin didn't travel anywhere without one of her family members and avoided the times of day when the streets were crowded. Everywhere she went, whether or not it was true, she felt all eyes were on her and every mouth whispered rumors about her attack. Shaking these feelings away was useless, as they always creeped back into her mind—especially as she tried to sleep.

One afternoon, Lin was returning from the riverbank with her friend Meilin who was unusually subdued—not her usual lively self. They were carrying heavy baskets of folded laundry. After a few minutes of pensive silence, Meilin finally spoke. "Lin, there's something I need to tell you."

Lin looked at her with a raised eyebrow, disturbed by the troubled tone to her voice. She hadn't talked about the attack with Meilin, and thinking about doing so tied her stomach in knots. It was hard enough to live with the memories, but saying the words out loud was impossible. She prayed that what she was about to say had nothing to do with drunken men in alleyways.

"What is it?"

Meilin bit her lip. "I'll tell you; but first, you must promise me you won't tell anybody. Okay?"

"It depends on what it is."

"No, Lin. Please!" Meilin's voice held a desperate pleading quality. "This must stay between you and me. Promise me!"

"Okay..." Lin whispered uncertainly. She had a bad feeling about this and briefly wondered if it was a mistake to leave the house today.

Meilin looked around to make sure no one was within earshot, then stepped closer to her friend.

"I'm pregnant..."

Lin stopped dead in her tracks, dropping the basket. It was just a whisper, but the words got louder each time Lin repeated them in her head, slowly processing the information. "Meilin!"

"Shhh..." Meilin looked around furtively. "Look, I would have preferred a more private place to tell you about my current... predicament. But I guess this is the best option at the moment. Honestly, I'm not willing to risk any member of your family overhearing. Just... please... keep walking, Lin."

Lin struggled to get a better grip on the basket as she picked it up, then resumed walking, still with a look of astonishment on her face. "You're pregnant? Are you *sure?*"

"Keep it down, Lin. And yes, I'm pretty sure. My flow hasn't come for two months, and I'm always nauseous." The look in her eyes was one of sheer terror, which Lin related to all too well. "That's the only possible explanation for this."

Lin looked at her friend's flat stomach, doubting. "Meilin... what happened?"

Her friend looked down, biting her lip. When she looked up, her eyes were wet with unshed tears.

"Meilin..."

"This wasn't supposed to happen. We just... I wanted to help..."

"I don't understand."

Meilin swallowed. "I just wanted to help. Things got very hard when Father left. My mother can barely even take care of us. The money we earn from cleaning barely helps. So... well, I saw a chance to make some extra money. And it was only three times!"

Lin felt her heart twist. "Oh, Meilin..." The girl was barely fourteen years old. A kid, just like herself.

"It was the stablehand at my mother's workplace. He offered me money..." Meilin faltered.

Lin saw her friend struggling with shame. She could already imagine the scornful looks that would be thrown her way if the news ever got out. She could already hear the whispers, feel the contempt.

"Meilin, I'm here for you. You know that, right?"

"Yes, I know. But, Lin, what am I going to do? Mother will kill me if she finds out. She's so stubborn. It's just that... we really needed the money!" Meilin's voice was desperate, entreating her friend to understand her desperate plight.

Lin inhaled a long breath and stopped walking. She placed her basket on the ground, then did the same with Meilin's. Pulling her into a hug, she held her friend, and neither of them spoke for a long time. Theirs was a hard life, requiring challenging decisions for survival. She didn't blame her friend for what she had done, and she was angry at the hypocrisy of their society.

There were women who took knickknacks from the houses of the wealthy people they worked for, confident they would never be suspected. They gave these items to their men to sell for a pittance. Yet it appeared as if it was okay to do these things, as long as they were kept hidden.

An unmarried pregnant girl would be held in disdain by the same women who slept with their husband's employers. In their society, it was okay to do shameful things, but they couldn't display their sinful triumphs or consequences. Shame would be brought upon Meilin's entire family, tarnishing them forever.

Pulling out of the hug, Lin looked at her friend, who was fighting tears. She didn't know what to say to her.

"Lin... what am I going to do?" She was fully crying now, dropping to her knees and sobbing into her hands.

"I really don't know..." The response came with sincerity as she crouched beside Meilin, just as those men did by her on that dark night. Lin helped Meilin stand and stroked her back until she could compose herself. They picked up their baskets, then walked another distance in silence, each lost in their respective thoughts.

"Jing!" Meilin said suddenly. "She'll know what to do."

Lin frowned. "Meilin, what are you thinking?"

"I have to get rid of it," the young pregnant girl's voice was cold, resolute. "Yes, that's what I must do. I can't have this child. We can barely feed ourselves as it is! I can't take care of another mouth."

Lin knew Meilin had good point; if anyone could help, it would be Jing. Jing would know what to do. She was always nice to the teenagers in the neighborhood and constantly offered advice should they become stuck in a difficult situation.

But Lin hadn't seen Jing since...

She took deep breaths to calm the racing of her heart. "Are you sure about this?" she asked, now also thinking an abortion could be more dangerous than having the baby in secret.

"I have no choice. Can you imagine what people will say if it gets out? If my mother finds out, it will kill her! Or she will kill me. So, no. I will not expose myself to that kind of ridicule." Meilin's voice was grim, determined. "I will not bring more shame to my family than I already have. I'd rather move to a new country on my own than put them through that."

"I'm not so sure that this is a good idea, though," Lin said as she paused to lift a strip of fabric from trailing on the mucky floor. "So many things could go wrong."

"Jing must have done this procedure many times, I'm sure. She will know what to do. She will! I just know it." Meilin started running then, the basket banging against her hip, and Lin struggled to run behind her.

Soon, they arrived at the Wong's home. Meilin still had to walk a little farther to get to her house, but before Lin went inside, Meilin said, "Remember, Lin, this is for your ears only. Please."

"Okay. Please be careful, my friend."

"I will. I'll let you know what happens." She smiled and continued down the road to her home, while Lin entered hers in disbelief.

THE FLIGHT OF THE BUTTERFLY

CHAPTER FIFTEEN

Two days later, Lin and her mother had just returned home after a long day when Meilin's mother, Fen, rushed in.

"Cheng!" she exclaimed breathlessly, her eyes wide with stark terror. "Cheng, something is wrong with Meilin. Please come. Please come quickly!"

Cheng dropped her belongings onto the dining table. "What's wrong?"

"Just... come quickly. Please. There is so much blood."

"Blood? Where? What do you mean?" But the woman was already out of the Wong's home. Cheng hurried after the her, her heart in her throat, and Lin followed a few steps behind.

An alarming sight greeted them at Meilin's house. She was writhing on her bed, uttering low moans of pain, her face contorted in anguish. Now and then, her body would arch off her bed and she would make a guttural sound. The whole sight was made even more grotesque by the amount of blood in the room. Meilin's clothes and bedding were soaked in it. Her hands were bloody, and her face was smeared with red, probably from rubbing her hands across it in a mindless gesture of pain. Her lips were bleeding from when she bit hard on them to keep from screaming.

Cheng felt an involuntary shudder run through her at witnessing the scene; one that was all too familiar to her. She had experienced three miscarriages in her life, and from what she could see, she quickly deduced what was happening.

"Cheng!" Fen turned to her. "Look at my girl. Is there any way you can help me? I don't know what's wrong. She's bleeding. Why is she bleeding so much?"

Cheng looked into the woman's eyes, knowing exactly what was happening to Meilin, but also realizing Fen didn't understand. "I don't know how to say this delicately, Fen, but... it looks like Meilin is losing a baby." She uttered the words in a gentle voice.

The woman's face crumpled, and she began to sob. "How is that even possible? I didn't even know she was pregnant! How is this possible? Did you know?" Fen asked Lin.

Lin nodded quietly. She then looked down as she grabbed her long pony tail.

Cheng held Fen close. "It'll be okay, Fen. Meilin will be okay."

Cheng turned to look over at her daughter's young friend, who was now gripping the bedding like her life depended on it. It was apparent there was nothing they could do at present. "Fen, for now, Meilin will have to ride out the pain. We must wait until the cramps ease on their own accord and then we will try to staunch the bleeding."

"I just... I don't know what to say. I mean... how...?" Fen's voice was broken. "How could she be pregnant? I didn't even—"

"Fen, don't worry about that now," Cheng said, at the same time sending a look to Lin; one that meant they were going to have a long talk about this.

Lin quietly looked at the floor again, evidently overwhelmed with guilt.

"What we need to do is to try to make her comfortable," her mother continued. "We'll worry about other things later."

Soon after, Meilin finally started to calm down. The writhing had reduced considerably, and she only now ocassionally rolled from one side to the other. Cheng took command of the situation then.

"Lin," she said, "go home and bring me my herbs. I'll give you a list of what I need, but bring anything else you think might help."

Lin took the list from her mother with shaking hands and raced home. When she returned, Cheng started pounding herbs in a small bowl. Fen held her daughter's weak body up while Lin managed to get her to drink some of the potion, after which she was allowed to lie down again. In a few minutes, Meilin drifted into a deep sleep, her face wet with tears and blood.

Fen covered her face, crying. "I didn't even know she was pregnant. I am so confused and... embarrassed."

166

Cheng put a comforting arm around her. "Don't be too hard on yourself."

Fen sobbed for a while, then squared her shoulders. "Thank you, Cheng," she stated as she surveyed the mess in front of her. "I should clean up now. Thank you so much."

"We can help, if you want," Lin said.

"No, please. You've already done enough. More than enough, in fact. Thank you."

Cheng understood the woman's need for solitude. "Okay, Fen. Don't be too hard on yourself... Or on your daughter. Let's go, Lin."

The woman nodded. "But, one more thing," she added, as they turned to leave. "I can trust you not to tell anyone, right? Please."

Cheng nodded. "Of course."

Fen turned to Lin, and Cheng also looked at her daughter.

Lin nodded. "Of course," she said. "Not a word. I promise."

Lin kept her head down, as they began to make their way home. They walked in silence for a while, then Cheng spoke.

"You knew she was pregnant." It wasn't a question.

Lin nodded bleakly.

"Why didn't you tell anybody?"

"She was afraid. I promised not to tell anyone, Mama. Of course, now I feel guilty for not telling you, the one person who could truly help."

"Yes, Lin. You could have told me—should have!"

"But I promised her! I really thought I was helping."

"Oh, Wu-Dip," Cheng sighed. "You are so naïve. What if Meilin had died? I understand that you were trying to be a good friend. But some secrets can be harmful."

Lin hung her head. "Will she be okay?" she asked in a low voice while staring at the ground.

"Yes, she will," Cheng replied. "A little scarred both inside and out, but okay."

"She only wanted to help," Lin said. "She just wanted to make some extra money for her family."

Cheng frowned as the implications of her daughter's words sunk in. She understood well what Lin meant. She looked her in the eyes and saw burning intensity there. "There are always other ways, baby. You should never stoop to selling your body for any reason. We may be poor, but we still have our pride. You remember that."

"But pride won't put food on our table, Mother!" Lin replied defiantly. "For the past week, we've had to depend on the scraps that Liu brings in for food. We cannot afford to be proud, anymore. And what about Jing? Why do you bother to help her if you know what she does to survive? You can't shame Meilin for trying to protect her family, just like you didn't shame Papa for going after Chan!"

Cheng stopped and stared at her daughter.

"Yes, I heard you two talking that night," Lin said darkly. "I know what happened."

Cheng grabbed her by her shoulders. "Listen to me, child. Sometimes a person becomes so poor, all she has is her pride. Nobody can take that away from her if she refuses to let it go. Remember that, Wu-Dip. Your pride and your reputation are your most important possessions. Do you hear me? Your father's situation was very different. He forgot he had a choice to back away from the situation. There is always another way to provide for your family. You cannot sink so low, especially when you haven't looked at all your options. Do you understand?"

Lin looked down once again, "Yes, Mother."

They walked the rest of the way in complete silence, lost in their own minds and the thoughts that haunted them.

That night, Zhang sat across from his wife at the dining table, listening to her talk about the events of the day. He sighed heavily and stood to guide her to their makeshift bed, catching a view of Liu and Lin sleeping out of the corner of his eye as he passed.

"You know what worries me?" Cheng said once they were settled in bed. "It's that it keeps getting harder and harder to care for our children. Liu depends on what he gets from the trash for clothes and sometimes food. Our daughter is blossoming, yet we can only dress her in clothes scavenged from the streets. I cannot even buy enough material to make decent clothes for our children." Her voice broke. "What are we going to do?"

Zhang had been pondering the answer to that very question for a while. After many months of soul searching and second thoughts, he had finally come to a decision. "Li Jong was talking about North America today. He was saying how it's a free land where anybody who truly wants to can have a good life. Unlike here. I think it's a sign."

"Again with your idea, Zhang?" She turned on her side to face him, and he did the same.

"Listen, Cheng. I think it's for the best. I've been thinking... They could live a much better life there than here."

"The United States?" Cheng's voice rose an octave. "You are such a stubborn man. You know we can't afford to send them. And I would never send my babies alone."

"Woman, we can't afford to keep them *here*! Maybe we only send Lin. Liu will be fine here. But Lin... she just doesn't have what it takes."

Cheng was pensive for a moment. "But... then it's possible that we'll never see her again! It's too far away. If anything, we must find a way for all of us to go, if that's the path we choose to take."

"You know we can't afford that. You just said that. Our Wu-Dip is special, and she deserves a chance to spread her wings. Yes, I want to stay together as a family, but there's nothing for her here. Besides, we can no longer care for our children. Sending Wu-Dip away will not only give her a fighting chance, but it would also reduce the burden on us. I think it would be better for us to take care of one child instead of two."

Cheng reared back from her husband. "Our children are not burdens! They are blessings."

Zhang grimaced. "Don't be difficult, honey. You know what I mean. I know they are blessings, but we can barely afford to take care of them. At least over there, Wu-Dip wouldn't have to wear clothes scavenged from the trash. Think about it. She could wear beautiful clothes, elegant shoes. She would be happy, healthy, and, most importantly, *safe*!"

Cheng shook her head on the rags that acted as her pillow. "No. I already told you last time. There must be another way—"

"What other choice do we have?" Zhang interrupted. "You are already working yourself to the bone. I work longer and longer hours too, yet what we make combined can barely put food on the table. Our son picks through refuse mounts for discarded objects that could prove useful to us. And our daughter works right beside you, scrubbing floors, heels bruised because the soles of her sandals have worn out and we cannot afford to replace them."

Cheng closed her eyes to hold back her tears, but they rolled down her cheeks, nonetheless. On seeing them, Zhang reached out and held his wife close to him. He kissed her forehead.

"Don't cry, Cheng. I just need you to understand that we have no choice. There is nothing for Lin here. At least there she will have a new shot at life. A blank slate that she can fill with whatever she wants. And I hear that in America, anything is possible. Our Wu-Dip could even become a wealthy woman with time, and maybe even take us all there eventually. Think about it. We have to let her go, Cheng. To help her, and to help ourselves."

"You know, Zhang, you keep referring to our daughter as fragile and delicate, but she is a strong woman," Cheng said, holding her husband's gaze steadily. "She's lived through poverty, a rough life, and now even assault. I really think you need to revise your opinion of her. Liu is prone to sickness, and Lin never gets sick. She is *strong*!"

Zhang stuttered for a moment, taken aback by the fire in his wife's eyes. Then finally, he said, "You're right... I'm sorry. She is a strong woman. I didn't mean it that way, Cheng."

Cheng didn't reply. Instead, she turned around, giving him her back.

Zhang stopped talking for a while, thinking about how to convince her. He still had an ace up his sleeve, and he had to play it now before he lost his courage. It had come to this.

"You know, my love," he whispered in her ear, "Lin is a strong woman. She is amazing. But as it is, she already worries about the state of our finances and living situation. You know that she is a warrior, not merely a survivor. What I am trying to say is... Well, I just don't want her to do anything stupid out of a misguided desire to help us. Look at what happened with Meilin."

He felt his wife shudder. This was his opportunity, and he continued, "This is our daughter's chance to have a better life, to have choices. In this place, we are condemned to live like this. In America, she can choose to be whatever she wants to be. You know her; she will succeed at anything there."

A sob shook Cheng's whole body, and he placed a gentle hand on her head. "Cheng, unfortunately, we have to send one of our own children away in order to survive. I wish it didn't have to be this way, but please understand what I've been trying to tell you. At least there our girl will have a fighting chance."

Cheng turned around, tears making her eyes shine in the darkness. "Where would she stay? Who would she stay with? She needs someone to watch over her; she's just a child. Besides, she only speaks Cantonese. How will she communicate without speaking the language? How will she interact with people if she can't even talk to them?"

"That's all been taken care of. I've been in contact with my cousin in Mexico. Remember I told you about him?"

Cheng frowned. "Chaoxiang? Chaoxiang Wong?"

"Yes. But he took a local name. His name is Carlos now. Carlos Wong."

THE FLIGHT OF THE BUTTERFLY

CHAPTER SIXTEEN

Cheng was quiet for a moment, then whispered, "Let's go talk in the kitchen. I don't want to wake the kids up."

The both got up as quietly as possible and exited the room, then grabbed two of the four chairs and sat facing each other.

"How did you even manage to reach him?" she asked.

Zhang shook his head. "It doesn't matter. What matters is that he has agreed to take our girl in. He's a rich man, it seems. He has many businesses and is doing well for himself. Wu-Dip could work for him while he arranges for her to be taught whatever she needs to know about the language and culture there. He's lived in Northern Mexico since he was an infant, so he knows better than anyone else how to help our girl find her feet. I hear there's a large community of Cantonese-speaking Chinese there too. And he's right on the border; it's the perfect place. He told me that it's easy for people there to go to the United States if they want to. He goes there himself every day. Once settled, she could take us all there."

It seemed like a good idea, but Cheng still felt apprehensive. Carlos Wong was the son of Zhang's uncle—his father's younger brother—a man known for his fierce temper and drunken fits of rage that were almost legendary. Things got even worse after his wife died in childbirth. It was rumored he had taken his baby son and new young wife to America for asylum after he killed a man, but those rumors were never validated.

What kind of man was Chaoxiang... Carlos Wong, a man raised by a notorious drunk known for his murderous temper? Of course, it was also possible that he was a redeemed man. An honorable man.

But, what if...?

"Zhang…" She sounded uneasy. "Isn't there anybody else that she could stay with? We don't know anything about Carlos…"

"There's nobody else," her husband interrupted, irritated. "Look, he very graciously offered to take her under his wing. It was even his idea that she go there. We should be grateful to him, Cheng. We have to take this chance. If we know Lin is safe with him, we can put all our energy into caring for Liu. It will be difficult, but for now, this is the best option for our children."

"He offered to take care of her?" she asked with narrowed eyes. "Why would he do that if he doesn't even know her?"

"Because he's a generous man who only wants the best for her. He's family, and that is what one does for family."

"If he is so generous, then why doesn't he send us some money instead? Or why can't we *all* go?" Cheng regretted the words immediately after they came out of her mouth.

Zhang turned a shocked face to her. "And how would we pay him back? You want us to accept charity? We may be poor, but we're not beggars. We are not beggars, Cheng! Don't be ungrateful. It will be challenging enough thanking him for taking in Lin."

"Oh, I see. But we can gratefully accept his *gracious*…" she spat out the word, "offer to take our girl into his care? His offer to cover all the traveling expenses? What's the difference?"

"The difference is that Lin will work for him in return. That was the agreement we made. She will work for him for a period of five years, during which he will serve as her guardian, protector, and sponsor. During this time, she will work in one of his businesses. Most likely one of his restaurants. After that time, she will be free to do what she wants."

"So, you're giving out five years of our daughter's life in exchange for a ship ticket and some shelter?" Cheng's voice was heavy with accusation.

Her husband ran his fingers down his face in frustration. He raised his voice, "Why are you fighting me on this? I thought you'd be happy that Lin has a chance for greatness. I thought we both agreed that Wu-Dip deserves to be in a better place!"

"Yes, I do want that. But I just didn't think that place would be halfway around the world! She is just a young girl, Zhang. Get that through your head."

Zhang gasped and shook his head. While very strong-willed, Cheng had never directly opposed him on anything before—or even raised her voice to him.

"Listen to me," the Wong patriarch began, picking his words carefully. "As always, I am only doing what is best for my family—"

"*Our* family," she interrupted softly.

He ignored her and kept going. "There is *nothing* for her here. This place is practically crawling with ruffians and thugs who would think nothing of taking advantage of our girl. And even if that never happens, what other option is open to her? Marriage to another laborer who will work himself to the ground for next to nothing? Scrubbing floors for the rest of her life?"

Cheng looked down and bit her lip. She let out a long deep sigh. Her eyes glazed.

"Listen, this trip will mean a new start for *our* child. She will begin a new life there with her uncle to guide her. She won't be alone. Family is family, no matter what part of the world you are in. And Carlos has given me his word that he will take good care of her and ensure that she has a good education. Like I said, it's what is best for her. She can have a future. Lin could learn Spanish *and* English there."

"That all sounds too good to be true."

"Cheng, Carlos is a wealthy man—influential and respected. Why would he lie to us? She deserves good. She deserves the best! Don't you agree?"

"I don't know," Cheng said, rubbing her temples where she could feel the beginnings of a headache. "I mean, yes, I do agree Lin deserves the best in life. But... something about this just doesn't feel right."

"I understand," her husband replied in a gentle voice. "You don't like the idea of her going so far, all alone..."

"It's not just that."

"Then, what is it?"

"I don't know. I just don't want her to go." She knew her husband was determined about this and would do what he had planned, regardless of what she thought about it. The thought of her daughter leaving for a distant land, probably never to be seen again, cut deeply in her heart, and she covered her mouth to keep in her gasp of pain. Her wet eyes met her husband's and saw the resolve in them.

Yes, he had already decided. Telling her was just a courtesy.

"Oh, my child," she turned to look at Lin through the open doorframe into the bedroom, sleeping soundly next to her brother. She was beautiful beyond words. She was her princess, and Cheng would do anything for her. A moonbeam fell across her pale face, giving her the look of some otherworldly entity gracing their humble home. Her facial features were relaxed, making her look like the innocent little girl that she accurately was. Each night, the look of terror on her face, brought by that terrible man, slowly disappeared until it had transformed into a flat smile.

Cheng stood up and walked toward the room. She stood there in silence, looking at her daughter. Seeing her face brought another sharp pain to Cheng's heart, and she wrapped her hands around her waist and bent over, crying softly. She felt that she had failed in her obligations as a mother.

Her husband came from behind and stood next to her. He placed a comforting hand on her shoulder, murmuring reassurances. "It'll be okay, Cheng. You'll see."

He sounded so confident that she wanted to believe him.

But she just couldn't. In her gut she knew there was something wrong in all of this.

Lin stood shivering, not from the gentle wind that caressed her skin, but from the greater chill that she felt deep within her bones. Her mother wrapped her arm around her, while her brother held on to her hand. They stood at the side of the road waiting for the bus that would take Lin on the first part of her long journey to Hong Kong. From there, she would board a boat to the port of Ensenada, Mexico. The other side of the world.

Her father had gone farther down the road to see if he could find out the reason for the bus's delay. Lin felt tears sting her eyes as she held on to her bag containing all of her belongings. There weren't many.

The night her parents had informed her about their decision, she had pleaded with them to let her stay, promising to do anything she could to lessen the burden on them. She promised to work harder, to be more frugal, more docile. But her father had remained unmoved, insisting this move was the best thing for her, while her mother remained silent, looking at her with eyes that spoke volumes.

After the rest of the family had gone to sleep, Lin remained awake, trying hard to stifle her sobs so they wouldn't wake anyone. But a hand had curled around hers, and when she turned, she saw her mother, eyes filled with unshed tears. They held on to each other and cried through the night, after which they had a whispered conversation that lasted well into the morning.

The tightening of her mother's hand around hers brought Lin back to the present. An old, empty bus was rolling toward them, and her father waved at them from the bus's open door. Her stomach clenched. She wasn't ready for this. She didn't want to leave her family, her friends, her home. She remembered the look of envy on Meilin's face when she learned about Lin's forthcoming trip.

"I wish I had this chance that you have," she had said, wistfully.

"I'd give anything to have our positions reversed," Lin had replied with feeling and without hesitation. She meant it.

The girls had hugged, thinking about all the memories they shared, good and bad. "Will I ever see you again?" Meilin asked.

"Yes," Lin said, but neither of them believed it. "We will always be Lin and Meilin!"

"Lin and Meilin, forever," her friend replied.

Now, as she watched the bus approach where she stood with her family on the roadside, she wished fervently that something would happen to keep her from going. Maybe a sudden thunderstorm. A hailstorm. Anything. But the bus came to a stop, and her father jumped off, grinning. A sour-faced young man jumped down beside him.

"This is Koeng," her father stated. "He will go with you to Hong Kong and take care of your boat ticket, among other things. He will take good care of you."

The man looked as if he could barely take care of himself. He had holes in his clothes and shoes, his hair was disheveled, and his smile showed yellow, crooked teeth.

Cheng closed the gap between her and her husband and whispered, "Zhang, are you sure?" though not quietly enough for Lin to not hear.

"Yes, I am. He is trustworthy. He will take care of our girl. Don't worry about it."

The Wong patriarch picked up Lin's meagre parcel and handed it over to the other man who promptly put it inside the bus, then stood aside, obviously waiting for them to say their goodbyes.

Liu hugged his sister fiercely. "Take care of yourself!" he said, trying to hide the moisture in his eyes but failing.

Lin thought about teasing him to lighten the mood, but his hug was so comforting, she couldn't bring herself to do it. She felt her heart breaking as she returned the hug. "I will, little brother. Take care of *Fuh* and *Mouh* for me. Okay?"

He nodded, not able to speak, then stepped away as their mother turned to face Lin.

"My child!" she exclaimed, looking at her daughter through misty eyes. She let her hands roam the contours of her daughter's face, as if she wanted to brand her features into the palms of her hands. "My child..." she cried once again and drew her into a tight embrace. "Don't forget what we discussed, okay?"

Just like her brother, Lin only nodded, as she was crying too hard to speak.

"Don't cry," her mother spoke in between sniffles. "You'll be fine. You will. You'll become a lady and wear pretty clothes and never have to worry about food again," she smiled through her tears.

"I'll be fine," Lin replied. "And I'll find a way to bring you to me. All of you."

Liar! said a voice in her mind. *You don't believe that.*

Be quiet, she snapped in her head. *I have to believe this. I have to!*

Believing it does not make it true.

"I love you, Wu-Dip. Always remember that."

178

"Yes, *Mouh*," she could barely say the words through her sobs. "I love you too."

Her mother kissed Lin's forehead and stepped aside to let her father speak to her.

"Wu-Dip..." he began, placing his big hands on her shaking shoulders. "I..." He stopped, as if it was finally dawning on him that he was sending his fourteen-year-old daughter to a strange, distant land, and that he might never see her again. As Lin stared into his eyes, she thought she saw him wishing; wishing that he could undo everything he had done in the past few weeks in preparation for this day.

"Yes, Papa?" she said, to encourage him. Maybe he'd changed his mind. She could only hope.

Her father took a deep breath and renewed his resolve.

"Lin... Wu-Dip," he started again. But still, he could not speak. There seemed to be a huge lump in his throat that he could not dislodge, no matter how hard he swallowed. Then the tears came.

Lin didn't remember ever seeing her father cry. Maybe he was right. Maybe there really was nothing for her here. Maybe her father knew best. She would be safer in this far away land. She would be better in America. And one day, when she was as successful as her uncle, she would bring them all along with her.

What are you doing? You're going into your own demise.

"Oh, *Fuh*!" Lin put her arms around him, laid her head on his chest, and cried for all that she was worth. "Father, please let me stay!" she cried quietly. It was one last desperate attempt, but her plea would go unheard.

"No, my child," he replied after clearing his throat. "This is a wonderful chance that you have. Please use it wisely. Your Uncle Carlos has promised to take very good care of you. All you must do is get there safely, and he'll take care of the rest. You know..." His voice finally broke, "that if I could help it, you would stay here with us. But I have no choice. Please understand this, my Wu-Dip." His eyes begged her to see reason with him.

"*Mouh* says you always have a choice," she replied. "*Fuh*... Papa, I'm scared. You have to find another way."

"This is the only way, Wu-Dip," he said, no longer able to face her, instead looking up at the sky. "This is the choice we must make."

"Yes, Papa," she said quietly. "If you think it's best."

At this point, Koeng made a small sound of annoyance, and they all turned to him. "We've wasted enough time," he affirmed. "We need to get going."

Lin sniffled and, with the help of her father, climbed into the empty bus and found a seat toward the back by a dirty window. As it began to roll away, she looked through the side and then the back windows, back at the faces of her family. She was certain that she was seeing them for the last time.

She waved, her eyes and cheeks puffy from crying, and blew them kisses. When they finally turned a corner, she buried her head in her hands and wept, thinking she wouldn't stop crying until she saw them again.

Cheng stared at the road, long after the bus had rolled out of sight. A cloud of foreboding hung over her; try as she might, she could not shake it. As she walked home with her family, she tried to dispel the feeling of doom that surrounded her, yet she couldn't. She just couldn't.

Something bugged her.

Why did she feel as though she had just sent her daughter to certain death?

May the love and protection of our ancestors go with you, Wu-Dip.

Hong Kong

Hong Kong awed Lin. It was bubbly, busy, and filled with people walking briskly down the streets, living out their lavish lives. While Guangzhou was striving to modernize and stay up to date, adding high rises and bridges each month, Hong Kong already felt like the future.

Nicely dressed men and women rode in nice cars, many walked, and others rode in buses. Every single person was determined to get to their destination in the shortest possible time. People spoke English fluently, and money was evident everywhere she looked. If only her parents had been blessed to live the life of the rich in this stunning city. Hong Kong; a remarkable place, to say the least.

Her bus travelled past the grand mansions on the hills and then toward the tall buildings in the city center, into what appeared to be a middle-class part of the city. It seemed to be near the harbor, if the stench of fish in the air was anything to go by.

The bus stopped before a rather dubious-looking tavern with a British flag hanging outside. Lin looked at her guide, confused. Surely he didn't mean for them to stay in this place that reeked of alcohol and cigarette smoke? As she stared at him in disbelief, he motioned for her to get out of the bus. So she picked up her small parcel, hugging her bundle protectively, and did as she was told.

At the entrance to the tavern, she took a frightened step backward when one of the men loitering there leered at her, showing teeth blackened by years of smoking.

"Come on," said Koeng, who held her elbow and steered her toward the building. "Ignore the men; they won't touch you as long as I'm here." For good measure, he scowled at the man, who shrugged and walked away, firing up a cigarette as he did.

The air in the tavern was thick with cigarette smoke. It was so thick that it disoriented Lin, and she would have stumbled if it hadn't been for Koeng's guiding hand on her elbow. They walked past the bar to another room where a young man sat behind a desk, flirting with a heavily made-up lady whose generous bosom was almost spilling out of her skimpy top.

"Hey, Koeng!" he greeted as they walked to where he sat. "I see you've got another one."

The look he sent Lin had her hugging her luggage even closer. He laughed at her reaction. "Calm down, little girl. I won't bite." Then he turned his attention to Koeng. "The usual?"

"Yup," he replied. After filling out all of the necessary paperwork and getting the keys, he asked, "Can we have a meal sent up? She hasn't eaten a thing all day."

"No problem, Koeng. She's going to need some more meat on those bones for her journey. Scrawny little thing."

The lady whispered something in his ear then, and he laughed aloud. "Let's hope not. This one has a look of innocence that will draw the wolves to her for sure." The voluptuous girl giggled like a drunk bird.

Lin had goosebumps on her skin. She hugged her bag, legs shaking, not knowing what to say. Not knowing what to think. Not knowing what to do.

Koeng steered Lin upstairs, "Come on, girl."

She followed him up the stairs and down a short hallway. Keong opened the door to a musty, damp room and led her in. Lin carefully walked forward, rubbing her arms in an unconscious gesture of discomfort. The bed looked hurriedly made, and there was a suspicious patch right in the middle of the sheets. A decrepit chair and table stood at one side of the room. There was a huge basin with a bucket of water beside it that was obviously meant for bathing. She gently lowered herself onto the edge of the bed, making sure to avoid the soiled sheets.

"Stay here," Koeng said grumpily. "Don't mind Mo Chou; that's just the way she is. Don't worry, she won't bother you."

Lin nodded and put her belongings on top of a wooden chair.

"Your meal will be brought up shortly. Eat and rest, Keong continued. "I need to go see about your travel arrangements."

"You're going to leave me here alone?" Lin asked, and there was no mistaking the apprehension in her voice.

"Just for a little while," he replied. "Don't worry. You'll be fine. I simply need to confirm your travel arrangements. It won't be long." Then, as if sensing her need for reassurance, he added, "Look... nobody will hurt you. Lock the door after I leave, if you want. And only open it when you hear one long knock and then two short ones. That will signify the arrival of your meal. I'll let them know. And I will knock the same way when I return."

She nodded, closing both arms into her stomach. He looked at her for a little while, then shook his head and left.

The young girl was petrified, and she had every reason to be. As the door closed, Lin gave free rein to the emotions swirling inside her. She was a bundle of fear, uncertainty, and anxious expectations.

She hadn't heard very much about Mexico until the recent days. Her uncle, Carlos Wong, was a successful businessman there. It was rumored that he even had top local government officials at his mercy. And he had offered to take her in. She wondered why. Would he really follow through on his promise to give her a better life? How did he intend to do that? She had heard the people in America spoke strange languages and ate weird foods. She could only speak Cantonese. How would she communicate? Would she be able to make new friends? Would she really be able to build a new life for herself? Was she even capable of doing that on her own?

Too many questions. So many uncertainties.

She sighed. She had no choice. Her parents had handed her an opportunity, and it would be wrong to waste it. She would do whatever it took to make them proud in this strange new land. Others had done it, and she would also succeed in this endeavor.

By the crack of dawn the following morning, Lin stood on the harbor, shivering in the chill of the morning air, her attention held by the cargo boat that would take her on the next leg of her journey. The place was a beehive of activity, filled with men busily loading various articles onto the boat, mostly in gigantic, red shipping containers. She made sure to stay out of their way while Koeng went to discuss in whispers with one of them. After a while, both of them walked to where Lin was standing.

"This is where I leave you," Koeng said. "Mr. Duong, here..." he gestured to the man beside him, "Will take you on board. Goodbye, Miss Wong. May you be well." With that, he turned and walked toward his bus.

Lin looked at his retreating back, her heart racing with anticipation and fear. She reached out for him, scared to be passed off to yet another stranger. While she was uncertain of what lay in wait for her, she had never been on a boat before, only small canoes in the canals and rivers back home. She wondered what it would be like.

"Well, come on," Duong said curtly as he led her through the bustling activity on the harbor.

After weaving their way through people and cargo alike, they came to a container that looked a lot like the other ones used to transport cargo, except this one wasn't empty; the inside had been transformed. Lin looked at Duong in confusion.

"Go inside," he said impatiently.

She looked again at the container, then Duong opened its large door farther so the sunlight spilled inside. She stepped in.

In the dim light of its interior, she saw she wasn't alone. There were other people in the container, all Chinese, and all bearing identical looks of anxiety and desperate hope on their faces. They all stared at her as she made her way in to find her place among them.

There were small dividers created for privacy of its tenants, but they were inefficient as the cloth used for them had holes, and the fabric was thin. There would be no privacy during this trip, and there was only one very public toilet in the back of the bolted container. About two dozen small pads lay on metal planks that would serve as their mattresses to sleep and sit. Some people had carton boxes and burlap sacks filled with personal items. Others clung tightly to their sole package containing their few possessions in life.

It was crowded and dark. She was used to small spaces, but this was different. For some reason, her chest tightened, and her stomach turned. Fighting the claustrophobia that was quickly sneaking up on her, she found herself in a spot near a girl that looked about her age.

The girl turned to look at her with friendly eyes. "Good morning," she said in a hushed tone. "My name is Ai. What's yours?"

"It's Lin. Lin Wong," she replied with a genuine smile.

"Lin Wong," the other girl repeated, as if tasting the name on her tongue. "I'm traveling with my family." She turned to indicate a man, a woman, and a little girl that sat huddled close to each other. "We're going to California. Where are you going?"

"Mexico," Lin replied quietly. When the girl looked around for her family, Lin elaborated. "I'm traveling alone."

"Oh, you must be very brave."

Lin simply smiled. She wasn't brave. She had no other choice; it was as simple as that.

About an hour later, the ship began to sail and their long journey to the Promised Land began. As time went on, she learned she was not the only young girl traveling alone to Mexico. There were several other girls in the container who sat quietly, their eyes betraying their anxiety and fear about what awaited them. Some of them from the mainland up north spoke Mandarin, and a few, those from Hong Kong, also spoke English.

Lin had no way of knowing all of their stories, but what disturbed her the most was the pure terror on some of the young girls' faces when the doors closed the final time. This was not the mere anxiety that Lin felt; it was fear for one's life—an emotion she knew all too well. Lin suspected these girls were here against their will, without the knowledge of their parents.

One of them couldn't seem to stop her tears or the quiet shaking that accompanied them. Another girl held her close, trying to offer solace in a hopeless situation. But there were also men traveling with their families, and grim-faced women with troubled eyes. The atmosphere in the container was a strange combination of hope and despair.

During the course of the journey, most of the passengers loosened up enough to engage in friendly discussions with each other. A camaraderie soon developed from the peculiarity of the situation, and they began to exchange stories and anecdotes, often speculating on the kind of life they hoped to have when they got to their various respective destinations.

One of them, a burly man with a robust sense of humor, regaled them with amusing stories about his thrilling misadventures. Some of them were going to the United States, while others said they would simply settle for Mexico, as they already had family there. One family had loved ones up north, in Vancouver.

The men talked about the various opportunities in trade and business that they could explore, while the women chatted about the various ways that they could supplement their husbands' income. They were all hopeful. Scared out of their minds. But hopeful, nonetheless.

Most of the passengers hoped that the move would be a huge step in their quest for a better standard of living. Only the young girls, who seemed to be closely guarded by an unsmiling woman with cold eyes, said nothing. Other than occasional whisperings with each other, they mostly kept to themselves.

Over time, Ai and Lin became good friends. When the boat ran into troubled seas and was tossed violently, both girls would sit close to each other, clutching their hands in terror. Lin learned that Ai's father had been a field worker outside Macau, but had decided to try to make his fortune in America after he had been unfairly dismissed from his job. Her mother had been a cook to one of the many wealthy families in the city. She had been unwilling to leave her friends, her family, and home behind, but she was also determined to support her husband's decision, regardless of the consequences. They had used their life savings to make this desired journey a reality.

"My family had to stay behind," Lin said when Ai finished her story. "I miss them, but my brother most of all. I wish I could see him grow up to be a man."

"Why are they sending you away?" Ai asked.

"They want to give me a better life. Liu has a better chance than me back home—he's strong and resourceful. And being a man, he is less likely to be... attacked." The word tasted bitter coming out of her mouth. "I'll be living with my uncle in Mexico, but I don't know the first thing about him. He is supposed to take me under his wing and teach me English and Spanish and everything about his home."

Ai tilted her head to the side. "Why do you seem so sad about that? This is a great opportunity. Most people that travel to the Americas don't even have a place to stay. You're ahead of the game."

A *game*. The irony of the word lingered in Lin's mind for some time.

"I'm afraid," she finally said. "What if my uncle isn't who my parents say he is? What if he's mean and nasty and doesn't look after me like he promised? I know I should be grateful, but I've never traveled anywhere else before. Things could go terribly wrong."

"Yes," Ai said, "but they could also go right. As long as you have a positive attitude, you can find the best in every situation. When you meet your uncle, treat him with the utmost respect and do everything he asks of you. Your patience and kindness will be rewarded by the universe."

Lin smiled, and Ai continued to talk about her family and the adventures she hoped to have with them. The longer the girls spoke, the more Lin realized this girl always chose to see the sunny side of life. She was happy for this cheerful girl, but she also envied her. Ai had the life Lin wished her family could have had. Once again, she wished her family was there with her—or that she was back home with them.

She remembered the name her parents fondly called her. *Wu-Dip.* Butterfly. Spreading beauty and growth to everything it touched. They had been calling her that since she was a baby. A butterfly had landed on her head when she was one, and Lin seemed to have enjoyed the company, smiling and playing with it. From that moment on, she became Wu-Dip.

Tears sprang to her eyes then, and she blinked them away. She would be strong for her parents. She would make them proud. She was their beautiful butterfly, and she would fly for them.

While the friendship that developed between the passengers helped to lessen the bleakness of their journey, there were still hiccups. Being in such closed quarters for such a long time took its toll. Occasional quarrels stemming from irritability and ill-temper broke out among the passengers. Once, one of the women got into a bitter argument with the guard of the teenage girls while they looked on, frightened.

The men also got into altercations, usually about differing opinions on politics and trade. On one occasion, some punches were thrown, and men were tossed against the walls. Thankfully, that was the only huge fight that occurred.

There was also the problem of space. Thirty-eight people were cramped into a very limited space, and this gave rise to problems when it came to sleep... or the bathroom situation. Sometimes, they slept practically on top of each other. Other times, some of them would opt to sleep while sitting up. *And the smells!* It was nauseating; as if the tossing of the waves wasn't enough.

Then there was the time one of the timid girls had suffered a panic attack. The stuffiness of the container did nothing to help her condition. The girl had struggled for what little air there was in the suffocating atmosphere while her friends fanned her with the hems of their tattered skirts. Eventually, her shaking and sobbing had reduced to whimpers, and one of the other women had drawn the girl to her, murmuring soothing words until she fell into an uneasy sleep.

There was no way to measure time in the container. It was hidden deep among the legitimate cargo. As a result, the sun could not get to it. The only way they knew it was daytime was when it got marginally brighter and the metal walls hotter. The large door could only be opened from the outside, and the only source of ventilation was a tiny window, which let in barely enough oxygen to go around.

The food was meagre and inconsistent. Sometimes they would be fed twice a day, sometimes once. The fare was usually watery soup and rice, or some unidentifiable maritime object which they had no choice but to eat in good faith. Often, the mothers would give their ration to their children so they could eat more. The round, five-gallon water container was refilled every two days by the large ship workers. But this was not enough for the large group inside.

Lin's friendship with Ai brought her closer to Ai's mother, Bao, and she came to really like the woman. Being around Bao gave her a little taste of home. Her features and the way she spoke reminded Lin of her own mother. At night, she'd snuggle close to her and imagine her family of four lying in the rags that they used as a bed. In many ways, Bao was similar to *Mouh*. She was warm, loving, and compassionate.

One night, when Ai was asleep, Lin felt queasy and couldn't find a comfortable position to sleep. Noticing this, Bao carefully shuffled over to her and held her in her arms. "Are you okay?" Bao asked.

Lin nodded.

"Why don't we talk to get your mind off things?"

Lin nodded again. "What would you like to talk about?"

"Why don't you tell me about what brought you here?"

"Bad things," she replied blatantly. "My home town is filled with poverty and apparently also with bad men looking to hurt young girls like me. My friend, Meilin, was forced to do some shameful things to help protect her family, and she got pregnant because of it."

Lin looked up at Bao who was listening intently, so she continued. "My mother didn't want that to happen to me. My parents want me to have a good life where I'm not forced to make those kinds of choices. They think, in my new life, I will always be clothed and fed, and I'll never have another worry."

"They sound like good parents," Bao said, squeezing her tightly. She caressed her cheek and said, "Why don't you close your eyes? Try to get some sleep, and I'll tell you about the time Ai almost broke her arm." Lin agreed, and focused on Bao's soothing voice as she fell asleep.

In the coming days, knowing everything Lin had been through, Bao treated Lin more like one of her own children. She even went as far as inviting her to share in her rations whenever she left it to her children. The good-natured woman fussed over Lin the same way she worried over her own daughter, and her kindness both lessened and sharpened the girl's pain at being separated from her own family.

At various points in time, some of the passengers fell seasick. One day, about half the inhabitants in the container were down with fevers and queasy stomachs, while the other half nursed them back to health. Once, the boat had endured a storm so violent they had all been convinced they were facing certain death. They could even hear the ship workers outside struggling and screaming to each other.

The boat had pitched sharply at different angles, causing the passengers in the container to roll over one another and try to hold on to whatever they could to avoid hurting anyone or themselves. The shaking had been so severe, it seemed as if the container had been thrown into the sea and was now being rocked to and fro by the waves.

Eventually, when the storm cleared, and they realized that they were still safely on the boat, they had to deal with the stench of vomit and other bodily liquids that fear had forced out of some of the passengers. It had taken a long and protracted shouting match with the hands on the boat before the mess was cleaned up and the place was made habitable again.

During the second leg of the trip, most of them were dehydrated, as the water ration was even more scarce. Some wanted to die.

All hope had been lost.

THE FLIGHT OF THE BUTTERFLY

CHAPTER SEVENTEEN

Ensenada, Baja California, Mexico

It came as a big relief they finally docked on calm waters. They were impatient to see what awaited them on the outside, but first, they were told to remain quiet until told otherwise. The Mexican Marina and Customs would be checking the large container boat. Not until their door opened were they able to talk or move about again. Lin clutched her new friend's hand tightly as they heard shouts in an unfamiliar language echo around their container. Should they be caught here, all would be for nought.

Once cleared, a few armed civilian men came first and took the young girls and their grim-faced guardian away. Some of them had broken down into inconsolable tears, while the others had simply looked on in listless resignation. They were marched to a large white van by the docks.

The rest of the passengers were led in small groups to the backside of the harbor where an enormous Mexican flag waved above them in the breeze. Eventually, some were let go, and a large group—including Lin, Ai, and her family—was taken to an air-conditioned bus. They hadn't felt a breath of cool air in a while.

They drove through the city on a road by the sea. The city's center was crowded with tourists and locals alike, all flitting about the countless small shops, and restaurants. The curious eyes of the fresh arrivals looked on with awe and excitement. They saw restaurants, stores, factories, parks, kids playing on the streets. On a crowded street, the bus stopped at a read light. Some of the passengers lowered the windows and Lin was able to hear snatches of a language that none of them understood from the people passing by next to the bus.

This place looked fun.

But this life wasn't for them, apparently. At least not yet. The bus would take them north, soon leaving the welcoming city behind.

Shortly after the bus was driven out of the city, they stopped on a dirt patch between mountains and the vast blue sea. There was another bus and several other cars with people standing. As the bus fully stopped, two men entered the bus and pointed to twelve of the passengers, including Lin, and beckoned to them. They were to go on the other bus.

Though nervous, Lin felt giddy with excitement. Somewhere along the tortuous journey, she had stopped dwelling on her separation from her family and had begun to see her situation as an adventure. She stopped focusing on the uncertainties awaiting her and started to explore the possibilities. Maybe she *would* learn the new language, get an education, and finally be all that her parents wanted her to be. She imagined herself returning to China after a few years and bringing her family to America.

All she had to do was be diligent at whatever her uncle assigned to her. Thankfully, she was used to hard work, and she was not one to shy away from it. Yes, she would take full advantage of this new chance given to her.

She turned to smile at Ai, whose eyes were filled with tears at this separation from her new friend. "Take care, my friend," Lin whispered, feeling the moisture in her own eyes. "And thank you. For everything."

"Be well, Lin Wong."

They hugged and then she hugged her newfound mother, Bao. There was no time to say anything after that, as Lin's group was taken to the older bus that didn't look as nice as the one that took the other group.

They would never see each other again.

A man with a gun said something and pointed towards the bus; and the small group climbed into the bus without any argument.

Lin found a seat at the back and tried to ignore the dead heat making her sweat out of every cell in her body. Lin learned from the discussion around her that the port where the ship had docked was called the Port of Ensenada in the state of Baja California. They were in

Mexico now. She also discovered that they had spent thirteen days in the hell on that cargo boat.

Only thirteen days!? It sure had felt like a lot longer than that.

This bus would take them east to Mexicali, a Mexican desert city on the US-Mexico border where they would learn Spanish and be sent to work in factories, restaurants, or stores owned by the local successful Chinese-Mexicans. Her uncle, Carlos Wong, was also supposed to meet with the bus and usher Lin into the new phase of her life. She felt almost heady with anticipation. Now that her new life was about to begin, she felt a rush of adrenaline that made her restless; she was eager to prove her worth to her uncle and learn all that she could about this new place. She was committed to the adventure.

As the bus sped through various unfamiliar landmarks, she looked out the window with twinkling eyes, eager to take in as much as she could about this strange new place. She looked with wonder at a large Jesus statue with open arms and the well-kept roads along the beach. She saw the endless sea on her left, while expansive brown mountains on her right made a giant wall, guarding the unknown. She gaped at the well-tended gardens and magnificent gates that hid even more splendid homes on top of the hills.

Eventually, the cities ended and so did their journey next to the ocean. It was all desert now. Then mountain. Then desert again. A lot of desert. She had never seen such rural, vacant settings. She wasn't used to such open space. The desert went on forever. So... brown. So... empty. She wondered if one day she could turn the vast desert into a luxurious home of her own. She would hire people to work for her and treat them like family. After all, why would anyone want to live in a huge mansion without being surrounded by people?

When they arrived at their destination, it was a dusty place. Flat, but urban, nonetheless. And though there weren't any tall buildings or rivers like back home, it was a city, indeed. There were a lot of cars, people walking around, and the air outside felt hot. Dry.

Finally, the bus got to a part of town that almost looked like home. Almost. There were buildings that had Chinese names, storefronts with Chinese lettering, restaurants that boasted having *authentic Chinese food*. Most of them were in Cantonese. She finally understood something.

That was a good sign. She smiled, a genuine smile she hadn't been able to muster in weeks.

The bus stopped a nondescript building by an alley. A couple of men led some of the passengers away, while six of them, including Lin, were asked to remain. The other five asked to wait were made up of two of the despairing girls and three old men; two of these men were Chinese, but had not been on the same boat as her.

She tried not to dwell on any of that, though, as she was just happy to have arrived safely. All she wanted was for her uncle to come and take her to his home. She imagined herself cleaning, scrubbing floors, and quickly learning the tricks of any trade he introduced her to.

If only she could let her mother know she was okay.

As she and her group waited, a tall, muscular man with tattoos all over his body and a long scar that ran down the left side of his face walked toward them. He was not Chinese. She wondered what he wanted.

He spoke over his shoulder to another shorter, hairy man that reminded her of a bear. Lin couldn't catch anything other than, "Hong Kong." The bear man nodded, and Mr. Tattoos made an affirmative-sounding grunt.

He scrutinized each of the girls closely, as if she were a piece of merchandise he was trying to determine the worth of. It made Lin feel uncomfortable, and she wondered when her uncle would come for her, or why he would send Mr. Tattoos and Mr. Bear instead.

Meanwhile, Mr. Tattoos turned to look at two of the men from the docks, said something else Lin couldn't understand, and handed one of them a parcel. Then he motioned for the group to come close to him. As they did, he called, "Lee Wong? Lin Wong?"

Lin raised confused eyes to him, then timidly raised her hand. He eyed her from head to toe, and she tried not to blush under the man's appraisal. She was not used to such directness. Her personal space was being invaded.

What was going on? Who was this man, and where was her uncle? She had so many questions to ask, but she couldn't speak Spanish... or English. So she decided to simply keep quiet and save her questions for her uncle. Maybe he would have some explanations for her. Maybe he was too busy with a business deal to come for her himself. Maybe he was eagerly waiting for her right this minute.

She took a deep, calming breath and tried to smother the doubts rising within her. Of course he was waiting for her. He had made all this possible. Everything was fine. She just had to be patient. Again. She had endured the long journey across the Pacific Ocean; this should be a piece of cake.

But as the big man gave a satisfied nod and turned away, Lin felt the worry begin to chip at her optimism like an insistent woodpecker. She had the distinct feeling she had just been sized up. But for what?

Where was her Uncle Carlos?

The man said something to her while making hand gestures. Though she didn't know for certain what he'd said, she assumed he'd told her to follow him.

Soon, I will understand this language.

The two muscular men walked away without waiting for a response. She hurried to keep up with them, clutching her bag with both hands, as they led the way to where a long, black, brand-new car with tinted windows was parked.

Mr. Bear opened the door of the backseat for her. He said something else curtly as he motioned with his hand for her to get inside. She got in, confused, and jumped when he slammed the door behind her. A chuckle made her jump again.

"Easy, girl. Calm down," a voice sounded in perfect Cantonese.

She understood!

It was a male voice, soft and cultured. It sent shivers down her back. She looked to her side and saw a neatly-dressed Chinese man smiling benevolently at her.

"Hello, Wu-Dip," he said, still smiling. "I'm Carlos Wong, your uncle."

Lin felt relief roll over her in waves.

"Uncle! Thank you for coming for me."

"How could I not?" he replied, looking at her in a way that made her want to squirm. "I promised your parents. How was your trip?"

Lin made a noncommittal response. She wished he would stop smiling. If he was trying to make her feel at ease, he was failing miserably. There was something insincere about it, something predatory about the look in his eyes.

And suddenly, she had the sinking feeling that things might not go the way she'd expected, after all.

CHAPTER EIGHTEEN

Mexicali, Mexico
1988

Carlos caressed his perfectly kept mustache as he regarded the pretty girl sitting beside him. It was almost unthinkable that this diamond came from the slums of Guangzhou. His upper lip curled in distaste as he remembered the dumps, dilapidated buildings, and refuse mounts that dotted the landscape next to the muddy Zhujiang River.

The last time that he had visited, he had nearly thrown up. The dwellers of the shanty town where his family came from lived like pigs, eating whatever they could scavenge, just to survive. He remembered the way their eyes had lit up at the sight of him, the pathetic way they offered effusive thanks whenever he deigned to merely talk to them. They were all pathetic, subservient animals, falling over themselves to please him. He had been very happy to get out of there as soon as possible and come back to the kingdom he had worked hard to build.

Still, his visit there had not been entirely a waste. After three long decades, he had finally met his cousin Zhang, who had happily talked to him about his wife—a woman who still retained vestiges of her beauty despite the hard life she led—and his princess of a daughter.

Carlos had met Lin, who had been only four or five at the time, but even then, he had seen the potential for great beauty in her. He had tried, even then, to convince his cousin to let the girl return to Mexico with him, but all of his entreaties had fallen on deaf ears.

THE FLIGHT OF THE BUTTERFLY

After returning to Mexicali, he had stayed in touch with his cousin through occasional letters, in which he dropped subtle hints about how much better his beautiful daughter would be in a place where she did not have to scrub floors for a living. In the letters, he wrote about the many possibilities and opportunities he would personally make sure were made available to her. Of course, he never elaborated on what form these opportunities would take or who exactly would benefit from them; a businessman never revealed his secrets.

And finally, after so many years, she was here, beside him, close enough for him to reach out and touch. He had to struggle to restrain his excitement and content himself with just looking.

"Are you hungry?" he asked Lin.

"Um, yeah. A little." Her voice, so sweet. The song of a nightingale.

"Don't worry. Soon you'll eat your heart's desire. Here, you'll be treated like a princess."

Lin simply smiled and looked out the window. She didn't notice the look on his face as he glanced at her bundle and tattered clothes in disgust. She also didn't seem to notice the way he wet his lips as he stared at her.

Carlos could not stop staring at this angel. She simply needed a new look, and that was an easy fix. She had beautiful skin, though it had the pallor that came from not being out in the sun enough. Again, this had a simple solution. He decided made a mental note to ensure she spent at least an hour everyday walking in the blazing Mexicali sun. Or better yet, sunbathing in one of his pools. She would get a nice tan, indeed. And that sure would be a nice view.

Her pink lips formed a perfectly shaped rosebud, and her black eyes, framed by those long, dark eyelashes, revealed an innocence that was sure to get any man's blood flowing. Her luxuriant, raven hair fell to the middle of her back in its thick braid, and he couldn't help but imagine that hair free, freshly washed, cascading down her back like a shimmering curtain.

He smiled to himself. Yes, he had struck gold this time. Her youth and innocence would be sure to bring him some serious profit. Proudly, he congratulated himself, as he had made yet another wise business decision. And this investment would bring about a wonderful return.

You are mine now, Lin.

Lin saw her uncle's smile in the periphery of her vision and tried to hold back a shudder. She felt like a lamb trapped in a corner by a wolf. Yet, this thought was unreasonable. Hadn't he been the soul of charm so far?

"I apologize again for not coming to meet you myself," he said, breaking the silence between them. He shuffled a little closer to her, and her muscles tensed. "When you have status like mine, you're expected not to be seen in certain places. This was for the best to protect you. I wanted to avoid any unnecessary publicity. I'm sure you understand."

Lin nodded, then once again looked out the window at the passing new surroundings. This would be her home now. She pushed her back deeper into the leather seat, hoping the man beside her would keep a safe distance.

I've come this far. This is all for my own good. She held on to reassuring words.

Still, no matter what she told herself, she couldn't shake the feeling that something was wrong. Very, very, wrong...

Lin remained uneasy throughout the car ride, as her uncle asked her questions about her journey and her family back home. She replied with short answers which she could tell he barely paid attention to anyway as he fiddled with his cufflinks.

Eventually, the car stopped in front of a building with a sign that Lin couldn't read. Mr. Tattoos opened the door for her uncle, who waved him over to Lin's side. She got out of the car, hugging her worn-out bundle of clothes close to her chest while she looked around. The building wasn't tall like the ones she'd seen in Hong Kong, but it looked nice. The parking lot wasn't big, but it was packed full of cars.

"Come in. Come in, please," her Uncle Carlos said, sweetly. "This is the Hotel Lucero."

The driver went ahead of them to open the door, and they stepped inside. Lin nearly stopped and stared, but her uncle's guiding hand on her elbow urged her along.

"I own this hotel," he explained. "I guess, in a way, you own it too. We're family, after all, and if you work hard enough, you could be running it one day. Doesn't that sound nice?"

Lin nodded, and for a moment, she got a taste of the life her parents wanted for her.

Carlos smirked, and she didn't know why. "This hotel is one of many in a vast chain across the northwestern part of the country. I worked for years to expand my empire and have gained the respect I deserve. Take it all in, because only a handful of people get a grand tour from the owner himself."

They walked past a busy reception area filled with people checking in and out. Concierges crossed in front of them, helping to haul luggage to an outdoor area where people awaited airport shuttles. They passed two pools and went straight into the last tower on the left where one of two elevators took them to the top floor. When they got out of the elevator, he courteously led her to a door, opened it, and motioned for her to go inside.

The room turned out to be a luxury suite that, according to her uncle, was reserved for him and designed to suit his specifications. Every piece in the suite spoke quality and wealth, with a large bed made made with imported sheets and an entire room with a dining set.

"Make yourself comfortable," her uncle ordered, gesturing to the extravagant chamber. "You said you were hungry."

As if in response, the young girl's stomach rumbled, reminding her that she hadn't eaten anything all day and had only drank one bottle of water during the five-hour bus ride from the port.

The man smiled. "That settles it. I'll have room service bring up a warm meal."

Lin nodded and was about to sit on a gold-accented white couch when Carlos interrupted. "We just had this room cleaned, so it's probably not a good idea for you to sit anywhere else until you're... proper. Why don't you go and wash off the grime and dirt of your journey?"

He led her to the bathroom then. In it was an ornate room with tile porcelain floors and a cupboard stocked with fresh towels, shampoos, and other essentials. He ran a hot bath for her, added special bath oils and sweet-smelling soap, then walked to the door.

"Once you get out of those clothes, someone will come in and dispose of them for you. Leave them outside of the bathroom. We'll find something better for you to wear. Like I said, take all the time you need, as I have plenty of business to attend to."

"Okay, Uncle."

"Oh, and Lin, don't worry if you hear noises in this side of the room. People will be coming in and out to prepare stuff for you. You can lock your door from the inside. Once you are done with everything, just make sure to stay in the room."

"Thank you, sir. I will."

Her uncle left, and Lin stood in the middle of the quiet room.

For a while, she remained there, looking at the sheer luxury that surrounded her. She had scrubbed baths like this before, but had never imagined that one day she would actually have the opportunity to use one herself.

Excitement swelled, and she giggled in sheer delight. She put her old belongings outside the bathroom and locked the door, then carefully lowered herself into the bath and sighed as the warm water soothed away the aches of travel. The oils and fragrance in the bath helped her to relax as she soaked in the warm water, luxuriating in the feel of the smoothness on her skin. She wished her family could see her now. Things were already looking up, and she was barely into her first day in this new promise land!

Here you will be treated like a princess, her uncle's words resonated in her mind. *I think father was right, after all. If only they could be here too.*

After her bath, thoroughly relaxed, she reached for one of the several fluffy towels with the hotel logo embroidered on it and wrapped herself in it. The sights and smells of a feast greeted her when she finally walked back into the adjoining room. Her mouth watered when she saw the variety of entrees laid out on the table. She smiled when she saw Chinese meals as well as other unfamiliar fancy looking dishes, and her eyes misted as she remembered when her family barely had enough to eat. She wondered if they had eaten already, and if they had eaten anything good.

I miss them so much.

THE FLIGHT OF THE BUTTERFLY

Lin shook off the cloud of melancholia that threatened to descend on her and looked around for her bundle. She walked to the table where she had dropped it, then got to her knees to search for it. It had disappeared. All of her clothes were gone! Everything she owned.

She turned around, confused, and noticed a beautiful gown on the bed. Her mouth dropped open as she picked it up. It was a knee-length chiffon dress, the color of lavender.

It's beautiful!

Its bodice was designed to fit snugly, while the flared skirt fell in soft waves. Beneath it were thin, pink, lacy undergarments that didn't cover much, which made her blush as she wondered who had picked them out. She had never worn this type of sexy underwear before, but she had always wondered. She couldn't wait to try them on.

Almost reverently, Lin put on the underwear and pulled the gown on and almost cried with wonder at the feel of the fabric on her skin. It was gorgeous; skillfully cut in such a way that accentuated her curves without being too obvious. Lin looked at herself in the floor-to-ceiling mirror in the room and couldn't believe her eyes. Was this her? It fit perfectly. She felt so pretty.

I am a princess!

The dress floated around her like a cloud as she twirled around in it. She had never seen anything so beautiful in her entire life. And it was for *her*? She was overcome with appreciation for her uncle and renewed her resolve to be diligent at whatever he gave her to do.

Lin felt like the princess from an American movie she once watched. She gave her reflection in the mirror another long look and saw through the mirror the two pairs of shoes by the bed, behind her. She had never worn high heels before, but these were beautiful.

She tried the first pair, but they didn't fit. Too big. Then she tried the second pair, and her toes slipped in effortlessly. Just her size, and just her luck. She stood up and saw her reflection once more. And there she was: a princess. A beautiful butterfly just emerged from her cocoon. She smiled with joyful tears.

She went to other side of the suite to have dinner. Hesitantly, she pulled herself onto a cushioned chair and slowly started eating. She wasn't used to eating alone, but everything tasted delicious, so she chowed down, savoring each bite. She tried a little bit of each dish and felt like she could eat for days.

"Ah! I see you found my little gifts," Carlos said as he walked silently into the room.

She screamed while chewing a piece of meat.

"Sorry," he chuckled. "I didn't mean to scare you. I'm glad you found everything I left for you."

She beamed at him. "Yes. Thank you so much, sir. I really appreciate this. And I promise I won't let you down in any task that you entrust to me."

At those words, his smile widened. "Yes. I certainly hope not. I'm giving you the life you've always wanted, Lin. Let's not do anything to ruin that."

Lin once again felt a quiver of unease at the way her uncle was looking at her, but she chose to ignore it and enjoy the food. She simply smiled.

Her uncle, on the other hand, continued to ogle her, as if stunned at the transformation created by a pretty dress and a good bath.

"I bet you can't find anything like this back home," he said, coming closer and dropping into the seat by her side.

"I'm sorry?" Lin replied.

"I mean the food."

"Oh. No," Lin said, swallowing. "We barely had any food. But... I miss my family." She stopped eating for a moment.

He stroked the top of her head. His touch felt icy. "I'm your family," he said. "Make sure you remember that."

"Yes, Uncle," she said. "You are. Would you like to join me? This is a lot of food."

"No, thank you, Lin," he said. "I have to excuse myself once more. I have a few things to do, but you can stay here and enjoy yourself. I've left some magazines and videos in Chinese for you on the coffee table, if you'd like something to do this evening. But make sure you get some rest too. You've had a long journey, and I need you at your best."

He stood up and so did she. He stared at here from head to toe.

"Wow..." He looked at her, a strange expression of awe on his face as he raised a hand to her cheek, stopping just short. "You look like an angel. Innocent and pure. Untainted beauty."

Lin blushed. She wasn't used to compliments. "I'm grateful, Uncle."

Uncle Carlos left, and Lin finished eating. By the end, she felt like her stomach would explode, something she'd never experienced before. And that send a pang of guilt washing over her. She reminded herself that this is what her parents wanted.

She took a brief look at the materials her uncle left for her, then stretched out on the bed realizing how tired she was. It was the most comfortable thing she had experienced in a very long time—or ever.

Darkness quickly fell, and Lin changed into a satin nightgown that either her uncle or someone else had laid out for her, and climbed under the soft, warm blankets. It had been an eventful day. The trip to this new city of Mexicali might have been scary, but it was worth all of the trouble. Today had been the best day of her life. Her uncle had proved to be the soul of courtesy.

Still, she couldn't help the nagging feeling that something was off about him. She remembered the way the tattooed man had sized her up and the few times it appeared her uncle was doing the same. Shivers rippled down her spine.

Stop imagining things, Lin. Just be a good girl and be grateful. And some day, the whole family will be here too. For now, just rest, as your new life awaits tomorrow.

CHAPTER NINETEEN

Lin didn't hear her uncle steal into the room later that night. For a while, he simply stood and stared, noting how relaxed her facial features were in sleep, the perfect image of innocence. No longer able to control himself, he bent over her and pressed his lips to hers.

She awoke to the sensation of being kissed and drew away, her heart pounding. "Who's there?" she whispered as she tried to get her bearings in the dim room.

"It's me, princess. Don't be afraid."

Her stomach tightened with dread as his fingers trailed over her. "Uncle? What are you doing?"

He hushed her gently. "Quiet now."

The memory of her assault came back to her, and she realized that this time she would have no savior. What could one do when the person supposed to protect her was trying to hurt her?

"Please, no," she begged, recoiling from her uncle's breath and hands on her. "Please..." She tried to push him away, but the weight of him on top of her was too much. "No... No! Stop!"

"Be quiet, you ungrateful puppy," he said in a firm voice now. "You promised to be diligent at whatever I would give you to do, didn't you? Well, this is what I'll have you do. Stop fighting me. Nothing in life is free. Don't you appreciate everything I've given you so far?"

Still, she continued to struggle until he lifted his hand and slapped her hard. The force of the blow shocked her into stillness for a brief moment, but she wasn't about to give up. Out of desperation, when his hand came up to caress her face, she bit down, hard.

"Why, you...!" He called her several dirty names. "You like to fight like an animal, is that it? Fine. Then, I'll treat you like one!"

And he made good on his threat.

Lin curled into a ball and cried. She was a bloody mess on the mattress, both literally and figuratively. She lay in a fetal position in pain, confused, and overcome with shame. It was all too much. She thought of her father's unwavering belief that the move to her uncle would be the best thing for her, and cried harder. She could no longer sleep. Her innocence was gone.

Carlos got out of bed and headed for the bathroom. Lin looked at the door, thinking she could run, but where would she go? When he returned, she pretended to be asleep, and he slid in next to her. She quivered for most of the night, holding on to the blood-stained sheets as if they were some sort of protection from the satisfied monster that lay next to her, sound asleep.

Eventually, exhaustion won.

The next morning, Lin woke to see her uncle was already up and dressed. Fixing his tie in the mirror, he said, "Take a shower, then get dressed. And do something with that hair; you're a mess." He finished getting ready and turned to her. "I'll lay out one of the dresses I had my men bring you. Don't take long. We must leave soon. Your new life awaits."

She obeyed immediately, afraid of what any defiance would cost her. The words "your new life awaits" echoed in her mind, and her terror seethed. As she reluctantly undressed, she saw the marks on her neck. The swelling and bruising around right eye. And the rest below.

Lin cried silently. As she headed to the shower, she could still feel the pain seeping through her entire body. Though she wept, she tried to keep her whimpers silent, or at least masked by the falling water. If he heard her, she feared she'd be beaten again. Or worse.

When she got out, she put on a black dress left for her that was half the length of the previous one. The high heels were the same. Under different circumstances, she would've felt pretty. But now, all she felt was dirty. She was no longer the princess of the previous night; she was a slut—Carlos's slut. Oh, how fast life had changed in one night.

The same two muscular men from the day before waited for her by the door, and they escorted her downstairs, one on each side. She felt like a prisoner being taken to the gallows. Still, she thought, maybe she could escape from these men. Could she find a place to go where they wouldn't find her? Yes. It was worth the try. Any fate would be better than whatever they had in store for her.

She bided her time, waiting for the right moment to make her move when the men were distracted. Where would she go, though? She couldn't even communicate. If she was to get out, she would be lost, cursed to roam the streets forever.

It didn't matter. It was still better than this.

"Where are you taking me? Where is my... uncle?"

Of course, these two didn't understand a word she said. What if she cried for help? The hotel was busy; someone would do something—right?

When they got outside and began moving toward one of the parked cars, Lin decided to act. Instinctively, she broke away from the men and ran as fast as her legs would take her. But it was hard in the heels. She took them off, leaving them behind, and continued to run barefoot on the coarse, burning asphalt.

"Help! Anyone. Please, help!"

The element of surprise was on her side. But not for long.

The men ran after her, caught up, and overtook her. She made to dodge around Mr. Bear, but he reached out and grabbed her. He tightened his grip on her arm so hard that she winced in pain, then lifted her up with both hands, pinning her arms to her sides, his nails digging into her skin. She kicked her legs and screamed as he dragged her back to the car, and though hotel employees looked on grimly, none made any attempt to help her.

And then Lin remembered. Her uncle owned this hotel; she had no doubt all of its employees were under his control. None of them would help her. And with the extent of his power, she didn't think anybody would. The thought brought tears back to her eyes and forced her cries to falter.

Mr. Bear said something to his companion, amusement evident in his tone. They both laughed. He slapped her and then he licked her face. Lin shivered in disgust.

Mr. Tattoos said something in his language while shoving her into the backseat. He took the seat next to her, and the other man climbed into the driver's seat. They drove for a long time, and Lin watched with a sinking heart as the view outside the car changed from well-tended streets and houses to older, dilapidated buildings. She was back at the place with Chinese signs and small alleys.

Finally, the car stopped in front of a warehouse, and they got out. Before Lin had time to wonder what it was, she was led inside the cold, dimly lit building and down a steep staircase to the basement.

The large concrete cellar was full of casino machines, some covered with sheets and others gathering dust. Mr. Bear urged her forward, and they made their way to a room in the back without windows. The door had a padlock, and he opened it. The room was sparsely furnished with only a bed and a table. He pushed her in and closed the door behind her.

Lin cringed when the door banged. She was trapped. A prisoner. Or was she?

But all hopes of escape were stifled when she heard the padlock click outside. She felt the prickling of warm tears in her eyes and let them flow unrestrained down her cheeks. She screamed and kicked the door. She punched it. She spit at it. And she screamed some more. But no one came. No one cared. She was here, all alone, a prisoner in despair.

Tired and with a heavy heart, she climbed into the bed and curled into a ball in defeat, hoping that by doing so, she would be able to banish the world and be left alone.

Time passed. It felt eternal. It felt swift. She didn't know how long went by. And when a woman finally came, she brought food and water, then left without saying a word. At regular intervals, that same middle-aged woman, always followed by an armed guard, would bring her meals and water. She also brought toiletries and would change the bucket that served as Lin's bathroom. The woman sent her a disturbed look each time she replaced the untouched meals with a fresh one.

On one occasion, the woman came and told Lin something which she didn't understand. So the woman used body motions to make her understand. She wanted Lin to eat. She insinuated that the men, Carlos's men—or perhaps the monster himself—would be upset if she didn't eat. But Lin didn't care anymore.

Leave me alone. I'd rather just die.

Sometime after, Carlos himself came down to her room. He stood at the doorway, scowling with displeasure at her exhausted body, so much leaner in only a matter of days. Her eyes widened as she saw him, and she backed into the farthest corner, fear spilling from every pore. The wall felt cold against her back, and she pictured herself at home with her family while trying to keep her tears at bay. She finally cared.

Get away! Not you! Anyone but you.

"Good. I'm glad to see you're still afraid of me. But I hear you've not been eating. Why?"

Lin said nothing, just looked at him with terror in her eyes.

"Is this a childish attempt to spite me?" his voice was mocking. "It's useless, you know. Now," his gaze fell on the plate of food on the concrete floor, "eat. Eat a lot. You need to gain weight. You're like a stick."

She didn't move.

"Oh, you want to be a *wild* animal now, huh?" His voice grew louder. "Then I guess I'll have to tame you. Eat, Lin. Now!"

She said nothing, neither did she make any move to pick up the plate. She remained on top of the bed, cornered like scared vermin.

Slowly, he picked up the plate of food and brought it to her on the bed. "I said... eat."

"No." She tried pushing herself deeper into the wall, as if that was possible, and rested her head on her knees.

"I said *eat*, stupid girl!"

"*No!*" she cried, suddenly picking up the plate and hurling it at him. Its contents scattered all over the place, across the bed, floor, and...

Carlos swore as food particles landed on his expensive suit. Without hesitation, he pulled her to him by her hair. "You dare to defy me, you insignificant, little *butterfly*? I will crush you! You are nothing but a worm."

Lin continued to cry.

The monster dragged her outside the room toward the larger warehouse chamber. "I will teach you a lesson, little girl. And you will learn. I'll only teach it once, but trust me, once will be enough."

He threw her against a slot machine and kicked her several times until she could barely move, let alone breath. And after a serious beating, Carlos Wong, her own uncle, forcefully had his way with her, ensuring that he caused her as much pain as he could. She was humiliated in ways she'd never felt.

As she lay on the floor, the monster stood, laughing at her while fixing his pants and belt. She could barely see him through the blood that dripped from her scalp and clung to her eyelashes. As he put his coat back on, he told her, "Lin, this is going to be your life now. You will be tied in your room until it is time to eat, use the bathroom, or you have a visitor. These visitors will be my clients, and they will do to you as they please. You hear me?"

She didn't say anything. She couldn't speak. Blood dripped from her face. From her legs. From her soul.

"And this new life begins now. So, next time I say eat, you eat. Next time I say jump, you jump. Next time I say bend over, you oblige. And you will enjoy every... single... moment... You hear me, bitch? I will send someone down."

Shortly after he left, another guard came to the room with a piece of rope. The guard looked with disgust at the bloody scene. Then he looked at her with... with empathy. Silently, he picked her up and carried her back to the room. He placed her on the bed and tied her hands and legs to the bed posts while murmuring something... soothing, something remorseful. The man didn't enjoy doing this but didn't seem to have a choice.

The familiar middle-aged woman came down next. She brought alcohol, bandages, and other first aid items to tend to the bruises on Lin's face, the blood that seeped from her skin, and then cleaned up the room as if nothing had happened.

And so, this became a routine. This was her life now. Lin would be tied hands and feet to the bed, untied only when it was time to eat or her uncle sent his *clients* to her.

She finally started eating. She had consider starving herself to death to end the torture of this nightmare she was living. But as the weeks went by, her hunger got the best of her. So, instead, she would binge. She would eat and eat.

Maybe if I get fat, he and the clients won't like me anymore.

But that wasn't the case. Carlos himself visited her every day without fail, constantly looking for new ways to demean her and break her spirit. And that is how she kept time. Every time he came, she knew it was a new day. And the days turned into weeks. And the weeks turned into months. And her hell felt eternal.

Every night, Lin cried and prayed for death. Her dreams were filled with snatches of her old life back in Guangzhou. It seemed so long ago. Now, every day, she woke into the same nightmare. A nightmare from which she couldn't wake.

Eventually, Lin found ways to adapt. She learnt to detach her mind from her body whenever her uncle or one of his clients was using her. Sometimes, it was multiple clients at the same time. She was taken in every possible way. Sometimes they brought foreign objects and toys. Sometimes they were sweet. Some were curious and nervous. Most were vicious.

Carlos trained her to be sultry, sexy, or scared, depending on what the client had paid for. If she didn't cooperate, it would be worse. It always hurt when clients had their way with her, both physically and emotionally. But she had to pretend to enjoy it, if that is what was required. The clients even had permission to be violent with her, as long as the damage wasn't visible or permanent. And, almost always, the clients chose to be violent—including the women.

She learned to close her mind to it all, learned to send her mind to the past when her present became too much, learned to read her uncle's clients. She mastered the art of hiding her emotions under a placid expression. She learned to act. She learned to survive.

The middle-aged woman started bringing her pills. At first, Lin was hesitant, but soon, she realized that they helped. They masked the pain.

Then she brought more—different ones. These helped her escape. Though not literally, she was certainly not present when the clients came. And she began to trust the woman.

Still, deep down through the haze of drugs, Lin longed for freedom. The only time she left the room was when the guard took her to the bathroom down the dark hall to shower. She was finally allowed to use that toilet too. It was a perk for being a good girl. She was brought new clothes and finally had options. But she would wear them for herself, not the clients. The clients seemed to enjoy her more this way, anyway.

After some time, the haze that kept her safe began to dissipate. The pills weren't doing their job effectively. She needed more and more and more.

Lin, what has happened to you? This is not okay! You need to get out. Get out. OUT!

Escape. Freedom. Flight. These were the words that kept her going every waking moment. She knew she was designed for more than simply the pleasure of men. She was a butterfly! She was meant to fly freely through the open sky. Her parents had told her so.

Her parents...

What would her parents think of her now? She was embarrassed. Would they even want her back, all broken like this? Would her little brother still look up to her?

Your pride and your reputation are your most important possessions, Lin. Mother's words echoed in her mind. She needed to get out. No more pills. No more clients. This wasn't her.

If only she could reach them! But she had no way to do so. They were most likely worried. Terrified they hadn't heard from her. But then again, her uncle could have lied to them and sent letters on her behalf. Of course, they probably thought she was doing great—perhaps they were even proud of her.

If only they knew.

Carlos's investment had paid off greatly. All his clients loved her. She was getting better and better. And prettier too. Most clients wanted to repeat, and word of her spread. It had been too easy. Yes, she was his niece, but no one would ever know.

Lin didn't know that Carlos Wong—her uncle, the Dragon, the monster himself—had lied to her parents about her journey to Mexico. He had sent word that she hadn't made it to the Mexican coast alive. He told them this was normal, due to the harsh conditions people endured in search of a better life. In the eyes of her parents, and to the rest of the world, Lin Wong was no more.

THE FLIGHT OF THE BUTTERFLY

CHAPTER TWENTY

Mexicali, Mexico
July 1989

Seven months passed. The year 1988 ended and a new year began. And these months flew by—though each day felt eternal.

Lin remembered how she had spent all of New Year's Day catering to her uncle's clients from both sides of the border. It had been a busy day. In fact, today had been a record—forty-two men and three women in the same day. Several of them were American businessmen, celebrating something on the Mexican side of the border. She was exhausted, both physically and emotionally.

Lin reminisced when, as a child, she would hope fervently that the New Chinese Year would bring her good things. Not anymore. The only thing she wanted now was to leave her present life one way or another.

Her birthday also came and went, unmarked and uncelebrated. She didn't mind. She hadn't even been keeping track of the days anymore. She'd given up. There was no way of knowing for sure what time or day it was except for her meals and Carlos's visits.

But then, she noticed something terrifying: her flow had ceased.

No! No, no, no. This couldn't be! She couldn't be pregnant. *No, please! Not here. Not like this.* She was too young. She could die!

And what would be her uncle's reaction be when he found out? She knew him to be a ruthless man. What would he do to her? Pregnant, she was of no use to him.

Or so she thought.

Pregnant. A baby inside me. A life that depends on me.

When she first realized she was pregnant, she wondered why her uncle hadn't taken any precautions. And the thought made her quiver. What would he do now? Nonetheless, the idea both terrified and fascinated her. There was a child growing inside her, depending on her for sustenance. She was important in the world again. And she felt a rush of maternal love for this child that was still a mass of tissues in her uterus. She wondered if it was a boy or girl. It was probably too early to tell, anyway.

But suddenly, another thought came to her that brought her back to reality.

She had been with so many men that she had no way of knowing who the father of her unborn baby was. The thought filled her with deep sorrow. It could be anyone. It could even be her own uncle. The monster! She had lost count months back.

This was not the kind of life she had hoped to have. Tied to a bed in the basement of a warehouse, at the mercy of her uncle and the men he sent to her. Pregnant as a teenager. A trafficked sex slave.

To them, she was nothing but a plaything, a prop with which they could act out their most intimate fantasies. And they did. They took her every way possible, even in ways she didn't even know were possible. She felt burning in her chest and took deep breaths until it subsided.

But Lin would not give in to her grief. She needed to find a way to protect her child. There had to be a way. She had a purpose now: her baby.

As it turned out, surprisingly, her uncle Carlos was pleased at the news of her pregnancy. Apparently, his creative businessman's mind had already seen the way he could turn this into a profitable venture.

"I ain't even mad! I have some clients who particularly enjoy being with pregnant women," he told her. "I'll just send them to you."

"I don't understand!" She was repulsed by the thought.

"Oh, honey. There is a fetish for every degenerate out there, and they are willing to pay good money for their fantasy. And then, when the child is born, I will just sell it to the highest bidder for a handsome price, followed by fixing you so that such *accidents* never occur again. You see, little butterfly, this situation is a win-win for me, no matter what."

And so, Lin found that she was still working for her uncle, even while pregnant. At first, she had been confused when her uncle had told her that the pregnancy would not hinder the continued flow of clients trooping to her. Then, as understanding dawned on her, she got angry.

Tears streamed down her cheeks as her uncle hovered over her. She implored. "You can't do this to a pregnant woman—just leave me alone to have the baby in peace. I don't know if I can handle the changes my body is going through and still be used in such vile ways. And please, whatever happens, don't take away this baby from me."

"Deal with it," he huffed. "Stop complaining about every little thing. You owe me for all I've given you."

She wanted to spit out her retort but bit her tongue. But she knew well that he would win this fight. The fact that he was telling his business plans to her face—of continuing to exploit her while pregnant, of taking away her baby after he or she was born—like nothing, almost like discussing an entreprise proposal with an employee, only made him that much more heartless.

And after the conversation, the monster had forced himself on her. As usual.

How was it possible for there to be such evil, sick people in this world? She could not comprehend it. And to think they were family. She abhorred the thought.

I hate my life. I just want to die... But I want this baby to live. This is all I have.

Mexicali
January 1990

Torturous months later, when Lin had cried about having terrible aches in her back, the middle-aged woman had been sent down to give her a massage. Though they never talked, Lin felt a close connection with her. She was nice and nurturing. By the way she interacted with her, she truly cared. She hurried to her side and helped her up, shaking her head, as if marveling at this new manifestation of her boss's cruelty.

Even though the girl was pregnant and now approaching her due date, the man still kept her tied to the bed. How could anybody be so cold? So evil!

Lin scowled as the rope was loosened from her wrists and ankles. Her feet had started swelling, causing the rope to burn into her skin. She was very grateful for the relief, even if it was only for a little while. She rubbed a hand over her stomach, wondering how the baby was doing. She hoped the less than ideal conditions in which she lived would not affect it. The baby had become her sole reason for living. When alone, she would sing to it, tell it stories about her past, her family, her home.

And when it was born, she hoped she would be allowed to at least see it before it was taken away from her, for she had no doubt she would not be allowed to raise her child. But she loved this baby so much already! It was a part of her.

After the massage, she thanked the other woman with her eyes as she was once again tied down. At least the ache had eased for the time being.

Later that night, a young client arrived. He seemed nervous about being with a pregnant, young Chinese prostitute. Still, he walked into the room curiously. When he approached the girl's bed, he saw her groaning in pain, straining against the ropes that bound her hands and feet. Beads of sweat clung to her forehead and upper lip. As he watched, she arched off the bed, giving a small whimper of pain, tears leaking out the sides of both her eyes.

Her water broke.

The man gagged, as if suddenly losing all desire to do anything. He turned toward the wall and threw up. And though her eyes were tightly closed now, she felt the ropes around her wrists loosen, then the ones around her ankles. When Lin looked again, the room was empty—and the door was open. She heard the young guy running away, still gagging.

The excruciating pain in her belly grew. It felt like someone was methodically squeezing her internal organs until they could take no more pressure. When the tightening passed, she lay in bed for a few moments, breathing hard. She'd heard of contractions before.

Lin was in labor. Her time had come.

And her bonds were absent.

And the door was wide open.

She was free?

She was free!

I am free!

She wasn't imagining this. She knew that whenever the clients came, the guards outside left. She could run now. To where, though? She wouldn't survive a day out there. But that didn't matter, she could get away from here. Somewhere. Anywhere. As long as it was away from this place of torture and slavery.

She'd had this same thought from day one, but never had a chance to act on it. This could be that chance. She could almost taste the freedom.

I must get out of here—now!

Lin didn't know when the guards would return; she knew she had to be quick. But she could barely walk! She stood up, grabbed a blanket, and made her way out the room, straight toward the only way out: the stairway.

The whole building was quiet, and Lin tried her best to tiptoe up the stairs. She was leaking, but it wouldn't stop her.

At the top, there was a tall wall with several windows near the ceiling. Noise and lights broke through from the other side. It looked like a casino of sorts. And there was a door there.

As quietly as she could, she sneaked through the apparently abandoned warehouse, going the opposite way, until she came to what looked like the back door. She unlocked it, and it opened onto a narrow barely lit back alley. No one was there. No cars. No armed guards. No one. Just some large trash bins.

Lin, for once, was grateful for her uncle's arrogance. He was too confident she would never escape her room.

A gust of cold wind took her breath away. The wintry air stole into her lungs, and she wrapped the blanket around her. Another contraction bent her over, and she took long, gasping breaths until the pain eased.

I have to get out of here. I must get out of here! Go, Lin!

Blinded by the pain and numbed by the cold, she stumbled to her feet and staggered away from the building. She didn't know where she was going, and she didn't care. All she knew was that she needed to get as far away from the warehouse as possible.

Her breathing came in short bursts as she labored through the night, stopping at intervals to ride out the pain of yet another contraction. As she walked, she hallucinated her mother.

Mother? What are you doing here?

Keep moving, my child. Don't stop. Keep moving.

But I am so tired. The pain is so bad!

I know. I know, my girl. But you are strong. You're resilient, Wu-Dip. You can do this. Keep moving. Don't stop!

Encouraged by the words of her vision, or delusion, she pressed on in the cold, biting her lip until it bled to keep from crying out in pain.

A strong wave of pain brought Lin to her knees. She gasped with its intensity and arched her back reflexively in response to it.

I'm going to die. I can't walk anymore. Just let me die.

No, my child. She heard her mother's voice in her head once again, this time clearer. *Don't give up. Do this for your child, Wu-Dip. Get up. You know you can. Get up.*

She tried to stand, but her legs refused to bear her weight. *I can't, mother. I can't. I am sorry…*

A butterfly breaks out of its cocoon to begin its life, Wu-Dip. Break out of this cocoon of pain. You can do it.

Lin closed her eyes tightly and mustered all the strength she had left, ignoring the constant cold creeping into her skin. With a grunt, she got to her feet, then continued to stagger through the night farther into the lonely dark alleys. Lin inadvertently stepped into the blanket she was carrying and it fell, but she couldn't bend down to pick it up, so left it behind. But soon, she could walk anymore and collapsed in another alley, making sure to hide behind a large trash container. Though she hadn't seen a soul, she was afraid to be discovered by anyone.

Lin felt a strong urge to push, but restrained herself with a great effort. She took off her gown and spread it on the floor, arranging it into a comfortable bundle. Then, positioning herself over it, she began to push with everything she had.

Blood drenched her legs, and she cried out in pain, breathing hard. Her legs buckled and ached to close. Things around her started to go blurry, but she forced herself to focus. She couldn't lose consciousness. Not now! She had to stay strong, stay present for her baby. This was for her baby.

Once again, she felt the urge to push. She got back to her previous position and pushed harder, soiling herself.

Exhausted, in pain, dirty, wet, and cold, she continued.

Come baby, come out!

She clenched her teeth with the effort and felt gratified when the pain sky-rocketed and she felt the head of her baby begin to crown. She couldn't stop now. She took deep breaths to gather her energy back, then pushed with all of her strength.

Slowly, the baby slid out of her and onto the bundle, closely followed by the placenta. She noticed she'd defecated herself too, but didn't pay much attention to that.

Overjoyed and relieved that it was out, she sat back and gathered her baby up, bundled in the fabric of her gown. She held it close to her, warming it with her own skin, and looked around for a sharp object by the trash bin. Finding a discarded tin, she used its sharp edge to cut the umbilical cord.

The newborn cried.

A quick check revealed it was a girl. It was a gentle, tiny thing. A beautiful, yet fragile girl. "My child," she moaned, looking into the face of her crying baby. "Shhh... It's ok, my butterfly," she said, rocking it. She cleaned the baby as best as she could with her gown and continued to whisper in her ear, "You are my life now. You are my everything."

The baby wouldn't stop crying.

Gently rocking back and forth, Lin began to sing some of the songs of her childhood to the newborn. Once more, overwhelmed by the shivering cold, she felt her vision blur, but forced herself to stay conscious. She needed to take care of her baby.

But she was so weak. So... so... weak...

Her eyes kept closing, when approaching footsteps prompted her to cower farther into the shadows. Despite that, she couldn't stop her whimpering or that of her child's. She watched the shadow of the newcomer lengthen, as whoever it was got closer.

Suddenly, everything went silent. She couldn't hear the sound of the wind anymore. She couldn't hear the cry of her newborn. She couldn't hear the steps of whoever was coming. All she could hear was the sound of her own heartbeat.

Finally, the sound of a shoe making contact with the asphalt and broken glass on the ground shattered the silence and it creeped horror into her veins. Then all the sounds returned at once.

She looked up, and the silohuette of a young man came into view.

At first she trembled in fear, but then her eyes widened when she saw the shiny, blue butterfly pendant resting on his chest.

It was a sign. It had to be.

The young boy ran to her and muttered something in his language, evidently concerned. He studied the scene, taking in her state of nakedness, her shivering, and the newborn in her arms. He looked around, and seeing no one, he quickly tried covering Lin with his own jacket which he quickly shed.

"*¿Hablas español?*" he asked.

Lin understood what he was asking. She shook her head.

The teenage boy said something else as he stood up. He signaled for her to wait and that he would be back.

No, don't leave!

As he turned, Lin suddenly felt a burst of energy that propelled her to her feet and urged her to stop him. She called to him before he had the chance to run off. He stopped and turned around, closing the gap between them once again. She carefully placed her baby in his arms, much to his apparent shock. She sent him a pleading look, then stroked her baby's cheek and kissed her face, then stroked his face too, leaving a smear of blood on it.

"Wu-Dip," she said, smiling weakly.

Her name is Wu-Dip.

"Ooh? Deep?" he vocalized in confusion, arms trembling.

She smiled and repeated herself, "Wu-Dip." This time her voice was frailer.

Wu-Dip. My butterfly.

She sank down to the ground, exhausted. She welcomed the darkness. Her daughter was in safe hands. She knew in her heart that her baby would be okay, and this brought her peace. Through the cascades of hemorrhage, through the sting of hypothermia, through the agonizing pain, Lin remained in peace; her baby was safe.

Lin's parents would never hear from her again. For a while now, they had assumed she was dead. Her lifeless body would soon be found by Wong's goons. But none of those things mattered anymore. Lin's legacy would continue with her baby girl.

Fly, Wu-Dip. Fly.

She closed her eyes and breathed her last breath with a smile on her face.

PART 3

• • •

Lucho

CHAPTER TWENTY-ONE

Ejido Sinaloa, Eastern Outskirts of Mexicali
Summer 1988

The cold crept into the room that morning like a thief on a mission. What remained of the once blazing fire were ashes that were fast becoming cold. Luis "Lucho" Fuentes rolled on his makeshift bed on the floor. Dawn hadn't broken yet, and the wind still howled like a wolf in search of a mate.

The dingy room was crowded with another three little bodies beside his: Pedro, Andres, and Santos. Being the oldest at twelve, Lucho had decided to sleep on the ground on a doubled-up blanket with a long piece of cloth protecting him from the whistling wind. The only bed in the room he left for his younger brothers. They would huddle together and pray the wood they had gathered in the fireplace would last the cold night. Their home was not much better than a shack. It was one of the many houses that dotted the sprawling plains of the south-eastern rural outskirts of Mexicali.

Lucho and his brothers hardly saw their mother, Sofia. For as long as he could remember, Lucho had never seen her in a sober mood. There was always an unfinished bottle with her. Her temper too was something to contend with. She would rant and curse any moving thing. She always told Lucho he would end up like his father: a worthless man that would only come around when it was time to get her pregnant. *How?* Lucho always wondered. He had seen many men but couldn't readily place the one who, with the help of his mother, had brought him into this cruel world.

THE FLIGHT OF THE BUTTERFLY

A whimper came from the creaking bed where one of the restless bodies fidgeted atop it. Lucho opened his eyes slowly and looked at the dirty ceiling; it was mostly covered by pieces of clothing, tied from one end of the wooden house to the other. This was to keep the afternoon heat away during the summer and fall months.

He stood up slowly, with groggy half-open eye lids. He hadn't caught a wink of sleep all night because of Santos's consistent complaints of hunger. Lucho had pleaded with him to wait until morning. By then, there would be enough light to rummage for food in the trash bins behind the supermarket in their underprivileged community.

"Lucho, I cannot wait anymore. My stomach is killing me," Santos said in a broken voice.

Lucho peered through the dark at the face of his brother. The other two breathed in a regular pattern. They were both awake, but were not crying.

"I am sorry, Santos. There is nothing I can do now. The night is still very much around. Hold on for a little while." Lucho stretched his hand in the dark and felt Santos's teary face where he sat on the edge of the bed. Using the back of his palm, Lucho wiped his brother's face dry and ruffled his coarse hair.

"I am really hungry, Lucho," the young lad insisted.

But Luis had nothing to say to him. He was lost in thought.

"I am hungry, and I can't sleep," the child whimpered, sniffing yet again.

The other two boys rolled over on the bed and jumped down. They groped around the side and stood next to Lucho, one to his left and the other to his right.

"When will *Mami* return?" Pedro asked.

He had dropped his head down on Lucho's right shoulder. The question made Lucho cringe. He didn't know what to tell his immediate younger brother. What use was their mother coming back if all she did was cuss all day and drink until nightfall?

"She will return soon, lil' bro. She will."

"Will she bring food?" Andres asked.

"Will she bring me a big cake like the one we saw on that piece of paper you showed us?" Santos added.

"Oh, yes, Santos," Lucho said, though he fought hard to hold back a tear. This wasn't unusual to him. The only way to calm Santos down was to distract him and tell him imaginary stories about having an abundance of food to eat; not just the meager amount they were used to.

"She will!" he continued. "She will not only bring cakes, but she will also bring chocolate—huge bars like the ones in the pictures. She will bring milk and lots of sodas. And then after eating, she will take us out, and we'll drive to the beach in San Felipe. There, we will run around with our arms spread open wide, the wind blowing through our hair. We will chase the sea and run back when it turns to chase us. Santos, we will be a big happy family with a dad that will always carry us on his shoulders."

Lucho paused to gather his thoughts.

"Go on, Luis... go on," Santos squirmed from the bed, and all the boys gathered on the floor by Lucho. The tears were gone from his face and voice, replaced by hope.

"We will go to school like the children in the city. We will work hard, and when the time comes, we'll become doctors and lawyers. Then we will have our own children. You, Santos, will become a good father, and maybe even the president, some day!"

As if on a cue, the two boys beside Luis screamed hooray and together began clapping their hands. By then, light was peeking through the window shutter that was banging noisily in the wind. Lucho looked at Santos, who had a smile on his face.

"It is morning," Lucho said, "and joy comes with it."

Corona, California
Spring 2019

As the man walked up the street, the bag of groceries he held swung from side to side. He smiled satisfactorily to himself. Even though he wasn't where he had envisaged being, he was not where he used to be. He was happily married to one of the most enchanting ladies on Earth, and he had the two most beautiful children. Yes, he was blessed beyond measure, and he was grateful for that.

There were times when he compared himself with Job in the Bible. Truly, his latter had been better than his beginning. He was one who had entered this country illegally and had gone through hell surviving the streets. What had he *not* been involved in? Drugs, gangs, stealing; check, check, check. Luis "Lucho" Fuentes had done it all.

Standing at five feet, nine inches, he had a full head of thick, black hair—although it had started thinning, slightly—his eyes were dark, and his shoulders straight and strong, giving the impression of one able to carry the burden of anyone close to him. His smile came with a dimple, and the scar of a deep cut lay slightly below his elbow. When he walked, his stride was determined, as resolute and confident as the way he spoke.

Now, it was evening, and he was grocery shopping. He had promised to make a special delicacy for his family for dinner, and he was gathering the ingredients to deliver on that promise. They had a reason to celebrate, after all. His son, a prodigy who at fifteen had already finished high school, had recently been offered a full-ride scholarship to study Philosophy at the University of California, Riverside—and Luis couldn't be prouder.

His son reminded him a lot of his younger brother, Santos. As a child, Santos was always teary-eyed and wouldn't sleep at night unless Luis told him imaginary stories of his future. Thinking of Santos made him smile remorsefully.

He turned the corner and crossed the road as he headed to the looming red-and-white Bullseye storefront. Back in his car were four large and heavy grocery bags, but this wouldn't take long. He stepped into the store, and on his way to his office, waved to some of the employees.

At his desk, he grabbed his coat and some reports. He couldn't wait to get home to his wife and kids. He was weary and could use a long shower.

Once done, he found his way back to the parking lot, and after unlocking the car, he dumped the contents of his hands onto the passenger seat. He settled in, turned the ignition, and started the drive on the I-15 toward South Corona.

As he drove up the driveway of the beautiful home where he lived with his family, with a white fence around a luscious, green yard and a porch with a loose board he hadn't gotten around to fixing, he saw his son at the door of the garage with a large grin on his face. He parked the car on the driveway, and his son ran over to hug him as he disembarked.

"Hi, *Papi*, how was your day?"

"Very good, son." He took out the grocery bags and left the car unlocked so Sebastian could help him with his remaining items.

Stepping into the foyer, Luis Fuentes pulled off his shoes. As he hung his coat on the rack inside the closet beside the door, he heard light footsteps echoing through the house, heading toward him. Luis smiled to himself as his soon-to-be thirteen-year-old daughter pounced on him.

"*Buenas noches, Papi,*" she greeted as he planted a kiss on her head of sun-streaked red hair—hair she had inherited from her mother. Her honey-colored eyes were twinkling with excitement, and he knew well that most of it was because she was turning thirteen the next day.

"*Buenas noches,* Alejandra. Where is *Mami?*" Luis asked as his daughter took the groceries he had deposited in the hall.

"She's in the kitchen," Alejandra said, heading in the stated direction.

Luis followed her, eager to see his wife. It had been a long day at work, and he was glad to be home, surrounded by the ones he loved the most: his family.

As he got closer to the kitchen, he could hear the chattering voices of his wife and daughter as well as smell the delicious aroma from the stove. Stepping into the room, he smiled. It was beautiful, with granite countertops and fully stocked cupboards. His wife had put in so much effort and time into making it perfect just for her. She called it her room of solitude. Large bay windows opened onto their large yard out back, which had a gazebo in the corner, a large vegetable garden lining the perimeter, and a patio set.

Luis watched his wife as she placed a pan in the oven. He walked toward her and wrapped her in his arms. Kissing her lightly on the lips, he greeted her. "*Hola, mi amor.* I said I was going to take care of dinner tonight."

"Yes, I know. It's just I decided to help you out a little and prepare dessert. You know, make things a little less stressful for you." Samantha smiled up at her husband as she brushed imaginary lint off his sleeve. "And judging by how tired you look, I'm glad I did. You should get some rest. I can make—"

"No, babe. I promised Sebastian I would prepare something special for him, and I want to. Don't worry about me. A cold shower, and in the blink of an eye, I will be as good as new."

"All right. But are you up for..." Samantha looked behind her to make sure Alejandra was not listening—she was busy unpacking the groceries—and lowered her voice as she said, "Are you up for the celebration tomorrow? We could postpone 'till Sunday, after service."

"Trust me, *mi amor*; I am perfectly fine. You know how much I enjoy cooking for the kiddos, so Alejandra's celebration tomorrow won't be a burden. Besides, look at our little girl's eyes! Do you really want to break her heart?" Luis gently turned his wife toward Alejandra, who was at that moment putting fruit away and humming a song.

"Oh, all right. But her eyes don't have that same effect on me, like they do on you. I wonder why that is!" Samantha mused as she started unpacking the remaining bag.

"Maybe it's because they are a replica of yours; and you know how much you love having your way just by using the power of those eyes alone. She's learning from the master, herself," Lucho whispered as he slapped his wife's bottom gently.

Samantha chuckled and lightly swatted him on the shoulder. "Ok, then, Lucho. Go on and have that shower so you can get started on dinner. The kids will be complaining soon; you know how impatient they are."

"Yes, my lady! *Como usted mande.* You're the boss." Luis gave a mock bow, and with a smile playing on his lips, he left the kitchen.

Later that evening, as Luis stirred a mixture of garlic, onion, lemon, olive oil, chili powder, and salt, his actions became mechanical. As he added the cilantro and lemon pepper, his mind was already several years away, to a time in his past.

Ejido Sinaloa, Mexicali
Summer 1988

Lucho roamed the unpaved streets of the dwellings at the eastern rural outskirts of the city. He hoped he would be able to find some food here, or at least some money to buy food. The people who lived in the area might have also been poor, but the very fact they could afford a hard roof over their heads and a house made of bricks, instead of the wooden shack of a home that he and his brothers had nearby, proved they certainly were doing better than them.

Hearing a voice, he hid behind a wall and watched a woman come out of a room whose door had certainly seen better days. He watched her for a minute, and as she walked toward him, the twelve-year-old boy hid in the shadows.

As soon as he was sure she had gone down the stairs, Lucho tiptoed toward the chosen door of this apartment. The owner was not around, but he couldn't say the same about the other neighbors.

Casting a cursory glance behind him, he brought out his beloved lock pick which he had been fashioned from nails from a lumberyard. It didn't take long before he was in, and Lucho's eyes scanned the scantily furnished living room.

There isn't much time, he cautioned himself.

He headed toward the kitchen. There was a fridge next to the only window. Opening it revealed a half-full carton of milk, as well as half a loaf of bread.

This will do for a while. The boy smiled to himself.

But he was not finished yet.

He dumped his finds in a plastic bag he had brought along and headed to the next room, straight for the worn dresser which stood next to a creaking bed.

To his delight, the dresser was unlocked. That most likely meant that there were no valuables within it. All the same, he ransacked the drawers, pulling them out and dumping their contents around him. As expected, he found nothing valuable.

Lucho scanned the room quickly and then studied the mattress. With all his might, he pushed it over and raised the wooden stands below it. A perspiring Luis was rewarded with a brown envelope. Opening it, he counted four-hundred pesos in total. This brought a smile to his lips, a motion that had eluded him for as long as he could remember.

As he was about to leave the room, he stopped, and with a groan, returned two-hundred pesos. Guilt. He had a conscience, after all.

After that, as quickly as his legs could take him, he ran out of the complex with his prize, not once looking back.

Corona, California
Spring 2019

The ding of the oven indicating the enchiladas were ready snapped Luis out of his flashback. He quickly retrieved them and smiled as he inhaled the delicious aroma. He got to work garnishing the enchiladas with the cilantro-based *mojo de ajo* he had made, along with some freshly diced tomato. Then he turned to the red rice he had left to sit, removed the bay leaf, and fluffed it. Finally, he turned to the beans and further seasoned the pot after tasting them.

"Alejandra, please set the table. Dinner is ready!" he called.

"Ok, *Papi!*" she replied excitedly.

The delicious aroma of enchiladas, roasted salsa, beans, and red rice circulated in the room as the Fuentes family sat down to enjoy their meal.

"This smells delicious. Thank you, Pa!" Sebastian said after they had prayed.

Lucho smiled. "*De nada, mijo.* You're very much welcome."

The dinner consisted of an overly excited Alejandra going on and on about her birthday celebration the next day. Every spoonful that went into her mouth was followed by talk on what the occasion would consist of.

"Yeah... yeah," Sebastian finally groaned halfway through the meal. "You do know that it's not going to be a big occasion, right? Just close friends and family. It's not your *quinceañera* yet, you fool!"

"Yes, I know that. But that doesn't mean all the games I've mentioned can't take place. It's going to be so much fun!" she squealed excitedly.

"Of course, it is," Sebastian agreed sarcastically with a roll of his large, dark-brown eyes—the eyes of his father.

"Anyway..." Alejandra said, loud enough to show Sebastian she had chosen to ignore him. She turned to her mother, bouncing up and down. "There's going to be a *piñata* too, right?"

"You want a *piñata* at your party? I thought you're too grown for that now?" Sebastian teased with twinkling eyes.

"A whole case of Mexican candy at my disposal? There is no way I'm outgrowing that—ever!" Alejandra shook her head vigorously, her ponytail bouncing. "The very thought makes me miserable. Besides, if you don't want any candy, then you don't have to have any."

"No, I'll have some too," her brother responded with a mouth full of food.

Samantha reached over and touched her daughter's chin, lightly. "Yes, my baby girl. Whatever you want. But go on and finish your meal so we can finish the plans."

This reassurance caused Alejandra to increase the speed at which she dug into her food, much to the humor of her parents and brother. The dessert of *tres leches* cake, which Samantha had prepared, rounded off the meal.

While Sebastian and Alejandra cleaned up the kitchen, Luis and Samantha reclined in deck chairs underneath the pergola of their rooftop garden, which was already filled with blossoming flowers as spring progressed. The yard of the house was large, and they had divided it between a vegetable garden and a playing space for the kids.

Together, they had created a marvelous wonderland on their rooftop. The rooftop garden was of a cedar patio design. It consisted of ornamental plants, the pergola, wooden dining furniture, lounge furniture, swings attached to the pergola, and an outdoor kitchenette. It was beautiful and well organized, with enough space for the blooming flowers, relaxation, and entertainment.

A set of spiraling staircases on either side of the house led from the ground level up to the roof, so guests did not have to go through the stress of passing through their home to get to the rooftop whenever they visited.

"It's so beautiful out here..." Samantha said softly.

They were both wrapped up in a crocheted wool blanket knitted by Alejandra, their chairs drawn close.

Luis chuckled lightly. "You always say that."

"That's because it always is, *mi amor*. God has been so faithful and loving to us!" Samantha said, a happy smile curling up her lips.

"I know, my love. He truly has." Luis kissed her head of red hair, and they both settled into a comfortable silence, staring at the beauty that lay all around them.

The next day dawned bright and clear. There was not a speck of rain in sight, much to the delight of Alejandra who was up by 5 a.m., giddy to get the preparations started. The party was to start a little before noon, and as soon as everyone was up, courtesy of Alejandra's consistent knocking on every door, they got to work cooking and organizing the decorations. While the ladies took charge of the food, the men took charge of setting up the whole house for the party.

A couple of hours before noon, everything was ready. The food had been laid out on linen on the long dining table with sparkling silverware. The grill was filled and ready to start its work, and the *piñata* had been hung up on the tallest tree in their backyard. Alejandra looked around in awe at all they had accomplished.

By 11 a.m., the guests started arriving. Samantha's parents arrived first, bearing gifts for Alejandra, as well as Sebastian.

"Congratulations to both of you!" their grandfather said after the hugs and pleasantries. More guests had started arriving, and the children had run off to greet their friends. "You have two beautiful children right there. Your home is blessed."

"Thank you, Daddy." Samantha hugged him again and walked off with her mother to welcome the new guests.

Samantha's father, Jose Gomez, towered over Luis at six feet, two inches. He smiled at his son-in-law with a full, white-bearded face. He had not always liked Luis for his daughter, though; he had only succumbed to the union after pleas from Samantha and his wife. But in a matter of a couple of years into their marriage, Luis had proven himself to him. Now, they were closer than ever.

"Thank you, Don Jose," Lucho said.

Don Jose shook his head, his balding white hair matching the scruff on his face. "That's no problem, Luis. Come on, let's start grilling. This *carne* is not going to cook itself."

At every family occasion, the men were always in charge of the barbecue, whether at the Gomez's in the Riverside hills or the Fuentes' in South Corona, and by noon, the rooftop and the backyard were thriving. Food and conversation were flowing. The *piñata* had already been broken, and all the children had had their fill. The party was a combination of American and Mexican food. The *carne asada* tacos seemed to be a favorite among the guests. There were also ice cream sundaes for dessert.

As Luis stood over the heat of the grill, he heard a familiar voice calling his name. His head snapped up, and he smiled at the sight of Pedro and Andres. They were hugging Sebastian and Alejandra. Luis sighed.

If only Santos could be here.

THE FLIGHT OF THE BUTTERFLY

CHAPTER TWENTY-TWO

Mexicali Rural Outskirts
Fall 1988

"Lucho, how did you hurt yourself?" Pedro asked, staring unblinkingly at the bleeding gash on his oldest brother's arm.

Today had been a successful day for Lucho, in the grand scheme of things. He had been lucky enough to get into the big house just inside town. It had been unoccupied up until a few days ago. He usually didn't go that close to the city, but his friend, Marcos, had informed him that the owners had moved in and were loaded. So, Lucho had set out for the house which was about a forty-minute walk away—though on an empty stomach it seemed like an eternity.

True to Marcos's word, there had been a lot of food in the kitchen, and Lucho had grabbed as much as he could carry. This time, however, he had not been able to find any money.

The problem had been leaving the compound undetected. He had been noticed, and the dogs pursued him. That was what had caused him to go scurrying over the high fence, and he had fallen smack on his face on the other side. At least he had survived and had plenty of food to show for his efforts.

Of course, he was not going to tell Pedro any of these things. He didn't want him more worried than he already was.

"It's nothing, Pedro," Lucho said as he cleaned his wound with some water. "Don't worry about it. I just scratched it against the chain-link fence around that big house close to town while I was scaling over it."

Pedro sat down next to his brother and took the bloodied cloth Lucho was using to dab at his arm. "Well, let me help."

They were seated in front of their crumbling house at the end of the dirt road. The sun was soon to set, and with it, yet another day had passed that their mother did not remember their existence.

"It's okay, Pedro. As long as I was able to bring home some food, it doesn't matter if I got hurt. The little ones should eat first. Where are they?" Lucho asked, looking around.

"Playing soccer at the field," Pedro responded. "They should be back soon."

There was an improvised dirt field at the end of the colony, with actual goal posts and ratty equipment that had been donated by some organization. The people of the community had come together and cleaned up a space within the trash piles and created a field, marked with lines and everything. The kids would spend countless hours playing soccer—that is, whenever one could find or afford to buy a ball.

Pedro took the heavy bag of stolen food from his older brother and headed inside. As he walked away, he asked no one in particular, "Why would someone have multiple kids when they can't even care for one?" It was a question they had all asked often.

Soon, their mother would breeze in and demand she be fed from the gains of Lucho's hard work. He shook his head in fatigue, taking in a deep breath.

Right on cue, the scruffy woman staggered up the dirt driveway, muttering profanities to herself. Her hair was a mess, and she reeked of alcohol. "Lucho, what are you doing out here? Go look after your brothers!" she shouted, then slammed the door as she went inside.

Outside the house, Lucho remained deep in thought. He was tired of their situation. He loved his brothers, there was no doubt about that, but he was tired of having to always scrape together food, of getting into trouble to provide for them while their so-called mother chugged on liquor wherever she found it, only returning to cause pain whenever she deemed fit through incessant shouting, vomiting, and drunken spews. Sometimes, Lucho felt it was better when she was away. He was sincerely tired and wished for a way out of this misery.

As he sat there, his mind tossed and turned the conversation he'd had with Marcos yesterday. They had sat off to the side of the soccer field while a few of their friends kicked the one good ball around.

"I'm leaving tomorrow," he said blatantly.

"Leaving?" Lucho scrunched his face in disbelief. "Where?"

"To the city. Where else? I'm smart enough to know there's nothing life can offer me out here. Who wants to live in a poor, rural *rancho*? You should be smart too and leave with me. We're going to die in our homes that you can barely call homes, unless we do something about it."

Lucho shook his head, tapping a deflated ball with his fist. "I can't leave; you know that. My brothers are too important to me, and they're too young for me to travel that far with all three of them. It would be too chaotic."

A crashing bottle inside the house broke Luis's concentration. His mother yelled, and Santos started to cry. With a heavy sigh, Luis dragged himself inside the house to protect his family.

Again.

Their mother left before the sun went up on Sunday morning, and another week without her began. As the days went on and the week ended once more, the older boys dreaded the arrival of their crazy mother's antics. Every weekend, their mother would show up and begin her drunken spews like clockwork. Santos, on the other hand, young and eager, always craved her presence. He was still quite naïve and not fully aware of the harsh realities that life had thrown at them.

As usual, she arrived that weekend holding a bottle of booze in one hand and a strong-smelling pipe in the other. She burst through the door without a hello, settled on the floor, and lit the end of the pipe. Luis could not help but wonder what she was smoking this time.

Her red and bloodshot eyes looked around at the four boys, and they settled on Lucho. She was a lot quieter than her last visit, and Luis didn't know if that was more dangerous or not.

Glaring at him, she asked, "Where's the food? We got anything in this dump?"

Lucho shook his head as he whispered in response, "No."

This answer brought about a string of expletives aimed at Lucho. She stood, swaying back and forth as she flailed her arms and spouted every Spanish curse word under the blistering sun.

Pedro and Andres retreated to the bed, staying out of sight.

Santos began to sob. "Why are you yelling?" he asked her and collapsed to the floor.

To round it off, their mother spat at Lucho, smiling mischievously. She then turned to Santos and motioned for the sobbing boy to approach her. "Come here, my baby," she said, leaning down to hug him.

Suddenly, she slapped him lightly on the face, and at once, his silent sobs were snuffed out. "That's right," she said. "You're learning exactly what happens when you cry like that. It gives mommy a headache. I'll let your brothers slap you around next time."

The woman pulled out a few one- and two-peso coins from the pocket of her alcohol drenched coat and handed it to Andres.

Andres hesitantly held out his hand, and she dropped the coins in his palm. "What are these for?"

"Go on," she said, nodding her head toward the door. The boys resisted the urge to plug their noses at the stench that came from her. "Take that sobbing mess out of here. All of you get out and get something for yourselves... but not that one." She pointed at Luis, who stood near the door, leaning against the wall.

"It's okay, bros," Lucho said, "You don't have to get me anything."

Andres collected Santos and pulled him outside. The youngest brother begged for their mother to come, but she was focused on Luis. Pedro stayed behind, watching Lucho and his mother apprehensively from his position on the bed. And as soon as the other two left, she took Lucho's ear and dragged him into the inner room of the house.

Lucho stumbled along without a word, though his ear burned. He knew better than to try to reason with his mother. But this didn't stop his brother from calling out.

"*Mami*, don't do that!" Pedro cried. "You're hurting him!"

But his pleas for mercy fell on deaf ears. Without letting go of Lucho's ear, their mother stomped over to Pedro and slapped him hard. He squeaked from the burning sensation on his cheek. "Behave," she said firmly, then turned her attention back to her eldest. "You are getting a job," she slurred as she jabbed at his chest.

Lucho looked up at her, confused, and this resulted in a hard slap on the cheek.

"Don't give me that stupid look!" she shouted.

While Lucho was still reeling from the sting on his left cheek, she pushed him to the dirt floor and stood over him. As he stared up at the looming creature before him, he felt a mixture of several feelings, ranging from pain to disgust to hate. But also, pity. He could easily overpower her; but he wouldn't. She was still his mother, even though she didn't act like one.

"My job is taking care of my brothers," Lucho whispered.

"No, that's my job."

"Since when?"

"Don't talk back to me," she said, kicking his gut. Her attack was weak, but Lucho pretended it paralyzed him. "You're working at a lumberyard."

"What about school?"

"You heard me. School is not for you. You are going to work over at the lumberyard at the edge of the city. All your earnings will be given to me by the owner, so don't be expecting any. I will use that money to care for your brothers. Don't worry, you will still get to live here. It's about an hour walk every morning and then again back in the evening. Don't think you can skip out on it. I'll know if you're not there. You don't think I'll let you out of my sight and give you leeway to do as you please, do you? Do you?" She crouched beside him and held his chin firmly in her grip. "You start tomorrow." Then she dropped him.

As she turned to leave, Lucho mustered all the courage he had and replied, "I will not." Standing up, he brushed himself off. "I know that whatever earnings I get will be used to buy your drinks and not for my brothers' welfare."

His mother turned around slowly. "Are you talking back at me, boy? Huh?" Her hand flew across his cheek once more, much harder than before. Lucho stumbled with the force, prompting his brother to catch him from falling.

"No, *Mami!*" Pedro shouted. "He didn't mean it. Don't hurt him."

"It's okay, Pedro," Lucho said softly, brushing his brother's protective arms away from his middle.

"Both of you, shut up!" She slapped Lucho again, and this time, Pedro looked away.

Lucho backed into the wall as his mother neared. And one slap led to another, and then another; all that Lucho could do was sit on the ground, hunched over while she poured all her frustrations on him. Better him than his brothers, he told himself.

Lucho tried to stop his legs from shaking as he pulled them into his chest; he would not show her weakness. But the woman yanked on his ear to pull him to stand. "You will work there, understood? Or else, I will kill you! I cannot have a useless child around here." She spat in his face once more and swayed out of the room.

As soon as the door slammed, Pedro jumped from the bed to tend to his brother. "I am so sorry, Lucho. I am so sorry!" He helped Luis to get to his feet. "What will you do? I don't think she is lying that she will kill you."

"I know," Lucho said, looking into his brother's pained eyes. This was the push that he needed. "I must get out of here, Pedro, and I have to leave you all behind. My only fear is that you will face the brunt of her anger." The words spilled out of his mouth, tasting bitter on his tongue.

Pedro remained silent for a moment. At first, his eyebrows contorted into a frown, eager to object to losing his eldest brother. But when his eyes dropped to scan their dilapidated home, his brow softened.

"It doesn't matter, Lucho. It really doesn't." Pedro shook his head. "I don't care about that. You must go."

Just before dawn, while his brothers were all asleep and his mother was half-asleep, still nursing her bottle, Lucho snuck out of the only home he had ever known. It had not really been a home, but his brothers were there. He had a family.

He didn't want to leave his brothers behind and knew they would pay for what he was doing. But he couldn't stay any longer, so he began the long walk toward the city through the arduous desert.

By the time the sun had risen and was blistering his skin underneath his thin clothes, he had reached the lumberyard at the edge of the urban part of the city. The twelve-year-old looked around, searching for something useful. In the midst of silence, Lucho heard voices nearing; his heart bounced up to his throat. Quickly, and as quietly as possible, he climbed into the back of a delivery truck that appeared as if it had just been loaded.

If they find me, I'll be in so much trouble!

The adult male voices grew in volume. Lucho covered his mouth with one hand, trying his best to not let any noise alert them, and used his other to balance himself. He swallowed as he waited in fear, unseen among the mountains of parcels. Two shadows passed by the truck doorway. One separated from the other and entered the cabin meters from where Lucho crouched, only a thin, metal wall between them. The other pulled the doors closed, plunging him into darkness.

Moments later, the engine started running and then they were moving. He could only hope that they were moving toward the city center. But it didn't matter, really; he would hitch a ride wherever the truck took him. And there, he would start all over again.

He hoped Marcos was right about the city. Either way, it couldn't be any worse than what he had back home.

THE FLIGHT OF THE BUTTERFLY

CHAPTER TWENTY-THREE

Corona, California
Spring 2019

"Hey, Lucho! Where did you drift off to, bro?"

Luis felt a hand on his shoulder. His eyes darted up, and he saw his brother, Pedro, looking at him worriedly. "Are you okay?"

Luis forced a smile. "*Si*, Pedro. Don't worry about me. *¿Cómo estás tú?*"

"*Muy bien*, bro. I am doing great, thanks for asking. But... are *you* sure you're okay?" Pedro still had a concerned look on his face. He had always been the worrier among them, Lucho thought with a smile.

"What's funny?"

"It's nothing. *En serio*, I am fine. Steak?" Luis asked him, motioning to the grill.

"Uh... *gracias*, bro... but I'd rather wait for the next batch. You can have this one," Pedro said, wrinkling his nose.

Luis looked down, and his eyes widened when he saw the black pieces of meat, coated with char. He shook his head. He had been so deep in his thoughts that he had burned the steaks.

Pedro had started laughing and didn't see Andres creep up behind him. As soon as Andres pushed him, the cup of apple juice he was holding spilled onto his shirt, and in the twist of a few seconds, it was Luis who was now laughing. The look on Pedro's face was quite hilarious.

"Andres!" Pedro glared at his brother, who took shelter behind Luis. "You ruined my shirt, you fool!"

"Sorry, bro! That was not the plan. The plan was actually to make you spill it on your pants," the gleeful Andres replied.

"Why, you little bastard..."

Lucho slapped his brother gently on the back. "It's okay, Pedro. You know how crazy Andres can be. Go on, talk to Sam. She'll help you out with one of my shirts."

"Thanks." Pedro threw one last dirty look at Andres and left, in search of his sister-in-law.

"Andres..." Lucho rounded on the youngest brother, "will you ever stop being so mischievous?"

"Oh, come on, man! Admit it was at least a bit funny."

"It was, but only for the first few seconds. You're always scaring us, fool," Luis said as he dumped the burned steaks in a trash can beside him.

"Okay, okay. *Fine!*" Andres whined. "I'll apologize to him when he returns... maybe. But for now, go on, brosky, you've been here for a while." He waved his brother away. "Go have some fun with your family. I'll take charge here. At least I won't burn the meat."

Lucho ignored the subtle jab, untied his apron and left it and the grilling utensils with his brother. "*Orale, simón!* Sounds good to me. Thanks, man."

Luis smiled as he approached his laughing children who were deep in conversation with their friends. He ruffled their hair as he walked past them, heading toward the pastor, who had just arrived and was chatting with Samantha's parents.

As time went by and the sun dipped lower in the sky, Samantha finally brought out the chocolate cake, decorated with thirteen candles. Everyone gathered around the table to sing to Alejandra and clapped when she blew the candles out. The guests continued to converse and indulge in cake, and soon, deep oranges and reds overtook the sky, and friends and family started to disperse.

When nightfall came, Pastor Terry officially ended the party with a short prayer for the stragglers that remained. The guests returned home, and the kids went to their rooms. Luis got ready for bed and leaned against the doorframe of their master bathroom.

"That gleeful smile on Alejandra's face completely melted my heart, *mi amor*. I am so glad I am getting things right in our lives. The mistakes of my past..." Luis choked on the words he was about to say.

"Oh, babe!" Samantha rushed from the bathroom with her long, red hair braided down her back. She took her husband's hand and led him to the bed so they could sink down together. "The mistakes of your past are just that... in the past. Old things have passed away, and behold, all things have become new. We have a beautiful and blessed family." She placed a tender hand on his cheek. "I'm proud of you, and the kids are, too. Pedro and Andres, as well. We are *all* proud of you! Don't let the past weigh you down. We've all made mistakes. It's part of being human, Lucho."

Lucho held his wife's hand to his face and closed his eyes. Two young faces hid in the blackness. "But... Santos... and Woo Deep... Every day, I wonder about that little girl. What of her? Is she still alive? Is she okay? I can't help it that the past keeps resurfacing in my thoughts." He opened his eyes to stare at his wife, but now they were filled with tears. "And maybe I could've done something for Santos..."

"Oh, my love! Come here," Samantha sighed as she cradled him in her arms, just as she did whenever Lucho felt his past was coming back to haunt him. He had told her of the little girl he had fathered for almost a year, and despite their efforts, it was impossible for them to know what had become of her.

With Santos, on the other hand, it was easy; his fate was definite and known. That was why, up until this day, Lucho felt he had never done anything right in his past.

Mexicali, Mexico
Fall 1989

Lucho adjusted his position on the bed of dirty newspapers. The night was chilly, and he could feel himself coming down with a cold. His eyes darted around the pavement, glancing over Pato and Addy, who were on the far end of the street, huddled together as they also tried to dull the bite of the cold. He might as well join them.

Lucho stood up quite giddily, as the effects of his earlier sniff had not yet worn off, and made his way toward them. They handed over the plastic bag which he accepted gratefully. Putting his nose in, he took a long, good sniff of the glue that lay within it. This brought about a fit of coughing, but he did not mind. He felt good.

He took another long sniff and returned the bag to Addy. Lucho sat back and rested against the glass partition of the bus stop they were occupying. His mind was far away. He thought about his brothers, but in an instant, he brushed them off, pushing them to the back of his mind. This was no time to think about them; it was happy thoughts time.

He had been living on the streets for five months now, and life couldn't be greater. He was living freely, doing as he pleased, and whenever he got food, he didn't have to think about sharing it with anyone.

The summer had been difficult, though. Doing odd jobs under the blistering Mexicali sun's rays had not been fun, and he was glad it was over... for this year, at least.

Now, the days were warm, and the nights were cold. He knew that with winter coming, there would be no more warm days. And he would soon have to worry about the freezing temperatures of the desert city nights. Still, he would rather bear the cold than toil through that scorching summer.

He pulled the bag from Addy's grasp and returned to his sniffing.

"Tomorr... tomorrow is Saturday. You... you guys..." Pato slurred. He had been on a consistent sniffing spree since sundown and was already very high.

"Uh huh. We know that... What about it?" Addy asked.

She pushed Lucho's head away from the bag and took another sniff, earning a glare from him.

"Well... cust... customers, of course. The *gabacho* tourists will be arriving at the border to come into town, stupids. It will be the perfect hunting ground for easy cash..."

"Hunting ground? Like animals?" Addy asked again, quite confused.

"No, dummy." Pato pushed at her head, and this caused her to slap him in retaliation. "I meant there will be enough pesos there for us. We just... just need to find the right set... of people. You know, those... with bul...ging pockets."

"Oh, *simón*! Perfect!" Addy exclaimed, but that excitement lasted barely a minute before she fell into a drug induced sleep.

She was soon followed by Pato; Lucho was left alone in silence.

He could not help but remember that his birthday was in a few weeks' time. He would be turning thirteen. He would make a lot of money tomorrow, he resolved. Then, he would be able to get something stronger for Pato, Addy, and himself. Maybe some of the good, much stronger stuff; the one that they called heroin was making its way around the area. He grinned to himself, satisfied with his plan.

Saturday, just like every other day in the life of the young runaway, consisted of hustling around with a window wiper, cleaning windshields.

Come late afternoon, Lucho hitchhiked the first part of the trip back to his abode, and for the remainder of the distance, he walked. That was his usual. They were not permitted to sleep on the streets, of course, and he didn't need the police to raid their pavement and send them away or throw them behind bars. Minors were supposed to be in school during the day, not living as the homeless, wandering the streets. And if they found them, they would surely take them. If he was taken in, his mother would probably come for him then. He shook his head at the bitter thought of his mother stumbling toward him and dragging him back by the ear.

By the time he reached the pavement of Lopez Mateos Boulevard, it was almost sundown. This was where he called home; no one here would try to take away his earnings.

As Lucho got closer to the boulevard, he slowed down. He was elated because, just as he had anticipated, he had made a lot of money at the border. A lot for a kid like him, at least. It was a matter of perspective.

As he crossed the road, a car without license plates sped past. He didn't notice much about the car, except for the tinted windows. And then, all hell broke loose. Its windows rolled down, and Lucho saw a black object reflecting the rays of the sun. He realized it was the barrel of a gun and dodged for the closest cover he could find: a tree.

In a matter of a few seconds, the occupants of the car had emptied the barrels of their guns into the body of a fellow street kid: Wen. Lucho looked on in horror. The driver alighted the car, approached Wen, and emptied his barrel into the unmoving boy's torso. The man reloaded and emptied the gun a final time into Wen's head.

Lucho was at a vantage position where he could see everything as it happened. He swallowed and held his mouth with two hands to prevent the outburst that was about to erupt from it.

Lucho heard the driver speak to the seventeen-year-old's lifeless body. "The dragon sends his regards."

The driver, a tall and thin light-skinned Mexican cowboy, spat on Wen and returned to the car to drive off. Only when the car's brake lights disappeared in the distance, did Lucho feel able to emerge from of his hiding spot.

He approached Wen's body cautiously and almost threw up at the sight that lay before him. Wen's body and clothes were all ridden with bullet holes, and his blood, dark and sticky, pooled around him like a shadow. His head was the most terrifying sight; it had been bashed in by the force of the bullets that had made contact with it. Parts of his brain were on the ground beside shards of skull, mushy, disintegrated, and soggy from the blood that pooled around him.

Suddenly, Lucho felt lightheaded. He turned away from the mutilated corpse and threw up right on the side of the street.

What had Wen done that was so bad he had to die such a painful and terrifyingly gruesome death? He was only a few years older than him. As Lucho heaved once more, he felt a hand on his shoulder. It was Addy.

She pulled him up. "Let's go, Lucho."

"But... but... Wen..." Luis said tearfully.

He had not known Wen very well, but to think the guy had died so badly made him feel terrible.

"He is gone. We have to leave now!" Addy urged him.

She placed her hand in his and started to run. Lucho didn't notice when his legs started pumping, but when he looked back, Wen was out of sight.

Corona, California
Spring 2019

Luis stood at the kitchen sink and watched birds fly around, just out of reach. He refilled his mug, and after inhaling the aroma of the strong brew, he slowly sipped it. He heard his wife's voice calling out to him, and soon, she was in the kitchen. She gave him a quick kiss on the lips and hurried him out of the house. Alejandra was already seated in the car, waiting for him.

"Come on, *Papi*. Let's go!" she urged him.

"You seem excited," he teased her with a grin as he turned the key in the ignition.

He pulled out of their detached two-car garage. As he did, Alejandra waved at her mother and shouted, as was customary for her every morning she left for school.

"See you later, alligator!"

"In a while, crocodile!" Samantha replied from the front porch.

Luis tried to hide the smile that was threatening to show on his lips. Those exact words had been a pattern for his wife and daughter ever since elementary school. Some things just never change. He chuckled lightly to himself. He liked it, and he didn't want any of this to change.

The drive to La Sierra Preparatory School in Riverside was in no way quiet, because it consisted of the young girl going on and on about her party. Lucho just smiled. She was not talking about it in a boastful or proud manner; on the contrary, she was being grateful and very happy.

Soon enough, they arrived at the drop-off driveway. Luis peeked at his watch; it was just ten minutes past eight. As soon as he cut the engine, Alejandra threw her slim arms around his shoulders and squealed.

"*Muchas gracias, Papi*! I love you."

Luis laughed and kissed her on the head. "I love you too, baby. Just keep being the good girl that you've always been."

"Of course!" She nodded, hugged him one more time, kissed him on the cheek, and ran out of the car to meet a trio of her friends who were waiting for her by the gated entrance.

"Good morning, Mr. Fuentes!" the three girls chorused as they waved hello.

"Good morning, girls. How are your parents?" he asked.

"They are doing well, sir," one of the girls said as the other two bobbed their respective heads in agreement.

"Okay, girls. Well... take care and be good." Luis nodded and shifted gears.

Before he pulled out, he stopped. Sticking his head out the window, he asked, "Do you have basketball practice today after school, Ali?"

"Yes, I do!" Alejandra nodded.

"Okay, then. See you later, *mi amor*."

"Bye, *Papi*." Alejandra waved as he pulled away.

Luis drove his silver sedan into the Bullseye parking lot in The Crossings outlet stores in South Corona. As he walked in, he was bombarded by greetings, which he returned heartily. His eyes darted around the cases and boxes that surrounded the back room, making sure that everything was in order to be placed on the sales floor. When he was satisfied that all was prepared, he headed to his office, where he said a short prayer for the day that lay ahead of him. The man pulled out his cell phone and dialed his wife. She picked up on the second ring.

"*Hola, mi amor*." Her beautiful voice floating from the other end sounded as creamy as chocolate, and he couldn't help the smile that crept up his face.

"Hi, babe. How's your day going?"

"It's going well so far. But it just started." She laughed quietly. "I trust you're at the office already, and Alejandra is—"

"She is already in class by now. What time is your meeting?" he enquired.

"It's at noon. And—"

"And you sound nervous." He chuckled softly. "Don't worry so much; you can do this! What did we discuss with the kids last night before bed?" he reminded her.

"Instead of worrying so much about issues in our lives, we should turn to God with our burdens."

"And...?"

He could tell Samantha was smiling; her spirits were already lifted.

"And if God always feeds the birds of the air, who do not gather food, and array the lilies of the field who neither toil nor spin, and clothes the grasses of the field who tomorrow will be cast into the oven... why then should we worry about anything, when our Father in Heaven knows what we have need of?'"

"Exactly! Cast your cares upon Him and do not worry. He is in control. Okay?"

"You're right." She let out a long sigh, as if releasing stress from her lungs. "Thanks for being here and reminding me that my faith shouldn't waver. And thanks for checking in on me."

"Go on and get ready for that meeting. And know this... even if this does not go through, there will be other opportunities. Do not stress about it."

"I know. Okay, then; I'll talk to you later. I love you, Lucho."

She hung up, leaving Luis staring at the phone happily. He believed she would land a great job soon. Samantha had been working at a design firm for years. But earlier in the year, a few weeks after she had been promoted to Interior Design Director, the company had folded, and of course, all its employees had lost their jobs. But Lucho had faith that her big break was fast approaching.

Luis got back to work. He went through some reports and the inventories, as well as consumers' evaluations for the past week. He was the store team leader, who functioned as a manager of this large Bullseye branch—one of the biggest in Southern California—and he always put his best efforts into his job. Luis believed that customer satisfaction was one of the most important aspects to a successful business. It built trust between the merchant and its customers, and that trust leads to loyalty.

Luis's head snapped up when he heard loud noises—the clanking of metal, shouts. As he rounded his desk to go outside and investigate, his door burst open. It was one of the checkout cashiers, Monica.

"Oh, good! Mr. Fuentes, you have to come quick," she gasped.

"Why? What is wrong?" Lucho was already out of his office, headed toward the source of the ruckus with long strides; Monica struggled to keep up.

The noise was coming from the baby section of the store, so whatever was happening had to be major for him to hear it from his office on the other side of the building.

"A shoplifter was caught! Well... two, actually," Monica informed him.

"Teenagers getting up to mischief, I'm guessing?"

"No—it's two little boys!"

CHAPTER TWENTY-FOUR

Mexicali, Mexico
Winter 1989

The young boy took a long sniff from the packet in his hands. He shook his head as the effect of the substance hit him like a train. He sniffed, coughed and then wiped his nose with the back of his hand. Standing up, he stretched his muscles, kicked his legs out, and flexed his arms. He had been sat for a long time, tightly between two cars encasing the small convenience store.

He started forward and then quickly returned to the other side of the corner. No, he needed more courage. He stuck his nose in the bag, inhaled, and became numb.

Perfect.

He pulled up the hood of the sweatshirt he had taken from a clothesline earlier in the week, and with his back hunched over, headed for the store entrance.

The muffled ringing of the overhead bell accompanied him inside. He looked around the store, his eyes settling on the cashier. He was a young man with matted brown hair and hooded brows. His lips were moving, but the boy couldn't hear anything. It was just a muffled sound.

The boy turned away and started walking down the aisle, looking for what he desperately needed. At the top shelf in the second aisle, he found it: canned foods. He looked over at the storekeeper and saw he was floating. *Man, that fix was powerful.*

The boy shook his head to wipe away the murkiness, threw three cans of food into a basket, and continued down another aisle that led to linen. As soon as he saw it, his red, drugged eyes lit up.

The boy pulled the long, wool blanket out of its packaging and, looking back at the cashier and seeing that he was paying him no attention, he wrapped the blanket around the three cans of food and placed it back in its wrapping. Then, carrying the package in one hand, he moved stealthily toward the door. Once close to the counter, he bent low and kept going until he was out.

But the bell rang, muffled above his head as the cool, winter air hit him in the face. In the mixture of sensations, the boy didn't think to run. He was thrown to the ground, his cheek pushed into the pavement.

"You thief!" he heard a voice shout.

He rolled over and saw the cashier looming over him. He kicked the boy in the ribs and he felt the sharp pain jetting through him. As he curled up, another blow landed on his back. And then another one.

He words like "thief," "druggy," and "*tecolín*." But he didn't care if he was all of those things. He just wanted the pain to stop, and he welcomed the soothing feeling that was suddenly hovering over him. He was now fully numbed to the pain.

A warm hand landed on his shoulder, but he wanted to drift away. The hand kept shaking him, bringing him back to the pain. He opened his eyes and saw a man's faces inches away from his own. The man was talking. "It's going to be okay."

The boy opened his eyes when he heard voices; one expressing fuming anger. The boy looked around the room and saw two men—the younger cashier and the older man he had seen before... before what? He must have blacked out. He was no longer outside the store, limp on the cold concrete. Now, he was inside, away from the bitter winter and lying a bed softer than any he had ever slept upon.

"He is a thief, Juan!" the cashier said to the older man.

"So, what? You seem to have forgotten your past. Were you not in a much worse situation than he is now? Were you better than him? Why can't you temper justice with mercy when you know fully well that you have been in his shoes?"

The two men, older and younger, stared at each other for a moment in tense silence. Until the young man drooped his head in shame.

"I'm sorry, Juan. It just bothers me when people take something that doesn't belong to them. It's not fair to those who pay, that's all. It won't happen again."

"I hear you, and I understand. But here's the thing... you promise to change now, but tomorrow, you'll be back to your old ways." Juan reproached him. "Go ahead. Go handle the inventory for the night. I'll deal with him."

The younger man nodded and quickly left the room. On the bed, the young boy's eyes traveled through the space of the room, searchingly. Where was he? Was he being held captive?

Juan turned toward him and noticed he had stirred. He approached the boy quietly.

"How do you feel?" he said gently.

The boy tried to sit up in the bed, but the pain was too much. Juan reached forward, fluffed his pillow, and helped him rest against them. The boy nodded his thanks.

"I guess I should not have asked that question. You obviously feel terrible." The man was talking, but the boy kept staring at him blankly.

"What is your name?" the older man asked him, now grinning.

The boy studied him intently, wondering whether to trust the man or not. But he had saved him from being beaten to death and left for the rats... So, he responded in a voice that was barely a whisper.

"My name is Luis. But everyone calls me *Lucho*."

"Lucho?"

Luis nodded but said nothing else.

"You want to tell me how you ended up living on the streets?"

Lucho gave his back to the man in silence, rolling over on the bed, though it hurt him to do so; not a single sound ensued from him. Juan sighed.

"Okay, let's retrace a little here, Lucho. I didn't mean to push too fast. How about you tell me why you stole what you did?"

"We are hungry and freezing our asses off, so we needed food and the blanket. Simple as that," Lucho answered without looking at the man.

Lucho shivered slightly. Juan adjusted the warmer around the boy to make sure it was wrapped around him snugly.

"*We?*" The man quirked his eyebrows. "Who is *we?*"

"My friends and me. Pato, Addy, and I," Lucho said, then paused as a wave of nausea rocked his body. "I don't feel good..."

"Yes, I think you are right. My friend is on his way, Lucho. If I take you to the hospital, they will ask countless questions which could leave you in a worse and vulnerable situation. So, I figured I'd call a friend of mine to come check you out here."

"I want to leave. Please...?"

"Sure, you can. Just as soon as you get your injuries treated and something for the pain, then you can be on your merry way." Juan grinned at Lucho, who had finally turned to face him again.

The boy studied the older man's face. There was kindness in his eyes. A smile. A few fain scars, covered by neatly kept facial hair.

"Who are you?" he asked.

"I am Juan. Juan Fuentes. I am actually the owner of the store you tried to steal from," the elderly man explained.

"Fuentes?" Lucho frowned. "That is *my* last name too! And the other guy... who is that fool? Also, where the heck are we?"

"That *fool*," Juan chuckled, "is my assistant. He manages the store when I am not here. His name is Manuel; we call him Manny. Manny is actually a very nice young man, once you get to know him. And to your second question... we are in the backroom of the store."

"You said—" Lucho stopped as he felt a bout of dizziness submerge his thoughts. He closed his eyes, waiting for it to pass, then continued. "You said he was worse than me."

"Everybody has made mistakes in their past," Juan said. "Wrong decisions. Intentional bad decisions. But the important thing is to not let those decisions rule you or control you. We must let our past refine us, not define us. One must be able to move on from it and start anew. We all have things that we are ashamed of, but we must learn not to cast the first stone, especially when there is a speck in our eyes. *That* was what I meant."

Lucho didn't respond. He was deep in thought, swallowing what he had just heard. It made sense. It made *a lot* of sense.

Juan continued. "Go on, now. Get some rest. My friend will be here any minute."

The man stood up from the chair beside the bed.

"Mr. Juan... why did you help me?" the now groggy Lucho asked as the man was walking away.

"Keep this in mind, Lucho. Always temper justice with mercy. You do not know the reason a person commits an action. As the Bible says, be quick to listen and slow to anger, be slow to speak, and always be merciful. Do to others as you want others to do to you. *That*, my friend, is the golden rule."

Corona, California
Spring 2019

Monica led Luis to the section where the thieves were. He gasped when they rounded the final corner. Many toys had been knocked from the shelves, and a glass case had been smashed open, its glittering shards littered across the floor.

"Monica, get this cleaned up immediately," Luis motioned to the mess. "I'll have a chat with these boys."

Monica bustled away immediately while another employee directed customers away from the commotion. Luis pulled the two blond boys away to a quiet corner and crouched to look straight into their eyes. Their clothes were dirty, and they looked famished.

"Why did you do that? Why did you take that romper and toy ventilator? Why did you smash the case? If you needed help, you should have found someone with a key."

At first, neither of them spoke. The younger one had tears in his eyes, evidently frightened.

"It's for... for our baby sister," the taller one stammered. "And the glass was an accident. I was standing on that stroller to reach the top shelf."

Luis looked at the boys intently; Monica was right. They were only little; nine or ten years of age at most.

"She... um... she has a cold, and she doesn't breathe easy," the boy continued. "I thought that... We saw a TV show where the sick person used a ventilator thing to breathe, so we figured we would help her and find one. But... we don't have any money."

What do you mean, she doesn't breathe easily?" Luis asked with genuine concern. "Where do you live?"

"With... with our aunt. She doesn't think Maui is... that she's sick. But we know she is! She was hot this morning, but Auntie Caroline wouldn't listen," the younger one said while a tear rolled down his dirty cheek.

"You know how to get home, right? Where is it?" Luis asked, determination flashing in his eyes. He was glad there was a law to deal with reckless guardians. He, himself, understood how difficult this was for a child.

He got the address from the boys, then guided them to the entrance of the store. As he walked out, the boys fast at his heels, he called an ambulance as well as his friend at the Corona Police Department, providing them the address. He fastened the belts of the boys in the back seat of his car and started the drive toward the community of Homegardens, about three miles north.

As his car sped down the road, within the stated limits, he asked the boys further questions as he stared at them through the rear-view mirror. "Does your aunt know where you are?"

The boys looked at each other, then shook their heads.

"Where are your parents?"

The younger one rested his head on his brother's shoulder. The brother patted his head, then looked at Luis. "They died a couple years ago from an overdose," he said. "That's what auntie told us. We're not sure what that means."

"We have to live with Auntie Caroline because she's our only relative," the younger one said, "She's our dad's cousin, but we didn't see her much when our parents were alive. She promised them she'd take care of us."

"Tell me more about your auntie, boys."

Billy, the older brother took the lead. "Well, Auntie Caroline doesn't like children. At least, she doesn't like us."

"What do you mean? How do you know she doesn't like you guys?" Luis replied, raised brow, concern on his face.

"She only likes to drink her stinky juice!" said Aaron, the younger of the siblings.

"She does drink a lot of beer," added the older boy. "And when she does, she's not very nice."

"She's never nice!" interjected his little brother. "She doesn't even want us to go to school anymore."

Luis swallowed hard. He could picture the whole scene on his mind. Though only an assumption, he could imagine this Caroline lady, an addict, incapable of taking care of young children. She probably had a questionable past, but getting the kids meant receiving a government check. Anger soared within him. But also, empathy for the boys. Billy and Aaron Denning, the boys, deserved better than this.

"How long has it been since you've been to school, boys?" Luis asked while looking at them through the mirror.

"Like almost two years now," said Billy.

Two years! Luis's knuckles whitened around the steering wheel. *For goodness' sake!* he thought, though he didn't let his anger show elsewhere.

Did she not have neighbors? Had the entire neighborhood been ignorant to the kids' existence for the past two years? Their little sister, Maui, had been born just six months before their parents' deaths. Where were social services? Didn't they come to check on the kids? This didn't make any sense.

Luis curled his right hand into a fist and clenched his teeth.

As he pulled into the parking lot of a rundown home, two police cars pulled up beside him. An ambulance was there already. He studied the surroundings with disgust. The house could not easily be noticed from the street because of the overgrown bushes abutting the lawn. They were high, and the grass had obviously not been mowed for over a year. Families of snakes and other dangerous creatures could have made this small jungle their home by now. This further fueled Luis's anger. There was a liquor store on the corner and a sex shop across the street. This was no place for young children.

If this Caroline Denning could not take care of them, why had she not told the executor of their parents' wills? He mused. *Oh, for sure, there was good money involved for her.*

One of the officers, Steve Gilbert, who was Luis's good friend and a fellow church member, approached him. "We're going in now, Luis. Stay here with the kids."

"But—" Luis started to protest.

"Lucho..." Steve threw him a stern look.

"Fine. I hear you. I will stay here with the boys..." Luis agreed.

"Good." Steve nodded before turning to the other officers. "Let's move in!"

Luis made sure the boys were in the car and leaned against it while the scene played before his eyes. Two officers had been stationed beside his car. Luis did not know if it was to protect the boys or to prevent himself from going in. He shook his head; he was not *that* volatile.

While the officers approached the house, he watched the police photographer take pictures of the environment. That was good. The pictures would be perfect evidence in a hearing. He hoped they would shoot some videos too.

At a loud banging, his eyes darted back to the door. The police officers were shouting now.

"Open up, Miss Denning!"

Luis knew that even if she didn't answer them, they were going to break the door down. There was reasonable cause to go in without a warrant—a child's life was in danger.

After receiving no reply, the officers broke down the door and rushed in, followed by the photographer. Luis hopped from one foot to another impatiently. He sincerely hoped they weren't too late.

After what seemed like hours, Steve and the others emerged. He was holding a small, blanketed bundle, and in tow a stringy, dirty-haired, obviously wasted woman, was being led by the cops, her hands in cuffs. The paramedics rushed to Steve and took the fragile toddler from him. Luis stopped them long enough to ask which hospital they were taking the baby to.

"I need to head back to the precinct to fill out all the paperwork, but I'll need the boys' statements too," Officer Gilbert informed his friend. "I can take them in my squad car."

"Does it have to be now?" Luis asked. "I'm sure the boys could use a checkup at the hospital too. And they must be very eager to see how their sister is doing. I will take them to the hospital and stay there for the rest of the afternoon. You can stop by later with your social workers and whoever else. How does that sound?"

"I mean, you're right, I guess." He heaved a hefty sigh. "I can wait to talk to them. See you later, bro. This was a good catch. I pray the baby girl is okay." Steve patted Luis on the back, and just as he was about to leave, he stopped and turned around. "That reminds me! I'm stationing two officers to shadow you for the meantime."

"Why? That's completely unnecessary."

"No, it isn't. This woman was more than just an addict; she was a distributor and producer. We found several stashes of methamphetamines and a crap-load of heroine hidden around the house. Who knows the people she could have ties to? It's just a precaution, as well as standard procedure."

"Okay." Luis shrugged, though this did set a seed of unease in his stomach. For now, he ignored it. He obviously didn't have a choice.

At the Corona Regional Medical Center, Luis found a nurse who directed him and the boys to the pediatric ward. There, they met a doctor in the waiting room, looking to get information.

"What's the problem, doctor?" Luis asked.

"Are you the family of the girl?" She asked.

"Well, not exactly, but..."

"Unfortunately, HIPPA law prohibits me from releasing information to non-family members."

"These are her brothers. She has no family. For the moment, we are acting as foster parents," Luis said between truth and fabrication, seeing there was no other way.

The young doctor stared at him, then at the kids. "She has a lung infection," she informed them, directing her gaze to the young boys, "which was already progressing at a rapid rate. We're lucky it didn't develop into pneumonia. With her malnourishment, she wouldn't have survived had she gotten it. We can only hope we caught the infection in time. She's receiving treatment now."

Luis wondered if the boys understood what was being said to them.

"Can we see Maui?" the older of the boys asked.

"So, she is fine, then?" asked the younger one.

It was obvious they hadn't understood all the doctor had said, but they had taken away one important detail—their sister would be okay.

"Sure, but not just yet. Remember, she's still very fragile. You won't be able to get too close." The doctor turned her attention to Luis. "I'll call a nurse to take them to her."

The doctor left, and they each took a seat. A few minutes later, she returned with a male nurse, who lead the boys away. The doctor remained with Luis.

"I didn't want to say this in front of the kids," she begins gently, descending onto the seat beside him. "Her situation is quite delicate. Tonight is going to be a trying one, if she makes it through. Only then will we know if she's in the clear. But if she—"

"She will, doctor. She will," Luis said firmly. "Those boys are not going to lose their sister."

The doctor smiled. "All right, sir. All we can do now is pray and hope she survives the night." With that, the doctor excused herself and left.

Luis exhaled and pulled out his phone to call Samantha. He explained to her in detail everything that had occurred and where he was now.

"Oh my goodness! That's terrible. The poor babies! Why are people so heartless? We'll be praying over here, *mi amor*. Don't worry about Alejandra; I'll pick her up from school."

"Thank you, *chula*. How was the meeting?"

"It was excellent. Thank God! We'll try to come over in the evening if we can. Just be strong for those boys. They've been through so much already. I love you, Lucho."

"I love you too, Sam." Luis hung up, then caught a passing nurse. "Excuse me, can you tell me where the pediatric intensive care unit is? Another nurse just led a couple of young boys there to see their sister."

The nurse gave him directions, and a minute later, he found the two boys peering through a large glass partition, separating them from their sister. He walked up to the boys and held them close. Their faces were wet and cheeks puffy and red; they had been crying.

"Do you believe in God?" Luis asked as he crouched to their height.

"Sometimes, I guess. Mommy took us to church a few times and told us about Him," Billy, the older one, said. "But Auntie never did."

"Well, believe in Him always, kids. I trust He can heal your baby sister. I think she will be all right."

"Okay." They both nodded.

"Which one is she?" Luis asked.

He was looking inside the room beyond the glass partition; there were three young creatures in beds under glass, cylindrical cases. The boys pointed to her. She was the one closest to them.

As soon as his eyes fell on her, Luis felt his chest fill with sadness. What the little girl had to face so young in life was terrible. She was scrawny, and her brown hair curled around her ears. How was she over two? She didn't look more than a year old! Tiny. Bony. She was attached to a respirator, making her chest and tummy rise in a constant rhythm.

The sight of her brought back memories of the little girl he had been a father to so young: *Woo Deep*. His eyes moistened. He had no idea if his little Woo Deep ever made it. He hoped that Maui would.

THE FLIGHT OF THE BUTTERFLY

CHAPTER TWENTY-FIVE

Mexicali, Mexico
Winter 1988

Lucho scaled over the bamboo fence and hid behind the thick bushes that lay beyond it. He ducked down just as he heard approaching footsteps. Angry voices accompanied them.

"Where is he? Where did that rat disappear to?"

"I have no idea. But if I find him..." A smacking sound and a yelp followed this.

"No idea? No idea? I told you not to let him out of your sight! Go on, fan the area!"

The footsteps retreated.

All the same, Lucho waited in his hiding spot for a while longer before he finally crept out, grinning at having outsmarted the crooks. He ran his hand through his greasy brown hair. Whistling and skipping, he headed home with the proceeds of the day's struggle.

As he crossed the road, he could not understand for the life of him why those guys had been so selfish. It wasn't like they didn't have enough. They did; they just wanted to have it all for themselves.

Lucho had been lucky to be outside the jewelry store when those crooks had robbed it. They had gotten away from the police, but not from him. He had tracked them all the way back to their hiding place. And what did he do? Nothing much, really. He simply waited for them to drink themselves to sleep, then took his share of the loot. There was nothing wrong with stealing from a thief. Right?

If he hadn't stumbled over that empty bottle, they wouldn't have woken up and gone after him. It would have been a clean hit.

Either way, it was all good now. Not only had he been able to make away with a sizeable sum that would not only last him a comfortable amount of time and pay off some loans, but he had also gotten away with it and had just pawned the jewels and received a good amount of cash for them.

A breeze blustered down the road as he strolled, and he felt it bite at his skin through the thin layers of his clothes; he shivered.

There is a thrift shop just at the end of the block. He told himself as he turned the corner. *I can just go in and get something that will keep me warm for the winter. After all, I did just rake in a large sum. I can afford it.*

He rolled his eyes at the thought. Why should he waste his hard-earned money when he could get it cheaper or at no cost? He pushed the voice to the back of his head and continued to the residential district he had in mind.

Hours later, the glee Lucho felt as he strutted down the street, head held high, was great. He had succeeded in snagging a brand-new jacket with all the logos of the NBA teams stitched on it from the rail of a house. He felt proud of himself, of course. Now what they needed were blankets.

Addy and Pato were busy, as well. As they did every year, they went around gathering protection and food for the cold winter days and nights ahead. They knew from experience that things were about to become much more difficult, so they had to be prepared. Just like a bear gathered food prior to hibernation, they were gathering resources for the winter.

He shivered a little as the wind blew harder and hastened his footsteps, adjusting the strap of the tattered bag around his shoulder. It was already dark; the moon was out, but it cast little light, and there were no stars visible. His path was only lit by the streetlights and the outer lights of shops along the road.

Lucho skipped over a pool of stagnant water in his path and turned the corner. He took in a deep breath as he studied the large street that lay before him. The houses inside the gated community were large and showed promise of a lot to offer. So, why was he not making the bold step?

He studied his hands, taking note of the already fading scars which constantly reminded him of all he had suffered in these past years. He had been caught on some of his capers, and, unlike Señor Juan, his targets had not taken kindly to his actions.

Pulling the jacket collar up in a feeble attempt to battle the cold, he crossed the road, heading toward the gate that separated the street from the rest of them.

Los Arcos was an older neighborhood, but most residents were still either upper middle class or straight-up rich. The houses were large and fancy, and from what he could see, all the houses but one had their porch lights on. That could only mean that all of them were home except that house. He would need to be careful not to be seen by either the neighbors or the security guards patrolling the community.

At that moment, Lucho thought of Señor Juan. He had believed in him and wanted him to change for the better. The man believed Lucho was destined for better things. Was he wrong? As soon as Lucho had felt better, he left, even though Señor Juan had given him the choice to stay with him.

He shook his head, trying to clear away every thought of the man who had saved his life. He didn't like thinking of Señor Juan because then he imagined the life he could have had. Well... it was a good thing then that the memories only came when he was sober, which was not very often these days. Most times, he was strung up on the latest fad in town: cannabis. He chuckled lightly as he hid behind the shrubs that framed the street gate.

He heard a sound and, standing on tiptoe, he looked through the iron rungs of the gate and saw a car backing out of a driveway. The outer lights of the house which had previously been on were now off. The car headed in his direction, headlights beaming. The gate opened at once, and Luis stared at the back of the retreating car intently until it disappeared from his view.

Looking around, he hastily scaled the tall fence, earning himself a small scratch on his arm. The street was lit up, and he had to be very fast if he intended to avoid detection.

"Crap!" he swore as he bent low and hid behind the security post by a small park. He had almost been spotted by a security guard who was entering the small building.

He could hear the man moving around inside now, but the sound of a window shutter opening above Lucho sent him scrambling away. His heart pounded in his chest as he sprinted as quickly as his legs could take him across the neatly cut lawns of the neighborhood. There, another guard doing his rounds was headed in Lucho's direction. He dove behind a shrub that lined the sidewalk.

Every house on the street was separated from their neighbor by a tall wall of cement blocks. They would shield him from any neighbor looking his way.

Lucho quickly jumped over the fence separating him from a darkened house and bent low in the yard. The house was dark, but who could tell there were no surprises waiting for him inside? Still low, he rounded the house and ended up in the backyard. It was a beautiful patio. Large. Fancy. Nice pool. He hoped there was no dog on site.

Very stealthily, he approached the back of the house and peeked in through a window. He saw nothing. It was pitch black but for the rays of outside light filtering in through the window. He would just have to find his way around with the light from the neighbor's yard. The most stupid thing he could do was switch on the lights in a house that he intended to steal from.

Using his ever-trusted lock picks, he had the backdoor open in less than two minutes. Quietly, he entered the house and made sure to close the door behind him, all the while not making a sound.

Where can I find what I need? he pondered. From what he could see, he was in a kitchen, and it was huge. Extravagant. *First things first, food.*

He headed for some cabinets next to the sink, opened them, but got no results; only dishware. With a groan of frustration, he moved on to another large cabinet door. He pulled at it, and the cupboard opened up, hitting him with an icy blast of cold air.

A fridge!

He started pulling out containers of food and grinned with pleasure as he pulled one out, opened it, and inhaled the delicious aroma. Whoever owned the house was a good cook, that was for sure. But then again, they probably had a chef that worked for them.

When he was content, he closed the door and headed out of the kitchen, pulling out the plastic bags he had tucked away in his backpack.

As Lucho traced his way up a set of stairs, he could not help but think back to the first time he had ever seen a fridge. He was a young kid. He had gone to Marcos's house, and when he had seen the white box in the kitchen, he had been baffled. That was why he had been dazed when he had seen the one downstairs; he had thought fridges were always that way: tall, white boxes, not large two-door, light-wooden cabinets that blended with the rest of the kitchen.

As soon as Lucho alighted the stairs onto the landing, he turned left. He had no idea where he was going. He stopped at the first door he came to and opened it.

As soon as he stepped in, he knew that it would be a waste of precious time to search the room. There was a wooden crib in the middle; he did not need anyone to tell him that babies did not keep valuables.

He went on to the next door and met a sewing room of sorts. And the next one was a bedroom.

The outside light from the neighbors cast a beam in the room, allowing him to move around. He started at the dresser, pulling out clothes and underwear. It was a boy's room, and from the size of the clothes, they had to be around the same age. The walls were covered with posters of Mexican rock bands. He recognized a couple of them.

He took one of the posters down and folded it before slipping it in his backpack. It would look nice back in the warehouse. He then headed to a cabinet and pulled it open: more clothes. He grabbed a handful of some of the fancier garments and shoved them into a bag. He pushed around, still searching, until finally, his hands lay on something coarse. He put his head in to see what it was and ended up sneezing. He pulled out the packet with delight.

Who would have thought a rich boy would delve into drugs! He chuckled as he took a whiff of the green substance.

Ah! This here sure is some strong stuff. I guess weed is a friend to everyone. Luis snickered.

He looked in and saw two more packets. He grabbed them all, left the room, and headed in the direction he came from. By this time,

Lucho was very impatient. He could not accept that the only thing that he had gotten from a huge house like this was food and dope. He needed cash.

Lucho entered the room and knew at once that his search had not been in vain. The dresser was crowded with all kinds of jewelry. It looked expensive. The occupants had probably been in a hurry, maybe late for an engagement or party. The woman of the household probably tried multiple items before finally choosing one and leaving all the others behind, visible. It was just his luck—and theirs too. He selected the newest from the collection and then turned toward the walk-in closet.

By the time he was done searching, the floor around him was strewn with clothes. Underneath all the clothes was nothing. He headed to a desk against a wall and pulled at a drawer, but it did not bulge. It was locked, and he doubted the key was anywhere around. Something valuable had to be in it if it was locked.

He looked around the room hastily, in the hope of getting something to pry it open. Finding nothing, he had to turn his sights to the single-standing dresser. Coats were hung in it.

After checking coat after coat and coming up empty, he finally found a wallet with a wad of cash in it. The boy grabbed everything and hurried down the stairs. He snuck out through the backdoor just as he heard a car pull up the driveway, followed by arguing. Out of curiosity, he hid in the shrubs, and their conversation drifted to him. The kitchen light was switched on, and he heard a woman's voice.

"I absolutely cannot believe you forgot your wallet, Alberto. I was so embarrassed!"

"It's not my fault! You were the one who told me to change my coat!" a man's voice followed.

"Well... did you have to be so dumb that you forgot to take your wallet out?" the woman responded, this time, louder.

"Says the woman who had to cheat in order to graduate back in college!" the man retaliated.

"How dare you!"

At this point, Lucho was already bored with the argument and was about to step out of the shrubs, when he heard light footsteps. He hid again and saw the silhouette of a tall boy walking toward where he was.

The tall boy looked around and, convinced he was alone, pulled a packet from his back pocket and took a long whiff of it a couple of times. He quickly dusted his hands and nose and hurried back into the house.

So, that was the dope-taking son!

He hurried out of his hiding place, and as quickly as he could, took off down the street. As soon he was out of the community, having jumped the perimeter wall, he knew he was home free.

Corona, California
Spring 2019

Luis breathed a deep sigh of relief when the doctor told him Maui was going to be okay. He felt like a weight had been lifted off of his shoulders. He couldn't contain his joy and quickly pulled out his phone to share the good news with Samantha. As he did, he checked the time. It was just after 8 a.m.

Samantha had visited the hospital the previous night and had left with the boys, who had taken an instant liking to her. She had been able to ease their fears and reassure them that their sister would be fine. Lucho, on the other hand, had spent the night in front of the pediatric intensive care unit, praying for the safety of all the children beyond the glass. God had answered his prayer, and he quickly gave a new prayer of thanks.

On the fourth ring, Samantha picked up. "*Buenos días, mi amor.* Did you sleep well?" her singsong tone floated through the phone.

"I cannot say yes to that, but I can happily say that joy comes in the morning," Luis told her, his voice brimming with happiness.

"Maui's going to be okay?" Samantha asked.

"*Si, mi amor.* By noon, she should be out of the intensive care. You can bring the boys over then. How does that sound?"

"Perfect! I'll let the kids know. They're all going to be so thrilled." Samantha's joy could be felt from where he was.

"Yes, do that. I'm going to call the office to check on things. I'll talk to you later." Luis hung up.

His phone call to Bullseye was brief. He just wanted to check everything was running smoothly; he believed in his team and knew he could trust them with the effective running of the business in his absence.

After calling the office, he called Steve. There were major issues he had to discuss with him, and as soon as Samantha and the kids arrived, he was going to head over to the precinct.

Just like the doctor had said, by noon, Maui was transferred to the pediatric ward. As soon as the baby set eyes on Luis, she had smiled widely. Now, she was fast asleep, and Luis was seated beside her. He watched her intently, his eyes following every rise and fall of her small chest, making sure it would not cease. Her breathing was normal now. Luis smiled, relieved.

"Lucho..." Luis heard soft whispering, and with great difficulty due to his high level of fatigue, he opened his eyes and set them on the loveliest woman in the world: his Samantha.

"Hi, babe!" He stroked her cheek causing her to chuckle lightly.

"The kids are here with me. How is Maui?" She moved aside so he could see the four, smiling children. In the few hours that the boys had been with his family, they seemed happier. There was a light in their eyes that hadn't been there yesterday morning.

"She's okay," Lucho replied. "The doctor said she is recovering fast and that if there are no complications, she can be released by Thursday." And to his surprise, the grinning smiles of his family diminished all at once. "What is it? Why the dull faces?"

"Well... we were all hoping that Maui would be well enough to be released this evening. Thursday? That's two whole days away," Samantha said. The four children behind her nodded simultaneously.

Luis chuckled and pulled Samantha close to him. He put his arms around her waist and gave her a kiss on the lips, much to the mixed protests of their kids and the chuckling of the two boys. Luis turned to them. "She is my wife, and we love each other. Now, do not worry about Maui. The doctors are just being extra careful and want to make sure that she is safe and sound. You got that?" They all nodded. Luis turned to his wife and kissed her again, and as before, the kids reacted the same way.

Samantha rolled her eyes at the children and kissed her husband again. This time, all the children groaned. She smiled. "Kids, look after Maui. Your father and I have something we need to discuss."

Sam and Luis headed out into the hallway. As soon as the door closed behind them, Samantha pulled Lucho toward the elevators.

"Where are we heading? We can just talk out here in the lobby," Luis protested, confused.

"No way. You're going to get some food into that stomach of yours first before we talk about anything!" Samantha said, a stubborn look on her face, daring him to say otherwise.

He knew by now that arguing with Samantha when she was like this was a waste of time. They *all* knew. Sebastian and Alejandra never tried to push further with their demands whenever she had that look. Still, he tried.

"Really, Sam. I'm not hungry."

"You haven't had anything substantial to eat since last night. So, don't argue with me. You're getting breakfast. Period," she said with a tone of finality and punched the down button in the elevator as they got in.

At the cafeteria, she pulled him to the counter and ordered their breakfast, unblinkingly and decisively. Pulling out a chair in the center of the large, rectangular room, she pointed at it. He sat and started poking the horrid-looking food, inspecting every single bite like someone who suspected poison.

"Come on, *mi Luchito*," Samantha said with a grin. "Eat!"

He looked up at her, about to say something, but couldn't help but smile when he saw her glittering green eyes. He chuckled and resumed his meal. Finally, he scraped the last of the scrambled eggs off his plate and washed it down with the orange juice.

"Do you want any more?"

"No! Thank you, babe. The food is... um... I mean, not exactly the best. I think I'll pass. I am hungry for your food and not... *this*... whatever this is." He motioned to the plate as the cafeteria staff took his tray away.

Samantha poked his arm as the lady left. "Don't be mean! She can hear you."

"Okay, but I am pretty sure she knows it is terrible, as well," Luis stated, raising his hands in surrender.

"Oh, dear..." Samantha chuckled. "Well, let's discuss something important. I would absolutely love for us to adopt the kids."

"Sammie?!" Luis exclaimed in surprise.

"Lucho... think about it. Where do you think those kids will end up? Their only living relative, their meth-junkie aunt, is in jail. And even if she wasn't, she's in no way fit to raise those kids, evident in the way she has done these past couple of years. Those kids will be headed into the system if we don't do something, and you know it. If they're lucky, they might eventually be adopted. But what are the chances someone will want to take all three? And let's be honest, Maui is the only one with a chance of being adopted. The remaining two will probably end up in foster care."

Samantha paused and took a long drink of her iced tea while her husband watched her in silence. Then she continued. "You know this already, Luis. Those kids will be better off with us. I know we can give them the love, care, and guidance they need to become outstanding people. There was a reason those boys chose this particular Bullseye store; maybe we are meant to help them!"

Luis just kept staring at her with the same amused look on his face.

"Lucho, why are you so quiet? Why that look? Say something already, *mi amor*." Samantha nudged her husband.

Still, Luis didn't say anything.

"Okay, babe. Now I'm getting upset."

"Upset? Why?" he finally said.

"Well, not upset. Confused. Concerned, maybe. You're not saying anything. To be honest, I'm just scared of what you're going to say about all this. And when I rehearsed it in my mind, it sounded better."

"Oh, so you practiced this?" He laughed.

"Yes. And in my imagined scenario your reactions had been... better. More enthusiastic."

"Well... I mean, you've come at me with everything you've got. But you really haven't let me pitch anything in," Luis said quietly.

"Okay, okay... I know. I'm sorry. I've been saying so much. I know I can be overbearing."

"Samantha..."

Her eyes widened. *Oh, no.* He never called her by her full name.

"Babe..." he corrected himself, and she relaxed, eager to listen. "I know you mean well. Don't worry. Besides, it seems to me like... like we *both* want the same thing..." he said, his smile widening.

Samantha's smile grew to match his. "Really?"

"Yes! I completely agree with you. I think it would be wonderful for us to adopt the kids too. They need a loving and Christian home to grow in. I see nothing wrong with us being that home. If anything, I was more scared of what *you* would have to say about it! With all of my friends on the police force, I'm sure this process can run smoothly. We won't have to go through much red tape." He stopped to think for a moment. "Well, I actually don't know for sure. But I hope not."

Samantha let out a joyful yelp and hugged Luis across the table. "I guess our home is about to get bigger, then."

"I guess so. Are you happy now that we settled on such a large house? At first, you were complaining about its size, saying the kids would go off to college and it would be just the two of us—"

"Yeah, yeah. I was wrong, and you were right, as usual..." She kissed his forehead. "You saw far into the future, *mi amor*. And yes, I'm glad you convinced me we should get that house. It's going to feel much fuller for a while."

"I couldn't agree with you more." Luis kissed his wife on the cheek. It was a very happy day, and he felt absolutely blessed. And in his heart, he thanked God with all the love he could give, and more.

THE FLIGHT OF THE BUTTERFLY

CHAPTER TWENTY-SIX

Mexicali, Mexico
Winter 1990

The winter was terribly harsh and defiant. The usual cold morning air was fortified by the previous night's rain, and this made it colder than usual.

Lucho gave the woman her change and tugged his coat closer to him. His teeth were chattering, and he really needed to get out of this cold. He looked down at the box full of packages of gum on the sidewalk. He could always continue the next day. He had made enough money to tide them over for the weekend. They had spent the last sum he got paying their debts. It was a good thing the snotty rich kid had some weed stashed in his room. Otherwise, they would have been stranded.

This would do, he told himself. He just needed to get out of the freezing weather. The night had been disastrous, and now, the early morning was worse.

Lucho gathered up the packages and started on his way home. He needed to rest his head. It hurt badly. He jogged up the road, trying to get a little warmer. But not looking where he was going, he stumbled and fell face-first onto wet cement. Groaning, he tried to get up, when his eyes caught something stuck to the edge of the sidewalk. He disentangled it and held it in his hand. It was a sterling-silver chain adorned by a stunning, bejeweled blue-topaz butterfly. It was beautiful.

This will definitely get me a little sum.

He cleaned it and placed it in his pocket. Then, as best as he could, he cleaned himself off and continued toward home. But, just then, he felt... weird.

The niggling feeling persisted as he crossed the road. He took out the chain and studied it intently; it was in good condition, and he was sure it was valuable.

His eyes lingered on the butterfly, surrounded by sparkling rocks. What kind of rocks or gemstones were they? Diamonds? Sapphire? Zircon? Who knew? He wasn't sure, since this type of thing wasn't really his cup of tea. Everything he'd learned came from the pawn shop where he sold his stuff. But, even if it was cheap or fake, it sure was a pretty piece of jewelry. And that is all he needed to know.

Heaving another sigh, he clasped the chain around his neck, and as he did, the niggling feeling went away. *On second thought, I might keep this one for myself.*

At the intersection, while Lucho waited for a chance to cross, he heard a dreaded rumbling: thunder. He looked up, and his fears were confirmed; the sky was getting darker, a sign of incoming rain. From the way the air temperature suddenly dropped and the little daylight was snuffed out, he knew it was going to be heavy.

Making up his mind in an instant, he turned south, instead of east. He would have to pass through a shorter and faster route—though it was riskier. He crossed the rim of Chapultepec Park and then the boulevard. Dipping into an alley, he rushed through it to La Chinesca.

His feet felt heavy as he got closer to Chinatown. It wasn't just Chinese immigrants that lived here, anymore; it was full of all kinds of people. And it wasn't exactly safe, either. It was the home base of crime lords and prostitutes, along with their dangerous pimps, and it was full of bars and other not very reputable businesses. Mexicali was growing, and it had been changing drastically in the last couple of years, and city officials had been trying to clean up the area; new businesses and cute Mexican curious shops were replacing the sketchy stores. But it was still unsafe, especially during the late, dark hours of the night.

Lucho had no choice, though. It was the fastest way to get across this part of the city. If he passed through La Chinesca, he knew he would beat the rain. Passing through the main city streets would most likely cause him to be trapped in the spontaneous brown rivers that always arose because of the strong rains. This desert city wasn't built for such weather.

Why did I have to sell at the border today? Why did I have to go so far from home? He beat himself up mentally. *Just a few more turns,* Lucho kept telling himself as he walked through the already crowded streets of La Chinesca, head bowed low, hands in his trouser pockets.

The feel of the handle of the knife within his pocket gave him little reassurance. He looked up and breathed in a deep breath when he realized he was out of the questionable area. He crossed the road and kept going. At this pace, he would be home soon.

Lucho stepped into another alley as he stifled a yawn. He could really use some rest, that was for sure. But his thoughts of sleep after a hot plate of food were cut short by a sound.

He listened closely and heard it again. It was quiet whimpering, barely noticeable if you were not listening for it.

Lucho followed the sound; the sight that he beheld shocked him. It was a bloodied, young Asian girl, and she was almost fully naked. But the sight that shocked him more was what lay in the girl's arms. It was tiny newborn wrapped in what looked like the girl's clothes. The whimpering was coming from both the girl and the infant.

Lucho approached them quietly and bent over the young girl. He could see she was still bleeding and was shivering as well. *Well, of course, she is shivering!* He scolded himself. *It's freezing tonight.*

She was losing so much blood. He tried to help her up, but she shook her head. Her large, damp eyes flitted over him and then they suddenly stopped; they gained a look he did not quite understand. He followed her eyes to himself and realized it was the butterfly necklace she was gazing at. It rested against his chest, shiny and beautiful.

"*¿Hablas español?*" She just stared at him, confused. She bit her lip and shook her head. "English?" Nothing. "Okay, let me get you some help. I'll be back as soon as possible. You stay here, okay?" Luis turned to leave when she called out to him, a shrill yelp in a foreign tongue.

He turned around.

She seemed to have suddenly gained a burst of energy. Standing up, she carefully placed the tiny baby in his hands, to his shock. She leaned forward, stroked the baby's cheek and kissed its face. She then turned to Luis, and with her bloody hand, stroked his cheek as well, leaving a wet mark.

"Let me—" He tried to leave. She needed help, quick.

"Wu-Dip..." she whispered, a weak smile playing on her lips.

"Woo Deep?" a confused Lucho asked.

He was frozen in the moment. There was a young, bloody, naked girl who didn't seem to speak his language, standing right in front of him. There was a baby, of all things, in his arms.

What do I do?

She placed her hand on her baby's cheek. Evidently, she had almost run out of the little strength she had left. She smiled softly and repeated, "Wu-Dip."

Before his very eyes, she gave up her spirit. Lucho watched as her thin hand slowly fell from her baby's face and to her side. Her knees wobbled beneath her, and she dropped.

Lucho reached out to the ground where she lay and closed her eyes. Her unmoving, naked body lying on the floor, wet and cold. Bloody. Lifeless.

Cradling the shivering infant in his arms, he wiped the blood from her body and headed out of the alley, toward home, not looking back.

CHAPTER TWENTY-SEVEN

Mexicali, Mexico
Winter 1990

Lucho arriving home with a newborn in his hands was a great shock to his friends and roommates. Home was an abandoned warehouse. Its windows and doors had been boarded up, leaving behind a dank and dark place—until Luis and his friends had found it. They had cleaned it up, furnished it, and made it home. It was the only one they had, and it worked for them.

Pato and Addy had been smoking a joint, sheltering themselves from the heavy rain and trying to keep warm, when Lucho walked in. Addy, who dropped the joint in astonishment, was the first to react. She was obviously the one who had smoked more from her unsteady gait.

"What is this, Lucho?" She peered at the baby with bloodshot eyes.

"It's a baby," Lucho said bluntly.

"I know it's a baby, *pendejo*. My question is, what is the baby doing here?" Her eyes widened. "Luis Fuentes, did you steal the *bambino*? What the hell is wrong with you!"

Lucho rolled his eyes and walked toward one of the overstuffed beds that the warehouse held. He gently placed the baby on a mound of sheets.

He turned around. "No, I did not steal the baby, Addy. Her mother is dead. She... she gave her to me."

"*What?*" This came from Pato. He had staggered to his feet, bewildered. "We already have enough mouths to feed, Lucho. Now, you are bringing in a fourth?"

"I couldn't let her die on the streets," Lucho said, again using the same blunt tone which conveyed the fact he was not ready for an argument.

"Yes, you could! What do you expect us to do with the kid?"

"She is staying, *Patricio*! And you might as well get that into your thick skull already." Lucho knew that Pato hated being called by his real name.

"Why, you...!" Pato lunged for Luis, but Addy stopped him.

"Calm down, both of you! Just... calm down," she pleaded.

Pato stared daggers at Lucho, but they were directed at the back of his head, because Lucho had turned his back to him and was bending over the little baby, trying to calm her down. She had started bawling when Pato had launched his attack.

For such a little thing, she sure has a large set of lungs! Lucho smiled.

As he held the little girl, trying to calm her, he saw three images in his mind that he had tried to suppress over the last two years: his little brothers. He had run out on them, and he could only wonder how they were. He regretted leaving them, and that was part of the reasons why he took drugs—to numb the pain.

He stroked the girl's cheek. He was not able to take care of his brothers, but *maybe...* maybe he would be able to take care of this little girl that had been born into a world full of despair and pain. She had no one; he had to help her. He just had to. Pato could rant as much as he wanted, but he was not going to get rid of the little baby girl.

But first things first, he had to get her some formula. Also, the winter was very harsh; he had to protect her from the cold. He needed to get good clothing for her, as well. There was so much to do! And he didn't remember much about how to raise a baby.

Lucho heard a sound behind him and quickly turned.

Addy stretched out her hands. "May I hold her?"

Lucho couldn't help the doubt that spread across his face. Could he really trust that Addy would do no harm to the baby? Could she protect her from the threat that Pato posed, at least?

Addy must have noticed his look. "I'm not going to hurt the baby, Lucho. Here, give her to me. There is no way she will survive with this place like this. She is not like us; she is fragile. The cold will mar her. Go get what is needed. I will care for her."

Lucho weighed the options before him. Addy was right, he had to leave the child in her care. Carefully, he placed the baby in her arms.

"Oh," Addy gasped as soon as she set her eyes on the little one, "she is such a beautiful *bambina*. What is her name?"

"Woo Deep."

"*Woo Deep*? That's a funny name."

"Yeah, maybe. But that's her name, and it's not going to change."

"Woo Deep... You are such a pretty little thing!" Addy sat on the bed, rocking the little girl. It was as if her natural, maternal instincts had taken over. She was good. She was loving. She was nurturing, protective. Addy opened her blouse and wrapped it around the baby, giving her skin-to-skin contact to keep her warm.

Who is this person? Lucho wondered. He understood Addy had fallen for the child. He could see it in her actions.

"Nice necklace, by the way," Addy told Lucho without looking at him; she was still fixated on the baby.

"Thanks. I'm going to keep this one. Somehow, I feel like it's my connection to Woo Deep," Lucho said as he inspected his newfound ornament.

He smiled. He knew she would be safe. Addy would protect her at any cost. And with that, Lucho left the premises on his mission to find whatever the baby needed.

He found his way to the large store a few blocks away. Luckily, this day had been a great day financially for him, and with all the money he had made, he bought formula, bottles, newborn diapers, baby wash, wipes, two blankets, a warmer, and some newborn onesies and other clothes for Woo Deep. Then he went back home.

But he stopped to get some nails on the way back. They would need to put up some extra boards to reduce the cold drifting into their home. Woo Deep would not be able to withstand the cold nights they had been experiencing.

Lastly, he bought a small heater at a discounted price. It was the floor model at an electronics store on the corner next to the warehouse. He had been wanting to get it, or steal it, for some time. And now, he had a reason to do so.

He ran back to the place he called home and was surprised yet again that day. Pato was laughing as he held Woo Deep in his hands. They were all in love with the baby.

"What took you so long, Lucho? Don't you know that Woo Deep has not tasted any food since her birth? Hurry up, dude!" Pato scolded him. He was truly concerned.

Lucho, still reeling with surprise at the turn of events, did as he was told. He poured some of the formula into a bottle after cleaning it and then warmed it. Pato removed it from the warmer and fed it to Woo Deep, who spat it out.

"Oh! Is she sick?" asked Pato with fear in his voice.

"No, dummy," Lucho said, taking the bottle from him and feeling it. "It's too hot. I would have rejected it too. She might be a baby, but that doesn't mean she would allow herself to get hurt."

"Oh... my bad." Pato scratched his head.

"That's okay, man." Lucho placed the bottle in cold water for a few minutes and then fed her the formula again. This time, once she was able to connect with the tip, she drank it up quickly, The poor baby was starving.

"We can do this... Right, guys?" Lucho said as he watched the tiny infant.

"Sure, we can." Addy stood to her feet quickly. She took Woo Deep from Pato's hands and sat down on her bed. The little girl was blissfully unaware of them all as she drank her meal.

"Good. However, there is one thing we must stop. It will not be good for little Woo Deep," Lucho said very slowly. It was going to be a very difficult thing for him to do, but he knew he had to do it. They all had to.

"What's that?" Pato asked.

"The drugs."

"Oh, come on..." Pato protested, pouting like a toddler.

"Guys... Woo Deep needs clean air to live in. It's not right for her to be surrounded by... people like us, you know? And this is a big open space, but we all share it. Now, we are sharing it with her too."

"I will try, man. Try..." Pato groaned. "But I won't promise anything."

"I'm in." Addy nodded absentmindedly as she carried the baby, rocking her from one place to another.

"Great. I think we are going to be good parents to Woo Deep," Lucho declared with more certainty than he felt.

At fifteen years old, he would certainly try his best.

Corona, California
Spring 2019

Luis looked around the police captain's office of the police station, taking in the whole room in one glance. Plaques. Pictures of family. Pictures with friends. Baseball trophies. Even college banners of what Luis assumed was the captain's alma matter.

The Captain was a good friend of Steve Gilbert, and Steve had told Luis in confidence that the Captain would see that the children's case was handled appropriately from all angles.

"Hi, Mr. Fuentes. Sorry I kept you waiting." The Captain stepped into the office. He shook hands with Luis and motioned for him to take his seat.

"That's okay. Thanks for taking the time to meet me. I know you run a tight schedule."

"Don't worry about that. Anyway, to the issue at hand. We have received the boys' statements, and this is pretty much a settled case. I mean, that whole house was a mess: the lawn overgrown, banister falling apart, shattered windows... really the place itself was a death-trap."

The Captain leaned across his desk, his expression grim and his hands clasped in front of him. "But the meth lab is the killer here. It's amazing how those kids survived these past couple of years. That little girl almost having pneumonia is not a surprise. Last winter was freezing and from the looks of that house, those kids were in no way sheltered from the cold."

"Wow..." was all Luis could say.

"You can say that again. Even if the charges of neglect and child abuse are dropped, she's done. It turns out she's a wanted criminal. If only you knew! Her entire family were criminals, but apparently, she's all that's left."

"Wait..." Luis straightened in his chair, "did you say child abuse?"

"Oh, yes. The boys mentioned so in their statements. They were her punching bags, apparently."

Luis grunted, then cursed. His knuckles whitened around the arms of the chair.

The Captain sighed. "Listen, Luis... Can I call you Luis? We have her for drug production, distribution, substance use—and also in the presence of children. Trust me; she also has quite a long rap sheet prior to this. Home invasion, battery, the list goes on. Believe me when I say that she's not going anywhere."

"Okay, then..." Luis ran his hand over his brow. "I trust in the system. It's just so sad that these kids had to go through these horrible things and that such people exist."

"You got that right, Luis," the Captain said. "Now, for the kids—"

"Yes. That is the main issue I wanted to discuss with you," Luis interrupted.

"You and your wife want to adopt them... Right?"

"How did you know that?"

"Oh, come on, now..." The Captain chuckled heartily. "Isn't it obvious? I know that defiant look you have in your eyes. When someone gets like this, they are like a mother hen defending her chicks."

This caused Luis to burst into laughter. "That's very true, Captain."

"Look, I understand you have already developed protective instincts toward those kids, and I know for a fact you don't intend to let them out of your sight."

Luis sat forward now. "What do we have to do to get custody of them?"

"We would need to meet with the executor of their parents' wills, for a start. And actually, in this case, it goes way beyond that; he was supposed to be an overseer of the kids' care, ensuring that were well cared for. He wasn't doing that, of course, because if he was, he should have gotten those kids away from Miss Denning a long time ago. They could very well be in cahoots. Anyway, being that the kids have no other living relative, you will need to make an application at Social Services, and—"

"Is that going to take long?"

"Well... investigations will be carried out on you *and* your family. The aim is to ensure that you are all capable of and will give the kids the good and loving home they deserve."

Luis leaned back in his chair. "We want to do that. That's not a problem."

"Oh, I am very sure of that. It's all routine. Anyway, you and your family are upstanding and respectable members of the community. I'm sure you'll be granted permanent custody of the little ones. It's just going to take a little while. Don't expect it to be immediate."

"Okay. And until then, what? What about the kids?"

"You will be given temporary custody of them. Steve tells me that you and Mrs. Fuentes are wonderful people. I'm glad those kids aren't going to end up in the foster system. The world needs more people like you."

"Thank you, sir." Luis stood and shook hands with the Captain once again. "I will get started on the applications immediately."

"No problem. And, once again... thank you for the call. This was a big catch. You have no idea how much easier it would be for us if more people helped us find bad people like this."

"I bet. Well, thank you, Captain. You have a great evening."

Before he was out of the precinct, Luis was already on the phone with his wife, giving her an update on his progress so far. She was quite pleased with the fact it wouldn't be difficult to get custody of the three kids and was already preparing permanent space for them in the family home.

As he hung up, he started up his car and headed to City Hall. He hoped with all his might that before Maui was released, at least temporary custody would be granted so the kids would have a place to call home. The pain they had suffered the past years had been great, and it was time for them to be happy once more.

At a red light, he called his brother, Andres, asking him to meet him at City Hall. He was a corporate lawyer. Though he was not a family lawyer, Luis would feel better knowing his brother was present when he made the applications.

THE FLIGHT OF THE BUTTERFLY

Mexicali, Mexico
Fall 1991

The shrieking of little Woo Deep persisted throughout the night and by morning, her fever had gone up. Pato stood over the little girl, annoyed and smoking a joint. Lucho, coming in from the cool morning with some groceries, was astonished by the sight. In an instant, his hand was at Pato's throat and the joint lay crumpled on the floor. Pato coughed, angrily.

"Are you insane, Lucho?" Pato complained as he rubbed his throat and coughed some more. "What is wrong with you?"

"I should be asking *you* that question, Pato! How dare you smoke over Woo Deep? I thought we had all decided to stay away from that stuff! She is sick, and you are only making her sicker with that crap! Don't you have a brain within that head of yours?" Lucho pushed at Pato's head.

"So, what?" Pato retorted. "The girl keeps getting sicker and sicker! My smoking makes no difference! She is probably going to die, anyway."

"Shut up!" Again, Lucho grabbed for Pato's throat, but this time his friend knocked away his hand. Instead, Lucho placed himself protectively in front of the child. "Don't ever say those things. She is going to get better, Pato. She just needs some time to get stronger. That's all. But we have to do our part and help her!"

"Stronger?" Pato laughed bitterly. "Do not kid yourself, Lucho. From the very moment you brought that baby home, she has been sick. It's been... what? Eleven months by now, right? Doesn't she turn one in December? That girl is pretty much already dead, Lucho. I am pretty sure she is not even growing like a baby is supposed to. And the sooner you accept that and stop wasting money on her, the better! The better for all of us."

"Stop it, Pato," said Lucho in a warning tone, raising a finger to his face.

"Stop it? No, Lucho. You stop it, *baboso*. That girl has been sick all through the year. Do you honestly think she will survive the winter? If you do, then you are dumber than you look. Go look for a bin, dump her in it, and resume spending money on important things! Look at you; you are skin and bones yourself."

"Important things? Like what, huh, Pato? Like weed? That's what's important to you?"

"Yeah, not bad, right?" Pato picked up his joint and tried to straighten it out. "Better than wasting it on formula and milk for a baby that is dying anyway..."

Lucho shook his head and turned to the little girl. Sometime during their argument, she had quieted down. He placed a hand on her forehead and sighed. She was still hot and very restless.

Maybe Pato is right...

No! He can't be.

"Where is Addy?" Lucho asked Pato, who had settled in a chair and whose head was now obscured by white smoke.

"I don't know. Somewhere in the back room," came his hoarse response. He chuckled. "I think she is having a sniff. But unlike me, she cares about what it could do to that baby. You two are so... stupid."

Lucho lifted Woo Deep from the bed and left the warehouse. Hopefully, the cool air would drive the fever away. He couldn't believe his friends had gone back to drugs. He shook his head, disappointed.

He knew it was difficult to quit—he had felt the withdrawal effects himself—but since the moment he had decided to take care of Woo Deep, he had put all of that behind him. He was successful. The drugs, the stealing, the prostitutes... he had done away with it all. Pato and Addy had tried too, but they obviously couldn't stay away. They had tried sincerely to help with taking care of Woo Deep, but they just had not been able to.

For the past eleven months, he had taken care of the little girl in his arms. He looked down at her, a tear rolling down his cheek. She was no longer restless, she seemed to always relax in his hold. She knew his smell.

Giving up on stealing had made getting cash difficult, especially since he was feeding more than one mouth. But he had no choice. He knew that if harm ever befell him, Woo Deep would be alone. They had changed each other's lives forever. They were connected. They were one. And their lives depended on each other.

Woo Deep shivered a little in his arms, and he wrapped her up tighter with the blanket. He *loved* the girl; she was *his*! She had completely changed him for the better, and he didn't want to lose her. The thought made him sick. He wouldn't be able to take it if she died, but doubt always found a way to creep in.

Was Pato right? Not about dumping her in a bin, but about her not surviving the winter... he wondered. He feared. He panicked.

Lucho looked down at her and brushed away the strands of brown hair that had fallen over her eyes. He had to do what was best for her. As much as he loved her, he knew she would be better off somewhere else, and not in his care. He just had to *find* that somewhere else. It had to be a perfect place for her to be taken care of, nurtured, and loved. Unconditionally.

But he knew of no such place.

"Lucho, where you at?" Addy's voice came from behind him.

"I'm here," he answered.

He wasn't going to reprimand her for the drugs; he had done so many times already, to the point he had lost count. He was just glad she didn't do it in the presence of Woo Deep.

Addy approached quietly and watched the now sleeping baby in Lucho's arms for a moment before flicking her eyes up to his. "You okay?"

He sighed. "She keeps getting sicker."

"Yeah... I'm sorry. I'm not much help taking care of Woo Deep. I love her, I really do! But I'm not as good at taking care of her as you are. I tried, Lucho. I swear I did."

"It's okay, Addy. You've helped a lot. I know that..."

Addy nodded and was about to go back inside when Lucho stopped her.

"I'm going to give Woo Deep away."

Addy's eyes widened. "Away? Away to... to who?"

"I'm not sure yet. I was hoping you knew of somewhere."

Addy shook her head, her eyes squeezed closed, but tears still crept from under her lids. When she opened her eyes to look at him again, they were glassy and red.

"No. Please, don't do it. Is it because of the drugs? I will stop, I promise! I will get help. I don't want to lose her, Lucho. She is our baby! She is a ray of sunshine in our sad, empty, and otherwise meaningless lives."

"I know that, Addy. *Lo siento, pero* it is what is best for her. She needs to get better. She cannot live through the cold that winter is going to bring. We must let go of her, Addy. If we want her to survive, we have to."

Lucho held Addy as she cried, Woo Deep clutched between them. He was devastated as well, but this was their only option. Addy kept saying she could take care of Woo Deep, that she would get better in their care, but he knew that the little girl wouldn't.

The next morning, Lucho wrapped Woo Deep up in a blanket and they went out, following Addy's lead. Lucho knew that Addy had not resigned herself to the fact they had to let her go, but at least she would make sure the girl would be somewhere safe. He appreciated that.

They headed to the orphanage where Addy had grown up before she ran away a few years ago: *Casa Hogar San Jose.* Addy said it was a good place. She was raised there until she felt like she was old enough, at thirteen, to face the world on her own. That's when she met Lucho and Pato, roaming the streets.

As they made their way there, Addy was pensive.

"What's wrong? You know this is for the best."

"Yes, I know, Lucho. But it's not that."

"Then what is it?"

"Sometimes I wish I could go back to the orphanage. They loved me there. They were good people."

"And what happened? Your case wasn't like mine, Addy. Maybe they'll still take you back."

"No. It's too late for me now." A few steps in silence later, she continued, "But it is not too late for Woo Deep. I know they will take care of her there. They will, for sure."

Lucho walked in silence the rest of the way, with a knot in his throat. *I hope you are right, Addy. I hope they do.*

As soon as they arrived, Lucho glanced at the building. It felt right. And as they entered, it seemed like all eyes were on them. But Lucho did not care, as long as Woo Deep was safe.

A woman ran toward them and, quite reluctantly, Lucho tried to give the baby to her, all the while, Addy was wailing. The lady gave Addy a big hug. Addy hugged her back. Then the lady took the baby from Lucho's arms and took them into an inner office. A well-dressed man and two older women were there as well.

They asked him questions about Woo Deep. They asked questions about their living conditions. They asked Addy how she was doing and if she wanted and needed help. Addy said she was fine. Lucho told them all that had transpired when he found the baby.

"What is your name and how old are you, son?" one of the ladies asked him.

"My name is Lucho. I am sixteen."

The adults in the room looked at each other in surprise. How had this young man managed to care for this baby for almost a year?

"Lucho, what is your full name?" asked one of the ladies in charge.

"Luis Fuentes," he answered quickly. "But don't worry about me. Please, just promise me you will take care of Woo Deep. I would not bring her here if I had any other choice. Please nurture her, love her, and give her your best," Lucho pleaded, his eyes now welling up with tears.

They watched him with a mixture of awe and sadness; his altruism and generosity had got to them.

"We will, Lucho. And may God bless you for all the care you have shown the little one," the man told them both.

And so Lucho and Addy left Woo Deep behind after they had hugged her very tightly. At that moment, Lucho knew he was making the best decision for her as he watched nurses carrying her away. Yet, he could not help the sadness in his heart. Mixed feelings—joy and emptiness. Indescribable.

"She is going to return someday, Addy. I promise you she will. And we will meet her again," he said, trying to comfort his friend, but she only scoffed and walked ahead of him.

"We will meet her again..." he whispered. "You'll see."
I know we will meet again, Woo Deep. Fly now. You are free.

THE FLIGHT OF THE BUTTERFLY

CHAPTER TWENTY-EIGHT

Corona, California
Spring 2019

Thursday had been a happy day in the Fuentes' household, as not only was Maui released from the hospital, but they were also granted temporary custody of the kids. Dinner that evening was special—and noisy. Luis and Samantha were starting to understand what having five kids was like. But still, they did not mind.

Friday afternoon brought with it a visitor, unexpected but pleasant.

"Get the door, Alejandra!" Samantha called to her daughter, who was out in the yard with her new siblings.

"Yes, mom," she called.

A wide smile stretched over Alejandra's face as soon as she saw who it was. She pounced on him with a bear hug. "Grandpa!"

"Hello, little one!" Juan Fuentes ruffled her hair as he stepped into the foyer. "I am so sorry I missed your party, Ali."

She took his bags and gave him another large hug. "It's okay, Tata. It's not your fault you were under the weather. If memory serves me right, you did say you'd make it up to me." She winked at him, showing bright teeth with shiny metal braces.

"Oh, I will. Don't you worry about that!" Señor Juan chuckled.

She laughed and ran off to inform the rest of the household of his arrival.

The boys had trailed in behind her from the yard, and they were tucked in the corner, looking shy. Señor Juan squatted in front of them and smiled.

"You must be Billy and you must be Aaron, am I right?"

The boys nodded, and Billy asked. "Who are you?"

"That's Grandpa Juan, boys." Samantha said as she stepped in with a smile. "He's your Daddy Luis's father. You can call him *Tata*." She gave Juan a hug and a kiss on the cheek. "This is a surprise, but a pleasant one, all the same."

"How are you, my dear?" he asked heartily.

"We're all doing very well, praise God. I see you've met two of the latest additions to the family."

"Yes, I have!" Juan smiled down at the boys. He ruffled the hair of Aaron who giggled shyly. "Where is the third and youngest addition, Maui?"

"Lucho has her, of course. He won't let go of her."

"I can imagine. And where is that husband of yours?"

Samantha chuckled. "He's up in the garden."

The grandpa grunted and headed toward the staircase leading to the roof. "Look who's developed a green thumb. Who would've ever guessed!?"

Luis chuckled as soon as he heard the voice. He didn't have to turn around to know who it was. It was the man that had believed in him and given him so much when he was at his lowest. The man who had become his and his brothers' father. He turned and hugged Juan.

"Hi, *Pa*. Good to see you."

"Yeah. Sorry I didn't call ahead, son," Juan said as he crossed to the shaded bassinet.

"You know you're always welcome here, Pa. No need to call ahead."

"So, this is Maui, huh?" he asked as the baby slept.

"Yeah, that's our new baby. She likes the outdoors, so I bring her out here to nap while I garden."

Juan smiled. "She's cute." As he settled into the deck chair beside Maui, he asked, "And Pedro. Have you been able to contact him?"

"Yes, I have. He apologized for not getting your calls. He had an emergency over at Sacramento, but he should be back by now. His flight was to land by noon, I think," Luis said as he sat next to him.

"They are coming over tomorrow, right?"

"Yes. What is it that you want to tell us, though? Are you getting remarried?"

Juan chuckled. "You know I will always love my beloved Alejandra, God bless her soul. I can't remarry."

"She was an amazing woman, indeed. She was the best mother to my brothers and I," Luis said, but he raised his head and noticed the look on Juan's face. "What exactly do you want to tell us, Pa? Come on. You have that uncertain look on your face, like you aren't sure how we'll react."

"Not until tomorrow, son." Juan patted Luis on the knee and went back into the house.

With a thoughtful sigh, Luis stood from his chair and walked toward the edge of the roof to rest against the railing that framed the perimeter. He couldn't help but think back to a time in the past when his life had been very different.

San Bernardino, California
Summer 1992

Hot and sweaty, Lucho tapped on the car's window and was rewarded with a folded bill. He waved as the car drove off and pocketed his tip. It was a blistering summer afternoon in San Bernardino, and his job of washing car windows only worsened the heat. Still, he was glad he had a good job.

After work, making up his mind to get a cold drink, he started toward the convenience store attached to the gas station. On his way, a short squeak made him pause. There were many cars about, but no people. Perhaps it was a rat. But something about it made Lucho's hair stand on end. He adjusted his direction toward the sound but had barely made it two steps before a gunshot ricocheted from an alley.

Lucho had been in the U.S. since the winter of the previous year, the month after he gave Woo Deep up. He was here undocumented, having entered through the tunnels beneath the border, and he intended to remain undetected. He was finally doing ok. He had no plans of getting himself involved with the police. Yet, here he was moving toward trouble.

Soon enough, he heard shrieking, and he hastened his footsteps. He stepped into the alley and saw a man with a gun pointed at a girl as he tore at her skirt. Lucho lunged at him, and he fell to the ground, sending the pistol a few yards away. The girl slunk to the ground out of pure fear as she watched her attacked scramble to his feet and his weapon. Lucho put himself between them and held the girl close.

"Are you okay?" he asked repeatedly.

The girl shivered. Her blouse had become rags, and she wore only underwear on her bottom.

"He has my bag!"

Lucho turned around just in time to see the culprit disappearing around the corner.

What exactly do you think you are doing, Lucho? Why get yourself into such an issue knowing full well that you are not legal in this country? Stay out of it, Lucho.

He mentally slapped himself. *But she needs my help!*

"I will get it for you, all right?" he said as began to run. "Get to a safe place. Have the store call the police. I promise I will get it back."

He blocked out the warning voice in his head and increased his pace. He caught up with the man in an alley. Living in the streets, if anything, had made Lucho a fighter. As soon as he had knocked the gun out of the man's hand, getting the bag had been a piece of cake.

As he ran out of the alley, he heard a gunshot. It wasn't until he was on the road, blood seeping from his shoulder and adrenaline on high, that he realized that he had been shot.

Still, with his one good arm, he protected the bag. The shooter was approaching him, a maniacal look on his face. He was yelling something.

Lucho turned his face to the side and saw a car heading straight at him. Then he heard receding footsteps, honks of cars, and a siren.

Then, everything went dark.

"Lucho, can you hear me?" a voice said when Lucho stirred. His ears perked.

That voice, that calm, reassuring, and fatherly voice... Where had he heard it before? And why was he lying on a soft bed? His bed at the apartment he shared with some co-workers was certainly not this comfortable.

His eyes snapped open and immediately widened.

"It's good to see you again. I certainly never thought it would be in the U.S., though!" The face Lucho could never forget smiled down at him. It belonged to the only adult that had ever shown him love in all the years since he was born.

"Señor Juan?" he croaked, his eyes welling up. "What? How in the world? Where am I? Am I dead? Is it really you?"

"In the flesh, my boy." The man grinned down at him. "Honestly, I wonder why we are always meeting under such conditions."

Lucho tried to sit up, but winced as a jolt of pain shot through his arm. Señor Juan helped him by propping his cushions in such a way as allowing him to sit up.

"You got a bullet to your shoulder, my boy. It's going to hurt for a while."

"How did you... I mean, what are you doing here?" Lucho asked, still reeling from surprise.

He knew Mr. Juan was an American citizen and that he had businesses throughout Southern California and also on the southern part of the border, but he had never thought he would meet the man ever again. It had been a couple of years since the previous incident. And he was two-hundred miles away from his old home.

"I almost ran you over."

Then Lucho remembered. "That was you in the car!" he said. "How is the girl? Did she get her bag? Is she doing well? And the guy that robbed her!"

"Yes, she is fine, my boy. They also got the guy, don't worry about him. But you might be in some trouble."

"Yes, I know..." Lucho looked down at his bandaged hands. "I am not here legally..."

"That's all right. I'm having it worked on as we speak."

Lucho looked at him, more confused. "What do you mean?"

"Your papers, my boy. You've been in the country for how long now?"

"Um… since last winter."

"And how old are you?"

"I turned seventeen in September."

"Perfect. It's not going to be easy, but I really think we'll be able to do it. Don't worry about a thing."

"Do what, Señor Juan?" Lucho held his head. He had a headache, and it seemed like the man kept talking in circles.

"Legalize your stay here, of course," Señor Juan said, like it was the most natural thing in the world.

Lucho paused and mouthed a few words, but nothing came out. Finally, he managed, "You would do that… for me? Why? How?"

"Why wouldn't I? I want to help you. I want to help you be what you are meant to be. The question here is, do *you* want to help yourself?" Señor Juan looked down at him with concern, and at that moment, Lucho realized he was not worthless, that he was not meant to be a loser, and his eyes welled up with tears.

After he had a chance to recover, Lucho left the hospital and went straight to Mr. Fuentes's home. There, he met the most amazing and caring woman he had ever met: Alejandra, Juan's wife. The two of them did all that they could for him, and by year end, Luis Fuentes had a green card. They had adopted him.

All Lucho wanted to do was work hard, achieve great things, somehow get his brothers, and pay Mr. Juan and Doña Alejandra Fuentes back for all their kindness.

The couple could not have kids of their own, and the thought of adopting had always been on their mind; this was the perfect opportunity. All that Juan and his wife wanted Lucho to do was go to school, draw closer to God, and reach his full potential.

Colton, California
Spring 1993

One bright, spring morning in the year 1993, Lucho returned home from school to find the biggest surprise of his life: Pedro and Andres. The love and respect he had for the couple soared more than ever. They had searched for his brothers in Mexicali and somehow were able to find them. They had their paperwork done and had also adopted them.

The reunion had been bittersweet; Lucho found out that his mother had killed Santos during one of her drunken dazes two years earlier. It had been an accident, but she still had done the deed. She had run out on them right after that, and they never heard from her again.

Hearing this discouraged Lucho's belief in God. He had kept on studying, working hard to become something in life, and took care of those around him; but when it came to God, he shut Him out. Despite this, his new parents, Juan and Alejandra, still accepted him without judgement.

But Lucho was determined. God did not exist. There was too much evil in this world.

Riverside, California
Fall 2000

Meeting Samantha while working at a Bullseye store in Riverside had completely changed Luis's life. Though Juan had encouraged him to join his business after he graduated with an MBA in Business Administration, he had declined the offer. He loved and respected the man as a father, but still, the man had given him so much already, and he wanted to create his own path. Samantha, just like Juan and Alejandra, never gave up on him. Before dating him, she kept working on him, until finally, he agreed to go to her church. That day changed his life forever.

The pastor preached a message that touched Luis's heart. He talked about second chances. About forgiveness. He talked about letting go and allowing God to take lead in life.

Luis was adamant about resisting. *God can't be real*, he convinced himself. *And if He is, then He is not good. There is too much evil in this world. Second chances? Give me a break. People don't really deserve a second chance. Certainly not Sofia.*

The pastor then talked about how in spite of evil in the world, there is also beauty. There is hope. There is joy. And yes, second chances abound in all of us.

Luis struggled with a conflict in his heart. *Perhaps... there is truth in all of this.*

After the pastor finished his sermon, he made a call. Reluctantly at first, Luis was moved. He relieved his life until that moment. He saw then all the opportunities given to him for a better life. And he cried.

Have I been wrong all these years? I mean, I too was given a second chance. And a third. And so many more...

And that day, right there and then, after decades of skepticism and dissent, after the buildup of discouragement over his lifetime, Luis accepted Jesus in his heart. From then on, he was a new person. Like his brothers already had, he became a newborn Christian. And this would be his life now, next to Samantha.

Corona, California
Spring 2019

Sunday dinner was a happy one, filled with laughter and light-hearted chatter. Samantha announced good news: she had been offered a partner position in her old friend's company. She was going to provide her skills in the business, while her friend provided the capital.

Later in the evening, the three brothers and their adoptive father were seated in the roof garden, Pedro and Luis chatting, while Juan and Andres discussed business. Andres was running the family business. The four men hadn't sat like this since the New Year. Sometimes, it was one with the other, or two with another, but not the four of them all together.

"You know what your mom always used to tell me, guys?"

The brothers shook their heads, sitting up to listen.

Alejandra had been an amazing mother to them. After suffering at the hands of their birth mother for years, they had finally experienced the love of a mother for fourteen happy years.

She had died a month after Alejandra, the granddaughter, was born, following a long battle with cancer. She had promised she would see her first grandchild before she died. And she certainly had.

Luis and Samantha had decided to name their daughter after her, in her honor. They had all been devastated but were able to move past it, because they had each other and trusted God's promises.

"She used to say to me, 'Juan, we were not able to have our own kids, but God brought into our lives three amazing boys. And I love those boys more than anything. They are gifts from God!' You know, you boys always made us happy and proud. You still do," Juan said, and the brothers could do nothing but pat him on the back. They were always going to be grateful to God for Juan and Alejandra, their parents.

"What is it that you wanted to tell us, *Pa*?" Andres asked.

Señor Juan cleared his throat and sat up. "*Escuchenme bien.* I know you are all going to be upset about what I want to say to you, but I hope that you will keep an open mind and open hearts as well. Promise me that."

"Dad..." Pedro started saying.

"Promise me, sons! All of you," Juan insisted.

"Ok, fine, we promise," the brothers responded almost in unison, though they exchanged uneasy glances.

"Sofia contacted me," Juan said. "Your birth mother."

"You've got to be kidding me!" Andres was on his feet. "She is still alive? To think an evil woman like her is still breathing while *Mom* is dead is—"

"Andres!" Juan exclaimed, holding the Andres under a hard stare.

"I'm sorry, Pa, but he's right." Pedro said. "The good certainly do die young."

"You promised to keep an open mind, boys."

"This is us keeping an open mind, Pa!" Andres took his seat.

Juan turned to Luis, who had been quiet. "Luis?"

"I'm sorry, *Papi*, but that is going to be difficult. I mean... she did kill our youngest brother. Her own son! She should be rotting in prison, for all we care. It's really..." Luis choked on the words he was about to say and cleared his throat. "What would have happened to us if we never met you and Mom?"

"Very good question," Andres said turning to his father. "What would have happened if you hadn't rescued us?"

"You would have found another helper. God works in mysterious and amazing ways, my boys."

Pedro groaned. "How did she even find us?"

"You..." Juan replied.

"Me?"

"Yes, son. The Architectural Award Ceremony in San Diego," Juan explained.

"Oh."

"We were all present. And, somehow, she was there too. Hearing your name arose her suspicions. But the speech you gave about your background was what confirmed them. And then she came closer and recognized you. But she was scared."

"Ah. So, she's smarter now," Andres said. "She *should* be scared!"

"Andres... I understand how you boys feel. I'm your father, and I watched you boys grow up, living with the pain of losing your brother. It was not easy; I know that."

"What does she even want?" Luis asked coldly.

"Seeing me with you guys, she knew I would be the best person to approach. At first, she didn't know who I was, so she watched from a distance. But then she approached me. We had a good conversation after the event. She is dying. She just wants to see you before she goes."

"Why?" Pedro threw his hands out as he exclaimed. "I'm sorry, Dad, but no matter how much I think about it, all I feel is hate. I'm going through my mind, my memories, trying to locate one, *just one*, happy thought, just one time when she showed us care... but I can't, Dad. Nothing comes to mind, because she never did."

He stood up and hugged his father. "I'm going to bed, Dad. Let's discuss this when I've... had time to think. Because right now, all this is doing is making me mad."

"Me too. Goodnight, *Pa*." Andres hugged him and left too.

"Are you going to leave too?" Juan asked Luis.

"No, *Papi*. You're missing mom right now, so I will stay out here with you."

"*Gracias, mijo.*"

"I kinda wish the news you had for us really *was* that you were remarrying, to be honest," Luis said only partially joking.

This caused Juan to laugh heartily. They stayed outside for a while in silence, taking comfort from each other's presence, then went off to bed.

Monday morning came and brought with it plenty of rowdiness; but by 8 a.m., the three children had gone off to school, Maui was at daycare, and Samantha had gone to the far side of Riverside with Sebastian and Tata Juan; they had gone for a campus tour of the university.

The three brothers had a late breakfast and discussed all that had transpired the previous night. Neither Pedro nor Andres were ready to go home yet. They had informed Luis and his wife that they would be spending spring break with them.

"All right, we will go see Sofia, then," Pedro said after almost an hour of discussion. "Let's see what she has to say."

"I know what she has to say. She wants to cry, beg, apologize, and explain why she was a despicable mother. You watch movies, don't you? That's definitely it! Finally, her conscience got to her, I bet!" Andres said with a laugh, though his eyes remained cold.

Luis chuckled. "Probably true. But, either way, we'll still go see her. Take care of the house, bros. I have to go."

"Yeah, yeah. Whatever. Have a good day at work," Pedro replied.

"I might just attack her..." Andres whispered to his brother.

"No, you won't," Luis said from the doorway. "We will be there with you. We are all in this together, okay? She didn't succeed in tearing us down when we were younger, and she won't now."

Pedro nodded. "No, she won't."

PART 4

• • • •

The Flight of the Butterfly

CHAPTER TWENTY-NINE

Corona, California
Spring 2019

Lucho arrived at the store to find a party in the lunchroom. "What is this for?" he chuckled once the cheering had quieted. "Mr. Fuentes, this is to congratulate you all on the new additions to the Fuentes clan!" came a reply from one of the younger employees. She handed him a little cupcake as she said this, and Lucho smiled down at the five little stick figures iced on top.

He thanked his team, and they celebrated together for a little, before they all went back to work as usual.

Luis was busy in the storage room a couple of hours later, when he heard a quiet knock. He looked up to see Monica.

"Hey, boss man. I just wanted to inform you that someone came looking for you last Friday. I don't know if it was important or not, but you've been so busy, I didn't want to bug you about it until you came back."

"Oh, ok. Thanks. Who was it?"

"Um... well, she didn't really say her name. She was petite with brown hair... a very pretty lady. Late twenties, maybe? I don't know. Anyway, she asked if you still work here, and I said yes. I think she'll back this week."

"Thank you, Monica. I'll keep an eye out for her."

Monica ducked back onto the sales floor, and Luis turned back to the inventory. But all the while, his mind kept drifting back to what Monica had said. Who was the lady that had come looking for him? He didn't know anyone who fit that description. At least, from the top of his head, he couldn't think of anyone.

About two hours later, Luis was preoccupied with the inventory once more, when he heard another knock and a voice.

"Yes?"

"Someone is here to see you, boss," said one of the newer employees.

"I'll be right there," Luis replied. *What is it now? Let me guess, an angry customer? I hope it doesn't have to do with the kids.*

Quickly, he rounded up his recordings and went toward the store entrance. But despite his inner ramblings, he wondered if it was the same person Monica had told him about.

A Few Hours Earlier

Genesis heaved a sigh of relief as the traffic finally started to lessen on the 91-freeway going eastbound. She stepped on the gas and moved forward. Glancing at her wristwatch, she took note of the time. It was just past 9:30 a.m. She hoped she would be able to meet Luis Fuentes today. She had checked on him the previous Friday, but he had been out.

It hadn't been a great weekend. She'd had to find a quick place to move into with Jay. It wasn't where they wanted to live, but it was for safety reasons. She hated moving. She was also driving without a license, since the next available appointment at the DMV wouldn't be for another two weeks.

Her father was also angry at her for not being entirely truthful about her trip, but his main concern had to do with being kept in the dark about her abduction. The fact that she had been in trouble, and he didn't know anything about it, infuriated him. And of course, once she and Jay told him, he was livid.

No; the weekend had not been the best.

She rounded a bend, and as she did, her stomach rumbled, reminding her she hadn't had anything to eat yet. She would have to grab some food once she got to Corona. She had left home early and had skipped breakfast.

She had also taken too long deciding on an outfit that morning. Nothing had convinced her. She finally settled on a semi-casual black dress and some wedges for her feet. Not too fancy. Not too revealing. Just... normal. Whatever that meant. Then she spent an unusual amount of time perfecting her hair and an equal amount of time deciding on her makeup.

What earrings would look good? Ugh! Why was she so nervous? What if this guy wasn't even him? But... what if he was? What would she even say to him? Would he even be glad to see her? And why was she trying to look pretty? Why would that even matter?

She had too many questions. She was trembling, and the hunger didn't help either. Her stomach kept growling.

Genesis finally arrived on the I-15 freeway. The traffic had been heavy, and as soon as she got onto I-15 South, she drove to the first restaurant she saw. She had to drive around the block before she found a parking space.

When she settled in at the café, Genesis was met with more frustration, as it took a while before she was attended. And it felt like it was taking forever for her to receive her order. She thought about going somewhere else, but by that time, there was a long queue at the door. She guessed they were all there for some sort of *Monday Morning Special.* It would be difficult to get out, and if she so much as stood up, she would not be able to get a seat again.

While waiting for her order, Genesis tried calling Jay, but she got redirected to his voicemail. She hung up the call. She was not used to being the one ignored. It sucked. She just wanted to talk to him; he was great at helping her be calm.

He's just busy, not ignoring me.

Just as she put her phone down, a plate appeared before her. Genesis surveyed the food before her intently. Her eyes moved from the soggy pancake to the burned eggs and then the sloppily buttered toast.

Coffee, ah, that would be good. She raised it to her lips and gagged as soon as it hit her tongue.

Who serves cold coffee! she wondered, very much annoyed.

She looked back at the crowd and wondered why on Earth anyone would choose to eat at such a place? Not tasting anything else, Genesis placed a couple dollar bills on the table and left. She could only hope that she met Luis Fuentes this morning, or else she would have to take the risk and try out another restaurant in the area before heading back home, once again defeated. If it was him, maybe they could go out for some food!

Don't move too fast, Gigi! she cautioned herself.

What if it wasn't him? Or what if he wanted nothing to do with her? The doubts were back. Her hands trembled as she started the car. But there was no turning back now.

Genesis pulled into the expansive parking lot of The Crossings, a large shopping center where the Bullseye retail store was located. She parked the car and turned the engine off. She took a long, deep breath, and then stepped out. The parking lot was a lot less crowded than Friday, she noticed.

Walking into the large store, she was greeted by the same lady she had met the previous week.

"Hi. Uh... is Mr. Fuentes around, by any chance?" Genesis inquired.

The lady stood up. "Sure. I'll go get the manager."

The manager... nice.

"Thank you," Genesis responded with a smile.

She let her eyes feast on the contents of the shelves nearest her; this was a huge store! She hoped that in a couple of years, she would be shopping here with Jay for their little one... *or little ones.* She sighed when she thought of her fiancé. She really hoped he wasn't still mad at her.

"Hi! Can I help you, miss?"

Genesis was interrupted from her thoughts by a warm and friendly voice. Slowly, she turned around. She took in the sight of the man before her. Khakis, red polo. A handsome man with salt-and-pepper hair, maybe in his mid-forties.

"Hi," she replied with a cracking voice. "My name is Genesis Gill. I'm from the L.A. Chronicle."

"Oh, wow. The Chronicle, huh? And how may I be of service, Miss Gill?"

Genesis stared at him, not really knowing what to say. He seemed confused.

Say something, G!

"I'm sorry. Actually, I'm not here on behalf of the paper. It's just that I... um..." She stammered to a halt, all words failing her.

The man looked at her with concern now. "Is everything okay?"

"Are you..." She cleared her throat and fixed a strand of hair that had fallen over her face. "Are you Luis Fuentes from Mexicali, Baja California, by any chance?" she asked carefully, though she knew in her guts that she was right.

She could feel it. The man who towered above her with his cheery oval face and confused smile was the one who had kept her alive for the first eleven months of her life. She just knew it in her heart.

He fixed her with a quizzical stare. "Yes. I am he. Can I...? I mean, how do you even—"

His question was interrupted when Gigi crushed him in a tight hug, leaving him stunned. Eventually, he relaxed and hugged her back, albeit gently. And finally, she pulled away with tears in her eyes.

"I am so sorry, but I don't think I know you, miss. Please tell me what this is about?"

Genesis gathered her thoughts and wiped her tears. "Actually, *I* am sorry. Like I said, my name is Genesis Gill," she said nervously. "I know I already said that, but you might know me as... *Wu-Dip, or Woo Deep.*"

Luis's mouth fell open. His eyes became glassy, and in a matter of a few seconds, he also broke down in tears. As he hugged Genesis once more he kept whispering, "Woo Deep."

After she was finally able to pull herself together, Genesis let go. "I have so many questions for you."

He looked at her, smiling. "So do I. I honestly don't even know where to start at. How have you been? Where have you been? What do you do? How did you find me? What's been going on with you?" Questions kept tumbling from Luis, leaving Gigi no chance to respond.

And yet Genesis couldn't help the large grin on her face. The reunion was going better than all the scenarios she had envisioned—and he kept going.

"You are so... grown. You look so healthy, happy, and stunning. I am so proud. Do you really work for The Chronicle? I mean, look at you! Woo Deep, all grown up!"

"Actually, Lucho... Can I call you that?"

"Only close family and people from my past call me *Lucho*."

Genesis's smile turned into a frown. "Oh, I see."

"So of course you can call me that! You are both of those things, after all."

Genesis beamed once again. "Well, Lucho, are you free to go get something to eat, by any chance? I'm starving. And I figured we can talk over brunch, if you don't mind. And I promise that I'll tell you everything."

"Sure, I am. Let me just talk to my employees. Do you have a place in mind?" Luis was also grinning from ear-to-ear.

"Not really," Genesis said quickly. "I'm not familiar with the area."

"That's okay. I know a place!" Luis doled out some instructions to the other employees and then left the store with Genesis. "Do you like Mexican?"

She nodded. "I sure do!"

"Great. It's not far from here. Come on, I'll drive."

They got into his car parked just outside the entrance. Hanging from the rear-view mirror was a beautiful blue-topaz and sterling-silver butterfly pendant necklace.

"That's a beautiful necklace," Gigi said, inspecting it in her hands without removing it from the mirror.

With a smile, Lucho put the car in gear. "Actually... that butterfly is you. I've had this piece since the same day I found you."

Genesis's eyes scanned through the menu at *Luna*. There was so much to choose from. The place was trendy and fancy, but cozy. Smooth jazz played in the background. She looked up and saw Luis watching her. He smiled.

"I still can't believe this is real. Should I order for you?"

She nodded. "Yes, please. And I agree. This is really happening!"

Luis ordered, calling the waiter by name. Apparently, they knew him; he was a regular.

"Rodrigo, can we also have the guacamole with mango and your chipotle salsa, *por favor*," Luis said. He then turned to Genesis. "I'm sure you will *love* it."

With a smile, Genesis agreed. "I'm sure I will. It all sounds delicious!" she said.

Their food and drinks came in a couple of minutes. Genesis had ordered horchata, and Luis got jamaica. They ate in silence for a while, and it was only after their second helpings were brought that they started talking again. Partially it was the hunger. Another reason was the nerves.

But Genesis answered all of Luis's questions, one by one. There were hundreds of them. He wanted to know how she was, who had taken her in, and if she been well looked after. He wanted to know her entire life story, and she gladly shared.

"I always wondered what happened to you, *mija!*" Luis smiled through tears. "My little Woo Deep. I really wanted to care for you, but... you were just too sick. I did what I thought was best..." He started to cry.

Genesis grabbed his hands. "You are an important part of my life. You gave me strength, shelter, food... and *love* when no one else would have done so. You gave me up because that was the only way to save me. Now, that is true sacrifice!"

Genesis squeezed Luis's hand with her small one. "I will be forever indebted to you, Lucho. You were a sixteen-year-old boy who barely had anything. But the little you did have, you shared with me. You kept me alive! You shared your life! Thank you."

They were both crying again. Luis smiled through wet eyes. "You don't know this, but you changed my life, as well. You changed who I was forever."

"I guess we were in each other's lives for a reason, then."

"Yes, we were."

"By the way," she said, "it's Wu-Dip, not Woo Deep. It means butterfly in Cantonese."

Luis smiled and almost laughed. "Wu-Dip. Butterfly. The necklace. It all makes sense now. All these years, and I had no idea."

Genesis beamed.

They sat there for the rest of the afternoon, talking about their lives. Luis told her about his life before he saved her, and about his family. He showed her pictures, and she also showed him hers. He was glad to know Addy was alive, and he concluded to try to reach out and help as well.

As they were saying their goodbyes, Luis said, "You know what, butterfly, I lost you once before, but I'm determined not to lose you again. Now that you're back in my life, will you stay?"

"I'd love that... Lucho." They hugged once again. "I'd love that very much."

Finally, they parted ways with a promise to get together soon, along with their families, hopefully by the weekend.

That afternoon, Luis went home and broke the good news to his family during dinner. If there was anyone as excited as he was, it was his daughter Alejandra.

She was a fan of Gigi Gill's works in The *L.A. Chronicle* and was thrilled she would finally get to meet her. Alejandra had written a homework paper earlier in the school year about sex slaves and sex rings in California, and Gigi's pieces had been a fundamental part of her research. Never in his life would Luis have imagined that this eminent journalist was his Woo Deep.

This was a small world, after all.

On her own end, Genesis arrived home to find Jay seated in the dark, waiting for her. He picked up a large bouquet of red roses from beside him and handed it to her as he turned on a lamp. Genesis smiled and gave him a kiss.

"Thank you, Jay. For everything. I have such good news."

"I can't wait to hear it. But just so you know, your dad is pissed."

"I know. I'm visiting him this evening to make peace."

"Good luck."

Genesis took a deep breath. "Ugh, I know. I'll need it." She put her purse and keys away and sat down on the couch. Jay joined her.

"Anyway, come on! Tell me all about your trip! I want to hear it all."

"Oh, my goodness. I don't even know where to even begin."

"How about at the beginning?"

They both laughed.

"Alright. So, the year was 1990..."

Back at Luis's house, the day after he met Genesis, Luis and his brothers went to see their mother in the hospital. Just like Andres predicted, she had nothing else to offer them but an apology.

"I'm so sorry, my babies," she croaked out, holding Andres's hand, though he looked down at the contact with mild disgust. "I was messed up for so many years. When your father left me to take care of Luis when he was born, I was young, scared, and alone. I didn't know how to care for a child by myself, and that's when I really dove into the drugs and alcohol."

"That's no excuse," Luis said. He tried to make his voice sound harsh, but in all honesty, he had done the same thing she did. When he was alone and scared, he had turned to drugs for comfort. He didn't have the strength to say no and find a better path.

"I know, my baby," Sofia said, then coughed harshly. "You are my first born, and I should have treated you better. Didn't you like that job I got you? Remember? At the lumberyard?"

Luis scoffed. Had she not even noticed his absence? "I never went to that job."

"Then who was giving me all that money?"

Pedro and Andres looked at each other and laughed. "I'm still surprised they let young boys like us work there," Pedro said.

Luis gasped. "You took my job? You never told me! It was so far from home."

"You left us!" Pedro said. "We had to find some way to provide for ourselves. We managed. Besides, Sofia here sure wasn't doing anything, so we never complained."

"Hey, I know I wasn't exactly mother of the year, but I did my best!" she protested, then fell into another coughing fit.

The men looked at each other, not knowing what to say at that comment.

Your best? You treated us poorly and weren't even around most of the time. And when you were, you abused us! Luis chose not to say anything and ignored her, instead choosing to address his brother.

"I'm so sorry you had to do that. I had no idea," Luis said. "You guys were definitely way better off without me then. I shouldn't have held you back and left much sooner."

"Don't start a pity party, bro," Andres said, patting Luis's back. "Your departure just pushed us to work harder. We wanted you there, of course, but we survived on our own. Don't let any guilt consume you, okay? That day you left, when you didn't return by nightfall, we knew you were gone for good. Besides, it wasn't your fault you had to go."

"I'm somewhat to blame for that..." Sofia mumbled.

Somewhat?

The men stared at her, and she shrugged. So they got ready to leave. They'd had enough of her antics and concluded she hadn't changed since she left them. But before they left the room, Sofia asked, "Where's your brother?"

"What?" Luis asked.

"My little Santos!" she beamed. "He was always so happy to see me. Why didn't he come? He's my youngest baby. Where did he go? We used to have so many laughs..."

"Laughs?" Andres stepped forward, clenching his fists.

Luis held his arm out to stop him from going any farther. "Sofia, do you remember what you did to him?" Luis asked.

"What I—" She covered her mouth with both hands. "I did something to him? Oh, my brain has been so foggy lately. I don't even remember the last time I spoke to him. Will he be coming to visit? I need to see my baby."

Luis looked at his brothers, then back at their mother. "He's... running a little late. He told me to tell you that he misses you, that he loves you, and that he can't wait to see you."

"Oh, good!" she squealed, clapping wildly. She fell into another coughing fit, and Luis led his brothers out the door.

"Why the hell didn't you tell her, bro?" Andres asked. "Or do you think she was faking it?"

"She's dying," he said firmly. "Everyone should have one good memory before they die, even if they are confused about the past."

"She doesn't deserve you, bro," Pedro said. "She doesn't deserve any of us."

"We need to forgive her. None of us deserve anything, either, but we were given a second chance." They remained silent as they walked. "Actually," Luis said as he stopped before exiting the building, "Can we say a prayer for her?"

Andres and Pedro looked at each other, then reluctantly huddled with Luis in the lobby. Luis felt the anger they held for her slowly dissipate. They made their peace with her and forgave her. It was a heavy weight lifted from all of their shoulders. It felt good to not have any rancor against their mother.

The next day, Sofia died in her sleep, at peace with God.

THE FLIGHT OF THE BUTTERFLY

CHAPTER THIRTY

Orange, California
November 2019

"I'd stopped believing in myself. But finding out about my survival story as a newborn, how strong of a fighter I was, and how life placed very important people in my path, rekindled my belief and love for myself and for life. Whether you believe in a greater being or not, I know that someone or something had been there with me, even when I chose not to recognize it. And this supreme entity paved the way for my survival. It's true, after all, that with time and through difficulty, life turns coal into diamonds, sand into pearls, and caterpillars into butterflies."

Genesis paused from reading to look across the small crowd of attentive faces, eager for her to continue. "Now, the flight and the journey of the butterfly is indeed completed, and I am once again home, at last," she finished.

The audience that surrounded her in her kitchen broke into applause. She placed the issue of the *L.A. Chronicle* that she had been reading on the table as her family, old and new, all approached her, enveloping her in hugs.

"*The Flight of the Butterfly* it truly is a befitting name for your story, my dear," her father said, picking up the *Chronicle* to look at her words on the page. "You've always been mine and your mother's beautiful butterfly."

"Thanks, Dad." She hugged him tightly, but lingered a little longer as he tried to pull away.

Alejandra was next in line, and Gigi hugged her tightly.

"All right, everyone... let's eat!" Samantha called.

They all hurried to the large table that had been improvised to fit everyone. They were having a large family brunch at Genesis and Jay's small apartment in the city of Orange to celebrate Genesis's story in the paper. It hadn't been easy getting Macy to approve it, especially after the article she'd produced after her return from Mexico.

Mr. Macy said it had lacked direction, and he didn't know if he was ready to read another piece she had such a personal connection to. But the moment he read the new article, however, he was eager to publish it. "It's filled with raw emotion," he'd said. Just the piece the *Chronicle* had been waiting for. It would surely go viral.

Genesis looked around the crowded table of her new place, and her heart swelled. They barely fit in their new home, but she wouldn't change it for anything in the world. She was surrounded by people she loved and who loved her back—her dad, Jay and his mom, along with his sister Julia and her family, Das and a handsome date he brought along from Mexicali, and Luis and his family, consisting of his wife, kids, father, and brothers.

She felt so blessed. In the blink of an eye, her family had expanded.

Gigi would never find out the identity of her real parents. The search for who her mother was had led nowhere, as there seemed to be no record of her death or any traces of her identity. Who her biological father was, was an even greater mystery. But she had made peace with this fact, because in the process of searching for her roots, she'd found a new family.

She had found her identity and purpose. She had found joy. She had made peace with herself. And her family was here with her.

Her journey was complete. She was blessed beyond measure; and for that, she was eternally thankful.

Jay kissed her on the cheek. "Earth to Genesis," he whispered in her ear. "Are you there, babe?"

She was pensive. Lost in thought, but happy ones.

"I'm right here, my Blue Jay," she whispered back with a smile. "I'm here, more than ever. I'm home with my family, where I belong." She then looked him in the eyes and blurted out, "*I love you!*"

Jay's smile couldn't be bigger. After a moment of processing, he asked her, "Are you ready to tell them the real reason you invited them all here today?" He stood and hugged her from behind as she sat on the edge of the table.

Her phone rang. An unknown number, so she ignored it. This was much more important.

A deep grin crossed her lips, and she stood tall in the center of the room. "Hey, everyone!" she screamed.

The crowd paused and turned their attention to her. Her phone rang again. She sent it to voicemail and put it back on the table.

"We're getting married today!" she exclaimed. "We're going to the court after this!"

Jaws dropped throughout the room. They all erupted with applause and cheers as the news sunk in. Gigi looked around, her face beaming between smiles and joyful tears. There was no better way to celebrate family and new beginnings than with an official union with the man she loved, surrounded by her past and present cherished ones.

Jay's phone rang. He stepped aside to answer.

"It's for you, babe," he said coming back with obvious confusion.

"Why on your phone?" she whispered.

He shrugged his shoulders. "Beats me."

"Who is it?"

"I don't know. I didn't ask. And No caller ID."

"Um, okay...?"

Gigi took Jay's phone, excused herself, and walked into the living room, away from the commotion.

"Hi, this is Gigi. Who's this?"

"Hello, Genesis."

She didn't recognize the raspy voice. "Who is this?"

The enigmatic male voice continued, "I've been looking for you. I've been digging around, and I've finally found you. I know who you are, Genesis. I mean, who you *really* are!"

Gigi looked at Jay from across the living room, who silently mouthed "*Who is it?*"

She shrugged, then spoke into the phone. "I'm sorry, I don't really have time to speak right now. If—"

"My name is Carlos Wong."

THE END

THE FLIGHT OF THE BUTTERFLY

<u>Human Trafficking Statistics</u>
(As of 2020)

- Human trafficking generates $9.5 billion yearly in the United States alone (United Nations).
- The average age of entry into prostitution for a child victim in the US is 13 years old (U.S. Department of Justice).
- The average victim may be forced to have sex up to 20-48 times a day (Polaris Project).
- Fewer than 100 beds are available in the United States for underage victims (Health and Human Services).
- A pimp can make $150,000-$200,000 per child each year, and the average pimp has 4 to 6 girls (U.S. Department of National Center for Missing and Exploited Children).
- One in three teens on the street will be lured toward prostitution within 48 hours of leaving home (National Runaway Safeline).
- Nearly 800,000 children go missing every year; that is roughly 2,185 children a day (National Center for Missing and Exploited Children).
- Adults purchase children for sex at least 2.5 million times a year in the United States (USA Today).
- Every two minutes, a child is exploited in the sex industry (Huffington Post).
- On average, a child might be raped by 6,000 men during a five-year period of servitude (Sun Sentinel).
- It is estimated that at least 100,000 to 300,000 children – boys and girls – are bought and sold for sex in the U.S. every year; some of these children are forcefully abducted, others are runaways, and still others are sold into the system by relatives and acquaintances (U.S. Department of Justice).
- For every 10 women rescued, there are 50 to 100 more women who are brought in by the traffickers (CNN).
- Immigrants, runaways, foster youth, and children in youth shelters are usually the prime targets for sex traffickers (Herald Tribune).
- Those being sold for sex have an average life expectancy of seven years, and those years are a living nightmare of endless rape, forced drugging, humiliation, degradation, threats, disease, pregnancies, abortions, miscarriages, torture, pain, and always the constant fear of being killed or, worse, having those you love being hurt or killed (National Center for Missing and Exploited Children).

Acknowledgements

To my wife, Zaidy, again, thank you. Without you, this book would still only be a dream. Thanks for your patience, courage, and love, but also for pushing me and believing in me all these years.

To my kids, Ojani and Zowie, thank you for being the inspiration to write my stories. Thank you for the smiles and for the memories.

To my parents, Oscar and Letty, thank you for always providing encouragement and support and for teaching me to care for those things that truly matter. *¡Los amo!* Apa, te extraño mucho. Nos veremos junto al río.

To my brothers, Oscar and Omar, thank you for going along with me on this journey. It's been great. Let's keep it going. Omar, a tí también te extraño. Can't wait for that glorious day.

And finally, I am thankful to God, from Whom all blessings flow.

About the Author

Obed Olivarría was born in Mexicali, Mexico and spent his youth as a fully bicultural transnational citizen. He has a passion for writing both fiction and nonfiction, public speaking, composing, arranging, and performing music, as well as traveling around the world. He loves the thrill of adrenaline-pumping activities, but also the quiet reflection he gets from writing and creating.

His love for books started at an early age, as his parents were eager readers and owned thousands of books. His passion for writing was born after winning a city-wide short story competition while in high school in Arizona. The publication of this in a local journal inspired him to continue creating worlds and characters in print.

Obed has worked as a youth and young adult pastor, as a graphic designer, as a session musician, as a consultant, as university dean, as school administrator, and school psychologist. Having worked at every level of the education system, from pre-k to university, has given him an expedition to the human psyche. He has a dynamic love of life.

Obed lives in sunny Orange County, California with his charming wife and two energetic children. Obed hopes to continue writing inspiring books that entertain, but also challenge the status quo. Personally, he would like to visit every country in the world, drawing inspiration from these travels for another great story.